Stevie Morgan is the pseudonym of zoologist and television presenter. She is the creator of *Independent*'s column, 'Beloved And Bonk' and 'In the Sticks'. Nicola Davies lives in Somerset with her two children, two dogs, thirteen chickens and three sheep.

Fly Away Peter

Stevie Morgan

FLAME
Hodder & Stoughton

First published in 2000 by Hodder & Stoughton
A division of Hodder Headline
First published in paperback in 1999
by Hodder & Stoughton
A Flame paperback

British Library Cataloguing in Publication Data
A CIP catalogue record for this book
is available from the British Library

ISBN 0 340 71804 8

Typeset by Hewer Text Ltd, Edinburgh
Printed and bound in Great Britain by
Mackays of Chatham plc, Chatham, Kent

Hodder and Stoughton
A division of Hodder Headline
338 Euston Road
London NWI 3BH

For the women in my family,
Mary and Katie.
And, of course, for Rona.

With thanks for being there to Ben S, Sue O, Katie V, Hazel N, Marlene G, Jeremy and Rachel, Jane and Roly W and to Simon, Joseph, Gabriel, Coral, Geoff, Joan and Chris for ever present support.

Chapter One

'We are very close to the end now,' said the Indian oncologist. His accent made it sound almost jaunty. I felt sure he must be giving me good news. As if he were announcing the last stop of a tedious journey. In a minute the hospital doors would swing open, like they do on a big bus, and we'd both walk out into the breeze. Reprieved.

I smiled at the doctor then; at his world-round face. Poor man must have been a miserable adolescent; acne had left his cheeks like a relief map of the world's oceans. There was the Mariana Trench, the Central Pacific Basin, the Plonet Deep and the Tasman Sea. We'd had a bad time last trip in the Tasman Sea I remembered. A bloody force seven. The passengers had started to make vomiting into an art form. Lars the first officer had been caught by a projectile jet of recycled bacon sandwich right in the middle of his uniform pips. 'Yo ho ho and a bottle of fucking rum,' he'd whispered as he took the poor sap below. Peter had found a retired accountant from York reciting Hiawatha in the nude on the upper decks, hallucinating on a double dose of sea sickness patches.

It was relief that made me smile more then. I thought thank God! We can get out of this coffin of a place. Get away from the bloody rain and the bloody nurses with their bloody cheerfulness and bloody black stockings. I thought about how I'd ring all our contacts, all the cruise organisers and expedition leaders. I'd get us a trip somewhere. Somebody was always dropping out at the last minute and they'd be so glad to get Pete and me. We could be in the Indian Ocean in a week. Less. Thank God. It was nearly the end the doctor said. Of course it was! How could I have lost my nerve in all this, even for a moment? It had all been a huge mistake, like babies getting swapped wrist bands and going home with the wrong mothers. It was inevitable in the underfunded NHS, where the admin staff had only the weekly lottery ticket and the chocky bickies in the desk drawer to offer hope. Peter had been given someone else's case history by mistake! We weren't meant to be here, in this hospital at all. And now the doctor was admitting the muddle, telling me that it would soon be sorted out and over.

'We are very close to the end now,' he said it again, 'a matter of weeks at the very most.' He sat close, his knees almost touching mine. His white coat made him look like an overstuffed laundry bag. He took my hand, yellow with faded tan against his plump brown one, and looked intently into my face. 'Do you understand Miss Bowen? Do you understand that we are nearly at the end?' That lilt, so much like the Cardigan accents of my father's family. But there was no jauntiness in it; I'd been mistaken. Clutching at straws, knowing I was drowning really.

Yes, I understood the end he was talking about. The end of all this whispering behind closed doors. The end of these suffocating corridors. The end of the radiographer flirting with the Dachau inmate who had been my lover. 'Hi Pete, lookin' good boy,' the nurse would say, poorly imitating his American accent. 'Feelin great gal. Ready for *anything* you wanna do!' he'd flirt back.

Dr Patel's straight dark hair had been carefully trained over the side plate of naked skin on his crown. Why the hell did he bother I wondered. Who cared if it was a slap head who told you the love of your life was going to die?

After that I stepped out of the little side room, where the

doctor sat over half a ream of official paperwork. How many different ways were there to document a death? The corridor was as dim as the bottom of a scummy swimming pool. Through the big observation window opposite I could see Peter and the radiographer in dumb show. Bantering as usual. Out of focus through the reinforced glass, and without the sounds of their voices they seemed a long way off. Peter lay under the huge curve of the equipment like a morsel in a giant's mouth, about to be popped in and chewed like a crisp. The nurse was skinny but still she turned his foetally curled body effortlessly. There was no weight to him any more. He floated on the surface of life like a leaf, so easily displaced.

The nasty plastic chairs were strewn with copies of knitting pattern magazines from 1994 and the occasional *Windsurfing Now!* dropped off by some junior registrar cleaning out his flat. I shoved them out of the way and watched Peter endure the attentions of the x-rays again. Without the flesh to pad out his wide frame it was hard for him to lie on his side like that. His shoulders stuck out so. It was like trying to balance a coat hanger on its end. Sometimes after a long session, his bones would wear right through the skin. It reminded me of that doll Daddy mended by nailing its arms to its shoulders. The nurse turned him again, almost with a fingertip, this time onto his back. He'd become so two-dimensional that lying down like that he all but disappeared. He was too flat, just a layer spread on the couch, the last scrape of jam from the jar.

This physical lessening of my husband was almost the worst thing, the hardest to endure without screaming all the time, and converting every day into one long tantrum. Peter had inhabited his body so completely, filled every finger, every fibre. I didn't see how this flattened husk could accommodate him. The way that a logged rain forest can no longer support its ridiculous diversity. I thought of the burned stumps we had seen in Sumatra, still smoking, stretching in all directions. Birds had hopped, confused on the blackened ground, with nowhere to go and an orang-utan had wandered lost, arms held, limp, above its head. Peter's habitat had been destroyed. It frightened me to see how powerful death was.

When we met, his depth and breadth had astonished me. How could anyone be that bulky? Was it the sort of fatness that supported wobble tsunamis after the slightest bodily impact? Or was it that plastic, stuck-on-muscle look that men got from bursting blood vessels in the gym and popping hormones? I was fascinated. From first sight I wanted to see him with his clothes off, just to find out. After a week of working with him, I could tell it was neither gluttony or vanity. It was simply him, the way he was; bone, muscle, a weft of Peterness made flesh. His physical being was quite unlike that of the young fit men on board, not quite at home in their bodies. For more than forty years Peter's personality had been seasoning his body, like good timber in mountain air. His sheer solidity was arousing because it was all him.

He laughed at me when I introduced myself.

'Myfanwy Bowen.'

'You're called *what*?'

'Myfanwy. It's Welsh. You know. From Wales.'

'I'm sorry, I just never heard it before. It's nice. Really. A nice name. Myfanwy? Myfanwy!'

When you are used to beating men off with a stick you can't 'do' seduction. Nevertheless, Peter became the first man I consciously seduced. Not that my seduction techniques were up to much, mostly consisting of cramming myself in beside him in the poop deck locker and helping him stack life-jackets at the end of the day. It was direct to the point of being humiliating. But I didn't have any other moves. I had no practice to fall back on. The only thing I felt good about was driving boats and that's a pretty useless kind of skill when you want to get someone into bed. And I was so bad at it all that I almost didn't spot when it had begun to work.

4

Late one night after a big do, dinner and dance for the passengers — the 'pacs' — I was roaming the empty decks. Urliss, the mad Nordic catering manager with two wives on each side of the Atlantic and a husky team in Lapland, and his boys, had cleared away all the stuff. Urliss understood all the little details that spelt out tropical paradise to someone who had spent forty years in an office in Croydon; the hanging pineapples, the lanterns, the banana leaves covered in rice salad.

The pacs were tucked up ready for the five a.m. start the next day. Even the botany lecturer had gone to his cabin, alone with a bottle of scotch and his halitosis again. I was wakeful, wallowing in my unrequited crush. I wandered into the dark lounge and flicked on the tiny light on the baby grand. Perfect. An opportunity for melancholy self-indulgence. Playing the piano was as private as sucking a thumb in a warm bed, and the same sort of deep animal comfort. I'd only ever played for Ma and me. In those days any sort of sadness took me back to her; a sick headache, a bad period and I could be crying all over again about her. So Peter was easily enough reason to play the saddest songs Ma and I used to play together. I tried out a few; 'There's A Place For Us', 'You'll Never Walk Alone' — we only ever went for the high octane schmaltz, fastest one-way ticket to a tear duct — but there was really only one to play. One that was the best and worst. I started the little tinkly introduction and shut my eyes to hear her voice, faltery, uncertain, frequently out of tune.

> Do I love you do I?
> Doesn't one and one make two?
> Do I love you do I?
> Does July need a sky of blue?

There she was again, half a cheek on the piano stool, shoes kicked off on the parquet floor, slowing her accompaniment to let me catch up with the melody. Our hands together on the keys, my skinny brown fingers and bitten cuticles, her joints swollen above the rings with arthritis, moving her fingers by swivelling her wrists, hands her arms' puppets. Both our eyes filling up at the last verse, and laughing at our sentimentality.

> Do I love you do I?
> Oh my dear it's so easy to see.
> Don't you know that I do?
> Don't I show you I do?
> Just as you love me?'

I opened my eyes. Peter was leaning on the piano looking at me. But I felt as if I'd been found cuddling a teddy bear wearing my first Babygro. I never told anyone I could play. It was like waking up in one of those dreams about going to school naked, and finding it was true. Seeing my face he stood up.

'I'm sorry. I guess you didn't want an audience. Good night, Myfanwy.' He turned away and walked across the room, dodging the armchairs, fading into the dark. I had as good as slapped him in the face. I had two seconds to drop my self-consciousness or he'd be gone and no amount of standing close and stacking life-jackets in my bikini was going to work.

'Don't go . . . D'you know that one?' He stopped. Waited. Then turned.

'Not all the words.'

'I've got it on tape, in my room. If you'd like to hear.' I nearly lost consciousness from the sense of my own daring.

He just said: 'Sure.'

I took him to my cabin. We lay down and listened to Cole Porter. Peter's side rose above me like the flanks of a liner in port. It's not true, I thought, that joke that says they're all the same height when they're lying down. His chest was fully six inches deeper than my own, and I'm not slight. Only with one arm folded into the wall and me on my side would his broad shoulders fit in my bunk. He was dense and heavy, packed tight with muscle on the bone, skin smooth and elastic over the flesh. He felt like a well-caulked vessel, snug and watertight, seaworthy in any storm. We had lain together listening to the songs, talking a little about the lyrics before he made any big moves. At last, as the tape ended he shifted his weight in the bunk so as to be able to hold me, and he held me tight. Never in all my life had I felt so safe as with this man, still almost a total stranger. Only my fear of seeming too young and inexperienced prevented me from crying.

A little later, when we'd got to the rumpled, clothes-burrowing stage, I got nervous again. I had this stupid thought that I couldn't get out of my head. Was he my first or my second? That's how naive I was. I didn't even know if the comprehensive fumbling with my first boyfriend counted as sex. I think I was afraid he could read my mind and hear my thoughts about my own inexperience. So to drown it out I decided to be bold again. We'd been drinking by then. His Southern Comfort, which I hate but said I liked. And after the first glass it wasn't too bad I suppose. I began to undo the buttons down the front of my best dress.

Very gently, very respectfully, he folded my hands out of the way. 'No,' he said, smiling. 'No. I want to do that.'

'No. I want to do that.' It was still, after our ten years, the most tender and erotic memory. Thinking of it as I watched Peter emerge from that radiography room, his feet dragging in hospital slippers, the thin legs poking from under the hospital gown, I felt so angry. I filled up with rage as surely as a glass filling with beer and the head spilling down the side. Rage. And a hopeless longing for him as he was, big and strong and well, and flattening me into that narrow bunk.

He slipped an arm, already like a whitened bone, through mine and I fell in with the shuffle that passed for his walk. We dragged along the scum green corridor ignoring the crappy magazines and the smell of drugs and disinfectant.

'What did Patel say? You were in there a while.'

'Good news,' I said, without really looking at him. 'We don't need to come back here.'

He stopped walking, and turned to me 'Hey, no more sessions with my cute radiographer. I thought you said it was good news?'

'Yeah, good news for me Casanova. I know what you two do in that cubicle.' I readjusted the bag on my shoulder. As long as I didn't look at him I could wisecrack. 'Anyway, you have to leave for Covent Garden right now, Darcy Bussell says she won't dance another step without you.'

He laughed so much he began to gasp. Then recovering, he asked, 'OK, so what did he really say?'

I couldn't look anywhere but his face then. And his smile was so much the same that I couldn't hold my features together, they wouldn't be commanded. Peter rubbed his hands up and down my arms, stick-like at my sides.

'He said . . .' I began to tell him, 'he said that . . . He said that . . .'

'I can guess what he said honey, you don't need to say it.' Stumbling a little he reached for me, and held me. *He* held *me*, even then it was that way round. 'That's OK. You don't need to say it.'

With nothing much more than his bones to hold around me, I felt then like I felt on that first night; that his arms were the safest place I'd ever find.

We got married. Silly old-fashioned sort of thing to do. But we did. I kept my name and my 'Miss'; 'Missus' makes me think of cross-over pinnies and pink slippers with the backs trodden down. We needed a base between trips, a home of sorts. So we bought a cabin by the sea, below Daddy's hill, with a peep view of the Preseli Mountains beyond. Pete always laughed at that 'Mountains'. 'They're pimples, sweetie. But very cute pimples.'

Our 'home' was a couple of beach huts and a wooden garage, but it had a view across the wide peachy strand to the sea.

Neither of us liked to be far from the sea for long. It had a living room with a fat woodburner we could cook on, a dodgy propane shower and a piano. So I could play songs and Peter could growl them out, pretending he couldn't sing. He'd learnt lots of Cole Porter lyrics by then. They made him laugh.

'As a true American I should know what a cayuse is. With Old King Cole's preoccupations it could be a kind of sex aid I guess.'

Sometimes I'd hear him singing something to himself and giggling quietly.

'Just turn me loose
Let me straddle my old saddle underneath the Western skies
On my cayuse
Let me wander over yonder til I see the mountains rise.'

We had a bedroom just bigger than the cabin we lived in on board most ships. 'I'm not sleepin' in a bunk when we're here. We gonna have a bed so big Warren Beatty could have a screw reunion in it.' The bed arrived in a lorry large enough to house the entire cast of *Miss Saigon*. It couldn't make it down the track. The delivery men — rotund twins, like Tweedle Dum and Tweedle Dee, only from Swansea — were all for taking it back to the shop.

'Can I talk to you guys for a moment, man to man?' Peter said to them, putting an arm around each of their shoulders and marching them into the garage. They were only kids really. Probably still living at home and giving their wages straight to Mam. I could see that they were flattered to be called men by this big burly American with the grey at the temples like a banker and the glamour of a movie star. Five minutes later the three of them were wheeling the bed on its casters across the hard sand. They carried it into the dunes and by the time they set it on the paving in front of the cabin it didn't seem to matter that it wouldn't fit through the door. All four of us sat on it and drank beers to celebrate its arrival. Peter made us all feel it was a party. When the men left there was a lather of enthusiastic hand-shaking and back-patting.

'If ever you're in Swansea like, you know. Come by and see us,' Tweedle Dum said.

'And. You know,' said Tweedle Dee, glancing at me from under his cowlick, 'take care like.'

'What was all that about?' I asked when they were out of sight.

'Tell you later. Shall we just sleep outside in this tonight, and I'll get it in tomorrow? You can lie back and think of Orion.'

It was a long dry summer spell. August. At bedtime it still wasn't raining so we went to bed in the outdoors, not with sleeping bags but proper linen and a duvet. We made the bed up, standing on opposite sides and smoothing the sheets neatly over the corners. The sky was pink and glowing and its light reflected upwards onto Pete's face from the white of the bed linen. It felt like some sort of ritual. We even got into bed in nightclothes and lay quite chaste for a while looking at the stars coming out. Three curlews flew over calling and dropped down to the edge of the incoming tide.

It was so glorious and so silly we began to laugh, and then to make love. We didn't notice the bed begin to move, not just in time with what we were doing, but consistently in a single direction. The dunes beneath the pavers had shifted slightly giving the improvised 'patio' a little gradient towards the sea.

Just as we were both temporarily insensible, the bed skittered over the edge of the paving stones and tipped us down the slope of the dunes into a particularly aggressive patch of marram. Being tipped into cold sand and having my just post-coital flesh lacerated by nasty xerophtic plants was not and is not my idea of a fun time. I stood naked in the dunes swearing.

'Wow. Creative,' said Peter, 'I didn't even know you knew those words. Do you know you have grass stickin' out of your butt. Could be a tail.' I ran to attack him but the spikey marram pricked my feet. My soles never got to be as hard as his. He laughed, walked behind me on his deck-hardened feet and gently removed the grass, caressing my bottom with such tenderness that I stopped yelling.

'Great butt. And I could get to like a tail. Who needs a fuckin' bed?' He rolled us in the quilt and the pillows on the sloping sand snug as a nest of larks.

'What did you tell the delivery men, to get them to carry the bed?'

'I told them you'd had a bed fetish and you could only fuck in a king sized. And that we'd been sleeping on a single mattress for two years. I guess you're so cute they took pity on me.'

The Monday after our last visit to the hospital there was a morning so bright white and blue it looked as if it had come straight off the celestial production line – the paint on it was still wet. Pete had faded, worn even thinner. Sitting by the wood-burner wrapped in every blanket we possessed he seemed, already, almost disembodied.

'Get out there. Smell that air for me,' he said.

'Why don't we take your chair outside?'

'No, you just go. Get those running shoes on. Another day in here with me and you'll be like Oprah before the diet.'

'Thanks.'

'You're welcome.'

'Will you be OK?'

'I'll struggle through the half-hour somehow.'

So I ran out over the sand, into the brightness reflected from the water. My blood sang. God forgive me but I rejoiced in that little escape from Peter's sickness.

I came back cold and breathless and called from the back door. Although I guess I knew. He was folded under the kitchen window. He must have got up from the chair where he'd slept the night, to watch me as I ran along the water line. I was pierced by the sensation that the last thing he saw was me, silhouetted against the sea. For a long time afterwards I found the fact that I had never turned to look towards the cabin whilst I was out unbearable.

'It would have been very quick,' the GP said when she came. 'A pulmonary embolism, a clot that blocked the blood flow to his lungs. A minute before he lost consciousness. No more. I promise.'

A minute seems to me a long time to fight for air. Like drowning.

Holding his hand, stroking the strange cold curve of his forehead, I felt all our ten years hover around me, all the memories clustering like relatives at the deathbed. And then, very gently, they landed on our furniture, our piano, on the roof of the cabin, on the dunes and then on things further and further out: on the everyday features of the landscape we had shared in sweet brief snatches. They settled like snow, a blanket of snow holding me cold and safe beneath.

> Don't you know that I do?
> Don't I show you I do?
> Just as you love me.

Chapter Two

'Tucker, you rat bag. I've come for dinner. Hellooo!' I leaned round the door of the glass porch, and shouted towards the hall.

There was the usual extraordinary muddle on the porch shelves, paintbrushes, half-squeezed tubes of acrylics, a selection of straw hats in which mice had made four-star accommodation, pot plants on the point of expiring from neglect and several items of antique veterinary equipment with which, presumably, Granda did unspeakable gynaecological things to his neighbour's Welsh Black cows.

The shoe selection on the floor told the story of the household: a progression of wellingtons, from red ones the size of a cup cake, through to black ones that, with the right lighting inside, could host a passable disco. Fourteen pairs in all, they were the only things in the whole house stored in some sort of order, lined up on either side of the porch. Each pair had its own tailor-made depression in the concrete floor with just enough room between to allow socked feet to approach their chosen wellie and step in.

Not a wellies day that day though. I kicked off my sandals outside and walked into the hall in bare feet. The worn flags were cool, and smooth as a horse's flank. From hooks all along the panelled side of the stairs hung coats and jackets in dusty almost geological strata, looking neglected now in the height of a proper hot summer.

Along the opposite wall a long narrow table with beautiful turned mahogany legs supported a mound of dog-chewed and age-faded slippers, the bottom ones probably dating back to Granda's time. I've always thought of this table with pity; it seems depressed, ashamed of how low it's fallen in the scheme of things. I imagine it moaning to itself 'not French polished since 1947, and don't even talk about the woodworm'. Although that would be an exaggeration because I remember it in Gee's front room in the sixties, at tea time with sponge and scones and her best Royal Albert tea set on it. But it's the sort of melodramatic object that *would* exaggerate.

The grandfather clock at the end of the hall is different. Not given to much comment these days. But it does still speak on some topics. On this particular summer's day it stirred from its silent stupor of unoiled cogs and ticked once, twice, three times. And stopped. As if on cue a shower began to run somewhere upstairs. There was a little frisson of distant giggling. A door closing. Well, I knew what that was.

Since A levels were over Julian and his skinny monosyllabic girl Vicky had discovered the joys of the 'carwash' as Peter used to call it.

'Why can't they do it up in the cow shed, or in the fields like we had to,' Idris grumbled constantly. 'There's never any bloody hot water now when I get home.'

'Hello-o.' I called once more, mostly to show Julian there was somebody in the house so I wouldn't find him and Vicky shagging on the landing.

No one else was in the house. Tucker would be up in her barn painting, her smaller kids running their usual riot all over the old farm, without a thought in her head about what anyone might eat for dinner. In other words situation normal in the Tucker-Bowen household.

I filled a jug from the tap over the butler's sink in the

kitchen and rescued the pot plants from certain death. As I put the jug back on the window-sill I noticed two tall bottles, one of green olive oil and the other of almost black balsamic vinegar, both with handwritten tags around their necks bearing something scribbled in expensive Italian. Nothing so culinarily aristocratic had ever been in Tucker's kitchen before. The closest this place had been to ingredients for good salad dressing was a congealed and lidless bottle of Branston Pickle, which I had once found in a cupboard. Finding anything even remotely edible was unusual.

I opened the freezer and found more unaccustomed bounty: big bags of prawns plump as fat princesses' fingers, salmon steaks, fillets of plaice stuffed with something that still managed to look exotic even under its layer of frosting. There were sweet things too – several tubs of 'luxury' ice cream and sorbet. Often the only thing in Tucker's freezer was a dead owl or a small oil painting that she wanted to keep wet.

Fascinated, I opened the fridge. Six bottles of *premier cru* Chablis and four bottles of champagne, French but a name I'd never heard of. Butter, natural yoghurt, fresh squeezed orange juice (six cartons) brown eggs, Parma ham. What was it all for and who the hell bought it? Usually, when I come for supper, I forage and just cook whatever I can find enough of to make a meal of sorts for all of us. Tucker's kids aren't picky, they couldn't afford to be, considering their mother's haphazard attitude to child nutrition. This food-rich fridge was unprecedented. I couldn't use any of this stuff without some sort of explanation.

I went out through the back door, shoving my feet into an ex-pair of Julian's flip-flops that he grew out of about four years ago. I grabbed the old flower basket from the top of the washing machine on the way. The back of the house is set into the hillside so the kitchen door opens to sunken courtyard, with steep sides lined with liverworts and grey slate. Just head height above me the day was hot, a different world. Climbing the mossy steps I gained ten degrees and progressed back to summer. It's the one thing I dislike about Tucker's house — Granda and Gee's old house — not being able to see the garden from the kitchen window. Or hear it. At the top of the steps, in the warmth again, children's voices screeching with delighted terror tumbled down the grass from the orchard.

Nothing's mown or cultivated in Tucker's garden. Except the little plot I dig and plant and sometimes can be bothered to weed. I started doing it out of sheer frustration really. To give myself some ingredients to enliven Uncle Jonas' Eeezy Cook rice and a tin of Spam, past its sell by date in 1992. I rummaged through it then, and plucked out handfuls of coriander, some spring onions and rocket and dropped them into the basket to collect on the way back to the kitchen. Prawns with fresh coriander, a rocket salad: almost a proper meal. I've no right to be rude about Tucker's catering; food just doesn't matter to her. She and Peter were alike in that. He never bothered what he ate either — salmon and new potatoes or deep fried Mars bar didn't matter to him — it was all just fuel. I never really cooked with Peter.

The lower doors of the barn were thrown wide and there was so much light coming in from the windows at the end that Tucker's almost entirely round body was edged in bright white. For a person who doesn't care about food she's a remarkable shape. Her two cubic feet of blonde hair was lit up like radioactive cotton wool.

She was standing in front of a huge red-smeared canvas with her paint-covered hands holding either side of her face as if giving herself a trial facelift. Only the slightest change in the tension of her neck signalled that she was pleased I'd arrived. I sometimes laugh at how we read each other.

'It's very . . . *bright* isn't it? What am I looking at?' I'm always rude about her work. I love it, mostly, but it scares me where she gets it from.

'Hmm. I've been standing here for some time trying to work

that out for myself. There's something that wants to come
through from that bottom corner.' In the lower left sector of the
picture a sort of face shape appeared to be pushing through the
surface of the painting, finding its way into the art world at a
place where the vermilion oil was thinnest.

'I think that's right. D'you think it could be, you know, one
of Idris' relatives making contact from the other world?' Tucker
dropped her hands, and gave herself a little shake.

'You are such a fucking philistine, Van.' No one else calls me
anything but Myfanwy. No one else calls her anything but Elen,
or mummy.

'No, I'm not. I just don't think paint has, you know, *free will*.
You do the paintings Tucker, they don't do themselves.'

'Not only a philistine but a cynic too. Bung those brushes in a
pot for me, luvvie.' Tucker wiped her hands on her overall, a pink
sheet with holes ripped in for arms. 'And then,' she said, '*then*
we'll go and open some *wine*. That'll be a first for you in this
house. Wine you didn't bring.' Having been so still Tucker was
now a kind of movement kaleidoscope, putting lids on tubes of
paint, dropping brushes into pots of turps, tidying canvases,
closing windows. She's got this talent for action she can turn on,
as if she's suddenly a speeded up film. I can't do that. I do
everything very steadily. In sequence.

'Who did bring all that. Food. You know and booze?'

'David.'

'David?'

'David. Jules' boy.'

'David the dancer! Yes. Yes.'

'Well, not David the dancer anymore . . . He got some, I
dunno, some dancery injury jobby,' Tucker doesn't understand
illness of any kind, like a dolphin doesn't understand dry land,
'had to give it up, almost, more than a year ago now anyway. I
s'pose you're past it at twenty-eight as a dancer anyway. So he's
going to America instead. America, New York. His dad's given
him a job. He's training some dancers for his father's next movie.

17

'So the dad's a what? You did say once . . .'

'Richard the bastard, my ex half-brother in bloody law. He's a Director with a capital bloody D. Dicky the Director and Dick Head.'

'Tucker. It's fifteen years ago?'

'Don't care. Still a bastard. But I don't say that to David. Big reconciliation after Jules died. He and Richard hadn't spoken for five years before that. I hate to say it but Dick has been good I think, about David having to stop dancing. He's more or less supporting him.'

'Why's he here?'

'Dunno really. Nice boy. Nice *man*. Nice. Funny. Clever. I think he's sort of saying hello and goodbye. I hadn't seen him for eight years. This America thing is . . . well he seems to think it's like emigrating. Like going to a colony on the moon or something. And he's sold his London flat and Jules' house is gone now so . . . Nowhere else for him I s'pose.'

'And the food?'

'All part of the hello goodbye stuff. And I think it's his new big thing. Food. Cooking. You know herbed loin of wood louse with a tickle of grouse feather vinegar. I suppose he never ate anything as a dancer so he's experimenting'.

'Can I make supper, you know, with some of it?'

'No. I'm going to put it in formaldehyde and sell it at my next show.' A child's scream covered the last syllable of her sentence and almost before she finished speaking Tucker began to run, moving her compact bulk with surprising acceleration. I'm in awe of mothers in general. That ability to do five things at once is enviable but being able to extract so much information from their children's non-verbal utterances is almost supernatural. To me the scream sounded just the same as the others that had played in the background all the time we'd been standing in the barn. But somehow Tucker could tell that this one was real pain, real terror, something that needed emergency action.

We rounded the corner of the barn, crossed four hundred yards of matted meadow grass and dock that had been a paddock and scrambled up the bank into the orchard. We were met by a wave of chaotic crying. Tucker's three youngest girls were clustered around a young man with a very round head and hair like a fuzz of black peach fluff.

This was David the possibly ex-dancer. Tucker's only nephew. Half-nephew. Less than half really as Tucker's dad's first and second families didn't really mix. Tucker's half-sister Jules had been close on twenty years her senior. David wasn't handsome like you imagine all dancers to be. My first thought was of some sort of alien, his eyes were too big for a real human, his nose too small and round and the five o'clock shadow over his jaw line looked like a disguise.

He was walking through the trees carrying a whimpering Agnes, Tucker's eldest girl. Her right arm was bent in an unnatural shape and cradled across her chest, and although she was clearly in pain, she was just as clearly revelling in the drama. Already at eleven imagining herself Michelle Pfeiffer to David's rather unlikely George Clooney.

'Elen, I'm so sorry . . .' David began.

'Mummy, I fell off the pear tree,' wailed Agnes.

'Agnes is too big for the pear tree now,' Jane sniffed. She had clearly been 'I-told-you so-ing' from the moment her sister hit the ground. She was upset because her advice had been flouted, not because her sister was hurt. Jane is going to be an accountant when she grows up I'm sure. Or an actuary. The little blonde twins looked genuinely distraught and were holding onto each other like distressed chimps: Jelly even had her finger in Moffy's mouth and Moffy was sucking it vigorously.

'Is Agnee gunna die Mummy?' asked Jelly. Moffy opened her mouth wide at this and let Jelly's finger drop as she began to howl.

'Jeezuz,' said Tucker. 'No, Jelly, she's not. Stop crying Moffy, it's not helpful.' Moffy shut her mouth and was silent as if someone had flipped a switch. Tucker was never fazed by disaster, merely irritated until she brought things under control.

'Agnes, I know it hurts but I'm sure you can walk to the house.'

'OK, Mummy.' David gently put her down. Agnes' broken arm was now the least concern, Tucker's approval was all. Everything had gone quiet.

'Ah. That's better,' said Tucker, smiling.

'But it does hurt.' Agnes almost whispered and began to cry again, quite undramatically this time. Tucker enfolded her and kissed her head.

'All right sweetheart.' She's not callous Tucker, just practical.

'God, Elen.' David's forehead folded into row on row of soft furrows. His eyes got bigger. I thought he too might cry. 'I'm so sorry. I should have . . .'

'Should have what? Prevented them from being children. It's an accident. All she's done is break her arm for God's sake!'

'Oh. Right. OK.' David studied his feet for a moment, gathering something together internally. Then looked around seeking eye contact with somebody, 'Is there anything I can do?'

I've been through this crisis management scene with Tucker so many times, on board ships with passengers dropping dead, going into labour, taking a swing at the crew. Once in a shark attack when Tucker and I had taken two inflatable motor boats – zodiacs – full of passengers snorkelling off Grande Comores. Some old cove had his bony shank gnawed whilst he was swimming. Word got round to the other forty punters in the water and they behaved as if Spielberg's *Jaws* was being re-shot right there and then.

Tucker and I had forty panicking coffin dodgers to get into the zodiacs and safely back to the ship. They all started flinging themselves onto one side of the boat, throwing snorkel gear in, hitting each other with flippers. You name it. She put a tourniquet on the guy's leg, and bullied the squealing oldsters into total submission. She even slapped some of their hands. She was so angry with them for losing their heads. She made them get out of the water slowly, one by one. And even though they were virtually soiling their swimsuits, Tucker's irritation was more impressive than a shark's teeth.

Anyway, I know to keep my mouth shut until Tucker is at the tiller of the situation again. So I waited, then said 'I'll cook supper, you take Agnes to Casualty. David can help.' He looked like he needed a lifeline.

'Yes. Yes, of course,' said David, smiling gratefully at me, the brow unfolding as instantly as a stretched concertina.

'Right. Good plan. I'll go now. Come on then, Aggie Paggie.' She steered Agnes down the path and David started to follow but I put a hand on his arm. Tucker would need a little peace to get Agnes into the car without Jane's advice or the twins' wailing.

'David. Shall we close the barn up? Take the kids down in a minute.'

'OK.'

'Jane, you run down to the barn, and finish closing the windows for me sweetie.'

'OK.' Given a practical task Jane was happy again.

'Moffy, Jelly? D'you want a carry?'

'Yes please.'

'OK. David take a child of your. Choosing!' I said.

We scooped up a twin each and crunched towards the barn in single file, David and Jelly leading the way.

Without Jelly's fingers for comfort Moffy had turned to her own and went into a dreamy stupor of comfort-sucking, leaning into my shoulder from the moment she was picked up. Jelly, however, was making the very most of her captive audience, sitting up in David's arms and explaining her world with gestures and hand movements straight out of a nineteenth-century opera.

'But Mummy says children is enough without dogs as well. And Daddy says he has enough bloody animals in work.'

'That's a shame. I had a dog when I was your age.'

'Where is he now then?'

'He died.'

'Oh, dear. Did you cry?'

'Yes, I did.'

'I think it's OK for boys to cry about dogs.'

With their two heads close together, even from the back I imagined some family resemblance between them. They went on with their conversation, Jelly giving more of her views about acceptable activities for boys – 'they shouldn't say girls can't do climbing' – David nodding solemnly. There was nothing for me to do but walk and watch the blue-shirted and blue-jeaned rear view of David as his rhythmic swing of a walk took him down the path before me.

Since Peter I hadn't really looked at anyone, man or woman. Not looked to notice anyway. Tucker and Idris and all their kids are so familiar to me, I hardly need even to see them to know what they're like; I've been able to spot Idris' walk at half a mile for the last twenty-five years and I'd probably know Tucker if a kidnapper sent me a section of her little toe. But anyone else apart from Dad? Or perhaps Graham? Other people's looks became a bar code my eyes swiped, to sort out those I knew from the rest of nondescript humanity.

Anyway, looking at men had always been risky. When I was young I had to spend more time making sure I wasn't being eyed up for purchase. So I got into the habit even before Peter of not looking at men. After Peter I saw people the way that computers read the post codes on envelopes: just the letters and the numbers, not the the cream vellum with the gold wax seal or the brown municipal with the crinkly cellophane window.

When I was first alone after Peter died I had a lot of visitors . . . old colleagues, local boys with no woman of their own, husbands looking to trade in the old model. But they could tell that I'd lost any hierarchical view of humanity. Washboard stomachs, good teeth, come-to-bed eyes, charisma, fast cars and fat wallets were as one to me with pension books and squints. They could be ninety-seven with no teeth and flatulence or thirty-five with all their own hair, and the only difference to me would be their names.

That kind of attitude in any woman is kind of off-putting, I suppose. So the visitors dried up. Tucker and her family became the only regular features of my social life. Graham too, in a way, our predictable chats when I dropped off my stuff for him to sell were for months my only conversations with anyone I wasn't related to. You don't meet many people living down the quiet end of a long beach in Wales. Which is, I suppose, the main reason to live there.

So I only looked at David at first for something to do with my eyes as I lugged the sleepy Moffy down the path. He was just another part of Tucker's family. Tucker's twenty-something semi-nephew. But after the first look I began to notice more than the post code on this particular envelope. He still held a dancer's shape. A sloping V from the corners of his horizontal shoulders to the waist, then strong perfectly proportioned legs.

The legs made me think of Peter. His legs were the second thing I'd noticed about him, as he walked down the corridor of A deck in front of me on my very first afternoon aboard *The Stellata*, my first expedition cruiser. His shoulders were the first thing. He was wearing a T-shirt, very clean, it being the first day of a trip with passengers needing a good impression. It had hung square from his shoulders, and the straight untucked hem ended far out beyond his hips underlining his shape as surely as a push up bra on a page three girl. His chinos were soft with age and the long well-upholstered legs showed their curves and straightnesses through the drape of the material. I was shocked at my reaction, afraid to find my fingers tingling with the desire to touch the fabric of the trousers, to lift the loose hem of the shirt and find a back. I was twenty-one years old and I had made my tomboy image into armour. So I didn't even know that what I was feeling was desire.

Walking behind David, I had the sensation of having just been reminded of something. Like smelling a scent from child-

23

hood after thirty years. I was so absorbed in looking and remembering, that when we reached the barn and David stopped walking I carried on into his back. My hands clasped around Moffy's legs making contact with his backside, and my face landing between his shoulder blades. For a tiny moment I felt that solidity of body, like bumping into a feature of the landscape. I smelled the warmth of living skin, so close and so intimate a smell.

'I'm so sorry. Where I was going. I didn't really see, I mean look. I wasn't concentrating.' I blushed horribly. Unmissably.

'That's OK. No harm done.'

'But I walked. You know. Right into your . . . your back and . . . I'm so clumsy.' My words were nearly always like ketchup, so hard to get them out in a steady stream. Since Peter I'd almost given up on complex communications. Sentences longer than four words were just too tricky. In stressful situations I'd turn myself upside down and shake to get them out and then they wouldn't stop coming in messy globlets. 'Are you. You know. All right. I didn't hurt you or anything. I didn't mean to. I'm so sorry.'

'No. Really, I'm fine. That's quite all right,' he said, then bent to put Jelly down and with his face turned I had a moment to collect myself.

Don't be so stupid. This is a boy, Tucker's nephew. If he believes you're a dirty old woman that's his problem because of course you're not . . . It was Peter you were thinking about after all. I took a deep breath and let my cheeks subside. Panic over.

Jane bounced out through the barn doors. 'I shut the windows and put the brushes in the pots and switched off the fan in the loo.'

'Brilliant. David and I'll shut the doors. Moffy down you go, you and Jane and Jelly go and see if there's something nice on television.' Talking to the children is always easier. Words come out in the order I plan; I don't have to squeeze and force.

'We've got *Die Hard with a Vengeance* to finish watching,' said Jane.

'No, I don't think so Jane.'

'Mummy says it's fine. Even for Moffy and Jelly.'

Moffy took her fingers out of her mouth to add her arguments. ' 'S' really funny. I seen it two whole times.'

'Really, Myfanwy. We've seen it loads. More than *Beauty and the Beast* even,' said Jane. I decided perhaps a lawyer rather than an accountant.

'OK. But if I get into trouble with Tucker, I'll kill all of you.'

The three girls ran down the garden to the house, like flower fairies fallen on lean times, hair on end, clothes ripped but with a pixie-like daintiness that perhaps Tucker had once had.

'Tripping off to see Brucey blow the bad guys away,' said David. 'I wish I'd grown up like that.' His face was folded again, puckered at the brow and round the eyes. I felt I'd walked into him a second time. Got too close by accident. But the longing was so clear I couldn't let the words go.

'Why?' I said. Instantly the puckering had gone. He turned to me, a smile spread neatly over his face like a yellow hanky and a hand thrust out in a gesture I guessed he'd learned almost before he could walk.

'I do apologise, I haven't even introduced myself. I'm David Wall, Elen's nephew.'

I took the hand, unexpectedly square and workmanlike. 'Oh. Right. Well. I'm . . . Myfanwy Bowen. Idris' cousin, which probably means we're related. Fourth cousins. Or something. Twice removed. You know.'

'I'm not very good at relatives. I'm ashamed to say I hadn't seen Elen for eight years before this week.' His charm was flawless, coating him now as quickly as the smile had concealed his face. It was like a suit of feathers, soft and overlapping, hiding all the skin beneath and rolling the world off like the droplets from a duck's back. It made me feel sorry for him because I know about that gap between the outside of yourself and the inside of yourself and how draughty a space it is.

I wasn't sure what to say next, I was often unsure what to say next. And when I said it it never sounded right any more. I used to know with Peter, what to say – something funny, or nothing even. And it nearly always came out right. But not since. I was a scratched record after Peter. A faulty CD.

David had no problem with saying things. With the crisis of Agnes over he was back 'on point'.

'Shall we do the doors? Elen showed me the knack on my first night here. It's such a wonderful building, it would make a marvellous rehearsal space.'

We each took one of the heavy oak sliding doors. 'The knack' was a single explosive upward jerk to get them moving on their rails, then a full weight of leaning to bring them to the centre so they could be locked together.

Since Tucker's work had become well known and valuable, a little security was worthwhile. Even if only to keep the twins from getting in and helping their mother's composition along a little: Moffy and Jelly never slept in the summer beyond five and various door locking measures had been instituted since they could walk to prevent early morning expeditions. In their third summer they had added their version of family portraits to twelve framed pictures ready to go to a Cork Street gallery.

It took us fully five minutes to get the doors shut and locked. Throughout the operation David chatted about Agnes falling from the pear tree, about Moffy and Jelly's various twinny bonkernesses and Jane's control streak. He was funny. Really funny and self-deprecating, joking about the fact that the first time he has responsibility for children and one of them breaks her arm.

It was all some sort of performance; all part of keeping inside away from outside. But it was at least a good one and made me laugh. I relaxed. Smiled. Here was a new part of Tucker's clan for me to enjoy. I let him see his attempt to charm was working, as well as it probably did with everyone else in his life. This was just the particular version for use on elderly relatives, maiden aunts, spinsters and widows of this parish.

We went down to the house. The girls were safely parked in front of their adult rated move. Explosions and gunfire inter-spersed with expletive-rich dialogue came from the sitting room followed by squeals of delighted terror. I suggested we should start cooking.

'OK I'll be sous chef. Tell me what you want chopping, peeling, shredding. I'll be kitchen slave,' David said. Then he went to the fridge and drew out one of the bottles of Chablis. He had it uncorked and poured in far too little time. A speed that suggested an unhealthy focus.

Seeing him strip the foil covering from the neck and plunge in the pointed end of the corkscrew I thought of a bear cub we'd seen in Alaska orphaned and therefore starving, who'd found a punter's back pack with chocolate in the pocket. In five seconds the pack was shredded and the Hershey bar gone.

'Glass of wine?' He'd already poured two. It didn't matter if I didn't drink one, he'd have them both anyway.

'Mmm. Please. Yes.'

'One of the perks of not dancing,' he said, 'drinking on a weekday night.' He downed almost a whole glass. There it was, a little bit of inside peeping between the feathers.

'Do you miss. Dancing?'

The smile spread again, the feathers closed over the skin. 'No. Not at all. It's a great relief really. It had got so painful. Not really. I still do some as a teacher, that's what I'll be doing on my father's film project. No. No I don't miss it.' It sounded as if he was slowly beginning to believe this self-propaganda. He must have been telling himself how he never missed dancing since the day he left Rambert. 'I'm finding out about everything else there is in life. Like food. I'm very keen on food just at the moment. I'd been eating dancer food for I dunno – all my life. Junk. Dancers don't eat all week and then stuff two hamburgers and milkshake after the performance. We get injured because our skeletons are made from the menu at the nearest burger bar! Eating real food and cooking has been a revelation to me! Shall I do some spring onions first?'

'Oh. Yes. And the coriander? I'll get the shrimps – prawns – whatever. Thawing.'

David concentrated on chopping for a moment as he'd earlier concentrated on his feet. Then very tentatively he asked, 'Do guests always do the cooking here?'

'Well. Starvation or poisoning or you know. Cook.' He laughed. A real laugh both layers outside and in, 'Lovely shrimps. I mean prawns,' I said.

'Great coriander. I grew lots in the window box of my flat last summer. First thing I'd ever grown.'

That was a surprise, an ex-dancer pottering over his window boxes.

'When I danced it was everything. All consuming, I didn't have a life outside it. And now I do.'

Even the duck-down armour charm couldn't make this sound any more convincing than Genghis Khan recommending the joys of macrame.

'Do Elen and Idris ever cook anything?' The wine was mellowing the performance a little, less the best behaviour tea with the vicar kind. This was now just his ordinary brand I guessed, used on friends and colleagues, so effortless they probably never realised that they were getting a face full of feathers.

'Burning toast. Idris is you know, accomplished at toast burning. Tucker does a brilliant instant black coffee.'

He laughed again. The sound made me smile. The funny fuzzy felt head thrown back, the big eyes creased up and folded away. Not handsome for sure. But engaging.

'They do like food though. I made everyone mushroom omelette the other night – the most wonderful fresh brown eggs from down the road – with a little drizzle of white truffle oil. They loved it. Even Jelly and Moffy. But I think all they ever eat when no one's here is Rice Krispies.'

Growing coriander, noticing egg quality and travelling three hundred miles with a bottle of truffle oil. Was this feathers or real skin? Inside or out?

'But that's you know what makes them. Lovely to cook for. They're so. Grateful.' More grateful than Peter had been. He could live for weeks on corned beef sandwiches or 'potato chips' and chocolate bars, then eat a real meal. Something proper that I'd make for him, (and myself out of desperation at the sight of another loaf of sliced white). Then he'd go back to the chip butties. I never understood it.

'Yes. Yes. You're right. They are.' David stopped chopping and looked at me with alien eyes wide. Suddenly intense and passionate, he continued to speak pacing about the kitchen 'Audiences are grateful like that too, because they could never do that with their own bodies. I always found that sad. All those people watching, not doing. Second-hand living. You have to do to be alive.' His assertions about not missing ballet became even more unbelievable. This was what was underneath the charm, a hunger for doing, for the sensation of being alive. He waved his knife around. 'Feeling you're alive. Expressing that you are alive. Knowing that you are alive. It's what humans are for.'

He stopped his pacing right in front of me, the knife held upwards, gripped like a sword about to do battle or swear allegiance to some hopeless cause. I think I most probably looked like a goldfish then, seeing this fierceness blazing through the soft charm, that was there to hide it and protect it.

But the charm did something else too – it muffled life. So David was a bit like me, with an outer layer to present to the world that somehow numbed and distanced us from the sing and sizzle of aliveness leaving us hungry to feel it.

David and I stood for a moment, me with a handful of frozen Pacific prawns, him with a Sabatier and green coriander-covered fingers and looked at each other. The skinny cherub of understanding flew over us fast and cleared off over the orchard, to bring a brief dream of lamb chops to the sheep on the hillside.

'More, you know, wine,' I said.

'Yes, please. Thank you.'

We turned back to the food without speaking again. Shelling seafood and chopping herbs seemed now to absorb all our attention. Right over our heads two lots of footsteps walked into the bathroom, and shut the door. The shower came on and tiny unmistakable sounds came to us through the water falling and the thick floorboards.

We took the dining table outside through the French windows onto the little lawn in front of the house that Idris always mowed with his dad's old push cutter, about as efficient as a pair of nail scissors. We laid the table with an old sheet and some night light candles David found in the airing cupboard. Then the idea of the meal as a kind of party seemed to catch on: Julian and Vicky appeared downstairs looking very clean and rather wet, and played art student and designer with a bit of cerise chiffon and some grey bricks, creating the kind of table decoration that blocks any view of the person opposite. But it did look pretty and they were unpretentious enough about it to let Jane and the twins add daisies in eggcups to the design. Just as we were ready to eat, a car stereo playing 'Bat out of Hell' at eardrum bursting volume came up the track from the main road.

'Oh. Good timing,' I said.

'Who the hell is playing that?' said David.

'Dad,' said Julian, 'it's his version of a mid-life crisis. Wanting to be Meatloaf instead of a vet.' Vicky did another simpering giggle and squirmed like something without a backbone. Idris' little red hatchback crunched into the yard beyond the lawn, windows down, music splurging rhythmically like blood from a sliced artery. Behind it Tucker's battered estate revved up with a beaming and be-plastered Agnes in the passenger's seat.

The whole family assembled. I'd only ever seen it happen at Christmas before. Rice Krispies and fish paste eaters though they are, they can rise to the occasion, Tucker's family. My family, I suppose. They tasted and savoured and wolfed everything that David and I brought to the table, proud joint cooks. They joked and talked and argued and asked for more. I drank more of David's lovely Chablis and got drunk, a little. I felt like a dog that turns round and round on its bed, because every position is comfortable and is home. David faded back into being another one of the Tucker clan, a bigger and more interesting variety of offspring. Agnes, sleepy with painkillers, fell asleep over pudding and Idris carried her to her bed. Soon after, Jane fell asleep on my lap, Moffy on Julian and Jelly on Vicky. I carried Jane to her bed, and when I came down Julian and Vicky had taken the twins upstairs too. They didn't reappear.

'Just listen out for that bloody shower,' said Idris. 'No hot water again. Ah well. Only young once.' The four adults moved to one end of the table. It was getting dark and cool, and midges were committing suicide in the candle flames but no one wanted to go in.

'It's not even the weekend or anybody's birthday,' said Tucker.

'Thank you,' Idris raised his glass, 'both of you. We're used to Myfanwy cooking for us, but David . . . Well. It's just lovely.'

Idris' accent, swings in strong after a little alcohol. That's when you hear which of the brothers – our fathers – stayed, and which left. I only have a lilt of Welshness when I'm angry otherwise my voice is a rootless, colourless English secondary school. 'Absolutely lovely,' sing-songed Idris. 'Even if I will have a hangover in surgery tomorrow. Actually at this rate I'll still be pissed. Ah well, at least little Fido can't complain to the BMA if I stick the thermometer in the wrong hole. More wine anyone? David?'

'A little.'

'Myfanwy?'

'No. I'm, you know, rushing. I mean rush cutting tomorrow.'

'*What* are you doing?' David asked.

'I'm going to cut rushes. For . . . well . . . I make, sort of . . .'

Why do I always have this problem about explaining what I do for a living? I'm not a prostitute or an arms dealer. I don't market child pornography, I'm not a management consultant. I'm not even an estate agent or a supermarket shelf filler. I could say I make furniture. Sort of. I mean I *do* make furniture. Chairs. And baskety things too from the rushes. I made them first for the cabin, for Peter and me. Then I made things for friends, then friends' friends, then for a friend's friend who worked in some posh London shops. And now just for the posh London shops. Plus a few commissions. And baskets for Graham's little tourist trap shop in Cardigan, too. The chairs pay the big bills, and in the summer the steady trickle of baskets selling from Graham's pays the little ones.

But the making is just the last part, only a tiny part of what I do in the winter, in my big workshop with the wood burner lit and the radio on. Collecting, that's really what I do. Foraging. I'm a hunter gatherer. The last this side of the Kalahari. I don't dig for edible roots or pull giant grubs from the stems of plants. I do hunter gathering for wood and stone and rushes.

Not the wood you'd find tame, square and stacked in some builders' merchant. I like wild wood, wood that's been around, that's seen some action and escaped with its life. My wood is pulled from sandbanks after storms, rescued from the bottom of a skip in a darkened back street, cut from the broken heart of an oak felled by age. By the time it's in my hands the wood I use has had a life. It's got history in it.

Stone has history too of course, but it's too long for humans and too boring. I can share a hundred years or more of life story with a worn plank from a shrimping boat but a pebble has two million years of lying still being part of a mountain. I can't listen to stones. They get put in my chairs as decoration, they don't have a say in things. Still, I don't like stone forced out of bed. So I don't use quarried stuff. I pick it up from the beach or the bottom of a stream.

There's no one bit that I can label and say it's what I do. No part that has more meaning than another. I'm grateful for it all, for the simple sharp pleasure I take in it, because after Peter I expected only the equivalent of a lifetime of hot needles in my eyes. Foraging was my new way to be alive when Peter wasn't anymore. My way to be alone with the sky and the sea and with all I could remember of him. I have no patterns, no pressures, no anxieties in my work. No rules even, no routine. Except in July. In July the rush *has* to be cut. 'It's your brush with stress and deadlines. The ordinary world Myfanwy,' Idris always says. Not that there's much stress associated with tootling about on a river meander in a coracle.

Tucker waited for a few seconds whilst I floundered about trying to decide which bit of all that to present for David's consumption and which bits I can manage to express with the fewest falterings. Then she stepped in. Each time it happens her patience runs out a little earlier. If I lived with Tucker I'd get to the stage where I didn't attempt to speak about work at all. I'd get as far as 'Um' and 'Er' and 'You know', perhaps once a fortnight. Except when we looked at *her* paintings.

'Myfanwy is an artist, but she'd never tell you that David. She makes fabulous chairs from found bits of wood and stones and woven rush. And beautiful baskets. They're extraordinary and they sell like hot cakes for thousands. She's collectible these days. You can see her chairs in Liberty's and Heal's.'

'And this time of year is her most trying. Terrible for you, isn't it, Myfanwy love?'

I stuck my tongue out at my cousin. 'Idris is just being . . . a prat. The . . . rushes. I have to cut them now. It has to be July. I have to . . . harvest . . . you know, enough. For the whole winter that is.'

'How do you do it? And where?'

'Why don't you just go along and watch?' said Tucker. 'You'd have him, wouldn't you Van?'

'It's quite . . . boring.' I wasn't sure about having a spectator, having David's charming chatter on the bank, distracting me. It would dilute the aloneness of the rushes, the concentration of reaching into gin-clear water to slice the white juicy stems.

'It's not boring. It's very picturesque. Take photos. They'd love it in America.'

'Well, I suppose given that my child care record is pretty useless I might as well go and leave you to paint and the girls to break limbs without assistance! If it's OK with you Myfanwy?' Looked like I didn't have a choice.

'Well. Whatever. Yes. I leave early. Seven thirty in the morning. Just come to the cabin.'

I went up to the loo before I drove home and sat briefly reading the adverts at the back of a year old Sunday magazine. David and Tucker's voices suddenly came up out of the open kitchen window to the bathroom above as they cleared the dishes.

'Does Myfanwy have a partner?'

'No. Not really. She was married, to Peter.'

'Divorced?'

'No. He died. About four, no, five years ago.'

'And she's still unattached?'

'I think Peter was a hard act to follow.'

Now wasn't that the truth?

Chapter Three

I know that some people do talk to their dead. Not in an Arthur Conan Doyle Ouija board-ish way but in the way Cliff Richard probably says he talks to God: chatting away to thin air about what was on special offer in the supermarket; or rather in Sir Cliff's case why playing Heathcliff is a glorification of His Name and not just a pathetic manifestation of having an ego larger than your brain. The thing about those sorts of chats is that the dead don't really say a lot about what's happened in their day. Neither I suppose does God. I don't like one-sided conversations. People who talk and never listen, or listen and never talk make me feel queasy.

So I don't talk to Peter. I hadn't talked to Peter for five years when I met David. That's a lot of silence. I sometimes thought about how we'd be together, if he came back from some other part of the universe. A whole continent of me was washed away when he died, I wasn't sure he'd recognise what got left behind as being his home planet.

I never talked but I did remember. I remembered all the time. A champion rememberer I was. Some days remembering was almost all of me, but most times just the backdrop. The stage. The set. The bone inside the flesh. I could do remembering like people can do playing CDs. Low level mood-music remembering: playing the atmosphere of one particular time all day whilst

doing something else. Digitally recorded symphonic remembering – every word, look, touch, every detail of setting – pin sharp.
Karaoke interactive remembering where I was back in the scene
we lived, replaying my part just as I did the first time. I had
complete control, I could stop, start, replay at the touch of
willpower. I was a virtuoso.

In ten years there are a lot of memories, a lot of CDs from
which to choose. Of course I had my favourites, my regulars that
I had on in the background, and my all-absorbing specials that I
saved for treats. I nearly always had something playing, some part
of my life with Peter, relived somewhere inside my head.

I was in 'mid remember' when David called the next morning.
A full symphonic digitised recording of the first day Peter and I
had together after our first night. I was at the part where we were
picking our way over the needle-sharp limestone, under the
casuarina trees on the seaward edge of one of the Aldabran
islands. Through the trunks of the trees the sea showed
impossibly turquoise and the shells of more than twenty giant
Aldabran tortoises made a series of dark hillocks against the
water.

We were coaxing and encouraging forty passengers over the
difficult terrain. They were a particularly tetchy group whose
previous life experiences had been confined to the insides of
office buildings and houses with decent plumbing. So their
greatest concern was to get through the morning without
spoiling their shoes. I caught Peter's eye. He was solemnly
explaining the impact of the tortoise population on the islands
vegetation to a small subgroup determined to wrest repeatable
fact from any situation. Mid-sentence he just smiled, without a
break in his words. Eyes and sea were for a moment the same
colour, so bright in the shade that everything else was invisible,
unimportant. Only those eyes and the sea existed in that remote
place for that second. The fact that he was actually talking about
tortoise shit only added to the emotional impact.

Always I stop the CD there and replay that little piece. But

David was half an hour early. I'd barely met the turquoise eyes and there was no time for a rerun.

I was out on the patio, in reverse triangle stand, that nasty yoga pose where you twist your torso back to front and tuck it in behind one leg. You feel fantastic when you stop. On bad days with my yoga I think that's the purpose of the thing, to just be relieved when it's over. I still do it though. Every morning. *Every* morning.

Wake up. Sit up. Get up. Leotard and joggers unhook from the door. Open the fridge, get the coffee. Kick the door shut. Make one half cup of espresso. If it's cold I put the cup on the window ledge inside. If it's warm I stand it outside on the paver nearest the kitchen door as it's the most level. And then I do my yoga, and sip coffee between poses. And every morning I do symphonic remembering of that first day. The first day I recognised as the first day of the rest of my life. The rest of my life that I imagined would never contain two mornings exactly alike. Being on your own allows you to be a fascist about your routine without any impediment of obligation or guilt. It allows routine to become an addiction.

But this morning here was David feathered with charm as before, a little red around the eyes, a little too newly shaven but apparently prepared: jeans and work boots and a plaid shirt, all the right costume for the part. But I was two 'navasanas' and a 'savasana' away from the end of my yoga. Not to mention the rest of the symphony.

'Am I early?' he said, forehead already concertinaed. I untucked my torso and stood up.

'Well. Yes.'

'Oh. You finish your yoga. I'll go and . . . make a coffee?' The charm feathers rearranged and settled into place.

'The . . . stuff. Coffee. Mugs. It's all . . . in there. You'll see.' I waved towards the open kitchen door.

'Right. Thanks.' He disappeared inside. I refolded my body. Recued the memory CD. But neither would play. My breathing was all over the place, my balance gone and the only thing I could hear in my head was Peter's rather flat Virginia voice saying 'Even their faeces have a significant impact on the environment here.' How I hate that word 'faeces'. Especially said like that: 'fee-sees' with that nasty high-frequency whistling quality to it. Peter saying 'fee-sees' infuriated me. Why did he have to pander to their prissy middle-class sensibilities with that word? Why didn't he just say 'shit' or 'crap' like he did the rest of the time? In five years of playing that memory I had never come across my own irritation before. I snatched up my cup so smartly that the remaining coffee spilt. 'Fee-sees' 'fee-sees', the CD went on in my head, quietly stuck. I slammed the kitchen door so the whole cabin shook and David jumped up from the chair by the window. He looked frightened; I must have seemed ready to hurl my mug against a wall.

'I've made some coffee. Would you like some?'

'I'll take it. Into the shower.'

'Right.' He stepped across the room and poured a cup from the espresso machine on the woodburner, speaking to me with his back turned, 'Look, I'm terribly sorry I came early. It's obviously not a good time.' He handed me the cup of coffee, 'I can easily go.' With his charm and manners he could have done that better. Made some excuse. Extracted himself from my bad temper quite seamlessly. But for some reason he wanted to stay so much that 'I can easily go' sounded more like 'drive a nail into my forehead but don't make me leave'.

Why was I making this lovely boy so unwelcome? There was no need now to be routinely unfriendly. Only young women were deemed beautiful by the world. At thirty-six I was safe, at the stage where people said things like 'she's good for her age isn't she?' Who exactly was I being irritated with anyway? David for arriving promptly or Peter for not keeping to the script I'd given him? My morning rituals that I prided myself on being so sustaining suddenly seemed as limp and pathetic as a train spotter's willie in a frost.

'No. No. I'm . . . sorry. I'm not, you know, used to anyone being here . . . anymore. I'll be five minutes.'

He sat down again then, discreetly looking out at the sea as I scuttled from shower to bedroom, got dressed, crunched my hair into a fat plait without brushing it.

Once again David leapt up, startled when I came into the room. 'It's OK. I'm not, you know, put out. I'm glad, really, you came.' He smiled then, a smile that went deeper than the ones I'd seen spread like camouflage over his face.

'Good. I just hope I can be of help.'

Well, he did look as if he might have been helpful. Reasonably strong, fit and young as he was he should have been helpful, but I suppose dance isn't much of a preparation for anything practical beyond tying shoelaces and lifting anorexics over your head.

There wasn't much to get ready before we could set off. My van is kept as prepared as a Baden Powell devotee at all times, with boxes of tools, waterproofs, wellies, boat gear all stowed away in the back. The roof rack is always on, a foraging find can happen anywhere and be of almost any size. I once found eight feet of oak pew in the paddling pool of a Cardiff park. All we needed to do was assemble a last few bits and get the coracle on top of the car, I do it on my own easily; they're built to be carried coracles, because you can't steer the damn things against a stiff breeze or current so the only way to get back up stream is to get out and walk with your boat on your back. So I left David to load it whilst I got the sorting table and some extra ropes.

I came back and just saved him from puncturing the pitched canvas on the end of the rack. Then he tried to close the van door on the paddle, narrowly avoiding smashing it, the window and his fingers. Then he dropped a cylinder of camping gas on his foot because he wasn't expecting it to be so heavy. By the time we got into the car to drive away I'd decided that I'd to watch out that he didn't drown or spontaneously combust before I got him home again. He was feeling the strain too because he lit a roll-up whilst we were still juddering down the track to the road.

'D'you mind if I smoke?'

'No. Just open the window.'

'Last remaining vice of a dancer. The junk food's gone, the obsession's gone, all I've got to get rid of now is this.'

'Doesn't look like you're, you know, *close* to giving up.' He drew on the fag as if it was the secret elixir of eternal life and shut his eyes.

'No.'

At that time of the morning, even in July when the caravans appear like zits overnight and ordinary meadows sprout orange tents, the road across the mountains – that Peter called pimples – is clear. I'd brought the car almost to the highest stretch before David had stopped luxuriating in the blue smoke streaming out through his nostrils. The visibility was astounding. The horizon so distant that even if you'd just watched footage of three hurricanes and a famine on the news you could still imagine the world to be a limitless succession of whale-back hills and knotted copses.

Peter and I had only ever come up here on days like this four or five times in the years we'd had the cabin. Once when we first knew about Peter being ill, we walked all day. We rested in the heather with all the larks in Wales singing over our heads and our backs against the standing stones on the highest rise. We touched their ancient lichen patches, baking in the sun like frilly fried eggs, and talked about time and death, and where all dreams go to. But those sorts of thoughts were recreational then, with Peter thirteen stone, wearing forty-four inch jackets and able to run from low tide to the cabin in twenty-five seconds. We knew as much about illness then as the *Titanic* knew about icebergs the day it was launched.

From the road I can see those stones, and driving past I

always remember that day, the long walking, the larks. The feeling of our existences being sandwiched briefly between great standing stones of oblivion. I play that day as I drive past as other people play Mahler's 'The Song of The Earth' or The Smiths.

But not this time. David threw the tiniest dog end through the window and wound it up.

'Ah. Now I'm human. How far are your rushes?'

'Another hour. About.'

'Right.' There was a rustling, the sort of noise a bird's primaries must make as they snap into line ready for flight. David's relentless charm was not going to allow the private replaying of 'The Last Song' or 'Heaven Knows I'm Miserable Now'

'Would you like to talk? Or shall I put the radio on?'

'Doesn't. Work.'

'All right then. Tell me about rushes, about your chairs.'

'No. You tell me about dancing. When you, you know, began and all.' He rolled another cigarette, and sighed.

'Ok. You probably know all my family history from Tucker but I'll tell it again anyway. My grandfather, Jiri Alstrom, was a selfish bastard when he was young – the women in my family seem to have a soft spot for selfish bastards. Anyway he left Granny Marjorie – who I never knew – when Mum was ten. He dropped her completely. Never gave her a penny, never came to see Mum. Mum didn't even know if he was alive or dead. But when Marjorie died, he sought her out. Came to see her. Helped Dad out with the finance for his first film – even before they were married – gave them the money for the house in Hammersmith.

'Then he used to come round to see me. He took me out every Tuesday afternoon until I went to school. The zoo, the Natural History Museum, The V and A were our favourites. Sometimes the Tate or just the tea rooms at the National. Then when I was bigger – five, I suppose, he took me to the ballet, and to concerts too. But it's the ballet I remember. It was, still is – even in bloody Florida – his big passion. That's probably how he spends his time when Susanne, his twenty-something new wife – lets him – watching videos of ballet. He'd sit right forward in his seat, and watch the dancers as if his eyes were held on needle points. He'd actually hold his breath sometimes without knowing it. I'd nudge him and say 'Grandad. Breathe. Breathe'. We saw some wonderful things together. We both escaped through it. He got away from being a fat old capitalist bastard and I got away from being a nervous wimp with a nail-biting addiction. I think it might have been the only time he really liked me. I was so shy and so frail. Frightened to speak. Spent all winter with earache. I don't think he believed that such a little scrap could be his flesh.

'Anyway. He was big benefactor to the big ballet companies – the Royal mostly, then Ballet Rambert too. He'd have charity "do's" at his place in Bayswater. Mum never went to one. But he'd bring me. Usually I got pretty bored, so I'd find some quiet corner and play ballets, in my head. I'd close my eyes and pretend I was a dancer. Prance around a bit I suppose. And one time, when I was eight, an ex-principal of the Royal saw me and told Grandad "The boy must dance" or some such luvvie nonsense.' David laughed, grimly. Sort of Hamlet seeing the funny side of skulls. And threw the end of the roly out of the window. 'And the rest is as they say history.' He looked out after the cigarette, over the open moor of the hilltops, and didn't look back when I spoke.

'So you went to . . . ballet school?'

'Yeah. The Royal. Then to Rambert when I left. Tipped for the top. Principal at twenty-one.'

I waited for more, for the hours of practice, for the high points of performance, for the big breaks and the setbacks. For the day the injury stopped him dancing. For the positivist propaganda of last night. But he leaned his fuzzy scalp on the window and sighed.

'All a bit of a waste now,' he said.

I'd had the same feeling the day I buried Peter.

He did turn out to have some practical skills. After we stopped talking he mended the radio. Pulled it out and fumbled around in the liquorice allsort wires at the back.

'Mum's stereo was always crap. I was forever fiddling with it to get it to play.'

So we passed the last part of the journey without speaking, hearing what the nation currently held to be their favourite classics: some monks doing what passes for barber shop in the lugubrious and echoey corners of Heaven, an Irish air played on six synthesisers and an electronic bagpipe and a fat tenor singing 'I Feel Pretty' from *West Side Story*. But I suppose that's the function of car radio, to remind you that there are other perspectives on the world that you can't even begin to understand.

It was already warm on the riverside. Damsel flies were doing Folies Bergères flitting over the water, black lace wings swinging like the skirts of French dancing girls. Swallows shot low over the water to drink, then out over the lolling heads of cattle to pick up a beak full of fat bluebottle. It wouldn't be long before the horse flies realised there was thin human hide on offer just feet away from the cows. The river surface was smooth enough to appear solid, not liquid, and only the hair-like wafting of the weed on its bed showed the water to be flowing at all. A few fields away a tractor was cutting grass for silage, late because of the wet June, the only high contrast sound in the background texture of insect whirr and faint bird doodlings. The rushes looked great. Well grown, long and just ready to flower. Perfect.

'I didn't know there were real places like this. I thought they only existed in Merchant Ivory movies,' said David, sinking down in the grass by the water a little dazed with sunshine and summer. He got up to help me but I motioned him to stay sitting. I didn't want the coracle punctured. I set up the sorting table to prepare and bundle the cut rushes. Put my ropes and pegs in the boat and launched her from the bank, light and easy as a leaf. Coracles are unlike any other craft. In most boats you feel 'in' the water, floating but definitely part of it. In a coracle you're like a pond skater, they float so high that you feel that the surface tension is what holds you up, like a trapeze. I still find I'm surprised on lifting the coracle out to find she's wet on the bottom.

I paddled her – she's a she, but I've never named her, it would be like giving a house name to a tent – to the opposite bank, got out, pegged two ropes, one at the downstream and one at the upstream end of the rush bed. Got in. Paddled back and pegged the ropes together on the opposite bank to make a triangle of handholds across the river; paddling with a boat loaded with rush is too hard, especially in the stiff breeze of a summer afternoon. I've learned to do it all this way myself, all trial and error, necessity and invention. Each stage of the rush-cutting I've wrested from the grasp of my own ignorance and inexperience. I've won the whole process for myself so even the simple pegging of ropes is deeply satisfying to me.

The last couple of years that Peter was alive I'd started making things. I made maybe one chair a year, a basket or two perhaps. I bought my rushes and I didn't know a coracle from a gypsy's horse. I'm not sure Peter would have like rush-cutting, although I know he would have loved the coracle. He would probably have spent the whole day paddling up the river in it exploring and I would have to have made two, one for me to work in and one for him to play.

He loved all boats. He used to go to great trouble to get himself rides in any sort of craft that was new to him, wherever we went. We were out one time taking a group of pacs round a little beach-side fishing village off Zanzibar. Pete just disappeared. 'You can cope sugar? I'll be back,' was all he said, leaving me with the two Misses Varney Chets and their identical bunions and the Modburys and their recollections of Sevenoaks through the ages. Trying to get them to think about anything apart from the heat was a struggle. It was only when Peter shot past waving from the tiller of a little fishing dhow with the boat's two owners beaming on the prow that they began to take any notice of their surroundings at all.

In my home-made boat out on the river I used to think of that moment: Peter's delight, so infectious even at fifty metres that my little band of overheated OAPs burst into spontaneous applause as he passed. I thought too of all the times in other boats; capsizing our dinghy to cool off on a hot day; ripping back to the ship in a zodiac across the glass calm of Arctic sea. It was a slide show, a loop of stills that clicked round in the back of my mind as I balanced the boat he never saw. It was the only boat I had now. I didn't go on the sea after Peter had gone.

By the time I was ready to take my scythe and cut I'd almost forgotten about David, still sitting and looking about him on the bank.

'You did all that so easily.'

'It's . . . practice. You know. Like pirouettes or . . . whatever. Do you want to . . . get in. The boat?'

'No. Not yet. I want to watch.'

And he did. Without a word. No questions. None of the incessant chattering charm I'd felt so apprehensive about. A friendly presence on the bank, neutral and approving as a dog. I cut rush for more than an hour without exchanging a word with him, undisturbed in my little world of clear green water and tiny fish darting from my hands as I reached to the white bases of the stems. Each time I had a boat full, unasked he came to the water's edge to unload the rush, smiling quietly and scooping the bundle quite efficiently in his arms. An armful of rushes is about the same size as a dancer I suppose.

When I'd cut nearly the whole bed, I showed David how to

sort the rushes and tie them into bundles. He seemed truly keen to help, beyond his politeness and charm.

And he was OK at it too. Careful, observant, dexterous. Perhaps rushes feel like the strings of ballet shoes. I didn't ask. From then, all day we worked as a team. I cut. He sorted and bundled. We smiled, said the occasional word but mostly we were silent at our tasks, part of the river and the sun and lazy bored cows staring at us from the opposite bank. We got into a rhythm so that when all the last bed was cut in late afternoon, I was sorry. I'd always done the job alone and assumed that was where all its joy lay. I was surprised to find I'd been wrong.

We loaded forty bundles of rushes into the van, crammed to the ceiling, then lifted the coracle, together this time onto the rack. I looked at David over the roof of the car as he tied the rope to hold the boat in place, far more businesslike than he'd been in the morning.

'David, you've been . . . brilliant. I've got so much done today.'

'I have had the best time! I could never have imagined how much fun this would be.' This wasn't charm. No face full of down. He was glowing, luminescing from the inside. Seeing his genuine pleasure in sharing this piece of my life, that before had been solely my own made me blush, as if he had told me I had good legs or a sexy mouth.

'You never even had a go in the. Coracle. Try now. We'll . . . untie it.'

David was reluctant. Afraid to damage my boat he said. But I made him. I wanted to see that glow again. I was sure he'd feel the magic of how she sat 'above' the surface.

In fact he fell in. Mum taught me to row almost before I could walk so I forget that for most people a boat is not merely an extension of their own bodies. Even with his good balance, it took just one gust to tip him over. The coracle bobbed up above him like a cheeky pony with a novice rider.

'Bugger!' he said as soon as he had stopped spluttering, then 'I'm sorry. Is your boat OK.'

'Fine. You OK?'

'Yeah. Can you help me out?'

I pulled him up the bank. Furious with the boat. I could have smacked her broad bottom as I hauled her out. But David was still neon glowing, even standing like a doused Labrador on the bank.

'Well, briefly that felt great. I mean, I was upright for a minute. Can I have a go another time?'

'Whenever you like.'

'Can I come rushing again?'

'Of course,' I said. I didn't even think about the further invasion of solitude. 'Come at the weekend. I'm cutting then.'

'Have you got any spare clothes? I can't sit in your van like this.'

So David travelled back dressed in the blue boiler suit that I kept in case I have to get under the car, with three inches of arm and leg sticking out and an arrangement of fly buttons that would have been indecent had he not wrung out his boxers and put them back on. Still he was undimmed, the fuzzy head that had leant depressed and smoking against my car window was floating high on a straight neck again.

'Nothing to some of the costumes I've had to wear,' he camped. And to prove it he posed in it on every one of the gates we had to open on the way back to the road. Lying across the top of the first one like a classic centrefold, like a swimmer about to do a racing dive on the second, walking like a Russian gymnast on the third. He was so funny, and so beautiful. I curled over the wheel laughing from deep inside as I hadn't for a long time. He made his whole body into a series of perfect little cartoons, and showed me for the first time the control and grace he'd had as a dancer. His whole body was intelligent, even his toes could think and do something marvellous with themselves. Watching his delight in his own physical being was like watching a foal running, or a raven doing victory rolls in an empty sky. He leapt off the last gate in a straddle tuck so high I winced waiting for the sound of cracking femurs as he landed. But he bounced up with impossible energy and threw himself into the front seat.

'I could never do that stuff when I was dancing. Way way too risky. Break a leg mucking about and miss a performance? Tut tut. I'll know about that last jump in the morning.' He rubbed his knees.

'Is that your injury?' He didn't answer but reached for his cigarettes, rolled one, lit it.

'Yeah,' he said 'Yeah, it is. But it's just boring that stuff, about giving up dancing. Boring. Tell me how you learnt about rushes and coracles and making chairs.'

'Oh. It's . . . too hard to talk. I'll just keep sticking.'

'I don't care. I want to know.'

So sticking, splodging words in awkward dollops at first, I told how the chairs began. About foraging. About walking beaches after storms, dragging half trees from hedgerows, always looking in every skip I pass. About the first coracle I made that sank. About the rushes; watching for next year's good patch, coming face to face with moorhens and pike as you cut; how the rush changes, fixing all the colours of summer as it dries. As I warmed up the ketchup speech flowed. It did that sometimes, when I talked to Tucker mostly, but never when I spoke about what I did. At least it never had before.

'It's all just an excuse to be outside all the time, looking at things. Doing what I feel like. It's only when the weather's really awful that I have to make things . . . and I can only do that because the things I've collected make me remember being outside where I was when I found them.'

No sticking. No splodging. I was amazed. So, by the look of him, was David. As we stopped at the end of a queue of traffic I noticed his roly burnt out between his limp fingers. He looked at me as if I were a UFO landed in the driver's seat. Aliens come to take him home perhaps.

'You didn't stick!' he said, still looking dazed.

'Well, I don't. Not always. Just mostly. It'll start again in a minute'.

'Can I come and see your chairs?'

'I've only got one at the moment. A commission. Yes.' I wondered as I answered, answering questions usually being a 'ketchup creation point' if somehow I had got permanently de-ketchupped, unstuck, de-ummed and erred forever. Probably not. I switched off the engine and we sat in silence.

'I don't believe it,' said David after a moment. 'A traffic jam here!'

'It's the bridge, they must be letting a big ship through. We're in for a wait.'

'Oh. OK. Underarm Bowling Association.'

'What?'

'Look. UBA. Haven't you played this before? We did it on coaches when we were on tour. Armenian Yachtsmen Titillate. AYT, that yellow Metro.'

A test of quick thinking plus having to speak the answers, this would put my ers back in if anything would.

'Aardvarks Raid Disco. It's a headline,' I said. 'The black Escort.'

'Brilliant. I can see it all. Aardvarks in overcoats and Homburgs with holes cut for their ears and machine guns.'

'Dark glasses too.'

'SHU. The green Citroën. Socialist Hairdressers . . . Understand!'

'I don't think Socialist Hairdressers would be very understanding.'

'P'raps you're right. No politically incorrect highlights, sir.'

'XHC. Ah! That's impossible!'

'No, there are lots of X words, you get to know when you've played this a few times: xenophobia, xerophyte – a plant thing – xerox . . .'

'OK. Xenophobia Hits Christmas! We've run out now until the traffic moves.'

'No, two new ones behind.' David unplugged his seat belt and twisted round eager for new material.

'WTT . . . Dunno.'

'Waikiki Toning Tables.'

'Great! Kinky Naughty Knights. KNK the old BMW.'

'Australian Brewers Trap. The white van.'

'There's lots for that one. Always are for A's. Austrian Barmaids Treat.'

'OK . . . Arkansas' Biggest Twerp. Guess who?'

'Angels Begin Training.'

'Annie's Biggest Tits.'

'So who's Annie? Arnie's Bollocks Tiny.'

'Oh, I know, that's from the back pages of one of those things like *OK* magazine! I'm sure I saw that last time I went to the dentist.'

The bridge opened. The traffic began to move and we hit a fresh seam of number plates as the traffic opposite streamed past.

'DYF. God. I'm stuck. That's impossible.' I said.

'Yachting, it's always good. Dogs Yachting Fraternity. What about yoghurt?'

'Dewberry Yoghurt Fool. It's in Delia's new book.'

'DFJ . . .'

Peter and I had played a word game waiting in the hospital for x-rays, for operations, for doctors.

'I packed my bag and in it I put pink knickers.' I began.

'Well, how practical. Why pink? You've never worn anything pink in your life!'

'I had pink spotted pyjamas when I was little.'

'OK. I packed my bag and in it I put pink knickers and a box of cookies.'

'They'll just get squashed.'

'Not if you wrap your knickers round 'em.'

'I packed my bag and in it I put pink knickers, a box of cookies and a grapefruit spoon. Because they never have them at hotels, and you end up squirting yourself in the eye when you should be enjoying breakfast in bed.'

It wasn't competitive. When the list got really long we'd give each other clues to keep the list lengthening. We learned our way around each other's filing systems. Sometimes I felt I could see into Peter's head and tell him how he'd labelled the little file he'd mislaid. '. . . red chillies, artichokes, a Williams' pear and. Ah, shit!'

'I'll give you a clue: and gravy.'

'Right! Williams' pears, roast potatoes, green peppers . . .' Peter always said about his mom's cooking that it was 'meat, roast potatoes and gravy'.

The day we did the pink knickers list was the day I noticed Patel's low parting. We packed all sorts of stuff that day.

'I packed my bag and in it I put pink knickers, a box of cookies, a grapefruit knife and a song.'

'You can't pack a song!'

'Sure I can. The score for "Do I Love You?" or even a CD.'

'OK. I packed my bag and in it I put, pink knickers, a box of cookies, a grapefruit knife, a song, your University of Idaho T-shirt. The one you wore on Aldabra on my first trip.'

'I packed my bag and in it I put, pink knickers, a box of cookies, a grapefruit knife, a song, Idaho T-shirt, your blue dress with buttons down the front.'

'Lost somewhere in the laundry room of *Princess of the Isles*.'

That day we packed something from every ocean we'd sailed, every island we'd visited, every year we'd spent together.

'The blue dress', whose buttons Peter had wanted to undo.

'The cowrie shell', the perfect one we found on Cosmoledo, and left behind for the hermit crabs.

'The yellow spinnaker', for the dinghy that I bought Peter as a wedding present.

'The Arctic fox', that walked two feet from us as we watched for polar bears on Spitzbergen.

'The bird sculpture', that my dad made Peter from two coat hangers.

'A handful of sand', from the dunes round the cabin.

When the nurse came to fetch Peter we were sitting hand-in-hand reciting our list together, like a rosary, checking that wherever we went from that place we took the same things in our bags.

'Come on, *DFJ*. Come on Myfanwy. Don't give up on me now! DFJ!' 'Dreadful. Demon. No . . . I can't, you know, think.' I was reummed and re-erred, ketchupped up again as the CD of my last memory game with Peter played with full digital accuracy in my head. For the first time I didn't want to listen. But there was no stop button to press.

David gave up on DFJ. The traffic thinned. We turned on the radio: classics for relaxation.

'Mogadon music,' said David, leaning against the window again, 'music for the living dead.'

Chapter Four

My parents always were pretty much off with the fairies. Surprising for a biochemist and his GP wife. They were too old by the sixties to wear love beads and drop out, and hippydom was a bit mainstream for them anyway. They both believed passionately that humankind would be saved by radical science. Not the sort of science they were paid to do in the lab or the surgery. No. But the sort they could conduct at weekends at the bottom of the garden.

In my earliest memory of them I am standing on my teddy to give me the height to see out of the open window. At the end of the lawn next to the stone birdbath, at the bottom of the two long beds of my father's experimental tea roses, is a huge vat, like a hot tub. My father dressed in a mandatory mad scientist's white coat is standing on a wooden stepladder and peering into the hatch at the top. My mother similarly clad is fussing over the small camping gas burner beneath the huge saucepan-like shape. Their intensity of purpose melts the rest of the garden, the house, and me into an undifferentiated blur. At the same moment they lift their heads and look at one another as if prompted by some signal. Both faces in profile are lit from within, my father says 'We could feed the world with this, Zoe!'

'I know, William. I know.'

That particular pre-Geldof attempt to banish famine forever, ended, my father later told me, when the neighbours complained about the smell from the autolysed yeast protein they were trying to produce in the hot tub.

They weren't joyless lunatics; they were happy in their madness. Happy to include me in it and make my life as interesting and fun as possible. And they had passions other than saving the world, or rather other passions they could use to save the world. My mother was convinced that the sea was our real home, that it was 'our watery cradle'. She would tell me her visions of a future when humans would live in communities of blue bubbles floating on the surface of the oceans. We would harness plankton for our food and ride around on trained dolphins. She kept faith with her dreams through sailing and swimming in the sea whenever she could. The sea was her religion, and in spite of the fact that we lived a hundred yards from the North Orbital she managed to pass me her skills of seamanship. We spent every holiday at her old friend's cottage on the Cardiganshire coast, just north of where Dad had grown up, endlessly launching Mummy's little sailing dinghy or her skiff and outboard from the steep unsuitable beach.

Both my parents believed in the therapeutic and transformational power of music. My mother even used it in the surgery to relax particularly nervous patients thirty years before 'Celtic Moods' got played in dentists' waiting rooms. My father bought a radiogram for work, and drove colleagues in the offices around his lab bonkers by playing the Dies Irae from Verdi's requiem at full soul-cracking volume whenever he really needed inspiration. At home they played music together, Daddy sang in a surprisingly sweet tenor voice and Mummy played. Show songs: *Oklahoma, Carousel, West Side Story* and the odd bit of folk, or old music hall. 'Love's Old Sweet Song' was their favourite.

> Just a song at twilight, when the lights are low
> And the flickering shadows softly come and go,
> Tho' the heart be weary, sad the day and long,
> Still to us at twilight comes love's old song
> Love's old sweet song.

Classical stuff they left to the professionals and played records of Beethoven, Mahler, and Mozart so loud the bricks spun with it. Just as other kids learn to make cakes or plant lettuce seeds through watching their parents I learned to play the piano. But until I met Peter it was like cake making, or seed planting, a private pleasure for home, not performance.

I think my mother was born strange and original, and stayed that way because no one ever showed her another way to be. The youngest of seven children — six brothers, the daughter of a Cornish doctor widowed at her birth, she was just allowed to grow up however she happened to. And that happened to be mostly in and on the sea. Her brothers' boats raised her as much as any human did.

My father's talent for eccentricity was learned in part from his own father, Granda Idris, farmer and part-time vet. Self taught, Idris the First was a cheaper fix for sick cows and women in labour than the chap from Haverfordwest with the degree from Swansea. The explorer Nansen was his hero and through Nansen he developed all sorts of daft ideas about the benefits of the Innuit diet. For the last twenty years of his life he never ate meat that hadn't been buried in the garden for a week, and he passed the winter smeared with goose fat and sealed inside lambskin underwear.

His wife Elspeth — Gee — and elder son Rees (my cousin Idris-the-vet's father) just got on dourly with making the farm pay. But they too had their moments. Gee's cakes for instance: tiered and stepped like the pyramids, up to ten layers of Victoria sponge coloured like a rainbow and shaped into boats, houses, globes. Worryingly unstable and lurid but delicious. She always made you take a second slice. Trying to destroy the evidence I think before Rees got home and told her off for being so daft. His only weakening to the family vice was naming all his sheep after movie stars. But youngest son William grew imaginings that even Granda Idris, Elspeth's cakes or Rees's Ava Gardner sheep couldn't cope with. Too bright for his own good they said, but it got him to university and far away to a salaried post in the white heat of technology.

Even my parents' first meeting was mad. They were both in Sarawak, as it was then in the late fifties. She as a Mission doctor trying to take the antiseptic joys of western medicine into a jungle where the nearest thing to disinfectant would only ever be spit. He on a fact-finding research trip, looking at how sago was grown and produced in the heart of the forest. One night curling up on a mat at the guest end of the men's longhouse he heard 'It's too damn hot!' coming from the other side of the compound. He shoved his feet sockless into his boots and groped his way out towards the sound. It was my mother in her Mission hut playing on the windup gramophone she had brought a hundred miles up river, one of her three discs. Cole Porter's 'Too Damn Hot', Glenn Miller's 'Chattanooga Choo Choo' and Kathleen Ferrier singing 'Blow the Wind Southerly'. They were both past their youth by then and had given up on anything but intellectual passions, so lust and love came as a shock.

They were married inside six months after the night in the Dyak hut.

I came late and unexpected into their lives; my mother was forty my father fifty odd. They named me out of the uneasiness my father felt about having run so far from the sheep and the hills; and out of the same sloppy nostalgia that had them singing 'Love's Old Sweet Song' of a Sunday night. But otherwise I did nothing to break their stride. I was just scooped up into all they were already so absorbed in. So I grew up feeling black and white to their glorious Technicolor, standing on the sidelines of their heroic lives. If my mother hadn't managed to drown when I was sixteen, I'd be there still, holding their coats and half-time oranges.

Daddy abdicated when she died. Resigned. Sold the house. Ran back to Wales and the next hilltop on, from where he had grown up, to try and rear sheep like his brother Rees. At sixteen I had to come too, but I didn't mind, it was my mother's will that had shot me up the academic ladder. Without her I was happy to jump off. I did two years at the local tech, ostensibly some kind of arts course. In reality a crash course in getting myself a life of my own. Before exams revealed just how little I'd done, I dropped out and got a job in the ships' chandlers – more a summer yachty's emporium – in the little town. I bought a moped to travel to work, and sailed Mum's dinghy at weekends. Sometimes Dad would come sailing but I think only so that he could pretend the girl at the tiller was Zoe. We did talk then more than ever we had before. I noticed him for the first time as a separate being, not just a part of the gestalt entity that had been William and Zoe. He had no idea how to be the parent of a young girl, so he didn't try. We shared the house like two adults. I began to call him William. Polite and friendly, gentle and companionable. I felt liked for my own sake.

I think it took him three years to suss that Mum's death was not temporary. But once he did, his eccentricity began to have an existence all its own. He sold the sheep and the land, all but two fields. He began sculpting, making strange objects from anything he came across and populating his last four acres with them. I was woken one night at three by a banging like all the demons of hell getting back to the gates without their keys. When I got up to investigate, I found my father in the kitchen with a hammer, a blowtorch and the bonnet of a car. He didn't even see me when I asked what he was doing.

His intensity demanded that I should be, once again, an audience, on the sidelines. But I'd come to like my little life. So I picked up an ad in a yachting mag one day, a cruise company wanted good zodiac drivers with RYA qualifications. Mum had made sure I'd got all the bits of paper to prove my skills. I applied. Five months later I was in the Med with a boat-load of coffin dodgers and five Swedish officers trying to get their hands down my knickers. And Tucker.

'Trouble is you look so good that you appeal to all tastes. Look. You can't help being beautiful. So just tell them to fuck off. Like this. Fuck. Off. Easy.' I can still see her, leaning against the opposite side of the bar, mouthing FUCK OFF very slowly and distinctly, with both thumbs up in encouragement over the shoulder of the hormonally challenged second officer as he attempted to fall down the front of my shirt. When I met Tucker I thought she was the sanest woman on the planet. Now sometimes when I look at her paintings I realise that she's married into a family that she was meant to be part of; Granda's steak burying, Elspeth's cakes, Rees's sheep, William's sculpture obsession and all.

In old age William's madness reached a plateau. Or perhaps a peak. A happy high place to inhabit, quite safely and contentedly. After I was married and we bought the cabin, and even more after Pete was gone, I found his world was as comforting and normal as the back garden famine solutions of my childhood. Now I've had my own life, I thought, I don't mind spectating his anymore. When I visited him, once, twice, maybe three times in a week, I was always reminded from where I got my foraging. William was the real master, because he never looked and still found things. More than thirty figures line the track to his house, all made of the found and the abandoned. A headless man with an Austin Seven radiator rib cage stands at the gateway, his fingers are knives and forks, bellows for a belly and penis combined, a rusting alarm clock for a heart, a gin bottle liver and two sawn scaffolding poles for his legs. Like all the sculptures – thirty or more – lining the track, he is held in place with two feet of the grade of concrete on which the World Trade Buildings stand. I didn't like to think of how I'd ever get them moved when Dad finally popped his clogs.

At eighty-seven he was still walking four miles every day to the shop and back. As a technophile he had a microwave oven and ate fabulously complicated gourmet meals, straight from their packets. The couple who run the shop – refugees from Coventry – got them in for him specially. He would test drive new dishes for the holiday market – green chicken curry, Thai pork with lemon grass and galangang. He never bought two of the same thing, so if I stopped to eat with him, he'd have Italian and I'd have Indian. His kitchen was as spotless as his lab had been. You could do gene therapy on his pine table. He only ever had to wash up a fork, a mug and a plastic container. *Those* got washed because they were incorporated into sculptures or whatever special investigation he had going on.

The day after 'rushing' with David it was natural dyes. He'd collected wool off the barbed wire of the fences round about, giggling about getting a 'valuable commodity' like wool for free. When I arrived the table was covered in neat rows of microwave dishes each with a little blob of wool sitting in a pool of liquid. Some were simply wet, some had taken a colour from the potion in which they were steeped. On the stove a saucepan of some vile concoction of earth and roots boiled. The fact that a trip to the library would provide the information he was extracting from first principles was irrelevant. He was joyfully reinventing the wheel for his own entertainment.

'Come and look at this.'

He never said hello, and nearly always greeted me by walking away to show what he'd been doing. We stood over the steaming saucepan.

'Nettle root. Not sure what it'll give but that's the nature of experimentation isn't it? But what I really want to show you is in the top field. I've got a big new project going up there. Come on.' Before I'd even uttered a word he'd walked away from me again.

'Will I need. Wellies?'

'No. No. *Come on.*' He strode off across the yard to the gate out into his two fields, moving fast enough to make me scurry. Watching him struggle with the catch on the gate I noticed he was suddenly thinner, the jeans and faded polo-shirt were emptier. I ran to catch up with him as he pushed the old metal gate open over the dried puddles and mayweed.

'Ha. Getting slow in your old age, Myfanwy! No. No. Only teasing, chook. You're as lovely as you ever were.' He patted my cheek, 'Like your mother, she'd be like a twenty year old if she were alive today.'

Before Peter and since, William was the only man from whom I could take a compliment about my looks. There was no transaction involved when Daddy told me I was beautiful. With other men a compliment seemed to be the first stage in negotiating some kind of deal, an opening bid. Or the prelude to some embarrassing display of macho posturing, revving engines (moped to sports car), downing shorts (in both senses), chest beating or peeing on lampposts.

But all that happened after adolescence. Luckily I was a knobbly, gawky little kid. Had I been a cute child all sorts of damage might have been done to me by other people's ideas of what little blonde girls ought to be like. At fifteen a late puberty did me the ultimate makeover and I started looking like something out of a high-class centrefold. In what felt like a span of time that was 'overnight', boys at school who I'd had perfectly normal relationships with based on insults and my unwomanly understanding of two-stroke engines began to behave like pithed rabbits in my presence. Girls who wore pink nail varnish began to want to be my friend. For a while Mummy's death was a distraction from it, but as I emerged from the fog of shock I couldn't ignore other people's perception of me. Beauty was like a uniform that I couldn't get out of, like being a policeman forced to wear a helmet and drive around in a panda car even off duty. I watched men and women glaze with their own assumptions when they met me: I was beautiful and therefore I must be a) stupid, b) incapable of anything more practical than undoing someone else's flies, and c) sexually like a battery, ever-ready.

I think the yachty shop did well out of my looks. Half the boys in Cardigan spent their Saturdays mooching around and buying small items for boats they didn't have. Rowlocks were the favourite. Usually requested by a lone boy with a group of mates outside the door hysterical with laughter. I never got a sensible word out of any of them.

It was all just so irritating. But when I began to work on ships it got scary as I began to work with grown up men. Men with wives and girlfriends and children, with whole lives behind them. The boys in the shop hardly knew what they wanted of me. But these men did know. I read the demands in their looks. Single words with big exclamation marks.

Trying to disguise myself made it worse. Wearing caps to cover my hair, baggy T-shirts, old swimsuits a size too big just added 'easy meat' to the list of 'stupid', 'incapable' and 'ever ready'. Tucker taught me the only thing that worked: act like an ice maiden and tell everyone to fuck off. 'You have to make 'em believe that if they even *think* about fucking you their dicks will fall off. And if they touch you they'll get five thousand volts *direct* to the balls.' After a month of Tucker's tuition I had every man on the ship behaving as if I was wired into the National Grid. After two months with the same men, they had even learned to stop seeing my blonde hair, my long legs, my breasts inside a wet bikini. They noticed my zodiac driving and how many margaritas I could take still standing, instead, which was just perfect with me. But it is why when I met Peter, seduction was so difficult.

As we reached the second field William was obviously very agitated. He stopped at a pile of recently dug earth and gestured over the whole area. 'Well? Well? What do think?'

The meadow, a slope to the west with a view to the roof of Tucker's barn and the sea, looked as if it had been ravaged by a set of giant moles. Forty or more piles of earth described a sinuous path across the grass. usually, given a moment or two I could get my head around even the most obscure of William's creations: the flying stag made from two half deck-chairs and an upright vacuum cleaner, the Kenwood mixer abstract, the portrait of my mother in chicken curry wrappers. But I couldn't see what these earthworks were all about, except that they certainly explained my father's weight loss; if he'd dug all these alone no wonder he was looking so frail.

'Did you. You know. Do all this digging yourself?'

'Of course. Who else? The fairies?' Considering how close he'd seemed to me to be to being stolen away to faery land all my life that wouldn't have surprised me.

'It's just that. Well. All this digging. Very. Tiring. For you.'

'What does that matter. I'm eighty-bloody-seven. I'm about to spend eternity with my feet up. The point is what do you think of it?'

'Well. I'm not . . . certain . . . That I can tell. What it is.' Fortunately that seemed to be the right answer.

'Ha. You can't at this distance. You'll need to go to the roof of Tucker's barn and look. Or the sea. Passing boats will spot it. I'm making mounds in a certain pattern, then I'll plant bulbs to mark it up.' He stamped on the earth pile, grinning gleefully. 'I'm getting a digger up here end of next week. So don't worry about my rest.' Once again he walked away before I was ready.

'But what is it?' I called after him down the field.

'My last masterpiece. You'll have to wait and see. Lunch? Nasi Goreng or Cumberland Pie? Oh, you'll have to move your hives. Can't risk the digger driver getting stung if he knocks them over'.

I tried to wheedle more out of him over the pie. But every time I asked anything about his earthworks he just grinned and insisted I taste a spoonful of Nasi Goreng.

Was he going to bequeath a 'White Horse' or a 'Rude Man' to Wales? Probably something more obscure and bonkers. But he was gleefully determined not to tell.

I drove to a farm sale this side of Carmarthen after lunch but I'd spent so much time wheedling I was late and all the good stuff had gone. Summer sales are often disappointing because the Cardiff antique dealers come out for the day in the sunshine. They can't bear the sight of their selection of overpriced 'austerity' deal tables so they trot out in the Range Rover and clean up all the interesting stuff, right down to the reclaimed timber and bits of old bannister that I might like to buy. I was leaving in disgust when a box caught my eye, an unsold lot of ripped damask curtains and broken tools. Down the bottom were two handleless wooden hay rakes. Solid and with all their own teeth like old farmers' wives. I could see them in a chair. And there was a hand scythe or a grass hook as my father always called them, with a lovely worn wood handle. David could have his own to cut rush with I thought.

I polished the scythe up a little when I got back to the van. Oiled its blade and then wrapped it in the better of the curtains to give to David. I'd deliver it on my way home.

Driving back I took my usual detour to take in the riverside picnic site where Peter and I had had an autumn barbecue with Alex and Becky just after they got married.

If I drove past there in October in the right light I'd sometimes see us all there. Alex playing with the fire, and Peter skimming stones on the big pool. Becky and me leaning against a tree and giggling like twelve year olds. But summer was the wrong time. In summer all I could remember was driving home in the dark after Becky and Alex had headed for the motorway. Peter suddenly pulled in undid his seat belt and grabbed me, kissing me so hard I couldn't breathe. Crossing the stream on the humpbacked bridge the memory of his mouth on my throat was usually strong enough to make me gasp. But today my memory ran on twenty minutes to Peter outside the car after we'd finished. Another detail, the sound of a heavy stream of urine hitting the beech leaves by the car door, then a belch. The sound filled the little valley and the sunny afternoon, and echoed fading behind me as I drove away. At speed.

Back on the main road I did deep breathing and paid great attention to exactly how the gear lever moved when I changed into fourth, and how my foot felt as I depressed the clutch. I put the radio on and planned a picnic for the next day's rush cutting. I thought purposefully about how to get David into the coracle this time without the swimming practice. Gradually the effort of looking out from myself lessened. The weather forecast was good. The rush was in perfect condition. It would be a lovely day.

Jelly and Moffy were playing ballets in the little walled garden at the front of the house when I arrived, with scraps of nylon nightie ineptly wrapped around their hipless hips. Agnes-was draped, pale and interesting, on cushions in the shade playing a board game with Jane. The whole thing looked as if it could have been lifted out of an Edwardian etching. Apart from Jane's orange trainers, and the 'dance explosion' coming from Julian's bedroom window. Only when I got close did I see how dejected they were all looking. Moffy and Jelly's playing was limp and half-hearted as if they were being run on flat batteries. Agnes and Jane threw the dice in slow motion.

'What's the matter with. You lot?'

'David's gone,' said Moffy flatly, coming and slipping a hand into mine.

'Yes,' said Jelly, attaching herself to the other arm. 'Gone to London to be mended.'

The dance explosion cut out upstairs and Julian leant out of the window.

'Mum's not here. She's taken the car in to be MOT'ed. David's gone.'

'I heard.'

'Don't know what you did to him but he was crippled after. He's gone back to London to see his doctor. Osteopath whatever. Then he said he might go to America early.'

'Right. Well. Tell Tucker. You know. I . . . called.'

'Yeah.' He ducked inside and flipped the on switch.

I detached the twins and left. I turned the van too fast. Went down the drive too fast. Let my heart beat too fast. I, who do everything steadily now, evenly with no drops or hillocks, was full of racing for the second time in one day. I parked in Cardigan, hooked the baskets over my arm and fetched up at Graham's shop with my head full of heartbeats and the sound of my dead husband's pee on a pile of leaves.

The closed sign hung at a slant against the glass and the little pine chests and blanket boxes and shelves were dark and lonely inside. But the pots of trailing lobelias either side of the door were streaming from the recent attentions of a watering can and there was a light on still at the back of the shop. The ordinary familiarity of it steadied me. This was one of the little rituals of my life. Yoga every morning, and a visit to Graham's back-street shop once a fortnight. Drop off my baskets, have a cup of tea and some chit chat, collect my money and go away.

Graham was as constant as his blue paint and blue lobelias. Old blue cotton trousers and checked cotton shirt in summer, brown cords, tweed jacket and Doonicanesque jersey in winter. Silky dark hair with a white streak and a line in conversation that never went beyond the last auction he bought at or the last big sale he made. Graham was one of the reasons that I had begun to suspect that I was safe from men these days. In two years of regular acquaintance he had never looked at me, apart from straight between the eyes. He was effortlessly impersonal, the most intimate thing he ever said was 'Thank you'.

He had the laid-back geniality of a local radio DJ doing the Eezy Listening show. I suspected that it was a manner that was more than skin deep, superficial to the bone in fact. Even after all our chat we still knew virtually nothing about each other. I assumed there was nothing to know about Graham. I thought of him as children think of teachers – that outside school hours they cease to exist. I suspected Graham might simply curl up inside a dresser after five and sleep until opening time the next day. He was very good at what he did. He bought cutesy pine furniture – nothing too big to fit into a hatchback – and some local craft stuff that made the pine look good. He kept his hanging baskets stocked winter and summer and he smiled.

I freed an arm and banged too hard on the glass. Graham appeared stooping from the back room, pushing his hair out of his eyes with one hand, as always. He slid back the last bolt and opened the door.

'This isn't your usual time,' he smiled. 'Good job you came, we sold out today. Big coach party from the Midlands. Streamed in bought the lot.' He gestured to the lazy Susan strung up to the high ceiling of the shop. It was empty but for the largest and most expensive rush basket.

'Tea?' he said, squeezing between me and a pile of painted key cupboards.

'Oh. Yes. Thanks.'

'Just dump the baskets on the dresser. I'll put 'em up in the morning.'

'You've got some. You know. Money. For me.'

'I have. I'll look at the book now in a minute.' One thing I know about Graham is that he's originally local, you hear it in his voice. 'Come on you. Through here and have this tea.' He left at eighteen, Idris said, and came back twenty years later with enough money to buy the shop and business outright, a slight Cardiff accent and a divorce. He had a dog, Idris said, which turned up at the surgery periodically for cortisone jabs. 'Vile it is,' Idris said, 'collie cross boxer I think. Never seen an uglier animal in twenty years of practice.' I'd never seen it at the shop so that was proof I supposed that Graham didn't sleep in the dresser. He must have a home to go to.

'I went to that. Sale. At the farm. Was in the paper.' I perched on the desk and put my feet on the chair. Graham handed me a tea.

'Oh, yeah? I couldn't go today. All these coach lot in 'ere.'

'Didn't miss much. I looked. For chests. You know. That you might like.'

'Oh, yeah? Thanks. Anything?'

'No.'

Normally, even at my most ketchupped conversation went a little better than this with Graham. He'd tell me something apparently funny about the customers usually. Or some retailer gossip about the butcher's two doors down getting done for having too high a sawdust content in their sausages or selling haggis to Americans as a Welsh delicacy. I'd tell him about something good I'd foraged or a new commission I'd got. But my arriving out of hours and pink with distraction had put both of us off our stride.

I drank my tea in silence. Graham downed his dregs and put his mug purposefully on the little sink drainer.

'Right. Right. I'll see how much I owe you then.'

He bent over a ledger, pushing buttons on a calculator, brow furrowed, white streak falling over his forehead. I looked at him, reading more than the post code for the first time. Looking at the envelope and the writing and the postmark of the stamp. A little under six foot I guessed. Heavy boned but too thin. Wide, solid forearms showing from the rolled-up sleeves, back muscles moving under the stretched fabric. Square hands, scratched and battered looking, with short thick fingers. Good legs by the looks of things. High cheekbones and a prominent curving nose. Oddly girly lashes and eyes like coal. Overall very nice really. More than nice. What Tucker would once have called 'Definite Mantotty'.

'Nice work, Myfanwy. Two hundred and seventy-six pounds and eighty-six pence. I'll write you a cheque.' He looked up smiling, then frowned. God knows what he read from my face then.

'Is there something the matter?'

'No. No. I. I . . .' I needed to think quickly to get back to faces and bodies as bar codes. Why had I suddenly noticed this man now? This boring man who could only ever talk about his bloody furniture and his bloody customers? Who wore terrible jerseys and shirts like a Texan tourist. What was I going to say? *I've just noticed you are rather attractive Graham, in spite of your terminal dullness.'* Or *'My pilot light which I thought had gone out appears to have burst into flame for some reason Graham.'*

Luckily I hit on my evicted bees. 'I was just . . . My Dad's told me to. Move. My bees that is. I was just wondering if. You . . .'

'You want somewhere to put the hives?'

'Yes'.

'How many?'

'Two.'

'Well. You can put them in my garden if you want. There's quite a lot of flowers. I'll be there Sunday, all day and after hours any other day. Oh and Thursday afternoon next week. That's if you want . . .'

'Lovely. Mmm. Thanks.' I almost snatched the cheque from his hand and left, much too fast. He caught up with me in the car park.

'You don't know where I live. Here.' He handed me a card with his name on one side and a tiny map printed on the other, 'It's the card I give my suppliers. No one's got lost yet. It's about fifteen minutes out of town.'

I got into the van and drove home. What was happening to me? Behaving like a schoolgirl over my best friend's nephew, finding my middle-aged retailer attractive, and unable to recall my beloved's kiss without the accompaniment of his flatulence, belching or urination.

Chapter Five

'Well I can't make head nor bloody tail of it. Here, you look.' Idris handed me the binoculars. Even from the roof of Tucker's barn, a viewpoint William recommended, the half-completed earthworks were still mystifying.

'Daft old bugger. It's probably some sanskrit swearword or something,' said Idris, leaning back against the slope of the roof.

'I can see the way the mounds are. Developing. There is a pattern. I suppose.' I handed the binoculars back. 'But I can't make out what it is. Can't see the whole field from here anyway. I saw him. Yesterday. He's very frail, Idris.'

'He's the best part of ninety. I should think he is bloody frail. No, I'm sorry, Myfanwy. I'm not being just my cynical old bastard self. He's over twenty-one. You don't get to be under twenty-one twice. He's his own man. If he wants to kill himself doing some bonkers art work or some message for passing space aliens then that's his choice. Right?'

'Oh. OK.' Idris has inherited some of Rees's irritation with his younger brother's eccentricities.

'Look. Why don't we just check on him every day now. Instead of every other day? I'll go after surgery tomorrow. Elen can pop in on Sunday morning and you can look in on him on Monday. Yes?'

'Yes. Thanks Idris. That's sensible. You'd better. Get down. You know. Get ready.'

'Oh bugger it. Takes me two seconds to get the DJ on. None of that tying nonsense with the bow, I've got one on a ribbon. Dead easy. Elen will be ages yet. I can stay out here for ten more minutes and we'll still be on time for the bloody dinner. Much rather have dinner up here. I think we ought to build a veranda or whatever on the barn. You could see the sea that way if it wasn't for the house. Another ten feet and I'd be able to send you smoke signals at the cabin. It's lovely.'

It *was* lovely. The first dry night for almost a week. In front of us the hills climbed like green billows up to William's earthwork at the top of the furthermost. Treetops crowded into the little valleys like foam, and the air, full of the moist breath of well-watered plants, split the evening sun into a gold mist. House martins squirted their chirping calls around the eaves and the tops of the girls' heads bobbed under the orchard trees. We could have been the prow of a great schooner bouncing the green curves all around the world.

'I've lived here all my life, Myfanwy. I'll die here, and I hardly ever look at it all.' Idris sighed. It wasn't like him to sigh. He had his father's dour practicality.

'But you're looking now.'

'I s'pose so. Oh God.' A second sigh more lugubrious and dramatic than the first. Perhaps this was where Agnes got her RADA standard tantrums from after all. I got the feeling he was waiting for a cue.

'What. Is it Idris.'

'I can't tell you how sick I am of being a bloody vet. I've had it with putting my hand up cows' backsides first thing on a Monday morning. I know this bloody job backwards and sideways. If I see another sodding dew claw this week I'm going to learn how to make collie curry. Or better still turn cannibal and sort out some of the lentil-brained dog owners around here.

I could throw in the cats as a kind of appetiser. Best use for the little bastards. Vanity and selfishness made fur!'

Idris had always moaned about his job, in the long tradition of comic moaning from Eeyore through to Victor Meldrew. But this was not comedy, not done to make Tucker roll her eyes and the children groan. And he was only just warming up, staring into the green distance and speaking with fierce low emphasis.

'And sheep. *Sheep*. Fucking sheep. Do you know how absolutely bog bloody stupid sheep are? They get tangled in a bit of bramble and it's "Oh God, I've got a thorn in my wool, I think I'll just drop dead". And horses. Jeezuz. They eat the wrong sort of bloody grass and they die. They're pathetic the lot of them, domestic animals. Don't hold a candle to something wild.' He sighed again and turned from the hills to look at me and lay his heavy hand on my arm.

'D'you know, some mad old bat brought me a fox the other week; car had hit it. Old vixen she was. She'd broken her pelvis in the accident. But she had an old break in her femur that had mended long ago and given her one leg four inches shorter than the others.' A smile of profound pleasure and admiration pushed its way across Idris' mouth at the memory of this wild fox, but as he finished telling me about her his eyes filled with tears. 'She'd been hunting and rearing cubs with the short leg. And with a broken pelvis, and gangrene mind, she was still ready to bite my hand off.' He shook his head laughing, crying together.

'And there I am wasting my bloody life trying to save animals that have barely got the will to live in the first place. Half of them end up wrapped in clingfilm on a shelf in Safeways. It's crazy. I want to do something with real animals. Wild ones. I've applied for a job in Kenya. Wildlife vet it is they want. Ten years' experience of practice. Well I got best part of twenty. I reckon I'm in with a chance. I've got an interview anyway.'

It occurred to me then that, unlike his relatives, Idris had never called sheep Yul, or Sophia, never made any sort of cake let alone one with sixteen tiers, never buried the Sunday joint with the potatoes or attempted to solve the world's food crisis in a DIY jacuzzi. This was his moment. And as our family's moments went, it was pretty tame. Almost amounting to sensible career development. I could just imagine Tucker painting under an acacia, smearing huge canvases with hot African colours, and the girls madly enslaving the hordes of nannies which in Kenya Tucker and Idris would be able to afford. Only Julian didn't quite fit. Showers were in limited supply the last time I was in the Serengeti.

'I think. It's wonderful,' I said, and squeezed the hand left on my arm.

'It wouldn't be forever. Just a few years perhaps.'

'What about. This. The house?'

'Oh, we'd tart it up a bit and rent it out. Could make a packet.'

'A holiday house. For some TV mogul!'

'Something like that. I'm not going bonkers like Granda am I Myfanwy?'

'Pass.'

Idris burst out laughing. 'OK. OK. If I start wearing sheepskin under my Y-fronts you can shoot me, all right? I'd better go.' He turned carefully and got onto the top of the ladder. 'I haven't told Elen any of this yet. So mum's the word, eh? I'm telling her tonight. Fingers crossed.' He disappeared over the edge.

Something was in the air for all the Bowens, then. William's last message to Martians. Idris off to commune with giraffes and me losing the post-Peter equilibrium that I'd worked so hard to establish. My world of remembering and solitary routine was unravelling. Starting with my Peter memorial CD collection. All week my Peter memories had behaved like virus infected files, throwing up weird faults, sticking, jumping or refusing to play at all.

On Saturday whilst I was doing my yoga and playing 'our

first morning' memory it stuck again on Peter saying 'fee-cees'. He repeated it over and over in his explanation of the impact of the giant tortoise population. He pointed out tortoise turds over and over. When he picked one up and tasted it offering pieces to the assembled passengers like Jesus handing out the fallen crumbs and fish bones to the five thousand I gave up on the yoga and the remembering, and went for a run instead with my Walkman playing full volume 'Poptastic Radio Local'.

For two days in a row I drove to the river to cut rushes and both there and back passed the standing stones where Peter and I had lain under the singing larks. Four times my memory stuck at a place I'd never remembered before: Peter telling the birds to 'shut the fuck up'. On the third day, I took a different route – a more direct one that saves twenty minutes on the journey and passes the garage where they sell the best tuna sandwiches in West Wales. I camped in the drizzle by the river for two nights to avoid the drive altogether.

All the time as I cut the rush on those days a loop of images played in my head. Not the usual one of Peter on all the boats we'd been on together. No. This was Peter losing his temper in every situation we'd shared from Cardigan Bay to the Aleutians. Here he was kicking the hoover in the cabin and dislocating his toe; here he was reducing some poor fat woman to tears for doing the wrong thing with her life-jacket; here he was shouting at a Malagasy taxi driver. Sometimes the images were in close up, showing his straight mouth and the spittle sticking to his teeth, or the vein throbbing in his neck, or his hands tensing into fists. Sometimes it was just the sound, echoey and distorted.

The loop played and played and I couldn't find a stop button. All I could do was drown it out with work. Every second I concentrated only on the next second and how to cram it full of effort.

By the end of five days' cutting, sorting, and bundling up the rush I was talking out loud to myself like a bag lady on meths.

But I'd cut almost all the rush I needed. I drove home on Wednesday night too tired to fire a neuron, shouting my own name to stay awake. I fell into bed without showering, playing music, or even undressing. Without any of the methodical little routines with which I had textured the predictable parts of my day for five years.

I woke on Thursday not at six thirty but at eleven, and instead of Peter's voice whispering 'Hiya honey' in my head there was my Dad banging at the door and shouting.

'The digger's coming, you've got to move the bees.' I threw on the day before's filthy clothes and ran outside. A very agitated and red-eyed William was practically dancing around his ancient Toyota pickup.

'The driver won't do it if the bees are still in the field.' he stopped pacing and grabbed my shoulders with shaking hands. 'He won't do it. You've got to move the bees.' Every muscle ached. Woken without the calm of routine my mind was spaghetti and my father was behaving as if the end of humanity was at hand because of a construction worker with a a bee phobia.

'Will. You. Shut. Up.' At least I didn't shout but I'd never said such a thing to my father before at any volume. He closed his mouth with a snap.

'Did you . . . shut the hives. Last night.'

'Yes.'

'Right. OK. I'll need your car. I've got. Rushes. Stuffed full in mine.'

Without another word we got into William's pickup. I drove. His failing eyesight and anarchic approach to road discipline were more than my nerves would stand. All the way up his junk-lined drive he mumbled on and on about the digger driver and the bees.

In my head a Peter CD started, something nice: Peter bringing me toast in bed balanced on one hand like a waiter. But as Peter opened his mouth to speak I found myself growling again, out loud: 'Oh, shut UP!'

The CD clicked to black.

'I wasn't saying anything!' claimed William.

The tattooed and balding driver was truly phobic. He had to go in the house and lock himself in the downstairs lavatory whilst I moved the closed hives into the back of William's car. My brain was still in the blender as I drove as gently as I could down my dad's unmetalled drive to the road. Where the hell was I taking these bees anyway? I rummaged in my trouser pockets and pulled out the folded card. After almost a week in with the fluff and coins it was only just possible to read the little map that showed where Graham's house was. 'Hafod yr Cwm' was the house name. My Welsh is non-existent really, (Grandad Bowen being mad and progressive embraced English and never spoke Welsh at home, not even to the farm boy or the kitchen help. Rees and William grew up the only monoglot English speakers in the district) but I can translate bits. Graham's home was 'The Shepherd's Summer House in the Valley'. It was more inter-esting than I'd expected: 'Arosfa', the Welsh 'Dunroamin' would have been less surprising.

'Hafod yr Cwm' turned out to be up another unmade track like my family's houses, a fifty-yard dip down from a hairpin bend at the end of a valley I didn't know. It was a tiny single storey stone house, with huge windows and French doors as if all the crumbling stonework of the old beast house had just been replaced with glass. Next to it was a barn three times bigger, with new doors and a patched roof. The buildings looked as if they had been simply placed in their meadow from above, the flowers and grasses brushed aside for a moment to make room. At its edge the meadow gave way to a woodland made of oak trees fresh from the set of some Druid drama documentary. None of it was what I'd expected at all. It just didn't match the sweaters.

There was a bit of vaguely paved hard standing by the barn door where the track petered out, and a mown path to the door of the house. Two vehicles were already parked. Graham's blue Bedford and a dark green delivery van with 'Davies' Pianos' written in tasteful white lettering down the side. As I drew up the piano van turned and drove away. Lost, I thought. What would Graham want with a piano? I'd never heard him even listening to the radio in the shop. Perhaps they were trying to deliver a baby grand to a recluse concert pianist preparing for her next European tour. Graham was often telling me how 'interesting people' were moving into the area and buying his cutesy furniture for their summer homes.

I stopped the car and got out. A breeze shimmered the flowers and grasses and dappled the shadows under the oak trees. My blender brain subsided into quiet. Even with the van's departing diesel to spoil it the atmosphere was extraordinary: like a smoothly iced lemon cake waiting on a perfect tea table, or a baby sleeping under a white coverlet in the open air.

'Oh. Hello!' Graham stepped out from the French window front door and came down the path wearing a revolting lime green T-shirt and sawn-off jeans. At least something about the situation was conforming to type. In spite of the sartorial offences it was an effort not to whisper in reply to his greeting, so strong was the influence of the buttercream calm and innocent leaf rustling.

'Oh. Yes. Hello. I've brought . . . My bees.' Looking at Graham again I was grateful for the T-shirt. Seeing him as 'Mantotty' again would have been the final straw that day.

'Right then. Where would you like to put them?'

'Anywhere. I mean. There's flowers. All over.' I gestured wildly to the meadow.

He helped me carry the hives around to the back of the house, where the meadow just continued for another acre or so to the edge of the wood. We put them on a slightly south-facing rise about a good stone's throw from the house.

'I won't need. To . . . leave them here. For long. Just until my dad's finished. Finished his. Construction.'

'Right 'o. No problem.'

'I'll let you have. Some honey.'

'Lovely job. Would you like a cup of tea?'

Normally there would be so many reasons to say no. Right from mentally wiring all men's genitalia into the mains, through reading people as bar codes to Graham's dodgy clothes sense. But this day I'd broken so many traditions, and I'd had nothing since lunch the day before. Anyway, I wanted to see how many more expectations Graham wasn't going to live up to.

'Coffee?'

'No problem. If instant's all right?'

The ugliest dog in the world — the result of some nasty weather in the canine gene pool — was shut in the kitchen. But what it lacked in looks — ie, everything — it made up for in obedience.

'Lie down,' said Graham, without any sort of emphasis or volume and it ran from our legs to its bed in the corner of the kitchen, its long rat tail beating a rhythm on the wicker of the basket.

Inside, Graham's house was just one big light space. A single room leading outside through three sets of glass doors. There was virtually nothing inside. A white galley kitchen area, a huge sofa along one wall, a futon rolled against another, a stereo system on the floor, a huge dresser. The walls were whitewashed. Everything was spotlessly clean. And in the middle of the floor was a beautiful shining baby grand. My fingers itched at the sight of the keyboard. It would sound wonderful. I pressed a few keys too gently to make a sound as I waited for my coffee.

'I made a bit of toast too,' said Graham. 'There's not much in the way of furniture I'm afraid. I usually just sit on the floor.' We sat on the ancient interleaved rugs that covered the floor. I recognised them as the sort of mixture one acquires from skips: nylon reproductions, rag rugs with bad spills and the occasional worn gem, a real Persian dignified and lovely in dilapidation.

'I didn't. Know you sold pianos.'

'I don't. I've just bought it. Can't afford lessons at the moment – I'm putting in a bathroom, expensive it is – but I'll muddle along with a book or two. Always wanted to play like. But my auntie told me I had the wrong sort of hands. Put me off.' He held up his hands and spread his fingers inspecting them. Palms like spades, digits like fat carrots.

'She was dead right of course. But then I want to play for myself, not for the Albert Hall or whatever. Here look, this bit of toast's got your name on it.'

I took the toast but couldn't bite. Buying a baby grand for God only knew how many thousands was rather more than just muddling through 'Old MacDonald' just to prove Auntie Flo didn't know spit.

'Why did you get. You know such a . . . I mean a baby grand?'

'Simple. It's beautiful. Isn't it? Very beautiful. I'm going to sit at it and have the windows open and one day I'll be able to play something . . . nice. Anyway it sounds lovely even if you can't play. Can you play? Artistic type. Bet you can.'

'Me? Oh. No. Not. You know. Really.' Not since Peter anyway. Not even alone now. Not for ages. 'But I know. What you mean. About playing in here. It will be nice. Very.'

I could feel just how very nice it would be, the open windows and the shimmering light outside, the shining piano and the keys yielding like muscled flesh. The experience Graham wanted, called me too, not with some little dinky voice in my head, but a great grabbing hand pulling at my guts with longing. I could just walk up to the piano now and play. Fill this light with notes and feel it going up my arms down my spine and into the earth again. But with Graham there? Impossible. Taking all my clothes off would be easier.

'If I ever progress beyond one finger scales I'll let you know!'

'I've got my dad's car. I'd better go.'

'Right'o. Sorry. I didn't want to keep you from your work, whatever.'

'If there's, you know, any problem. I live on the beach. You know the cabin?'

'Oh, aye. I know.'

'Or you can leave a message. At the vet's. Idris Bowen. You know. My cousin.'

'Have you got a phone?' Only Tucker's clan knew my phone number. I told other people I didn't have one. If the phone rang too often I got the feeling Peter would start to ring, and tell me he was still alive somewhere. I could see myself ending up chasing to Bali, or Tierra del Fuego, or the Aleutians to find a dead man.

'No. No, I haven't.'

'Right'o. Is there anything I need to do for the bees?'

'No. Just tell them. Your news.'

'What?'

'If you have news. You have to. Tell the bees first.'

'Oh. Right. No danger of that then. I haven't had any news for about five years.'

'Well. If you play, you know, a tune. For the first time. Tell them.'

Tell them I might go home now and see if my piano lid still opens, if the notes play, if my fingers work. I really might.

I really did. The piano was horribly out of tune, but my fingers still worked the notes and the Cole Porter song book was only a little mouldered. I'd get the tuner in, I decided. I'd broken another tradition that day.

Julian gave Tucker and Idris a lift to the dance en route to Vicky's house. The two of them tottered out to the car hand in hand like sixteen year olds on a first date.

Idris looks reasonably presentable in a DJ. It sort of smooths him out a bit and prevents his body looking, as it usually does, as if all its parts are at war.

Tucker, in spite of being shaped like a pig on its back legs always looks fabulous. Draped in bias cut velvet with the pearly skin of her arms and bosom exposed she is sex in a frock – her mountain of hair, her landscape of curves comprise a world of voluptuousness into which any man could escape for years. Idris is always fondling her bottom before they get to the end of the front path. Watching them go I wondered how affectionate they'd be at the end of the evening after Tucker knew Idris' plans.

The girls were officially tucked up, as they always were when I came to babysit. But we had our private ritual. As soon as the smell of melting chocolate snaked upstairs they'd come down. But not before. I could have my half hour of peace alone with the old house and its speaking furniture, its imprinted walls. After the misplaying memories, the broken routines and the sheer physical strain of five fourteen-hour days on the trot I just wanted to lie on the sofa in the sitting room and let the memory of Gee's tottering cakes wash over me: The background tinkle of the best china as Elspeth gossiped to Zoe and William – down for the weekend, or Easter – about people who had been dead for fifty years; the slam of the old back door as Idris and I ran up the back in our black wellingtons for Idris to show me the new calf, or dare me to go on the rope swing.

But even those fine hand-coloured pictures wouldn't come. Instead something much sadder and darker. Idris, face down on the living-room floor with one of Elspeth's old satin cushions clamped in his mouth, screaming between clenched teeth. It had been the night Susan died. A brain tumour at twenty-three and a six-month-old Julian in the cot upstairs. I was seventeen. Still crying over my mother. I had no idea what to do. I sat by his legs and stroked the back of an ankle.

It made me feel tireder still to see Idris lying there so long ago. I got up and went to the kitchen. Unwrapping the bitter chocolate to melt and chopping the fruit to dip I wondered how often Idris saw himself on the living-room floor or walked into the kitchen to find Susan's narrow back bent over the sink. Maybe that's what he was fed up with too: his hand permanently up a cow's backside and his head intermittently plunged into his past.

We had to have a video on with the chocolate fondue. That was part of the ritual. We sat on the big sofa with an old sheet across our knees to catch the drips. Not because either Idris or Tucker gave a damn about damaging the furniture but because chocolate drips would give away our secret.

'Oooh, this is my favourite bit. Coming up now. When they walk through the grass stuff the dinosaurs start grabbing them. It's reeeely good . . . and then . . .' said Jane.

'They could spit poison from their claws, you know, Myfanwy,' said Agnes solemnly, 'You can tell from the marks on the fossil bones.'

Moffy and Jelly were always totally hedonistic in their movie watching: 'Shhuttup. Shuutupp Jane and Agnes.'

'Ooee. I'm scared. More chocklit.'

Agnes couldn't always shut up, she was after all censor of the twins' viewing. 'Moffy. Jelly. Shut your eyes . . . Now! Keep 'em shut. OK, open 'em.'

Watching a film with junior Bowen girls was always much more absorbing than going to the cinema, always enough to drive away anything but the present moment. Immediate as the melt of chocolate in the mouth.

I was washing the bowl and generally disposing of the evidence when Idris and Tucker got home. Julian had brought Vicky back with him and I heard them running straight upstairs. No carwashes this week, Idris had told me.

'I heard Julian tell his mate on the phone that they're exploring tantric sex, whatever that is. But you don't need warm water for it apparently.'

As soon as they came into the kitchen I knew that Tucker had snapped up the idea of Kenya as she used to snap up changing ships or a new first officer. She could change direction as fast a fish. Even if Idris didn't get this job they'd be off somewhere else instead.

They leant against the worktop close together, squirming with the thought of the big thing they were going to do.

'Guess what?' said Tucker.

'No. What.'

'We're going to Kenya. Idris has applied for a wildlife vet's job. We can take the kids. It'll be fantastic.'

'Well,' said Idris, pretending to contain his excitement, 'it's not all signed and sealed you know. We can't get too excited . . .'

'Yes we can. I know we're going. I just know.'

I just knew too. The house knew. Everything knew. Life was taking a big lurch forward, a big about face. Inexorable as a season's change.

As I drove away, I caught sight of Idris and Tucker at their bedroom window; Idris with his face buried in Tucker's hair, already half lost in her beloved continent; Tucker, arms wrapped around him, hands already under the loosened edge of his shirt. They were in their new future. All I had was my old past, the memory of making love with my five years cold husband. It wasn't enough any more.

Chapter Six

After my mother drowned I lost my taste for being out in a good storm. It's sort of Captain Harris' doing that I got it back. Tucker always said that there was a future for Captain Harris on the Woolwich ferry. He was spectacularly inept. The company only kept him on because central casting would have had him behind the wheel of a big ship every time. Built like a deluxe double-walled brick outhouse he was the only thing on board that ever made Pete's ocean liner sides look like a dinghy. He had a voice like a foghorn and unshakeable self-confidence that covered him like anti-fouling paint. But after he'd run aground three times in a year and lost an anchor because he wouldn't listen to the river pilot we had on board, looking right for the part wasn't going to save him.

On what proved to be Captain H's last trip — a whale watching cruise round the Newfoundland coast — he missed the spring tide to take the *Princess* out of a harbour where he should never have risked anchoring. She was stuck on best advice for a fortnight. The passengers were taken off and, eventually, flown home. Peter being Expedition Leader had to stay around and sort out Disgruntled from Tunbridge Wells and worse, three ladies from Pittsburgh who had memorised every word Ralph Nader had ever said. Tucker and I got to skip off on full pay for a week or more.

Tucker got us a couple of berths on another sort of whale-watching trip: a tiny wooden sailboat captained by her old mate Hopp. As we were the only crew and the boat was barely twenty feet long Hopp was only just 'captain'. He'd been surveying whales all summer for the Canadian government and his crew of students had gone back to school come September first.

He needed us to sail *Freebird* (Hopp was an unreformed hippy, still wearing tie dye from the first time around) down the coast to dry dock for the winter near St Johns. It was an epically adventurous trip as Hopp's attitude to navigation was based on his perception of good karma rather than longitude and latitude. He was forever disconnecting the satellite navigation system and there we were some ugly scenes over the chart table. But mostly we were in sight of land and pretty safe anyway as the weather was quiet as a lamb, with nice manageable little breezes.

Then twenty hours off St Johns I was on watch at three a.m., steering a course by the compass in darkness so complete I wondered periodically if I'd gone blind quietly and without prior warning, when the edge of the first storm of the Arctic winter caught us. Within forty minutes the sea was tipping like a roller coaster and trying to hold any sort of course was a joke. It was the sort of thing my mum used to love. The sort of thing she taught me to deal with comfortably until the day it became the sort of thing that killed her.

I sat frozen for a few minutes waiting for Tucker, due on watch any minute, to emerge and let me escape. I stared at the blackness towards the hatch, willing a crack of light to show she was on her way. Nothing. I was going to have to get on with it, sweating palms and visions of my ma going down for the third time, and all. By the time she hauled her oil-skinned bulk out of the cabin, like dough expanding, I had everything under control. Mainsail and Genoa down, storm jib up, course set. And the fear too, burned off as I swore into the high-speed rain, damning Tucker's idle bones. But I was still ready to smack her one until the sea did it for me. As she came on deck we caught a bit of chop broadside and a fat arm of sea water caught her full in the face.

'Yo ho ho and a bottle of fucking rum,' she said, wiping her face. My anger went. My fear had gone. I rode out the storm all the way to St Johns, through the last of the dark and on into the light standing on the pulpit and whooping at the waves like a fairground ride. The wind chased us right into harbour so fast we made anchor in time for tea and cakes in a cafe in town.

So although I didn't sail after Peter died I still had my liking for rough weather and once I'd turned forager there were professional reasons for feeling a lift of the heart at the sound of thunder. A good stirring turned out the sea bed, brought up the lumber lying in the deeps forgotten and asleep, it worried at the edges of the land breaking off the loose and the unattended; everything from rotting bits of Victorian piers to dogs that weren't tied down. I once found a perfectly salt-mummified toy poodle, with its little red bow still in. After a storm there could be flotsam from any shore in the world. It showed the community of the sea, boundless from here to Antarctica, washing up the temperate, the tropical, the lost and the unwanted all onto my beaches.

Which is why the wet and stormy August that followed my rush-cutting July felt like a blessing almost. My Peter CDs were out of control, playing wild, mad and inaccurate. I had to do something to drive them away. There were almost no sustaining moments left. Sometimes I could summon his voice in bed as I woke: 'Hi honey'. Sometimes the blue eyes over my shoulder in the mirror. But most often now he came unasked, shouting, breathing in my ear, snoring, picking his nose, putting his hand down my knickers at traffic lights. Very close, very real. Unpredictable. Out of character. At night I dreamt of him in a boat far out at sea, calling important instructions. When I struggled to swim within earshot I found him saying 'Myfanwy, you got to cut your toenails!' or 'Myfanwy, you got to get me some more green socks!' By day he only spoke within range. His voice loud with all manner of banalities: sail names, capital cities, road numbers, grocery lists. So I went beachcombing in the eye of every storm, glad for weather that demanded my attention. I wanted the waves to shout him down, the wind to slap my face with wet hair and sting my hands with wild sand.

One afternoon in about a force eight, a dry gale but cold as October, I was searching a beach in South Pembrokeshire, far from home. Spray scoured off the sea and the sky was blown clean of cloud, almost clean of blueness. I found the edge of what looked like a nice grainy bit of old oak, I guessed, sticking out of the sand near the low tide mark. I loosened it all round, digging with my hands, then began to rock and worry it free.

After a morning's quiet, a mad Peter CD began to play, quietly at first behind the wind, then cranking up to a volume I felt sure must be audible outside my own head. It was a kind of rap, taken from a tool catalogue that had been lying around the cabin for years. Making a rap out of nail sizes and spanner types was definitely not something the real live Peter had ever done in my presence. Or had he? What was I remembering and what was I inventing?

> Loose pin, steel butt, padbolt, flush,
> Brass cleat, robe hook, vacuum brush.
>
> Gimlet, bradawl, portable vice,
> Drywall saw and trap for mice.
>
> Texture comb, adhesive trowel,
> Dust mask, gauntlet, long chrome rail

I pulled more and more frantically, but the wet sand had done its thixotropic trick. It clung to the wood more tightly the harder I worked. Peter's rap got faster. Faster still. He was really quite good. From what I'd heard on the radio I guessed if he'd done this alive I could have been left with more than a wooden cabin and a fibreglass dinghy.

Tee plate, snap cup, pop top wire,
D ring, screw ring, electric fire.

Washers, tappers, fibre discs,
Bow saw blades and flat wood bits.

Ratchet tie down, iron hawk,
Feeler gauge and spanner torque.

The wind worked into my hair and wriggled it free of its plait, got under my jacket and billowed it out, flapping like a loughed sail. I felt embedded in noise and chaos, that same 'wasp in jam' feeling you get in dreams. The only thought in my head was that I must get the wood out of the sand. I rocked my whole weight back and forth on it even as the waves began to replace the sand I'd scrabbled out. Cold water filled my boots and I still didn't have the presence of mind to just give up. I must have been the day's only highlight for the desperate holiday makers crouched in macs behind their stripy windbreaks; a mad woman with a halo of out-of-control clothing and hair, fighting with a buried plank as the tide washed over her.

Siphon, jumpleads, sealant, wrench,
Tin snip set and handy bench.

Jigsaw, sander, grinder, drill,
Combie driver, concrete sill.

Sliding doors and rim sash lock,
Plastic mortice, safety sock.

Then the sand, bored with the game spat out the plank just as I was leaning away from it with all my body. I shot back into an incoming seventh wave closely followed by the not-so-oak and not-so-interestingly grainy lump of timber, which hit me smartly on the head. That at least stopped the builders' merchant rap.

The ugliest dog in the world was standing over me, jowly as a Tory judge, when I opened my eyes. Standing over *her*, was Graham in a bright blue cagoule that made me want to close my eyes again immediately: dog and man in perfect harmony of awfulness.

But I sat up instead and there was a horrible squelching sound as my soaking clothes sat up with me. I was out of the wind tucked in behind rocks at the top of the beach. Graham crouched beside me and helped me prop my back against a boulder.

'Thank God for that. I thought I was going to have to do cardiac massage and call the ambulance.'

'What are you. Doing here?'

'Walking the dog.' It was too complicated to ask why he was walking the dog on a beach forty miles from home.

'Why aren't you. You know, in the shop?'

'It's Sunday, Myfanwy.'

'Oh. Right. Yes. Bees OK?'

'The bees are fine I think. I haven't told them anything, mind.'

'Oh. Good.'

'How do you feel now?'

'Oh. Fine.'

'You've had a nasty knock, you know. From that wood. And you were right under the water.'

'Did you . . . pull me out?'

'Yes. I saw you from over there. I was walking over to help, with the post, then you fell.'

'How did I get. Here?'

'Half walked, half dragged. Then you went out, phhht. Scared the living daylights out of me.'

'I can walk. To my car. I'll go home.' I got up, held the top of the rock for a moment and began to walk away. Graham followed.

'I don't think driving is a good idea. I can drop you home and bring you back tomorrow to get your car.'

'No. No. Really. I'm fine.' I stopped walking and turned to face him. The wind pushed the blue cagoule hood over his eyes along with the brown-and-white striped dollop of hair. Not mantotty today, that was for sure.

'Graham. I'm fine. I'll drive home.' That was the voltage to the goolies voice, and it worked as well as always. He actually stepped backwards.

'All right. If you're sure. I'll carry on walking the dog like.'
'Bye then.'

'Bye Myfanwy. C'mon Bet.' He strode off down the beach with Bet, the world's worst looking dog at his heels. The dog's embarrassingly pink and breast-like teats wobbled with every step, and the nasty cagoule pulled in unsightly creases over Graham's behind as he hunched his hands into the pockets.

I felt sorry then, seeing the two of them heading into the big flat sands alone. I hadn't even thanked him for being kind. Just treated him like a shark, when he'd never been anything but a goldfish and I wasn't even shark bait any more. Was I? I called after him, 'Thanks. Don't get cut off. By the tide.'

But the wind took my words and flew them out to sea. Graham didn't turn round. I was the one in danger of being cut off by the tide not him.

August wasn't entirely full of Peter behaving like Jack Nicholson on speed inside my head. There were quiet days at the end of the month. Days when any memory of him was absent. They were almost worse than socket wrench sonnets, whispered obscenities and stereo snoring. I felt cold and exposed as if my soul had had a very severe haircut and was now hat-less in sub zero temperatures. I stayed in on those days, as if it were really winter. I shored myself up in my workroom, with the month's haul of driftwood and the remaining bundles of last year's rush.

I had an excuse apart from comfort seeking; a short notice commission from old colleagues who wanted a chair to celebrate the birth of their first child. I made a wide low rocker, with layers of soft tight plaited rush like a great nest. The repeated rhythm of weaving the twisted green and gold leaves back and forth, back and forth was comforting, mind numbing. I think sometimes that rush is narcotic, like the hops that sent the cockney pickers to sleep on the trains back from Kent.

One Friday afternoon I was in a rush trance over the last bits of the chair. I'd made sure I knew what day it was after being caught without a clue by Graham.

It was a nice Friday-ish sort of Friday. Hopeful sort of weather that looked as if, given the encouragement of a Saturday morning to live up to it might even improve. No storms. No wind. Almost resembling summer again. All the same I didn't want to be in the outdoors and have to feel how much space there was around me without even Pete's mad alter ego to keep me company. Opening the door of my workshop let in enough of the world's uncertain sunshine to manage on my own.

I didn't hear any scrunch of the gravel yard outside the workshop. So when I felt that the top of my bent head was being watched, I assumed some new form of memory aberration. Perhaps Peter was now going to appear hologram-like before me, and was at that moment standing in the doorway ready to express views and behaviour his living personality had never allowed.

What could be next? Dean Martin impersonations? Reciting the First Amendment? Quoting Chairman Mao in the original Chinese? I kept my head down, concentrating harder and harder on the details of the rush, between my fingers. How did you speak to manifestations of your own mind? And if you spoke did they answer back?

'You didn't hear me come in, did you?'

Not Peter's voice at all. For a split second I thought that it might be the final memory breakdown, Peter speaking with someone else's voice. But it wasn't. It was David. Looking tanned, a little nervous but smiling a true smile, which seemed oddly catching.

'I said I'd come and see your chairs.'

I jumped up as if the rushes had suddenly turned to asps and found my tongue was ketchupped to the roof of my mouth. My tools clattered out of my lap with embarrassing volume but gave me the excuse to spend minutes possibly hours — days even — scrabbling around retrieving them from the corners of the workshop floor. I gathered tools, and time to compose myself, to shake out something in the way of words. As I unfolded from under the chair I came face to face with David. Also on hands and knees, unnecessarily or unintentionally very close.

'Oh. Hello,' I said, stuck half between kneeling and standing.

'Hello. How are you?' he said.

Maybe this uncomfortable half standing was something all dancers did. We didn't move anyway. His hair was still cut to the same dark duck-fluff fuzz. The eyes still too big, and with no nameable colour.

'Good. Well. OK. You know. Fine.'

'Good. Good.'

Good wasn't up to David's usual standard of easy conversation and flawless charm. Maybe this crouching face to face was just as uncomfortable for him as it was for me.

'You?'

'Better thanks. The injury flared up. That silly jumping I did the day I came with you. That's why I rushed off to London. Then I had to go to America, earlier than planned to help my dad. He was casting dancers so . . .' he trailed off, looking down at our uncomfortably folded limbs,

'Shall we stand up?' he said.

'Oh. Yes.' Standing straight with my face more than six inches from David's I felt less umm-ed and ketchupped.

'I've just been. You know. Finishing off this chair.'

'It's beautiful. Who's it for?' I sensed the unfurling of feathers again, the spreading of the charm, but it was uncertain, like the weather. Tentative.

'Old friends. It's to celebrate their first . . . baby.'

'Oh. Nice.'

So we had one 'good' and one 'oh nice'. David was definitely not on the form he'd been on when we first met. What had changed for him. Why was it that we were both being so awkward. Ketchup or no ketchup I had to make this situation work a little better.

'I finished the rush. Cutting it, I mean.' I sometimes wondered if I just had my grammar centre surgically removed if I would be able to speak more easily under stress. Like Yoda in *Return of the Jedi*. 'The rush cutting I finished,' I could have said and it might have come out in one go. I'll never know.

'Oh. Good. I'm sorry I didn't help. I just had to go to London . . .' once again he trailed off. I got the feeling he was as speech-stuck as I was. Maybe we could both have done with a course in grammar from an intergalactic guru.

'That's. Fine. Come and see. All the rush I cut. Loads!'

'Great!' He seemed as grateful as I for a reason to move, but still hesitated. I had to squeeze past him to get to the door. I couldn't understand why he wasn't moving out of the way. I took him round to the other end of the workshop, out into the sunshine and back into the dim of the airy dry cool of storage room.

A little sunlight found its way through the slats high on the walls and striped the only patch of the floor left free and uncovered. I loved my rush store, full at the end of summer like this. A hundred sage-and-corn-coloured bundles making me feel like a woman of property, pregnant with all the baskets and seats to be born over the winter. I turned away from David to gloat over my horde. But he was struck by the atmosphere too. The quiet. The green. The sweetish smell of the drying rushes.

'Wow! There's so much. D'you use all this?' That was better. A little genuine awe to oil the communication.

'Most. It's not ready. It needs more drying.' Once in there I couldn't help a little clucking, a little checking and caressing of bundles. Without me looking at him his confidence seemed to return a little.

'Myfanwy. We had such a lovely day that day. I really

enjoyed your company. I'm sorry I left without saying goodbye before.'

Why David thought it necessary to apologise I didn't understand. But then I hadn't really understood why I'd got so disappointed about his departure.

'It's OK. I didn't. You know. Expect you to.' I looked hard at the bundle of rush closest to me. I found two blackened stems and began to pull them out to stop the mould spreading through the bundle.

'Have I missed all the rush cutting now?' The stems were hard to disentangle. I had to pull each one very slowly.

'Yes.' Slower and slower I pulled. As long as I pulled I wouldn't have to look at David, looking so hard at me I felt it like breath. Like some sort of verbal demand.

'Oh. Because I'm not going to America again for a while now. I thought I might stay around here. I mean. At Elen's. There's nothing useful I can do for Elen once the kids are back in school. So I wondered if I could help you a bit. Somehow?'

'Oh. Well. Thanks.' My hand trembled and the stem broke with a little ripping sound. I continued pulling the new-torn end.

'I'd like to have come rush-cutting with you again. Have a go in the coracle, maybe stay afloat this time.'

I wondered what had happened in America, there was barely enough charm to cover his skin. He felt needy. Longing.

'So. What are you doing at the moment?'

'Finishing the chair. Beachcombing after the storms.'

'Oh. I don't suppose you need help with those.'

'No. Not really.'

The last centimetre of stem came free. I rolled and crushed it in my hand and looked up. The striped light brindled David's velvet head and gave each eye a single bright needle point of whiteness. His forehead had that crumpled velvet look, his mouth was a dark straight line. What harm could it do to let him keep me company? He wanted to. A lot.

'But the chair. It's almost finished. And I do need help with delivering it. Getting it into the van. Out again. It's got to go to Gloucestershire. So there's lots of driving.' The forehead smoothed, he stepped closer, no longer looking at me, but stroking the bundle of rush at my side.

'Maybe I could help then?'

'Yeah. You could.'

'We could find some more number plates on the way?'

'Tuesday morning. I'll pick you up.'

'Right. Tuesday then,' he said and left without another word or look.

I wasn't sure what I'd said or what he'd heard.

Chapter Seven

With Peter escaping the plot outline of memories and popping up out of character in inconvenient places I jumped when my phone rang. I answered it holding it a foot from my ear. But it was only Tucker.

'He's got it. We had the letter just now in the post.' Her voice was shaky down the phone. 'We'll go just after Christmas. Maybe before. Have Christmas out there. Maybe.'

'Great,' I said. 'Tucker that's. Brilliant. Brilliant. How's Idris?'

'Listen!' She held the phone out into the hallway: I could hear 'Do Anything For Love' playing in the sitting room and sounds of delighted squealing as four little girls pranced around their daddy. Idris would be standing on the sofa with an unplugged table lamp as a mike doing rock singer impersonations.

'I don't need to tell you what he's doing, do I?'

'No. Tucker. You don't sound pleased. You know. Excited.'

I guessed I knew why she wasn't bubbling with enthusiasm. After a good dinner and two bottles of Cabernet, Kenya is the place where cheetahs pose against the sunset and you can have a gourmet meal served under canvas. At eight a.m. on a Bank Holiday Saturday Kenya is the place with a style of health care and law enforcement that Europe lost in 1400. In the real world there were twenty-mile tailbacks to get over the Severn Bridge and under ten's dropping from cerebral malaria in downtown Nairobi.

Tucker was up for any sort of adventure for herself and Idris, but Moffy and Jelly, Agnes, Jane and even big boy Julian were another thing altogether.

'I am excited. It's just . . .' she sighed, 'bit of a slog to organise it all. Rent the house out, sort what we'll do about schools for the girls, sort out Julian. It's just . . . well. A lot!'

Tucker oppressed by a task she hadn't even begun? Had Tucker been a mountaineer she would have had her pitons into the first face without bothering to look to the peak to see how far it was to climb. It was one of the reasons she couldn't cook, because if she decided to make chocolate soufflé she wouldn't let a lack of eggs or chocolate get in the way. I didn't know what to say. Ketchupped into a silence that only Tucker could have read.

'OK, yeah. I know. Not like me. Give me time. Anyway. I do want to celebrate. It's Idris' triumph anyway. The weather forecast is good for tonight. Can we have a barby and a bonfire on the beach at the cabin?'

'Good. Idea. Yes. Leave it till seven. Give the grockels time to roost.'

'Will your dad come?'

'I'll ask him. I'm going up. To see him. Later.'

'Oh. I forgot to say. David's back. He arrived yesterday. He's staying for a while.'

There didn't seem to be any need to say I knew.

'Look at this Myfanwy!' William pounced on me the moment the van stopped, almost pulling me out into the yard. For once he didn't have to walk away to show me his latest enthusiasm, it covered him. From head to foot he was a mass of patches, little oblongs and squares of denim in various colours known only to the Taiwanese chemical industry. They each had printed-on stitch effect round the edge and were all slightly peeling at their corners.

'I found these amazing things in the market last Thursday. They iron on. You can mend almost anything with them.' My father had always been convinced that domesticity was a cinch, that all the complexities of cooking and needlework were only some sort of religious conspiracy that could be overcome with scientific logic. In William's world only my mother really knew about cooking.

'But only. You know. If your clothes really need mending.'

'Oh, for goodness sake, Myfanwy. This is an *experiment*. Of course my clothes didn't need mending! *I cut holes in them.* Now I know I'll be able to mend them when they do need it!' He was triumphant. I knew better than to try and argue or reason. 'And look at this. Inside, come on!' He scuttled off and disappeared through the back door like a spider into a crack. '*Come on!*'

His earthwork project he said was almost completed, but he'd gone on getting thinner as if he was being distilled down to his pure essence: Eau de William Bowen something you put behind your ears to give you visions of a parallel universe.

I followed him inside and found him bent over peering into the microwave his face lit up by its light. Here was proof of the distilling process, in the intensity of his attention, his whole consciousness focused on whatever was going around in the oven box. Microwaves do draw the attention – the way the light comes on as you hit the start button, as if the machine itself and its little revolving stage and spotlight bring the food into being from nothingness – but William's eyes were almost burning holes in the glass. I stood beside him and peered in too: a garment of some sort – ancient and of the kind of average colour you get to after a half million journeys round the washtub – was being 'cooked', whilst covered in more of the little Far Eastern miracle patches.

'You see,' said William, explaining to me as he'd explained everything from eclipses to dung beetles all my childhood, 'my theory is that the microwave can perform the same function as the iron. I merely have to press the patches into place over the fabric, and the heat of the microwave does the job of the iron.'

'Ping,' said the microwave, dumping the garment back into dark non-being as its light went out.

'Let's see!' Eagerly William pulled out the T-shirt and shook out the folds. Five patches fell to the floor. 'Oh! Oh!' With an odd little squeal of dismay William bent down to try and scrabble up the fallen scraps of material. He kept saying 'Oh dear! Oh dear!' as if something truly dreadful and shocking had happened. His hand shook. His face was pinched and confused, the focus and attention of a moment ago completely gone.

'I'll pick them up, Dad. It's OK,' I said. I retrieved the patches and put them in his hand.

'Thank you, Myfanwy,' he said, 'I can't think why I was so concerned about avoiding the iron. Silly. A very silly idea.'

'Shall I make. Some tea?'

'Yes. Yes. That would be very nice.'

He was lost. Limp. Perhaps this wasn't a distillation process after all. My father was evaporating, boiled off into the air by time.

It turned into a proper August Saturday, as near to scorching as it gets in Wales. Down the other end of the beach within five minutes barefoot teeter of ice creams and lavatories, little territories sprouted, boundaried by cooler boxes and windbreaks. Adults strove to maintain separateness, sprawled on lurid towels surrounded by as many portable trappings of their living rooms as possible. Children and dogs sluiced around between the grown-up encampments mixing anarchically, like the bits in soup.

After visiting William and collecting food and Aussie bubbly from town I took the chair outside and worked. The outdoors felt less empty with the bright dots of human activity on the sand half a mile away. I was committed to finishing the chair and the little cradle I'd decided to make, before departure on Tuesday. I hadn't given myself such a deadline for a long time and it felt good, mostly because being self-imposed and a novelty it didn't really count as a deadline at all.

I concentrated hard on every detail, the feel of my tools, the sand under my feet and the voices spirited in odd fits and starts by the breeze. Everything in the present tense nothing past, nothing future, nothing conditional. I kept out William's decline, Tucker and Idris' departure and Peter too. Even David and his mystifying needy crumpled forehead. It felt like yoga for my head, holding my thoughts in one position the way you hold a yoga pose, thinking about bits of your body you didn't even know you had.

The only thing that slipped in was something that seemed as strange and off kilter as Peter's rap: an image of Graham, picking out a tune with one finger with the ugliest dog in the world curled under the baby grand. It flashed into my mind and out again before there was any chance to wonder what the hell it was doing there.

I got the driftwood fire nicely glowing and the cast iron grill set up over the top and another fire going too, for sitting around and keeping warm later. I put out blankets and chairs and got the boules out for the kids to play with. I set the booze chilling. I pricked the sausages. I distributed night light candles in jars. This was our celebration ritual: for almost a decade the same lighting of fires, the same blankets laid out, the same plastic cups, the same old pink picnic table. Weddings, births, birthdays, first exhibitions, Julian's O levels, dry Christmases, even Peter's last birthday when he spent most of the time watching from the chair indoors. All had been marked in this way, with the scorching of Morgan's Family Butcher's best pork chipolatas and wine from the green mock glass beakers. With every event we celebrated, the ritual gathered another layer of significance for us all, like a coat of varnish deepening the colour on a painting.

Seeing the whole scene laid out and empty of its cast made me feel for the first time the meaning of Idris and Tucker's leaving. It was the end of this ritual. William was right, he was about to spend eternity resting. Any day, any year now, and then the only thing left to celebrate would be my birthday, alone with quarter of a pound of sausages and half a bottle of white wine. One picnic chair, one mock green glass and who knew what fantasies of a long dead husband playing about my head.

The gravel crunched. Distraction had, thank God, arrived. Tucker had William in the front seat of the Land Rover and everyone else was crammed in the back with the largest on the bottom layer and the smallest on the top. So Moffy and Jelly were first out, running across the gravel and dunes to me almost before the engine had stopped.

'David says we can help cook the fishes . . .'

' . . . and the "jean" thingies.'

'Aubergines!' David called from the car where he was having something complex explained to him by William, as my father lowered himself from the cab.

'Oh-burr-jeans, stupid,' said Jane, 'and he says Aggie and I can do some too.'

'OK girls, let's not start the evening with world war three shall we?' said Tucker, taking a box of bread and booze straight inside. 'All looks lovely, Van,' she called as she disappeared. 'Be useful girls, get the rest of the stuff from the car.'

They streamed back past Idris who, already a little pissed, was making stately progress from the back of the car as befitted a guest of honour. I hugged him as soon as he was in range.

'Giraffes,' I said into his ear, 'hunting dogs, hyenas, cheetahs. Well done!'

'Bloody mosquitoes and green mambas, Ethiopian bandits and sleeping sickness. That's all I've heard about from Elen all day. You'd think she'd never been further than Barry Island to hear her.'

'It's the girls. You know. Her babies. She's just letting off steam.'

'I s'pose. It is good though, eh? I'll be doing all the veterinary work at the research station after three months training under their outgoing vet. No more bloody sheep.'

'Wildebeests have bottoms. You know. To put your hand up on a Monday morning.'

'Arm up a wildebeest's bum? Ah bliss girl, seventh heaven compared with a bloody Friesian!'

David extracted himself from William's theory of clothes mending and greeted me as I poured champagne for Idris.

'Lovely to see you again, Myfanwy.' The feather armour was back. Doubly protective and iridescent. The 'again' his tone implied was 'again' after so long, not 'again' after twenty-four hours. Why did we both collude effortlessly in pretending his visit the day before had not happened.

'How. Are you? You've been to America?'

'Yes. Helping my father cast some dancers for his movie. I'm going back but not until early November. I could have stayed there, but . . . I decided not to.'

'We're going to use him shamelessly for free babysitting. Every night down the disco we'll be. A film set will seem like a peaceful refuge after a month with Jelly and Moffy.' We all laughed at Idris' little parental joke, but as I filled his plastic glass David looked out at me from under the charm visor.

'I know who to call on if I need grown-up help,' he said. The expression in his eyes was shockingly direct. I'd never noticed pupils dilating like that before. He made the words sound like *and I know who to call on if I need a good going over*. He had I concluded been hitting his own little supply of wine all afternoon.

'I'm going to find Tucker and William, they haven't had any champagne yet,' I said, almost running into the kitchen.

David's rebirth as gourmet and cook had quickened in his time away. Along with quietly boozing he'd spent the afternoon making a variety of barbecue delights: marinaded salmon steaks and aubergines stuffed with herbed cheese. Now he stood over the grill, happily poking sausages, tending to his creations and trying to prevent third degree burns for Jelly and Moffy as they 'helped'. Cooking was a very meagre attraction for Jane and Agnes when there was sea on offer.

William walked them down to the waves to keep an eye on their body boarding, although what he could possibly have done to rescue them, stick man that he now was, I couldn't imagine: shout, throw a bit of seaweed.

When Julian and the squirming Vicky finally arrived, no doubt after many detours on the walk down, they went to join the girls in the water whilst food finished cooking. Idris, Tucker and I put up the old scout tent that I kept for accommodating overnight guests, big enough to qualify for the definition marquee, but dung green and therefore still just a tent. It was part of the ritual for really big celebrations that everyone should stay, curled in a communal heap of duvets and sleeping bags round the central pole.

'You two can sleep inside,' I told Tucker as we spread the ground sheet. 'You know. In my bed. William can have the sofa bed in the kitchen.'

'Thanks, Van. We will, otherwise Moffy and Jelly will be jumping on my head all night.'

'Unless of course we give the lovebirds the seclusion of Myfanwy's room so they can shag each other senseless for the fifteenth time today. God I wish I had my son's stamina. I wish I'd *ever* had staying power like that.'

'Nothing wrong with your staying power, Idris. We'll take the bridal suite, please Van.'

'Lovely.'

'Of course, Elen,' said Idris draping himself around Tucker's ample neck and leering at me most unappealingly, 'that means the lovely Myfanwy and David will be unsupervised and sleeping under the same roof.'

'Mnnn?' said Tucker with a similar leer, 'she's always had to fight them off!'

'Don't be so bloody stupid. I'm thirty-six. I'm a widow. He's your nephew for God's sake. We'll be in this tent with six other people.'

'Wow. Haven't heard you so articulate in a while, Van.'

'Dear me. I think we hit a nerve Elen, don't you.'

'Piss off. Both of you. I'm getting the plates. Food must be ready by now.'

We sat around the non-cooking fire, stoked up now to keep us from the little sea breeze that had blown up as the sun sank. Jane and Agnes carried plates of sausages round to everyone, Moffy and Jelly tottered about with the tomato sauce. David brought round slivers of seared salmon and oozing slices of aubergine. We ate with our fingers and hunks of bread.

'We'll be able to eat out all the time in Kenya girls.'

'Except for the wet season, Daddy.'

'Won't the lions come and eat the sausages?'

'No, the mosquitoes and the snakes will come and eat us.'

'Oh, Tucker!'

'I'd like to propose a toast.' William carefully put down his plate of untouched food, and raised a glass. 'I'm delighted Idris has this great opportunity. I wish him and Elen the very best of luck!'

'Good luck!' We stood up. Raised the green plastic and toasted, even the girls with their squash. We were all in the middle of a drunken moment of familial sentimentality when Vicky's unfamiliar little voice squeaked up.

'Good luck? Good luck?' It was like a mouse shrieking and stamping its foot. 'You are so pathetic you lot. Just bloody pathetic. All you can think about is your big adventure in Kenya. What about poor Julian? What's he going to do? Where will he go out of term? You don't care about him Elen because you're not his real mother!' She threw her plastic glass on the sand, pushed past Elen and stomped off up the track towards the road. For a droopy child in her dress like a nylon nightie and her four-inch platforms, she did a good job of a righteously angered exit. We still had our glasses half raised. The sea slooshed insistently in the quiet. No one spoke. Then everyone turned to Julian like the orchestra towards a conductor.

Tucker began telling Julian how he *was* her son as far as she was concerned. Agnes and Jane clung to Tucker. Moffy and Jelly began to cry, the fire spat onto Idris' legs and he began to swear loudly amidst trying to ask Julian what was going on.

Julian looked completely astonished, white with shock. He put his drink down and ran, shouting over his shoulder that he'd talk later. 'I've got to check on Vicky.'

We were instantly sober amidst the wailing and worrying of the four girls.

'Well, what the bloody hell was that all about? She's had too much tantric sex that one. Maybe they ought to go back to the shower.'

'Oh, Idris! Julian must be feeling awful to have told Vicky all those things. Oh God! I've never thought of him as anything but my own.' Tucker was being over-emotional, not getting to grips with the crisis at all. Had it been a shark attack anyone in the water would simply be fish snacks for all Tucker would have done in this state.

'Oh, that wasn't Julian talking. That was Vicky. She's going to do psychology at Reading, she's just in bloody training is all.' Idris put his arm around her. 'Look love, it's OK. We'll go up to the house now and sort it out, all right. OK girls, enough drama. Cut the water works.'

'Yes. Yes. Oh, Idris, I'm sorry. I wanted you to have a real celebration.' Tucker was close to tears. A very rare situation indeed.

'What about? The prospect of black *and* green mambas in the bath?'

'Oh, Idris!'

'Look, I'll walk home,' said William. 'I'll start now.' Idris retrieved him from his determined exit.

'No. No problem, William, we'll drop you home. Elen's sober enough to drive.'

'Just . . .'

'OK. C'mon girls. Into the bus.'

I helped round up the confused and tired kids, and walked them to the car.

'You know, Elen. I'll have Julian. Here. In his holidays. You know,' I said.

'Thanks Van. Thanks love.' Thanks *love*? Tucker *was* in a state. She climbed into the driver's seat and wound down the window. 'We haven't got David!'

'I'll stay,' David called, 'help Myfanwy clear up. I can walk home later.'

Amid the distress of my relatives I felt a sudden little panic. 'No, it's fine. It won't take you know. Long. To clear up.'

'I insist,' he called.

There wasn't time for further debate. Idris had bundled the girls into the back and helped William in beside Elen. 'I'll speak to you tomorrow Van. I'll phone. Don't unplug it,' she said.

Then they were gone.

With those dilating pupils in mind I was very business like. I gave David and myself separate tasks. He cleared the food, the plates, the glasses. I shook out the blankets, folded the furniture and stowed it all away in my garage cum barn. We didn't have to go in and out of the house by the same door, we didn't have to speak. It was dark by the time we'd finished. I lingered outside blowing out the little makeshift jam-jar lanterns.

I could see David through the kitchen window, moving beautifully even with more units of alcohol than was good for him. He was finishing the drying up and the last bottle of champagne by turns. Very soon he would come to the end of both and come out looking for me. Meeting him out here in the uncertainty of the darkness was unwise. Not sensible. He was definitely drunk, possibly infatuated and indisputably Tucker's nephew. He was not out of his twenties and with more emotional baggage than a carousel in a Californian airport. I was past all that, in the calm cold predictable waters of widowhood, with a nice little float of memories to cruise me to my grave. The fact that the float was currently inflating, deflating and morphing into objects more resembling anchors than buoyancy aids was beside the point.

The last mock-glass glass and the last swig were imminent. Where was that troublesome and misbehaving dead husband when I needed him? No CDs – malfunctioning or otherwise – seemed to be available to help keep me and David, as 'nephew' and 'Auntie's best mate'. Best to be decisive then, what romantic overture could possibly happen under an electric strip light? I walked to the door and stepped boldly into my own kitchen.

'Oh! I wondered where you were. I've finished all the washing up. There wasn't much.'

'Oh. Right. Thanks.' I made an effort to look straight at him in an ordinary sort of way, but as I couldn't seem to think of what to say, I looked away again, around the room as if inspecting it. The mock glasses were dried and stacked on the table.

'I didn't know where to put them. So I just, dumped them there.'

'That's OK, I'll put them away. When you've. Gone.'

'I'm not very sober, I'm afraid. Would you mind if I made a cup of coffee. Before . . .'

'You go?'

'Well. Yes. Would you like one?'

'Fine.' I made a move towards the kettle, but he bounded beside me and took it from my hands,

'I'll do it. You sit down. I'll bring you one.'

Like someone in a dentist's waiting room, listening to the drill, I went to sit on my own sofa bed.

'I'm just going to light a couple of candles. My eyes are frightfully sore in this light.'

He lit two of the lanterns I'd brought inside and set them on the floor beside the sofa then switched off the strip light.

Immediately the room transformed. Under the electric light its shape and size had been clear; where one object ended and another began was a hard sharp line. But in the leaping shadows of the candle light we could have been anywhere from baronial hall to Bedouin tent. There were no boundaries between things, no lines, only shadowy mergings and overlaps.

David brought me a mug of coffee, teetering slightly across the floor, and sat down beside me.

'Thanks.'

'It's a pleasure. I've enjoyed the evening in spite of Vicky's little bombshell.'

'I don't think. It's much about . . . what Julian feels.'

'Maybe not.' He paused, and looked down at his mug in the way people do only when they are not about to drink from it but about to say something brave, foolish or insulting. 'Myfanwy, I've been thinking.' Instinctively I moved back a little, my money was on 'foolish'. Automatically he shuffled almost imperceptibly closer. 'About what happened this evening. I think it might be best if I left them all to it tonight. I was wondering if I could, maybe, just sleep here?' So direct and so reasonable a request, I couldn't refuse it without seeming paranoid, vain or both.

' . . . and I'm too pissed to walk anyway. Sorry.' He leant back into the sofa to emphasise his point, and slid his arm in sleepy stretch along the back of the settee behind me. I sat forward a little.

'Fine. The tent's, you know. Nice. To sleep in I mean.'

'Right. Thanks.' He sat forward too, bringing his arm behind me, resting it lightly across my shoulders. I sat very still, analysing how strange the contact of this alien limb felt, then moved just enough to break it. To put the arm back now, he'd have to move his whole body three inches, too much to be able to pretend it was just an accident. He wasn't going to pounce.

'I've put some blankets. In the tent. And a pillow.'

'Great.' David was talented at using words which when they arrived in my head had another meaning. *Great*, arrived as a very bitter and depressed version of *Oh bugger!*

'David.' My turn to look down at the surface of my coffee, like someone out of a bad made-for-TV movie. 'I'm really. Tired. I'm going to bed.' I got up. I'd been clear without being cruel. But he wasn't ready to give up.

'OK. Could you help me to the tent. I really am pretty wobbly.'

No points for subtlety but ten for persistence. I almost laughed. His rather endearing mixture of the shy and the direct made me feel old, so much older than him. This was what it was like to be a mother and have your son's best mate make a pass at you.

Any stir of temptation I'd felt was gone. I snapped on the light, David blinked and winced. I handed him a torch, and pecked him gently on the cheek. 'Just stagger. It's about twenty feet. Night.'

I was terribly tired. Too tired even for the sort of automatic pilot half-asleep sex you have with a spouse. The sort of sex you have through zips and button holes because getting properly naked is just too much effort and having to put a nightie back on afterwards would be a herculean task. So having to be awake for sex with someone new, keen to show all their moves would have been impossible, no matter who or what David had been.

I'd been tired all month. Worn out by Peter, making me remember him or making me forget. Coming and going at his will, not mine. I lay in the dark on my back feeling squashed between David's takeover bid and Peter's quiet occupation of my being. I think I fell asleep to escape.

I woke in the middle of a dream I hadn't had for a long time. It was a Peter 'CD' about making love. Something from our very early days together. Digitally remastered. Reframed to include new footage previously left on the cutting-room floor by the rose-coloured scissors that came into the hands of my subconscious after Peter died. The new editing had converted it from a memory of 'making love to or with' into one of 'being fucked by'.

We were in my cabin on the *Princess*. In the dark. Sweating and slightly drunk. Quite soon after getting our clothes off Peter had stopped speaking. No endearments, no whispered compliments or tendernesses. Just a sense of unstoppable purpose. Peter folded my legs back over my head like a male spider folding the female's fangs out of the way so he can safely insert his little packet of sperm. I felt as if I had been pruned back, reduced to a single female essential. I tried to move, to participate a little.

'Keep still!' he said. Quite sharply. 'Keep still!' I realised that my responses to his touch were not required. My presence in my body was irrelevant as he pounded in and out of me. I could think about something else if I wanted to, even do something else so long as I just kept still, useless legs pinned back out of the way. I could have got out a manicure set and started doing my toenails. As an afterthought, just before he fell off me insensible he said, 'Come if you can.' As if it was nothing to do with him.

At the time that order made me feel so ignorant. 'Oh,' I thought, 'there's something I'm not doing, something the woman is supposed to do when the man is doing this, and I'm too stupid to know what.' It was a long time before I twigged that folded double with thirteen stone of body leaning on the back of your legs there's nothing you can do to come. And Peter knew it.

Strangely, for a long time that incident was a private erotic icon: his power, his control, the way he just decided how he'd have me was a turn-on in those first few years when I was still too young and unconfident to know any better.

I woke as he said 'come if you can', full of him, and full of the humiliation I'd felt at the sense of my own inexperience. Furious at him for letting me think that's how it was meant to be for both of us. And furious that I should remember that time, that one time out of the many others when it had been different. Equal. Who came and when, the subject of joint attention. Pleasure not separately designated.

Going back to sleep and reliving the whole thing wasn't an attractive prospect. Outside it was light as day, with a big white moon in a navy blue sky. I got up, shoved on last night's dress with a jersey over the top, and went out through the French door of the bedroom, over the dunes and down onto the beach.

Everything in shadow was lava black, solid, everything moonlit was translucent. I trailed my feet through the edge of the water in the white light. The wavelets flirted this way and that with the moon's pull. I'd done this on so many shores. As I stared down, my feet appeared against backgrounds of sand, mud, rock, pebbles, with blue, green, grey, brown water over them, the pictures flitting like light on the eyelids in a moving car. Every picture with an emotional tag, an atmosphere of Peter.

I tried to hold one picture, something to take those folded legs away, but the images slipped like the water. The only one that stuck seemed at first bland and unimportant: a background of mud. A crowd of little red crabs comically milling around together like tourists at the Albert Memorial. As my foot came down amongst them they ran, legs twinkling at double speed and I heard Peter's voice say, 'Run away. Run away', a whispered undertone full of laughter. He didn't know I heard him. He was making a joke all for himself.

Laughing alone, revelling in the world and the life inside his own skull. That one tiny moment, the tone of his voice, the crab feet moving fast over the silt was Peter distilled, his hopeful and amused interaction with the planet. Thinking of that when he'd been alive was enough to prickle my eyes, now it stung afresh and took my breath away; along with thoughts of limb origami and spider sex.

The problem had always been that since Peter, the past had him in it, the future did not. I'd tried to think of something not in the past. It was too hard. The certainty of the past had trained my inner eye to look back as surely as gravity trains roots to grow down. As long as memory could offer some predictable moments amid the new chaos it had turned up, how could I find the way to look forward?

The tide was on the turn. Sluicing back and forth indecisively over the flattest part of the hard sand, reflecting the moonlight first one way, then the other. I'd walked almost the width of the beach, staring down at my own feet. I turned to go back and looked out over the sand and quietly encroaching water. Out on the only spit, nearly surrounded now, was David. He was dancing: leaping, twisting, his white shirt untucked from the baggy shorts and twirling around him like strands of cloud. In ten more minutes he would have to swim to get to shore. I started running.

He was still dancing when I got closer but he wouldn't hear me. 'You're going to be. Cut OFF!' I yelled.

'What?' he called back, and went on leaping.

He wanted me to rescue him, he hadn't given up. I could leave him to it. But it's not fair to do the ice maiden bit erratically, do it and stick to it. I'd been doing it in patches interspersed with little interglacials. I'd given him reasons to believe he was in with a chance. And he *was* Tucker's nephew. I had to wade out to the spit.

The water was already more than knee deep, so I took a little while. I called and called about the tide coming in. About how deep it would soon be. Even amidst his continued dance he must have heard and seen me. I knew he had when I got to the spit. He was at the other end. He stopped, looked at me then began to twist and leap towards me.

This was a performance, just for me. As the posing on the gate tops had been. But this was something much more fierce and wild. Standing my ground as he came closer felt risky in the way that standing in front of a galloping horse might be. I could hear the rush of his breath, the thud and give of the sand as he landed and took off again. The back of his shirt stuck down with sweat, his calves ran.

In five perfect impossibly high twisting leaps he was by my side, folded in a dancer's bow at my feet. He looked up at me and his face was smoothed, not with something spread on the outside but plumped up from within with pure absolute aliveness. I fully expected a declaration of some sort, but suddenly the smooth face crumpled. 'I can't move.'

'Like you couldn't. Walk to the tent?'

'No. My back. It's locked.'

The aliveness had left him. His face was back to its crushed velvet look. As the first waves washed over the spit he managed to half stand. The pain didn't look faked. He'd gone from almost supernatural powers of physical performance to this, in seconds. For the first time I really appreciated what he'd lost. It was as bad as a bird having its wings lopped off.

'David, we have to move. Now.' I'd sobered up. Regained the presence of my dead love through the bizarre agency of some Filipino fiddler crabs. 'Let's get into the water. Let it take your weight. I'll tow you.'

Peter, I think, would have appreciated the joke, me towing a dancer with a duff back off the spit. Although by the time we reached the shore proper I wasn't ready to laugh about much. Swimming in wet clothes is like running in nightmares, where your legs work but you still move backwards.

For a relatively small man David was a ton weight. It took another half hour to get him along the beach and up to the cabin, bent double and gritting his teeth.

I shoved him under the shower and peeled off most of his clothes, as matter of fact as skinning potatoes. He didn't say another word until I had him wrapped in a duvet and pumped with painkillers on the sofa. It was getting light-ish as we sat side by side bent over mugs of sweet tea.

'What can I say? I think you pretty much just saved my life.'

'Don't be. Dramatic. I'm not Lassie.'

'I think my life's turning into a kind of bad comedy. I set out to dazzle you and end up nearly drowning you. I'm so sorry Myfanwy.'

'Just. Drink your tea. Anyway. You did dazzle me. That leaping and dancing! I understand a bit about what you've lost.'

He lifted his head from the contemplation of the surface tension of tea with two sugars and looked at me like a dog patted for the first time.

'Do you? I can't do that stuff anymore without getting like this. If I take it really gently, pace myself I can cope – direct a rehearsal, whatever. But if I want to *dance*, here's what happens. I hated all the dancers I helped my father to cast, because they can still do it. I don't know if I can go back to work with people I'm so jealous of.' If he hadn't been so tired and so full of pills he would have cried. Instead his voice was flat, lifeless as a robot.

'Is that why, you came back?'

'Yes. And to see you.' He didn't wait for a reaction, he just began to talk quietly gaining momentum as he spoke. 'It's not *just* that you're beautiful. I *know* every man must tell you that. I *know* that's kind of boring. But it isn't just that. You've survived losing the most important thing to you. You've found another way to be. I saw your chairs in a shop in London. They had all the things you described to me in them. All the river, the summer, the beaches you walked. You've found somewhere else to put your life. How did you do that, Myfanwy?' His face lay before me then: open, quietly desperate. He saw my life as a new creation. No good telling him that I saw it as a bit of bad salvage, a few planks lashed to keep me afloat, my head always haunted by the same ghost.

One rescue was not going to be enough. He needed something profound in the way of life-jackets and buoyancy devices. However ill-equipped I felt, I was going to have to provide them because he'd asked. Because he believed I could. Because he'd chosen me to help.

So I told him I would try and help. I told him I'd be his friend but I didn't let him mention being my lover. I didn't tell him then how he'd chosen the wrong person to show him how to let go.

Chapter Eight

Peter's warm closeness had gone with the fiddler crabs by the time I woke in late morning. I was back to the uneasy feeling that he might suddenly manifest himself at the edges of my vision doing or saying something completely outrageous. Maybe it was his ghost teasing, I don't know. But when I got up and went to the loo, the nasty pink box chose to fall off the bathroom shelf. It fell into the sink as I brushed my teeth and flipped open releasing the remnant of what had been my contraceptive cap. Five years unused and unlooked at had not been kind to it. More use for straining tea now than keeping out sperm.

Sleeping on my sofa was a man who had made what my mother used to call 'a pass' at me. I had promised to help him in an emotional crisis. I had asked him to come with me to deliver the chair to Gloucestershire. A journey probably requiring an overnight stay. However detuned to the processes of seduction, however haunted by my dead husband I still felt, those were the facts.

Whether or not you believe objectively in angels, God or Elvis' continued existence, if Gabriel folded his wings to fit into the passenger seat of the car, or God took you to inspect the crab nebula or Elvis did 'Blue Suede Shoes' in your living-room you'd have to start having faith in something. So whether or not I *believed* I could incite the kind of physical passion that I did when

I was twenty, whether or not I believed I could go to bed with a person who was not Peter, were both irrelevant. The fact was, passion had clearly been sparked. David was — emotional rescues notwithstanding — as Tucker had once so gleefully said of Idris, 'definitely up for it'.

And if I looked objectively at my own melt-glaciation-melt behaviour then I had to conclude that maybe I was too.

David was, depending on how you looked at it, either a hopelessly unsuitable partner or the perfect possible fling. On one hand he was ten years my junior, with huge emotional backpacks and about to depart for America. On the other hand he was nearly ten years my junior, willing to take a risk and . . . about to depart for America. Tucker's policy with lovers, pre Idris, was 'never poop on your own doorstep'. So she never took anyone to bed who she knew was going to be on board for more than a month. Guest lecturers and short term expedition leaders were all game: officers, crew and zodiac drivers with long contracts were all out of bounds, no matter how gorgeous.

I couldn't risk any sort of 'lovers' policy' apart from the total abstinence that was the corollary of the 'zap their goolies' school of manhandling. Let one through the barrier and there'd be a flood. Peter was the only exception because I knew there would be no one after him.

But now. No danger of a flood. No Peter. At least, not in any sense anyone else would understand. So, anyone looking at the situation rationally would say I was in distinct danger of having a sex life again.

If that was the case then I ought to be organised and adult and get myself something more reliable in the form of contraception than a latex tea strainer. But getting a new cap felt like making a *decision* to have sex. Making a decision to go to bed with David. Supposing it happened and was a disaster? Or Peter suddenly popped up in my head demanding fidelity? Supposing it *didn't* happen and my new cap sat rotting, ready to jump out in synchrony with the last? I put the cap back in its nasty flesh-coloured holder, and shut the cabinet door on it. As I did, there, in the mirror was the glint of Peter's blue eyes. 'All right,' I told them testily, 'all right, I'm not going to.'

I got dressed, left David sleeping and went up to William's to do something to avoid any possible Peter whisperings in my head. I nearly turned straight back down the track as Tucker's car was parked outside. Leaving the cabin I thought of that song 'Little Susie' about the teenagers falling asleep watching some movie and therefore being apparently 'out all night' together. 'Out all night' with David, I felt that Tucker would need as much explanation as a fifties parent. But the longer I left it the more explanation would be required, so I got out of the car and went to look for them.

There was no reply to my yelling so I walked up to William's earthwork. The mounds and long banks of soil were smoothed now. They were greening too, sprouting opportunist plants in the late summer warmth. Two figures patrolled the shapes carved into the field looking like alien refugees; masked, boiler suited and equipped with back packs of weedkiller they waved their killing spray wands before them. Neither was Tucker. I sat down at the top of the field and waited for one of them to notice me.

The banks around the field were dotted with heather, catching up now after the delay of the wet August. Every sprig of bloom had a bumble bee colliding with one cluster of flowers, rummaging buzzily about, then butting into the next. I remembered my bees, completely neglected in Graham's garden for more than a month. My basket money too was uncollected and my new stock for Graham undelivered.

Forgetfulness of the present was just part of the story. I was still squirming with the thought of Cagoule man and ill-favoured dog slouching off down a rainy beach. Graham would be at the shop today and Bank Holiday Monday, charming the bus trippers. I could call in anytime and get things back to just business.

'Hiya! I didn't see you come!'

Julian lifted his mask and sneezed. He seemed pleased to see me.

'I'm so sorry about last night. You'd gone to such trouble you know, with the fires, and the booze and stuff.'

'Don't worry,' I said. Julian wriggled the back pack of weedkiller off and sat down beside me.

'I'd no idea that Vicky was going to say all that stuff about me and about Dad and Elen going to Kenya. All I said to her, when I found out about it, was well . . . I s'pose I was a bit like, pissed off, that they were just going to go and leave me to get on with college. But only for a minute. I mean I can like, go out there. In the holidays and stuff. So, it's OK.'

'You don't need to explain to me Julian. It's OK. Really.'

'Thanks, Myfanwy. It's awful at home today. Last night when they got back. Dad shouted at Vicky, I guess cos Elen was so upset about what she'd said. And then I protected Vicky because, well she is my girlfriend. I'm like furious with her for what she said but, she kind of meant well. Anyway, then Vicky said she wanted to go home, but I'd had too much to drive. So Elen said she'd do it, and Dad said no you're not driving that girl anywhere. Vicky got a taxi home and she was crying and saying she didn't want to see me any more. Then Dad and Elen had this huge row and they never row. Oh God. It's just a mess. So I came up here to help William, and get out the way.'

'Maybe I should pop in?'

'Oh I think that would be great. Take Mum out. She's so upset. She won't believe I never said anything like what Vicky said, you know about Elen not being my real Mum. Vicky, she just thinks too much.'

'Tell Elen I'll see her. The Goose tonight at seven. Idris can babysit. Or you can, if you're not out?'

'Don't think I've got a girlfriend any more, so I won't be going anywhere. Here comes William. What is all this stuff, Myfanwy? I can't make out what these shapes are.'

'With William, who knows? Could be. The meaning of life. Could be a shopping list.'

'Vicky thinks the meaning of life *is* a shopping list!'

'Jesus. That's the sort of thing. Husbands say.'

William reached us and removed his mask. He was bright as a robin. Alive and in control. None of the bewildered confusion I'd seen over the patches. He even looked a little plumper and I wondered if his and my own gloomy predictions about the shortness of his future were ill founded after all.

'Ah! Myfanwy. This boy is worth his weight in gold. Been up here since nine helping me. Marvellous. You can put your bees back here, you know. Now this is all done. Come on, let me show you round.'

Julian helped him out of the weedkiller outfit and as usual he set off in front of us, impatiently beckoning. As he walked us around the precise curves, points and flourishes of the thirty interlocking shapes he giggled at our mystification, delighted to hold a secret.

Julian whispered to me 'I think he's forgotten what the shapes mean.'

'Or maybe he never knew,' I said.

'Yeah. Aliens gave him the pattern in a dream.'

I got back to the cabin and David was up. I put a towel over the bathroom mirror when I went to the loo so there was no risk of blue eyes questioning me every time I went in there. Then I sat outside putting little cutesy additions onto the Moses basket and rocking chair, and David stretched and exercised in the sun.

Watching him coax his body back into action made me think of some mechanic with a classic car methodically cleaning its plugs, changing the oil and starting it up with just the right mix of throttle and choke.

He was infinitely patient and disciplined with himself. Never pushed a stretch too far too early, warmed every muscle carefully before working it. Wrapped limbs to seal in the heat when they weren't in use. After three hours of steady effort he was able to stand, walk and do basic dance movements without any wincing or sudden intakes of breath.

We didn't talk. I wove. He moved. The sun tracked across the dunes, the bright umbrellas sprouted up at the far end of the beach. Nothing but the present intruded.

At last he brought us each a coffee and sat beside me, carefully blowing the smoke from his cigarette into the wind, away. I disentangled myself from all the rush and wood, got up and did some stretching of my own, and sat down again with my coffee.

'My yoga's gone to hell. I'm stiff.'

'Well, you look perfect to me.'

'Are you in pain. Any more?'

'No, no. 'S fine. No problems.' Jauntily he tossed the dog end aside. With the physical pain gone he'd pushed everything back under the carpet. As elected helper it was my job to haul it all out and pick it over.

'Is that. The worst it's been?' He moved from beside me to kneeling in front of me, turning inquisitor with his dancer's articulate body.

'Wait a minute. You were de-ummed last night weren't you? What's happened?' Daylight had happened. Thinking had happened. Caps falling out of bathroom cupboards with uncomfortable questions had happened. Avoiding issues was happening for both of us. I looked away from his face and played with the fine white sand.

'Don't. Put . . . a spot light. You know. On it. Makes it. Worse.'

'I'm sorry. I just don't like to think I make you nervous.' He touched my arm, then stroked it elbow to wrist, elbow to wrist.

'David. You want my help still?'

'Yes.' The stroking went from elbow to shoulder. Leapt the strap of my top to go shoulder to ear, shoulder to ear.

'Then you have to. You know. Talk.'

'I'll talk. I'll talk about how beautiful you were in your

coracle. How wonderful your work is. How fabulous you were last night.'

'No. Talk about. Dancing. Your . . . father. About your mum dying.'

On went the stroking: shoulder to ear, ear to chin, chin to forehead, forehead to mouth, lip to lip. I shut my eyes to keep my concentration on my words, away from the almost forgotten fairy lights coming on in my nervous system.

'You've got to. Talk. About how to. Change.' Shutting my eyes had been a mistake, without eyes to monitor him, David took his stroking more seriously.

'You're so lovely to touch.'

I opened my eyes, caught the wrist of the stroking hand. Looked right at the alien eyes.

'I'm just, another. Distraction.'

'No. You are not a distraction. You make me feel alive. You help.'

'You can't fuck your way. Out of your problems.'

'I'm not fucking my way out of anything. I just want you.'

'David. David I can't.'

'Why not?'

'Because. I'm taking your aunt out for a drink.'

I got up. I showered. I dressed. I didn't look to see if David was still where I left him. I ran out of the cabin almost an hour before I needed to. I drove very slowly and still I got to the Goose early. It did at least give me time to compose myself ready for Tucker's entry. Tucker was going to know the moment she looked at me that I'd spent the afternoon in bed with her nephew. Even when I hadn't.

The Goose isn't particularly local for either of us. It's a safe place to talk without much risk of being disturbed by some acquaintance who's had too much to drink and wants to graduate to being a friend. The Goose is small, old, whitewashed, and its dark inside polished to shiny brown by a hundred years of beeswax and nicotine. It doesn't get any busier in the holiday season because the tourists don't find it, or if they do they don't stay once they've spoken to the landlord. His standard greeting after 'What will you have?' is 'Have you given any thought to your funeral expenses'.

He's not a local himself isn't Victor, but the aging villagers have taken him to their hearts, Birmingham accent and all, because he started a little private savings scheme for them. He's a retired undertaker, but still likes to keep his hand in with coffins so he helps his regulars put a bit aside for their cut price, wholesale bought funerals.

When some old bloke pays three pounds seventy-five for a half of lager you know he's going for the velvet lining and the brass handles.

I discovered the Goose after Peter died. One of my first commissions was for a TV producer with a holiday cottage three doors down from it, and we met in the pub to discuss what he wanted. He gave Victor a twenty and said 'Keep the change'. I thought it was a bit odd until I heard he'd died, not a year after I delivered his rocker.

I got my orange juice and lemonade, told Victor that I was 'sorted thank you for asking' and wriggled in behind a table in the corner. The bar was quieter than ever.

Early evening, still warm and sunny, the Goose's regulars would be out in their gardens picking runner beans for tea. The only other person in was a gent ready to collect on his savings behind the bar. As his hand lifted his pint it shook, so that the froth boiled like surf. It took him three attempts to get a sip of beer. When he caught me staring I looked away and walked my eyes over the dark framed floral prints on the walls. Among them were photographs of 'floral tributes' – wreaths of plastic gardenias and vases of synthetic lilies, crosses of red rosebuds and teddy bears made of peach carnations.

The local florist had evidently seen the opportunity offered by Victor's enterprising second string. I was so engrossed in these little snaps, new since my last visit to the Goose, that when the ugliest dog in the world dumped her flobbery head in my lap it came as a total surprise. I hadn't even heard the click click of her claws on the lino as she came in.

'Come away Bet,' said Graham, from the bar. He'd been in the shop, open to catch the tourist trade so he had the blue trousers and gingham shirt look. He'd caught the sun; sitting outside the shop over the last few days his forearms were as brown as wood. They looked incongruous with the line of pastel material above them, like a beard with a lace bonnet.

'No. S'right. She's fine just saying hello.' I patted the smooth dome of Bet's head and fiddled with her satin ears. She shut her eyes and sighed.

'Oh, Myfanwy. I didn't see it was you, coming in out of the sun like.' Graham walked to my table to greet me, standing above his dog and me. 'Can I get you anything. A drink. You know?'

I wanted to say how sorry I was for being so rude and ungrateful when he'd rescued me. Yet I didn't want him getting his feet under the table in case Tucker arrived either ready to spill the contents of both ventricles amongst the beer mats or to give me the KGB interview about David. But Graham's manner was exactly as it always had been in the shop; bright, breezy and superficial. No hint of killer planks or toast under baby grands. I could risk my apology.

'Graham, I'm so sorry. I was rude. That day. On the beach.'

Suddenly he looked down at Bet, and began scratching her back as if he had remembered that the secret of the universe was in the grasp of a flea somewhere in her fur.

'No worries. 'Sfine. Forgotten.' He coughed, stopped searching for the flea with the answer but still didn't look up as he spoke: 'I haven't hardly seen your bees.'

'It's been so wet. They'll get out more now. In the dry. I need to move them. Up to my dad's. For the last bit of heather.'

'Fine. Anytime after hours I can give you a hand.' Still he looked down at Bet, his hair flopping as always over and into his eyes.

'No. No. I can do it. I'll come over tomorrow. After it's. You know. Dark. If that's OK.'

'Fine Fine.'

He straightened up. Looked at me smiling, but with a tight mouth and switched-off eyes.

'Good.'

Right then. Oh. Could you drop off some baskets when you fetch the bees? I'll leave a cheque for the last lot. If I'm out like.'

'Great. Thank you.'

'And I can't get you anything?'

'No. No thank you.'

'Right then. I'll go outside. Bet, you know. She doesn't do well in the smoke.'

The bar was fresh as a daisy. The old guy in the corner was having enough trouble just breathing without inhaling as well. But Graham was obviously anxious to escape, so I just nodded and smiled. He snapped his fingers softly to bring Bet to heel and walked out with his pint into the last of the sun.

Tucker's hair was a halo on LSD as she caught the light in the doorway a moment after Graham and Bet had gone to find a quiet seat outside. Blinded by the slanting sun she took a moment to make me out in the gloom and I had time to look at her before she saw me. In the distorting, down-welling glow of the lights above the bar her face looked lumpy and pink. She had been crying on the drive over. Almost nothing made Tucker cry within a hundred miles of where anyone would actually see her. She noticed me, and raised an eyebrow towards the bar. I shook my head. She ordered herself a pint of lemonade. Her usual was a half of Guinness. I was definitely expecting ventricle contents rather than third degree.

'What a fuck awful day!' she said, as she plonked herself heavily onto the chair opposite me across the little dark table.

'What's happened?'

'I've been being a cow that's what happened. Julian swore he never told Vicky any of that stuff about me not being his "real" mother. And I screamed at him that I didn't believe him, so he took my car off to William's. Then Idris and I spent all day spatting and he tried to calm me down and I savaged him, and told him I wasn't going to Kenya with him, so he drove off somewhere. The girls are all howling. David came back about half an hour ago or so and I just ran out and left him with it all, poor sod. I got a taxi here.'

'You could at least drink. You know, sorrow drowning and all that.'

'Yeah, I could drink. In *theory*. Like in *theory* going to Kenya is no problem and in *theory* I know Julian's telling the truth.'

'OK. Tucker. OK. Don't bite me.'

'Why not? If you're shagging my nephew you deserve to be bitten.'

'Tucker! I thought you and Idris . . . I thought you'd be pleased.'

'Oh so you are then?'

'No!'

'So why did you say you thought I'd be pleased?' Tucker was fizzing for a fight. Her halo hair discharging electrons in blue sparks around her. So angry about something that she wanted to smash the world. If I happened to be the first casualty that was just tough. Tucker in this condition was like a nuclear reactor, careful decisive handling was necessary to avoid global meltdown.

'Hello. Hello. Earth to Tucker. What is this really about? You're off your head.'

'Yes. Yes I am.' The hair stopped sparking. She gulped lemonade and wiped her mouth on the back of her hand, quite demurely as a duchess might do at the end of the third gin bottle. Then she slumped like a washed up jellyfish. 'I'm pregnant,' she said, 'bloody, buggering, fucking, *arseholing* pregnant.' There was, it seemed, nothing wrong with the old guy's hearing, Tucker had just ruined his fourth attempt at a second sip, by sending it splurting from his lips at high speed.

I didn't have the first idea what to say. All the other times when Tucker had said 'I'm pregnant!' before, we had hugged and squealed and danced around the room for joy.

'OK Van, shut your mouth now or something will fly in there and roost.' She gulped more lemonade. Belched slightly, then put down her glass and looked at me, a charge once more beginning to build up on her head like a Liebig condenser. 'Well?' she said.

'Are you sure?'

'No, I'm just getting in a state for practice. Course I'm sure. I'm a week overdue. I did a test yesterday morning. Two bloody blue lines. Twice. Oh God!'

'I need clues. I mean. Why is that a bad thing?'

'*Why is it a bad thing??* Jesus, Van. Why d'you think?'

'I don't know. That's why I need clues.'

'OK, OK. Well it is Idris' in case you were thinking otherwise.'

'NO!' Well, yes, but only for a micro second.

'Because I can't have a baby in Kenya.'

'Fly back. Have it here. Go back when it's born.'

'Do you know the infant mortality rate out there?'

'Nonsense, Tucker. Your baby will live in a big house. With things like breakfast. And vaccinations. And mosquito nets.'

'OK. OK. So . . .'

'So?'

'What do you mean, "so?" '

'What's the real reason?' Tucker slurped again, slumped further.

'I'm ashamed of my real reasons.'

'Go on then.'

'I don't want this baby because I have had it with being bloody pregnant. I've had it with having footballs passed out of my parts and having to behave as if I'd been raped by a porcupine for six months afterwards. And breast feeding, and waking up every three damn minutes all night, and being sicked on. I don't want to be going through all that when I could be having a wonderful time painting giraffes.' She sounded just like Idris bemoaning the stupidity of sheep. 'I'm selfish now. I just don't want to do it all again.'

'Don't then.'

'Oh fine. I'll just a wave a bleeding magic wand.'

'Get a termination.'

'An abortion, you mean. I can't.'

'Why?'

'It's our baby.'

'How pregnant are you?'

'About six weeks.'

'Tucker. It's a bunch of cells.'

'I know. The size of a baked bean . . . But it feels, like they all did, Moffy and Jelly, Aggie and Jane . . . they all felt like this.'

'OK, then have it.'

'No!'

'Lesser of two evils Tucker.'

'But I can't get an abortion without telling Idris.'

'Who said don't tell him? Tell him.'

'He'll get all responsible and do something stupid like say Kenya's off because of the baby. Then nobody gets anything that they want. Not me, not him, not anybody!' She was just this side of wailing.

'Anyway,' she snivelled, 'he's stupid about babies. He loves them. He'll persuade me.'

'Listen to yourself, Tucker. Is Idris pregnant?'

'No.'

'Does he get the vagina like the Bayeaux tapestry?'

'No.'

'Does he get the cracked nipples?'

'No. But he would if he could.'

'But does he?'

'No.'

'OK. Whose decision?'

'You sound like me. That's the stuff I'd say.' Tucker looked at me from under her brows, like a sulky teenager in the head's office.

'Where d'you think I got it? So. Whose decision?' She sighed. Played with a beermat. Then visibly regrew a spine, and unslumped.

'Mine,' she said. 'My call.' She sighed. 'He'll be so hurt, so upset. He'll fight me for it. And all just when he's got his dream of raising injured cheetahs like furry Lazaruses.'

'You don't *have* to tell him.'

'I'm starting to throw up. He'll guess soon anyway.'

'Well OK. But you're a very fine liar. You could . . .'

'Would you have lied to Peter?'

I didn't answer and Tucker took it for a 'No'.

I drove her back. We were there by nine. Idris' car was back in front of the house by the time we got there, Tucker's too. We sat for a while before she got out.

'So are you shagging my nephew then?' she asked in a perfect imitation of Idris' accent.

'What's it to you missus?'

'Nothing. 'Sfine by me. I was just being bonkers in the pub. Nothing wrong with you a good going over wouldn't put right, I reckon.'

'Thanks Tucker. Sensitive. Like a butcher's slab.'

'That's me. No, Van. You've got to break your duck with someone, sometime, girl.'

'*Some*one. *Some*time.'

'Watch it Van. Your bar code could run out first with an attitude like that.'

'I'm not going to. To. Have . . .'

'Have-sex-with . . .'

'David.'

'No?'

'No.'

'What about this taking him with you to deliver a chair? You'll be away overnight?'

'Yes.'

'Mnnn?'

'He needs to talk about. His dancing. His mother. Therapy. No sex.'

She sighed. Shook her head and got out of the car. 'OK then. Night. Thanks, Van-let.' I shrugged,

'Good luck, old trout.' The door slammed shut, but Tucker opened it again, beaming, back to form.

'Hey, maybe I should keep it and you should get pregnant too and then come to Kenya and we'll paint and weave and breastfeed together. Yeah?'

'Piss off Tucker. Can I come and use your phone?'

'Course. Who are you ringing?'

I stood in the hall talking, dialling on the phone on the wall by the ever grumbling table. In the light bulb yellow it looked even more depressed than normal. I closed my eyes to shut it out, together with the slippers and the coats and the thought of the house full of people who would soon be gone. Baby or no baby. I could hear a murmur of voices from the kitchen, Tucker wouldn't hold off telling Idris for long once she'd decided. I wanted to get out fast, I'd had enough baby-talk for one night.

But not home. The thought of the cabin with David's bedding folded neatly on the sofa and Peter's eyes in the bathroom mirror, was about as attractive as a British Rail waiting room. I could just about manage to load the chair and the basket then all I had to do was drive. I rang Mandy and Clive.

'I can't make Tuesday. I'm driving to you. Tonight. Beat the traffic. Is that OK.'

'Oh yes. Bank Holiday Monday tomorrow of course. That's

fine. You'll be here what? Around one? I might be up. She's feeding every three hours.'

'Bad luck.'

'Are you coming alone?' Mandy asked.

'Yes.'

'Oh! Myfanwy. You don't sound sure. Something to tell us?'

'No. Nothing.'

'OK. I'll put you in the gallery then. You'll be away from the screaming. Key'll be in the door. See you at breakfast tomorrow then.'

I put the phone down and opened my eyes. David was standing in the porch, arms crossed head on one side, blocking my exit.

'You're taking the chair tonight?'

'Yes. I thought . . .'

'You could do it without me?'

'No. Not really.'

'So that's all right then. Lucky I'm free. Let's go.'

If I'd decided to argue I don't know what I could have said. He couldn't be blamed for keeping at it, with my signals still giving little blips of hot amidst the cold. Loading the chair alone would have been difficult. All I really knew was that I didn't want to go home. And with Tucker and Idris about to talk about life and death, David was really much better out of it.

Chapter Nine

We loaded the chair and then I drove. David smoked. Slept. Didn't talk. Maybe he could hear all the clanking going on inside me, as yet another bit of past got done over, relived. Maybe he didn't want to know about why I'd nearly set off without him. Anyway, he left me to the cat's eyes and the dark, sitting in the passenger's seat as he'd sat on the river bank.

Tucker didn't know just how good a job I'd done that night in the Goose at keeping my insides separate from my outsides. I'd never told her about the baby I could have had with Peter. So she didn't know what unrotted corpses she was raking up from the compost heap of my past.

It was all bad timing really. I had never told Tucker because she had too much on her plate when it happened. She'd just decided that being a wife and mum didn't mix with spending eight months a year on a cruise ship with five busloads of OAPs and fifty randy sailors. At home in Idris' house she was missing her mates, the travel and her four dry martinis a night. Plus the fact that Janey was only a month or so old when I found out; no matter how pro-abortion someone is give them a new-born of their own to hold and hormones seem to change opinions. So I didn't tell her and she never noticed. The only person I did tell was Peter. Sometimes, afterwards, I wished I hadn't. Which is why I thought for a moment that not telling Idris might be an option.

Peter and I had been working for the same company almost exclusively for five years at the time. They gave us good contracts, all on just two different ships. Mostly summers whale watching around the coast of Newfoundland and Labrador, winters in the Indian Ocean anywhere from Dar es Salaam to Trincomalee.

At first Peter was the part of our couple the Company really wanted — an experienced expedition leader and boatman, first class all round naturalist, entertaining lecturer. But after the first couple of contracts they cottoned on to the fact that I was one of the best zodiac drivers they had on their books, thanks to Mum. And I'd picked up enough of Pete's natural history knowledge to impress the passengers. And of course I was decorative. The pacs liked that. And they liked the fact that Pete and I were an item, quietly and discreetly bonkers about each other. We got wall to wall work. Which was what gave us the money to get the cabin and to take a little time each year off contract to be there.

It was a wonderful time. I saw so many things. Things that are not part of the Peter Memorial CD collection, so I can remember them without that sense of being somehow, haunted. Except perhaps a little by my mother and her vision of a world on floats, because day and night I was with the sea, in it or on it. The memories I keep from that time are all of the sea, and like the sound of surf inside a shell I can pick them up and live in them for a moment. Some are very simple, things that happened to my senses: a particular turquoise of a lagoon against a storm grey sky; a moon rise over open ocean; the smell of the land after a fortnight without sight of it.

But some are complicated, a combination of people, their lives and what we all saw together: tiny moments with every bit of the past and the present, crammed in, visible at a glance like a fabulously detailed miniature, rich with significance. Like the day

I was in a zodiac with a retired couple who'd been the brightest academic biologists of their generation. Sixty years on, still in love, but she was disappearing into Alzheimer's. The day before she'd come to me on the observation deck, as sweetly slight and pretty as she'd been at twenty 'I wonder,' she'd said with the kind of manners that went out with white wrist length gloves, 'I wonder if you could tell me who I am and where I am supposed to be?'

Anyway this day, I was returning them to the ship after a shore trip, and a swell came up beside the boat. In it, three dolphins held like figures in a glass paperweight. In that little second the husband held his wife back from oblivion, and we three humans stood and looked at three dolphins, all six of us miraculously up from chaos at the same tick of the clock.

These shells come up to my ears unpredictably. Awake or asleep. Sometimes I can forget one of them for months, and then it'll get thrown up by some sort of internal tide. The shearwater was like that.

It hadn't been an extraordinary event, particularly. Birds were always hitching rides and seeking refuge. But the shearwater had a meaning I'd never understood, only felt. I'd found it one afternoon behind the deck-chairs on the pool deck when we were cruising around Aride Island in the Seychelles. I thought it was a bit of burnt paper at first. When I picked it up it didn't struggle. The smooth chocolate body and little leathery webbed feet were quite cool, and still in my hands. But its eyes were bright. Alive. They fly at night, shearwaters, they don't like the heat even the ones that nest in the tropics, so I put it in our cabin ready to release at dusk.

It was a good opportunity for a show, so I assembled the pacs on the poop deck in the pink afterglow of a particularly dramatic sunset. I brought out the box and spieled the stuff about shearwaters I'd learned from Pete. Standing behind the pacs he caught my eye and winked.

Then I got the bird out. The timing was right, after their first cocktails they were ready to appreciate a little theatre. They gasped at the sight of this perfect calm little creature, with its dark eyes looking out so steadily at us all. I held it out over the sea, my two hands a platform for its feet. It sat. It simply sat and looked. It looked all around. At me. At the pacs. At the white rail of the deck above, at the metallic shiny surface of the sea, at the bright horizon.

It sat for fully five minutes until my arms began to ache. No one spoke. No one moved or even breathed hardly. The bird was uninjured, calm, well fed — I'd seen to that — but it would not decide to return to its life.

So I took it in my two hands, wings against its body, and threw it with all my strength into the air. It was a big risk decision. The audience had now so fully identified with the little beast that had it plummeted to its death under the wake I swear half the pacs present would have gone over after it. And first of all it did plummet. Tumbled, folded and all wrong. A metre above the sea, the straight brown wings clicked out, it wheeled and banked and headed off like a small missile into the heart of sunset. We watched until no one could be certain that the dot they saw was bird or a splodge on their bifocals. Then there was spontaneous applause, and not a single dry eye in the house. Not even Pete.

What had we all felt through that bird? The singleness of that little life out in the world? The singleness of our own little lives? Or something of the essence of parting? I didn't know, but my dreams knew because after it happened for real it washed up in my sleep. And the first time was just after my bad timing pregnancy.

I got pregnant because Pete and I had developed itchy feet. In spite of all we saw, shearwaters and all, or maybe because of it, we got greedy for new places and experiences. We started to look at the globe in our cabin and turn it to all the bits we hadn't explored. Mostly we turned it upside down to the place where the metal fitment held the plastic ball in place and obscured most of the continent and about a half of the Ross Sea: Antarctica.

Looking at the tiny writing though a magnifying glass I could see glaciers calving between the italic letters. Seals and penguins porpoised around the tip of Palmer Land, reaching like a lover's finger to Drake Strait and Tierra del Fuego beyond. In our bunk at night Peter would hold the globe above our heads and describe scenes from Antarctica.

'Right now, in the fall here, it's spring. The Austral Spring. The Big Melt. Biggest event on the planet. The krill are comin' out from under the ice, and the crabeater seals are getting their first prawn dinners. Mmm-mmm. Those krill, crushed against the teeth, cold and salty, taste so good.'

He'd wanted to go all his life he said, but not just for a week as a tourist. The company had a ship down there but getting on it as staff was like getting an equity card used to be I guess. You had to have Antarctic experience to get the work, but without the work, then no experience. So Peter and I stocked up on Company brownie points: We did tours of duty so long we forgot what a night on land felt like, accompanied the oldest ladies to their check-ins and never once told Captain Harris what a total idiot he really was. We never let the London Office forget that we wanted a shot at a season in Antarctica.

After three years of waiting we got our chance. Three months on board as assistant expedition leader for Pete and zodiac driver for me. The itinerary had everything we'd wanted to do on it. It was a dream ticket. We'd leave mid November and be back just after Valentine's Day in time to join our old ship at Mahe. The condition was that there were no half measures. We were down there for three months of non-stop work, then back in the tropics for two more straight months on board with almost no breaks.

We heard the news one evening in early March. We'd taken the pacs on the standard tour of Zanzibar town and one old girl had fallen badly. Pete and I had spent half a day wrangling to get her flown home. We'd scrambled back to the ship where Harris was wetting his substantial knickers about the hour's delay in sailing time. There were plumbing problems on A deck, two pacs had lost cameras, and the photocopier had eaten the next day's itinerary and gone up in smoke.

When we arrived back on board the reception office was an uproar of hot, tired pacs all demanding things, like a group of five years olds just before tea time. Harris was stomping about being insulting about 'Expedition Staff'. In the middle of it all were Clive and Mandy our regular work partners after Tucker packed in, dispensing sweetness and light in a measure that seemed unreasonable under the circumstances. They insisted on sorting everything out without our help and sent us packing to our cabin. On the bunk when we got there was a fax from London telling us about the Antarctic trip. Next to it was a bottle of champagne from Mandy and Clive and Lars.

Which is how I came to conceive. With champagne inside us and our longest held ambition under our belts we got careless. When the cap had pinged across the bathroom and stuck to the shower curtain for the fourth time I gave up, and Pete said what the hell. By the time I got home on brief leave in May I was throwing up as if every hour was a force ten in a herring boat, and bursting into tears if the kettle didn't boil. It would have been born in December somewhere off the Antarctic Peninsula. Impossible.

Even then I think I could have kept it from Peter, pretended I didn't realise until it was too late to do anything about it. It never occurred to him that something as stupid as an unintended pregnancy could happen to him. I could have passed off my nausea for weeks as a 'stomach bug'. But I had no reason not to tell him. I didn't realise my feelings about being pregnant were mixed until the moment I shared them.

I didn't know that part of me was proud of having conceived. Pleased and smiling far inside. We had made another human, half of me and half of Peter. A line to cast off into the future and hook us there. I didn't know that I wanted him to feel that too until the moment when he so obviously didn't.

'Get rid of it.' It was the very first thing he said. The very first. And pretty much the very last. If that was the way he felt there was nothing more to say or to ask.

Now I think that maybe he knew a clock was ticking for him too. Mine marking out the remaining eggs in the basket, his marking out the last months that he would have to live, to see crabeater seals making their first prawn dinners of the year.

He came with me to the hospital. He held me through the pain and the crying. But he never shed a tear of regret himself. And I never went to Antarctica. I got an infection after the abortion. For three months I felt as if a large bus had run over me and then reversed back for good measure. I had to be pumped full of so many antibiotics you could have disinfected a toilet with my blood.

So I failed the medical that you had to have before being allowed to go. Peter went alone, and in that winter I rocked Janey to sleep in my first rush and driftwood cradle and sold my first chair for money.

That's when I had the shearwater dream, after the abortion and all the time Pete was away. I dreamt it just how it had happened, with the steady brown eyes looking all around, and the held breath of the human audience. In my dream the shearwater lay on my hands every night. And I never knew what to do with it, I never threw it to the sea. Until one night months after my baby had been gone, but no different from the rest, I threw it. I saw it turn over against the sky, fall, spread its arm-wings and fly until it was a dot. My bird-child gone, forever.

I joined Pete in Mahe the next week. He'd got his crabeaters, his adelies, his whales. Less than two years later he was dead and I didn't have the child that would have left me half of him. I wondered what would have happened if I had kept the baby. Would I have lost Peter another way then?

Anyway, I didn't think about the shearwater again until that night on the motorway whilst the car sucked up cat's eyes. I thought about Tucker and I remembered the bird-babe going off over the sea in my dream. How big a difference her decision would make: another life or not another life. Where would I have been if I'd kept the child? Happily integrated into a cosy community of mothers? Making fish fingers and baked beans after school? Kept from indulgent solitude and mad remembering. Saved and damned by ordinary routine.

We slid under the lights of the junction and off into the sudden blackness of the lanes.

'Can we stop? I need a pee?' David unfolded and stretched. 'I've been asleep.'

'I know. Cross your legs? We'll be there soon.'

'Can't.'

I pulled into a gateway and switched off the headlights. David dived out of the car.

'Won't be a moment.'

It was very dark, all moonlight smothered by the cloud that the hot weekend had summoned. Something in the apparently uniform blanket in the sky above shifted and began to shed its load of water in juicy droplets that hit the dry ground with audible plips, like fingers drumming on cartridge paper. The cold splash through the open window and the smell of rain on the dry ground brought me wholly back from corpse raking and brain clanking to the present.

What was I going to do about David. I hadn't stopped him coming with me. I hadn't said I didn't like the way he touched me that afternoon, I'd just slid out from underneath the decision.

And now in half an hour we would be in Mandy and Clive's gallery, the little stone annex that doubled for guests and Clive's sculpture exhibitions. It had one bed, a large double on a wooden landing above the ground floor which was covered in bronze or stone figures. It wasn't just the only bed, it was the only bit of flat surface on which to lie in the whole place. My subconscious had made a series of clear decisions that led just one way, why was the rest of me putting up this ridiculous fight?

Like the flat you get when a wave and a trough meet I felt blankly neutral, cancelled out by the yeses and noes. Before I had time to think any further David leapt back into the car, shaking the rain off his back.

'I got bloody lost!' he laughed, 'it's so frigging dark I couldn't find the car. And I've dropped my fags. Bugger.' He was wide awake now and perky, probably with hopefulness. He sat up and swivelled to look at me as I negotiated the pirate's map of lane and track that led to Clive and Mandy's.

'I've never even asked who these people are!'

'Clive and Mandy. Old friends from when I worked on ships. With your aunt.'

'My "aunt"? Tucker you mean?'

'*Aunt* Elen.'

'Aunt Elen! Makes her sound like a Victorian spinster. She's hardly old enough to be my aunt anyway. Only twelve years. Twelve years is *almost* nothing. Anything less *is* nothing.' So much for the deterrence value of a reminder of our kind-of relatedness and age gap: David gently touched my leg, stroking my knee as he spoke.

'Where are we sleeping?' he asked.

'In the annex. The gallery thingy. At the bottom. Of. The. Garden.'

'Wow. What happened, you've been been de-ummed for days! What did I do?'

'You bloody. Know.'

The last half mile of track to the cottage offered a timely series of cold showers for David as he got in and out of the car to open the series of gates.

'I'm very wet,' he announced after the third.

'Sorry. That was the last one.'

'What is is about you and Elen. You live at the bottom of muddy tracks and so does everyone you know.'

'I do have. You know. Some normal friends. In flats even. With an entry phone.'

'I don't believe you.'

'OK that's it, we're here.'

'This is the middle of a field,' David said, peering through the windscreen as I turned off the lights.

David's genuine discomfort with the dark and the wet made me less nervous about the possibility of him feeling confident and hormonal enough to be predatory. It occurred to me that I could simply leave him in the car and run to the gallery and he'd be too scared to follow.

'Yes. But there's a house in the next field.' I reached into the back of the van and got out the big torch that is almost as bright as the floodlights on a football stadium, and the umbrella that's like the stadium itself. 'OK. Let's go.'

David clung to me, the torch, and the bottom of the umbrella as if his life depended on all three. I felt him relax as we rounded the hedge end and the gallery and its weedy outside light came into view. We propelled ourselves through the door and out of the rain, and fumbled around in the shooting torch beam for the light switch. Over the switch was a note with Mandy's neat print.

'Sorry, Myfan. Woodburner lit but no lights in here. Candles next to bed. Bet you have a torch. Love. M C and . . . J.'

'Oh. Blast!' Alone in a bed with a overhormoned young man, and nothing but candlelight and wood flame. Oh God! I did a quick mental search for any Peter CDs that might be lying playable in my brain. Nothing. Nothing. Not even a single solitary fiddler crab.

'S'OK. We don't need light do we?' David flicked off the torch and gingerly stroked the six inches of my bare arm above it. I moved it smartly away and switched it back on.

'Of course we do. Can't climb stairs. In pitch.' I led the way though the strange cloth-swathed figures towering above us. Clive had a big commission to repair and regild the Victorian statuary of various London memorials and state buildings. The gallery housed the completed ones, all swaddled up and ready to return to the city. Little bits of gilded nose and finger stuck out from the cloth wrappings making the still shapes seem extraordinarily human and alive. I felt watched as we climbed up the spiral stairs to the bed and tiny shower room.

Rain slashed on the sloping windows above, but the heart of the woodburner beat red and passionate. I lit the candle and the whole scene became sickeningly ideal for a seduction. Under the sloping roof and windows the bed nestled with its foamy covering of cream quilts and mounds of cushions that had never been there on previous visits. They were inviting, suggestive and body like. Beside it the pot-bellied stove popped and creaked away to itself throwing a languorous warmth and glow all around. The moving yellow light of the candle made the bed and its surroundings seem like a little floating world above the darkness of the floor and its assembly of still, golden giants below.

David wasn't wasting time. He began peeling wet clothes off, and was down to a bare chest before I had time to look away and blush. I kicked myself for colouring up, my cheeks so bright they were visible even in candlelight. Seeing that, David's feather charm spread for the first time that night.

'Oh. I'm sorry. I'm being very rude. I'm so cold and wet. I'm frozen. Is there a shower?'

'Yes, in there.'

Once again he disappeared. I knelt on the bed and began to arrange all the pillows and cushions in a Berlin wall down the centre. But my plumping and pushing of stuffed fabric got slower and slower. I sat on the duvet and felt enveloped in a cloud of downy sensuality. Even the furniture was conspiring.

Inside the shower room the water was hot, steam snaked under the door and David's little sounds of thawing pleasure came through the thin partition walls. It was an electric shower so the lack of light wasn't a power failure. I wondered if Tucker had perhaps rung ahead.

I flashed the torch around and found the light fittings to be without bulbs. This was Tucker leaving me out on deck a second time to face up to my fears. And that was the only argument against David, my fear of something I couldn't put a label on. Why bother resisting this anymore? Maybe it was a good idea? Maybe it was what I wanted.

'Oh. God. Hot water. The finest invention known to humankind.' David stepped out wrapped to the waist in a white towel. Still a little damp round the chest hair, the head peach fuzzy like the day I first saw him. Eyes not so wide as usual a little pinched with tiredness. The whole thing no classical beauty, and yet beautiful. Desirable. A good first start and no mistake. Perhaps it could be a way to help David as I'd promised.

'What's the matter?' he said.

'Nothing. Come and sit down. Talk to me.'

'You *know* I don't really want to *talk*, Myfanwy.' He was getting brave again. I wondered if he had half a bottle of something secreted in the shower.

'I thought. That's what. I was for. Talking to.'

'What do you want to hear?' He sat down beside me. I could smell the dampness and heat of him. He turned my head away and began to unplait my hair, very, very slowly.

'About your mother.'

'OK,' he sighed, and talked as he twisted hair around his fingers and brought his face closer and closer to my head until I could feel his breath, feel his mouth moving on my scalp. I tried to focus on his words, rather than his lips.

'Well. One day. When I was twelve I came home and the first thing I heard as I closed the front door was Mum crying. It wasn't particularly unusual. She could cry for an hour over the cat crapping behind the sofa. But this was different crying, and she was sitting under the kitchen table to do it. He'd gone. Came home from the end of shoot, and said he'd got his break. The chance to direct a real Hollywood movie. And that he didn't want to take her with him. That was it. No negotiation. He just went. Out of my life. Left me to cope with Mum and her weeping. Some days she didn't get up. Some weeks! I cooked for her. I dressed her sometimes. And it went on for years.' David hands massaged the back of my neck, the corners of my shoulders, 'Do you still want me to talk?'

'Mmmn. Yes. Did you. Miss him?'

'No! No. Well, yes. I suppose. But I hated him more than missed him. For leaving me alone to cope with Mum in such a state. I hated her for being that way. For relying on me so much. My hate got me into the Royal. I put its energy into dancing. Like a furnace generating electricity. I turned one form of energy into another. Hate gave me the jumps the dance critics raved about.'

'Did you. Go on. You know. Hating. Your mum.'

'For a long time.'

'How long?' The massaging stopped, the fairy lights inside me dimmed and David's words dried. This was the point about David that I'd missed. I was indeed a distraction. A means to distract his controlled outside into letting the inside speak.

Distraction was what he needed to talk. I turned back towards him and without looking, began to stroke the top of his head, rolling my palm around over the peach fuzz.

'Oh, God. Myfanwy.' He relaxed like a puppet whose strings had been suddenly snipped, and began to talk again. I felt a rush of power that I'd discovered this simple sensual key that was unlocking David at the first turn, and keeping me in control. In control felt safe. In control felt like the flat place where the wave and the trough meet.

'She came to every performance I ever did,' he went on. 'She was so proud. She was so grateful for all I'd done for her. She believed I loved her.'

'Didn't you?'

'I don't know. I felt hate. Hate is what I felt. Anger. Fury. At all those bloody days and years of her crying. All the time she was ill, I thought only a little while now. Only a little while. And I'll be free.' He turned, looked up at me, hands limp in his lap, his brow rumpled. He passed a hand across his head, to wipe mine away.

'I'm sorry. I'm being very self-indulgent.' The feather shield exterior began to close over him. I had to be decisive. I laid a hand on his leg feeling its hardness through the towel. He sighed, his brow unwrinkled he began to talk again. Such a simple key.

'I lied to her. I pretended to love, to be sympathetic. And all the time I was so angry, so trapped, so full of hate. When she watched me dance that's what she was seeing without knowing.' He reached to my face and began to caress its outline. His eyes were wide again now, soaked in sadness.

'What happened when she died?'

'I was there. When they turned everything off. I saw the readout on the screen go flat. Like the movies. And I stopped hating her. I loved her. But it was too late.' He was kissing and crying at the same time then sobbing into my shoulder, me with my arms around his strong naked back rocking him like you rock a baby.

'You loved her. All the time. With the hate. It was the *two* things that made you dance. You don't need to feel bad. You loved her. You did. You did.'

Running my hands over and over the perfection of that spine it seemed likely that there was nothing wrong with it, just a pus of guilt pressing on some nerves. I drew David down into the encompassing softness of the covers and pillows and wrapped as much of myself around him as I could. He cried and cried. Kissed my neck, my mouth, held on to me and cried more.

'You did love her,' I said in a lull between weeping showers.

His face was almost too close to focus, and anyway made smudgy by tears. His nose was running, which was oddly endearing.

'Mmm. Yes. I did. I did.'

'So that's OK. She knew you did. You weren't lying.'

'But I hated her!'

'You hated all that responsibility. Doing all that so young? It's hard. But you did it. You were wonderful. But it's all done now. You can just love her, and remember her.'

'Yes. yes.' And he cried again for a while, sniffed loudly and stopped.

'You're de-ummed again.'

'Mmm. Seem to be for while.'

'So much for Casanova. This is the second time I've drowned you in salt water instead of fucking your brains out,' he laughed and snivelled at the same time. 'Oh bugger it,' he said, sniffing monumentally, 'snot's no aphrodisiac is it?'

He fell asleep eventually, still crying a bit, still letting me tell him that he had loved his mother. I caressed his sleeping face and body, I was safe enough now to feel a little pure desire. Would this mothering sensuality be as close to sex as I ever felt comfortable about being again? It certainly was not the scene that Mandy and Tucker had plotted with clandestine phone calls and light bulb removal.

I arranged my arms and the pillows so that David's head could be on my shoulder without cutting off my circulation, and fell asleep.

The dream must have come very close to morning because I woke up straight out of it. It was just like before. Almost. The deck of the *Princess* in a tropical sunset. A silent assembly of passengers, but no Pete smiling in the background. And the bird on my hands sitting impassive and neutral and, apparently, motiveless. Sitting on my hands, held up and out over the limitless sea. Then Peter's eyes came, the way I see them deep inside the mirror. His eyes looking out through the dark beads of the bird's own. And then I woke up.

It was light but still raining. David had rolled himself into a ball of duvet and pillows and I was fully clothed outside the covers and cold as a corpse. What sort of intimacy was being a mouth to kiss and a shoulder to cry on? What did it mean?

What would it mean to a dead and possibly jealous husband

whose peering out of a sea bird's eyes might presage all sorts of ectoplasmic hi-jinks? When David woke and looked at me would Peter's blue eyes be hiding inside his big black ones?

Pre-caffeine anxieties I told myself. All the same I got up, snuck down the stairs and out into the warm mizzly rain. A line of stepping stone flags, sunk in mossy grass of an impossibly bright green sauntered in a freehand curve to the back door of Clive and Mandy's house. The kitchen window was open and breakfast type noises were coming out of it: fridge opening, sleepy monosyllabic conversation over-cheery radio, a kettle whistle. I didn't knock just leant over the top half of the stable door.

'Hello-oo.'

Mandy was sitting at the long oak table, thin white hands laced around a huge black mug, looking more like a harassed flower fairy than ever. Clive was marching around the kitchen in a very substantially belted towelling dressing gown with a tiny comma shaped bundle held to his shoulder with one huge blacksmith's hand.

He looked as if he might be demonstrating some new and important tactic to another year of the Sandhurst hopefuls who, in his other life, he used to convert into crack SAS material.

Mandy lit up like Peter Pan's sidekick as I called, and whirled me in a hug of perfect broderie anglaise and wispy blonde hair. Clive allowed himself to be kissed, nodded and smiled. About the highest emotion greeting I'd ever see him give to anyone who wasn't Mandy. The bundle didn't say anything.

'It's so absolutely lovely to see you. Sit down, sit down. Clive, pour her a coffee.' Mandy's voice is straight out of those nineteen-forties movies about wartime gals being 'frightfully brave'. Clive's would be at home on the Tory benches of the Lords and really will be if his elder brother doesn't pack in cocaine dealing when their dad pops his clogs.

'OK. Here. Hold this.' He passed the bundle to me with one hand, inside the fat end of it was a tiny face.

'Julia,' said Mandy, 'she's nearly eight pounds now.'

'Ugly little sod. Like her mother,' said Clive placing a mug in front of me. 'One sugar isn't it?' he added and gave my shoulder a tiny squeezing. He put a full plate in front of Mandy, 'Toast. Eat something. Friesians don't make milk out of air,' then tucked an escaping bit of hair behind her ear as she looked up to smile and thank him.

'Julia,' I said in my head, 'you are a very lucky girl. These people are from another planet, much nicer than Earth.'

'Right'o. I'll just put this child upstairs, so we can have breakfast in peace. C'mon Julia.' He scooped her from my lap, passing her from hand to hand via a definite little phase of flight. 'Same aerodynamics as a rugger ball,' he said and disappeared up the stairs.

'He's been wonderful, Myfanwy. As if he'd been handling babies all his life,' said Mandy. All her attention was with the sound of Clive's footsteps in the bedroom above, visualising him putting Julia in her cot.

'She should sleep for a while now,' Mandy said, and stretched in her chair like a sleepy cat. I doubted then my theory about the light bulbs. Ten days into their careers as parents neither Clive nor Mandy had the energy for promoting somebody else's love life. So if Tucker hadn't rung then David was going to come as a complete surprise. How was I going to explain David, from a standing start. I ran through a few potted versions in my head.

This is Tucker's nephew, David. Who is my friend, sounded so bare as to be foully incriminating.

This is my very close friend David. He's Tucker's nephew.

This is my sleeping partner David.

This is David and I don't know what to do about him.

Mandy and Clive had known Peter and me for so long. I didn't want them to think I was being unfaithful to him. I didn't want them to think I had thrown aside Peter's memory to jump into bed with someone new. Least of all when I wasn't. And hadn't. But David preempted any attempts at explanation. Clive was downstairs again and David had found his way to the back door.

'Hello! Good morning!'

From the looks on Clive and Mandy's faces it was obvious that light bulbs, cushions and candles had all been a complete coincidence and my conspiracy theory was up there with alien abductions and ethical foreign policies.

'Oh, yes. This is David. He's . . . going to help. With. You know. The chair.'

But nobody heard my ketchup blobs because David's performance instincts and full plumage charm had taken the stage. He stepped in through the door, tousled, unshaven but luminescing like a neon tube at midnight.

'Hello,' he said again, 'I'm David Wall. Myfanwy's friend.' There it was again. David's ability to make one word sound like something different, and stud a single syllable with a mosaic of imagery. This time 'friend' came complete with a little video of the most energetic sex any of us had ever seen. But although all three of us undoubtedly saw it, Mandy and Clive were too polite to react. Or perhaps they felt that, to a husband five years cold, unfaithfulness isn't a realistic concept.

'I came with her to help with the chair,' he beamed, shaking Mandy's hand earnestly as if she were a cross between the Dalai Lama and the Duchess of Kent. 'It's a little bulky and we thought you might have your hands full. Congratulations on your new addition by the way.'

'Very pleased to meet you David. Do come and have some breakfast.'

Mandy, Clive and David did a little ballet of charm. All of them on point exchanging snippets of life stories and opinions over the toast and coffee. At the end of forty minutes they were old friends and David was making free with their kitchen appliances.

'More toast anyone?' he said, 'Myfanwy, you've hardly had anything, and you did all the driving last night.'

'No, no. I'm fine. You know. Replete. Thanks.'

'Well, David, why don't we boys get the chair shifted, whilst we've peace upstairs. We can leave the girls to small talk.'

'No!' I said, rather too loudly. I didn't want Clive having any time alone with David. I could just imagine the images that David could manage to conjure whilst describing how we'd met and our limited subsequent 'relationship'. By the end of three sentences Clive would have a mental picture of David and me riding off into the sunset together, or remaking *From Here to Eternity* on a West Wales beach. 'No, the chair. It's all wrapped.' I blobbed, 'A surprise. I want you to see it. You know. Properly.'

'All right. If you're sure the two of you can manage. I'll open the French windows, you can bring it through that way. At least it's stopped raining.'

'Let's go, David.'

I set off towards the van at quite a pace. Sharing a duvet and a load of snot did not mean that David had the right to imply that we were an item. It did not give him the right to make remarks about my consumption of breakfast, as if he had some responsibility for my welfare, and therefore some rights to accompany it.

'Hey, wait for me!' David came squelching up beside me in a pair of outsize borrowed wellies. 'Oh, they're lovely people!'

'Yes.'

'They're going to love your chair and the cot.'

'Cradle.'

'Sorry.'

I opened the back of the van. 'Right. We'll take the chair. Together. Then you can unwrap. Then I'll. Come back for the cot. I mean cradle.'

'Fine.'

'You take those legs. I'll take this side. Ready? Lift.'

'Right!'

It was still wet underfoot and slippery. Vapour was beginning to rise from the meadow, twisting out of the grass; a whole colony of genies. We *pas de deux*-ed along the path, with the huge awkward shape of the upended chair between us. Speaking over the sea of bubble wrap that enveloped the chair, and glancing down at our sliding feet.

'It's solid. Didn't expect it to weigh this much.'

'It's the slate. In the seat.'

'Oh!'

'Is there something wrong?'

'No. Yes.'

'What is it?' Instinctively, David moved towards me. I tried to move away, but carrying each side of the chair as we were the result was a slow erratic revolve.

'You implied. In there. That we were . . .' That we were what? 'Going out'? 'Going steady'? 'Courting strong'? Or simply 'fucking'? What should I say?

'That we were. Lovers.' I concluded.

'I did not! I introduced myself as your friend.'

'Yes. But you said it. Like. Like something. Different.'

'What do you mean something different?' This was the David I'd seen that first night sparking around Tucker's kitchen with a carving knife: light the blue touch paper and retire to a safe distance.

'You made it sound. Like. Sex. Not friends. Sex.' Heat is supposed to make things flow more easily. Doesn't always work with my words, often they melt and stick together as anger warms me up.

'Well, I'm sorry!' Now it was his turn to walk away. But still holding the chair with me attached we just began to rotate the opposite way, a little faster than before.

'I'm so sorry that my feelings somehow slipped out. I think that spending a night in someone's arms and telling them your innermost secrets makes you a little more than just friends.'

'Don't. Shout.'

'Why bloody not? What are you afraid of?'

'Of. My friends. Embarrassing. Them.' He stopped walking,

and we stood looking over the chair again, not really aware of having moved halfway up the field, further from the house than ever.

'Well, I'm your friend, aren't I? I'm not embarrassing me.' He pushed the chair into me, forcing me back, then around and around widdershins again. 'Last night was important to me. Special. I said things, felt things, I've never said or felt before. You got close. You wanted to get in. You got in. It means something.'

'OK. OK. But not.' I stopped moving and pushed the chair back at him with a jolt, 'Not. That we're. Lovers.'

That was it. The paper had burnt to the gunpowder. Ignition.

'No. Oh, NO! Of course not. Because we didn't actually *fuck*, did we? You were just being my *therapist* when you kissed me.' He dropped his side of the chair and struggling with the weight I slipped, fell and lay in the wet grass, flailing like a landed fish. David fumed over me. 'That was sympathy I felt in your lips was it? Well, it felt like desire to me. Lust. Passion. But maybe I just haven't *had* enough women to know. Carry your own bloody chair.'

I've never seen anyone really turn on their heel before. Perhaps it takes a dancer's training to do it. But David did. Turned on his heel and marched off down the field towards the track. I slipped twice trying to get up, and by the time I was successfully upright he was out of sight. I knew he wouldn't have gone back to the house. I guessed he was running, already halfway to the main road. He'd hitch to the station and run to London. What was the point in chasing him? What was I going to say?

I got the chair onto my back like a tortoise's shell and staggered to the house with it. Clive was waiting in the sitting room with the French windows wide open.

'Mandy's feeding Julia. I wondered where you'd got to,' he said.' Didn't come looking. You know. Heard the row going on. Just the voices of course. I didn't actually hear . . . Where *is* David?'

'Gone. In Wooton by now I expect. In a taxi to the station.'

'Oh, God. I'm sorry. Lovers' tiff, eh?'

I pretended not to hear and went back to the car to fetch the cradle.

I hadn't been to Clive and Mandy's for more than a year. They had a lot to show me: the alterations to the house; Clive's studio and foundry. And of course the various unique and wondrous aspects of their baby. It got us through the awkwardness of David's departure. Stopped me having to speak about my life. Gave me enough distraction to keep floating just six inches outside of myself to look at what might be going on. And perhaps enough time for David to get to the station miss a train, come back.

'Oh, you'll love this,' said Mandy, as we crossed the strip of daisies and speedwell that separated the house from the newly restored barn. 'Even I got excited and normally I don't go much for all that Victoriana stuff.'

Clive steadied Julia the rugby ball with one hand and with the other threw open the double doors at the end of the stone building. Inside was an enclosure of light. Most of the walls had been replaced with glass and huge windows in the roof let the full sun of the Indian summer come cascading in. Inside the barn was the kind of yellowy glow you usually only see coming from hoards of pirate treasure in children's books. It came from statues, big sisters to the ones clothed in rags in the gallery. These were mostly unwrapped, huge Amazonian-limbed women, with Roman noses and steady eyes.

'They're fourteen feet tall,' said Clive. 'It's taken me weeks to do the gilding.'

The gold was so bright it seemed fluorescent; living. So that when I brushed against one of their arms I drew back as if at the unexpected touch of live skin. Light bounced off the statues so that walking between them I was in a kind of gold mist. I wandered, mesmerised. Clive was squirming inside his clothes with delight. But he's always believed he could hide his marsh-mallow interior by displays of brusque practicality. So he leant in close rubbing the gilded surfaces with a dirty critical thumb. Probably for the fiftieth time.

'They belong on the side of a Victorian chapel in Yorkshire. National Trust job. They were in the most frightful state when I got them. I had to recast a few noses and fingers. Thank the Lord they weren't male figures. I'd have spent two months todger moulding.'

'They're the virtues,' said Mandy, 'here's Hope, here's Faith, over there is Love.'

Their reproachful hands surrounded me. Their sad faces gazed down on my head. They looked pained as if they might be wearing thistles in their knickers to offset profane thoughts. But it worked. They did look virtuous.

I knew about virtue. A virtue was something you worked at. Like getting a six-pack stomach from doing lots of sit-ups. Since Peter I'd done lots of spiritual sit-ups to acquire the virtue of self-control, wilful detachment. I'd never considered that I could get myself anything really *nice* like Hope or Love by working at it. I'd always thought that those were things that you had or didn't by luck or circumstance. I'd lost Love, Hope and any sort of Faith in my own life when Peter died. It had never occurred to me before that I could *choose* to regain those things.

Clive had moved down to the end of the barn where one last statue stood in the corner. She was ungilded, black and brassy with a broken arm and a dented nose. The poor bet for the heavyweight championship.

'Here's the only one I haven't finished,' he said, 'she's Chastity.'

'I thought it was Faith. Hope. And *Charity*.'

'We did have Charity but she's already back in Yorkshire. The Victorians were pretty keen on Chastity.'

Of course they were! Hence the thistle-lined underwear. Chastity, well that was one virtue I had kept by effort of will. Looking at the sad drab giantess in front of me she seemed like a very poor choice indeed. Keeping Chastity I was wilfully turning away any chance of holding hands with her more attractive golden sisters.

'Truth's my favourite.' said Mandy, 'but you can't really see her through the packing. She's got a lovely face. Less kind of "we are not amused" than the others. Come and look, Myfanwy. There. If you squint up under that bit of wrapping you can just see.'

Standing next to Mandy I twisted round to peer up under the statue's coverings. Down a blue corridor of polythene sheeting a prettier version of the Mona Lisa smiled: Truth's sweet, golden face. I was short on her virtue too. From Truth's end of the plastic she could easily see the little psychological sleight of hand I'd pulled on myself since the moment I met David. I'd been putting a false beard and glasses on my feelings, because I was afraid. The blank gold eyes could see fear sitting on my chest, a fat stone bird without a label. It wasn't going to move until I could tell it by name to get going and let me get on with my life.

Chapter Ten

The Grim Reaper of invertebrates, who never has a moment's rest, had brought a world of bad news to my poor bees. There were tiny bodies in every part of both hives. They fell off the frames as I took them out, light and dry as empty sweet papers. And after the inhabitants of the Hymenopteran palace had died the ransacking had begun. Mice had got in and eaten most of the combs. In the second hive there were even signs that some enterprising mouse-mum had reared a litter of youngsters.

Every tiny blobbit of bee blood was on my conscience. In all the time the hives had been at Graham's I hadn't checked them once. All through the wet of late summer they'd been slowly starving without a loan of sugar to keep them through the cold flowerless weeks. Starvation had taken them where they stood. I found that stupidly touching. As if they'd been a human orchestra playing as the ship went down.

I'd started with the bees out of desperation when Peter was diagnosed. I tried to keep my cool. But in the face of words like 'cancer' and 'terminal', 'rational', 'calm' and 'hope' don't cut a lot of mustard. I did at least keep my panic to myself. Mental isometrics tightened my emotional sphincters so that I could act normally with Pete. But out on my own the panic spurted out as hyperactive straw-clutching. I read the label on every herbal remedy in every whole food shop for thirty miles. I got so I could do key word searches in the pages of health magazines just by flicking through them in the newsagent's.

Not that Pete would actually have tried any of the supplements, pills, potions, crystals, extracts, tinctures or distillates that I turned up, even if he hadn't been royally nauseous with side effects.

'It's pathetic!' he said, after I'd found some Sea Vegetable Extract with thirty different trace elements, 'I'm not going to start believing in witchcraft because I'm sick.'

'It's hardly blood sacrifice I'm talking about! All I'm asking you to do is take some vitamin pills.'

'Why don't you find me something to *eat*?' he yelled, 'something that doesn't make me throw up?'

I did. I found honey. I swotted up on the health benefits of all bee products: it seemed that bees, not dolphins were the potential saviours of human kind. Bees, apparently, produced substances that could combat every illness from alopecia to Alzheimer's. If only we ate nothing but bee food the apiarist authors suggested we could all be Olympic athletes at a hundred and fifty.

Organic wildflower honey was the best, they said. I tracked some down in the 'Pimples' at the bottom of a muddy lane. It was made by a little commune of ex-Brixton squatters, or rather their bees. I bought up almost all of their meagre supply, twelve fat jars full.

Peter ate the honey and wasn't sick but still he slipped a little further. I decided that honey I'd produced would have some extra 'positive' ingredient. Honey laced with love could save him.

I put an ad in the local rag and tracked down Alun Ap Rees, 95, and finally finding his ten hives 'a bit much like'. He looked rather like a bee. Neat and small and slightly rounded. I bought his kit, and two hives full of nice quiet bees.

He did teach me a bit, but he'd been keeping bees so long it was part of him. Explanations were difficult.

'Oh, now. Let me think,' he'd say, stopping dead still with a smoker on one hand and two hundred sleepy workers on the other, 'No. No. It's no good. I can't *tell* you how to do that. I'll have to show you. Tomorrow. We'll do that tomorrow.'

After three days of hit and miss tuition I was in at the deep end with two little boxy hives set up in William's top field. Round the cabin there was nothing but marram, thin pickings for hungry bees.

Alun's bees were used to experienced handling. With me they got stroppy and in the first month I was stung half to hell and back. I always seemed to be sitting in William's kitchen with one of us pulling stings out of me with a pair of his dissection kit tweezers.

'You know,' he told me one afternoon when I'd failed to put my veil on right and they'd got in to my head, 'a friend of your mother's once told me that you have to tell them news first. Before anyone else, you tell the bees. Keeps them sweet tempered apparently. Nonsense of course.' It was a piece of bee lore that I've come to love, but with fifty little barbs still pumping poison into my scalp I wasn't ready for it.

'There's just one thing I'd like to tell those bees now. And that's fuck off!'

'Myfanwy! Language!'

But then I got my first pot of honey. It smelt right and only had a few bee body parts in it.

'Hey. Same colour as your hair!' said Pete, and tasted it manfully. 'This is good!' He took a second spoon with real enthusiasm and kept it down. He swore he liked it better than the commune's product. He ate more, that was certain. Here at last was some help I could give. Something more than just spectating Peter's decline.

The stings got less after that. I thought I was improving. But it wasn't me. It was the bees. They were training me up nicely. Subtle and selfless, stealthily they slipped in their lessons without my noticing. Schooling me to be slow and calm. I watched them moving around on the comb apparently so purposeless but achieving so much. I sat next to the hives and watched their tiny comings and goings at the entrance. Lilliput made real. The sound, the smell, the constant movement. The hypnotic super entity of the swarm drew me in. I started noticing patches of flowers, wind direction, sunshine and cloud. I got bee tuned.

'What are you doing?' I asked Pete one night in bed, as he lifted my shirt and felt along my ribs like a doctor.

'Just checking you're not growing six legs and a pair of wings. Don't wear that stripy sweater any more. It makes me nervous.'

I drove up to tell William that Peter had died before I told anyone else. But the bees got the news first. William was in the top field. I passed the hives on my way to find him. 'He's gone,' I said, 'the honey didn't work.'

I tried to give the bees back to Alun. He wouldn't take them. 'You keep at it girl,' he said, 'saved my sanity when my Margaret died did the bees. And honey is good for grief.'

So in the spring I got back to hive rhythm. Retrained with just a few reminding stings. My bee tuning came back – spotting likely flower patches, tutting to myself on days when the wind would make flight difficult. I went to the hives almost every day just to watch the selfless comings and goings, soft as the drip-drip that wears through stone. the desireless purpose of the bees as they covered my hands, numbed my longing. By midsummer I had a subset of Peter CDs that I played to the humming of the hive as I worked the bees. they were part of the big memory-world that I built like a comb all round me.

I got their foraging mentality so completely that it made me look at everything in a new way. I stopped finding driftwood and shaped stone by accident. I started knowing where and when to look. Like the bees searching for nectar to make into honey, I searched for flotsam and made it into more and more chairs.

The little holidays from loss that the bees gave me that first summer without Peter came back close and real as my own breath. I stood looking down at the drifts of little corpses and felt miserably guilty. Rain began to patter on my protective bee gear. I looked out through the dark gauze at the meadow already wet from a week of rain. About to get wetter as the escape route up to the blue sky slid shut. Yellow grass, limp and sorry as dishcloths. Thistles drooping and slimy with the damp. Even the trees had bad posture. And forty thousand mini-ghosts waggled their antennae soulfully at me.

I sagged, my arms fell limp, my heart dropped to the bottom of my belly. I was at the bottom of the shabby little plug-hole into which I had been slipping for quite some time. Swirled down by Peter's mad ghost, by David, by Tucker's baby, and Idris' wildebeest and the memory of a sweetness that failed to save the day. It felt like the end of something more than just my career as an apiarist. I hadn't paid attention to the bees because Peter was so dead. Too dead now to bother with honey.

'Oh God. What happened? I swear I didn't spray the roses after you brought them here.' Graham had come to stand beside me, his blue cagoule hood pulled up over the flopping hair. I'd assumed he'd be out at this time on a weekday morning. 'Maybe they died of shock when I told them I could play a bit of Beethoven's Ninth.'

Hiding behind my now entirely unnecessary veil, I sighed audibly and swore in a melancholy sort of way, 'Poor bloody bees. Poor bloody bees.'

'Oh, damn it. Me and my big mouth. Myfanwy, I'm sorry. Joking here with you so upset. Come you in now. Out of this rain. Have some tea. Bit of toast and you'll be right. I'll help you sort the hives in a minute.'

I let him lead me away, over the meadow and inside. So much for the six-pack-stomach of self control, I was limp with sorrow. I felt I didn't have the energy to keep anything in or out any more.

'Bet. On your bed.' The dog did a high-speed slink into her basket, 'Good girl,' Graham said. The kitchen was more untidy than before. A flock of dirty mugs stood at the edge of the sink and the table was covered in papers. Through in the living room a futon was still unfolded and strewn with bedding. 'Oh. Sorry about the mess, like. Doing accounts today. Now that the tourist trade's dropped off.'

I drew my hands out of the gloves and lifted off my veil and hat. Graham turned away abruptly, as if I'd whipped off my kit down to my underwear. He clattered cups and kettle, milk and fridge door for a while until he'd left me enough time to get out of my bee armour.

'Can I just leave this on the floor?'

'Oh, yes. Bet won't touch it. Milk and sugar?'

'Mmm.'

'Come and sit for a minute,' he said, 'I've actually got chairs now!' He led the way through, past the piano to the second pair of huge French windows. Facing each other but turned slightly towards the view down the meadow were two of my chairs. I'd made them a year before. One a nest-like swirl of rush with driftwood arms and legs. The other upright as Canute's seat, made of planks I'd pulled from a rotting mesh of kelp in a storm on Ceibwr beach. I'd put a line of big 'sea jewels' — weathered glass — in pale blue and green, tiara-wise across its back. The last time I'd seen them was in a shop window in Knightsbridge.

I didn't know what to say. Whether to be alarmed or flattered. Certainly surprised. I didn't think my asymmetrical over-dramatic stuff would be Graham's scene at all.

'I've owned them for a while actually,' he said, as if apologising for some misdemeanour. 'Bought them in London. But they've been on loan. To a mate in a rented flat. His furniture was in storage and he likes nice stuff. Modern design. So I lent him these. Finally got 'em back last week!'

Graham must have paid the full whack for them. Five grand for the two, at least. 'You didn't . . . tell me.'

'Well. No. I dunno why. I didn't want to embarrass you I s'pose. Anyway. Sit down. They're good chairs.'

I'd seen my chairs in friends' houses before. Taken the praise.
But once stuff went to London shops. That was it. Goodbye. I
sat down in the Canute throne. The wood was cool and smooth.
I ran my hands over the arms, turned to touch the sea jewels.

'It's beautiful,' I said, as if it was someone else's work. I was
astounded. I'd thought my chairs were merely odd. Bought as
curiosities, sort of up-market Garfields.

'Yes. It is. They both are. I can never make up my mind
which is my favourite.'

'I remember finding, you know. All the bits of them.' And I
did. The stretch of river where I'd cut the rush and seen an otter
that year for the first time. The cove where the glass washed up.
The tantruming sea the day I found the planks. In a single glance
I recovered all the little moments of my life that were recorded in
those chairs I'd made.

I saw myself from a distance out under the sky foraging, like a
solitary bumble bee. Tiny, mad looking, behaving unlike any
other sort of human: there I was, the only figure on a beach in the
rain. Quartering up and down from high to low tide in my
oilskins like a demented kumquat. Here I was, struggling up a
cliff path, a load of rotting planks on my back, frightening the
family of holidaymakers. And far below and out on the rocks I
shook snowflakes off my hair and plunged two white arms into a
rock pool. Too distant to see my face or know anything about
what particular Peter CD might have been playing to me. All the
little moments caught like a shoal of fish in a net. *My* experience,
my living, made into something solid and real.

Somewhere inside me, in a place that *deserves* the name 'Islets
Of Langerhans' more than a few nodules of pancreas, an idea
burst its seed coat. It put out a tiny shoot: it was that the life I
had made alone was more than just occupational therapy for a
widow. It meant something. Counted for something. There was
the seed of a chance that what I'd done and been since Peter was,
perhaps, more than just a dish of cold leftovers with some well-
chosen spices.

Graham coughed slightly. My tea, I noticed, was quite cold. I had probably been staring into space like a lobotomised rodent for five minutes.

'Are you all right, now?' he asked.

'Oh. Yes. Fine. I'll finish my tea.'

'Right. I think there's a gap in the showers. I could help with the hives?'

'Yes, Graham. That would be lovely. Thank you.'

We left the house through the kitchen. Graham picked up my veil and gloves. 'Don't you need these?'

'Don't think so. Dead bees don't sting.'

With minimal but companionable conversation, Graham and I dismantled the hives and scraped them out. It felt like an exorcism. I imagined little bee ghosts spinning off into the void shrieking, as we worked. Then we stacked the bits in the back of the van and I left feeling steadier of mind and lighter of heart than I had since David had stomped off into a Gloucestershire meadow.

The day David made his dramatic exit was the day when the acceleration into the plug-hole slide had really picked up. All the way back from Mandy and Clive's I'd dismantled my behaviour to David and David's behaviour to me. I did a thorough job. By the time I got to Tucker's on Tuesday morning, I had a pile of tiny components that I couldn't even name. Let alone fit together. As I expected, David wasn't at Tucker's and she hadn't heard from him. But that was the last thing on her mind. She was alone in the house when I called. Kids at friends', Julian at Vicky's, Idris at work. But she wasn't in the barn painting: a bad sign.

'Tucker, why are you doing that?'

She was down on her hands and knees cleaning the kitchen floor. 'Because it's dirty.' The hair sparked but she didn't look up.

'I'll go then. Leave you to it.'

'No. No, Van.' She hauled her bulk upright. 'Sorry. I'll make us coffee.'

'No, I'll do it. Any of David's Blue Mountain left?'

'Yeah . . . in there.'

'So. What's happened.'

'I told Idris. He was furious.'

'Furious?'

'With me. He says I'm careless with my cap. That I must have put it in wrong. As if anyone can check it. All that stuff about "feeling your cervix through it like a nose". As if anyone has a *cervix* like a *nose* . . .'

'OK. OK, Tucker. So what did you say then?' Idris had, I guessed, tipped Tucker into proto meltdown. She could have said almost anything.

'And then I said . . .' she sighed and buried her fingers in her sparking hair.

'Oh Tucker! What did you say?'

'I said, "Well, nobody else's sperm ever got past it so maybe it's your fault".'

Idris had always been very touchy about Tucker's sexual past. She'd been knocking off both of the lecturers on the trip when he'd met her. He'd been a virgin the first time round, and Tucker was only his second lover. He made rather nervous jokes sometimes about the possibility of her 'having some on the side'. Never completely confident that for a sassy gal like Tucker he could be enough. So under the circumstances Tucker's retaliation was rash.

'And then he said,' Tucker went on,' how did I know that it was *his* sperm that got past this time.'

'And then?' I could guess what was coming.

'I hit him.'

'Bloody hell, Tucker.'

'Not hard. Just did one of those slaps that girlies in movies do when some old lardarse puts a hand up their skirt or something. Anyway, he left. Drove off. That was last night. I think he slept at the surgery. He was there when I rang this morning.'

'What did he say?'

' "Fuck off", the first time. Then I rang again and he said he'd talk when he got home. This coffee smells like cheese. Oh God I'm going to be sick again.'

I heard her make it to the bathroom. When she came back down she was white. She sagged into the kitchen chair. She seemed visibly less rounded. Only Tucker could be pregnant and lose weight.

'I never felt this bad with the others,' she said, 'there's no way I'm going through twelve weeks of grade one nausea. If he makes me I'll put syrup of figs in everything he eats for nine months.'

'D'you want me to babysit so you can go out and talk?'

'No. I know what I want you to do. But I can't ask.' Tucker never pussyfooted around a favour request like that. It must be big.

'What?'

'Talk to him for me. Explain it. He'll come home all full of his bloody neuroses about me shagging the postman or the milkman or the plumber. And I'll just get furious and it'll be a replay of this morning.'

'Oh. I can't,' I actually wailed. After making the little pile of emotional nuts and bolts on my van seat I didn't feel up to marriage guidance. But Tucker hardly ever *asked* for anything. And maybe rummaging around in someone else's life might make me feel better about the mausoleum that was apparently my own. 'All right. Greater love hath no woman that she should berate her cousin for her best mate.'

'Hey, Van. That's the longest sentence I've heard you do in ages.'

'I'm temporarily and intermittently de-ummed.' A little light bulb of curiosity snapped on over Tucker's head.

'So what happened with you and David then?'

'Nothing. Like I told you. Talking. Anyway I've got to go Tucker, if I'm going to catch Idris before he leaves surgery. Bye. I'll call if I have a result.'

I sat in the empty waiting-room whilst Idris dealt with his last patient of the session. After a few minutes a huge cardboard box emerged from the door of the consulting room. Behind it was a small haggard looking bottle blonde flanked by two wailing children, who leant and clung. As they cleared the doorway Idris beckoned me in.

'What are you doing here, Myfanwy?' He was already truculent, an Eeyore whose thistles had been 'Tiggered'.

'Have you got, you know. A few minutes. To . . . talk.' I could sense the sticky tomato-y feeling happening in my head, gumming up my words.

Idris was grumpily washing his hands and wrists, grumpily drying them. 'Well, no. I haven't. I've got to be at a farm halfway to Carmarthen in an hour. I suppose Elen sent you.'

This was going to be so much more difficult on ketchup setting. What in the last twenty-four hours had kept my speech flowing? Like tuning a radio to a fuzzy signal, first I picked up David in my arms asleep, fairy lights twinkling inside me as I stroked his back. But that didn't hold for long. What cleared my head and loosed my vocal cords was those big 'Head Girl' statues with the prickles in their panties, holding to ideals by willpower. I turned my dial to those blind gold eyes and heavy limbs and the knots and glitches in my sentences pulled out like the loops from a taut string.

'Yes. She did,' I said.

'Oh, right then.' Idris stood with his cleaned hands on his hips, 'What's the message, then. Tell me, then you can bugger off.'

'No message. I'm not sure what she wanted me to say. But can I come with you anyway? I've got nothing on this afternoon. We could talk in the car.'

'Oh. All right.' He went on grumping a bit as we walked to the car, but only for form's sake.

It was going to thunder again. We left the blue sky at the coast and drove in under piling cloud that looked no higher than the valley tops. I waited until we were clear of town to speak.

'Tucker told me about what happened. About the baby. About what she said to you.'

'I bet she did!'

'Whatever you think she *meant*, it's your baby. So she's right about it being as much your fault as hers.'

'So why did she say that. About. You know other men's . . . About it working for other men.'

'Because she had a lot of lovers before you Idris. You *know* that. But she's had no one since. Twelve years and no one but you.'

'How do you know? How do I know? How do either of us know she's not shagging her art dealer mates every time she goes up there?'

'Not much of an affair. That's about two fucks a year, Idris.'

'How do I know what she does all day in the house?'

'She works. She's obsessive. She's a painter. She has four little girls and one big boy.'

'I dunno. I dunno.'

'Yes you do. You *know* she's never been unfaithful to you.'

'Oh, fuck it.' To the almost aneurism-inducing surprise of the Land Rover behind us Idris swerved the car off the road and into a lay-by. He sat at the wheel breathing very hard and screwing up his eyes as if he'd just peeled a scout camp's worth of onions.

'What is it, Idris?'

'I wish she had been unfaithful. I wish she'd had every man for twenty miles around. I wish she'd fucked her dealers right in the middle of every gallery in Cork Street!' Idris spoke with even more conviction than he had about sheep intelligence. I got the nasty sinking feeling I'd got once before, after Peter's first set of blood tests. That deep gut level 'Oho', when you know that you've just hit the tip of a particularly unpleasant iceberg. I tuned in resolutely to 'Clive's big gold ladies', and put a hand on the nearest of Idris' tensed arms.

'C'mon boy. What is this all about?'

I must have had the magic touch for making men cry that week. Idris' face turned bright pink and hard, then dissolved into wavy lines and fat rivulets of tears. He hit his head rhythmically on the wheel in between words. And cried.

'I'm (hit) such (hit) a (hit) fucking (hit) idiot (hit).'

'Stop it, Idris. You'll knock yourself out. Think how stupid that'll look in A and E.'

'OK.' He stopped instantly sat up straight and sniffed as if breathing in the Red Sea.

'So,' I said. 'Now. Tell me what all this is about.'

'I've had an affair.'

I'd guessed that there was some sort of horrid subtext but hearing it out loud was still like being hit. Idris, dour and funny, perpetually out of sorts with everything from his underpants to his MP. This Idris had been doing dark, secret, intimate things with someone who wasn't Tucker.

Incomprehensible. I reeled. I recovered. I retuned, and sorted out the list of questions into a sensible order.

'Is it still going on?'

'No.'

'Do you love her?'

'God. No! No!'

'Do you still see her.'

'No. I only met her 'cos of her Afghan.'

'Her Afghan?'

'Afghan hound. Tarquin. Stomach tumour.'

'She called her dog *Tarquin*?'

'Yes. She did. And yes, I still went to bed with her.' The Eeyore truculence jumped up again.

'OK. OK. Idris, start from the beginning.'

'It was in the spring. April. I was feeling. Oh, God. Like death. Like dyin'. Like I wanted to put down every pet and every owner and every bloody farmer between here and Bangor. Elen was up in London. With another lot of fabulous work. Gorgeous pictures; you remember all that blue sea stuff she did last year?'

'Mmm. Lovely. Go on.'

'And she'd gone off all full of it. Of her art and her life. Looking like a big lovely ice cream sundae that you want to lick. And I just thought well, this is it boy. This is you. Arm up a cow's arse. That's about all you're good for. Not good enough for anybody. Anyway. So I was feeling bad this particular day. And I got called out at the end of the day to this Afghan hound by a woman down here on holiday. Jolene Sharp.'

I couldn't help a smirk: Jolene. Tarquin.

'Oh, fuck off Myfanwy. I'm bloody baring my soul here.'

'Sorry. Go on.'

'Anyway. It wasn't a house I'd been to before. Holiday house it was, near Cilgerran. She was there on her own with this dog. Very old it was, and ill. She'd come on holiday from Bristol to give the dog a last outing I think. And it went downhill faster than she expected. So. I got there. She was waiting at the window. This little white face and dark hair round it. Skinny. Big eyes. She let me in. Explained about the dog. I examined him. Said he'd be better put out of his misery. She didn't say much. Just nodded. I got the injection ready and she sat on the floor with her arms round the dog and it just shut its eyes and went. Quicker than anything.

'She was very upset then. Cried over the dog. Distraught. I didn't like to leave her. She seemed very alone and a bit I dunno, unbalanced I think. Anyway. So I made her some tea. Black tea it was. Wasn't any milk in the fridge. Made her sit down in the kitchen and talk. Her husband had left her, of course. She had the kids, three kids, living with her, but he'd taken them on holiday. She was alone for the first time. She looked so frightened. Wrapped her fingers round the mug as if it was going to save her. But she stopped crying after a while. Dried her eyes blew her nose and pulled herself together. I did notice, you know, that she was attractive. But even then I thought time's getting on I'd best get back. Julian holding the fort with the girls and all.

'I asked her if she wanted me to dispose of the body. She said she wanted to bury him in her garden. She'd drive back to Bristol that night she said. Could I help her get him to the car. So I did. He was bloody heavy. We went back inside for her to find her cheque book. She wrote the cheque. Gave it to me. Said thank you. Then she just broke down again. Apologising all the time for it but standing there at the door sobbing. Helpless with it. I didn't know what else to do. I put my arms round her. And she folded against me.' Idris stopped, his voice washed away in tears. He wiped his face, sighed. Began again.

'I saw the bend of the back of her neck, dark hair either side of it. Wispy. And I felt her body against mine. She stopped crying then. But she didn't move. I stroked the back of her neck. She laid her cheek against my jacket. We stood like that for a long time. Until it was obvious that there was something else happening to us. We just knew then. There was this atmosphere. We knew what was going to happen. She said "The bedroom's in here". So we went into the bedroom. We didn't roll about or anything. We sat on the bed and got undressed. Like we do at home I suppose. We got into bed. And then. We made love. And we both cried our eyes out. She cried about her husband leaving her and I cried about being a bloody vet with a wife too good for me.

'Then I got up. Got dressed. Came home. That's it. That was it.' There was silence. A lorry wooshed past too quickly and Idris' car rocked a little in the slipstream.

'It was so. I dunno. *Sweet* . . . A release from the practice and Elen being full of herself. It was like a holiday from my life. I feel terrible about it now. I almost wanted the baby to be someone else's when she told me. So I could feel less bad. So she might understand if I told her. Stupid.'

'Did you want it to go on. If she'd stayed, this Jolene.'

'I didn't know at first. On the first day after. Then. No. No. I'm sure now. But I don't wish it hadn't happened. It helped me. Made me see how bad I'd got. I hope it helped her. I wanted to tell Elen. But I can't say a lie. I can't say I wish it had never happened.'

'I think you could tell her.'

'Too scared. And now. Oh God. That night started it all for me. Changing things. Deciding to get out of the practice. And now there's all this baby mess. She can't go to Kenya pregnant. I can't leave her. I'll have to forget the whole bloody thing.'

'Idris. No. That's just what Elen's afraid of. That you won't get what you want and neither will she. You don't have to have this baby.'

'What, you mean an *abortion*?' It's never a pretty word. On Idris' lips it was like 'Hitler' or 'torture' or 'bestiality'.

'Tucker's less than nine weeks gone. It's not much more than a ball of cells.'

'It's what Julian, and Agnes, and Jane and Mary and Jessica were. It's like killing one of them.' It wouldn't have been helpful to tell him that was just what Tucker had said.

'That's crap, Idris. A list of ingredients isn't a cake. It's not killing. It's just sending it back.'

'Oh, God. I don't know. I don't know what to think.' He hit the wheel and his fist made a horrible cracking sound. Immediately he creased in pain and drew the hand towards him staring at it as if it were some surprising animal that had just appeared under the dashboard.

'Fuck. I've broken something. It hurts like bloody hell. I can't move these two fingers.' He cradled the hurt hand and looked up, bewildered.

'I think I'd have coped with the sheepskin underwear better than this,' I said.

'You what?'

'Where's your mobile, Idris. We'd better. You know. Phone

the farm and say you're not coming. Then I'll drive you to Casualty and get your hand x-rayed. Then I'll take you home.'

Two broken fingers and a cracked wrist. I called Tucker while Idris was getting bandaged up.

'Well??' she said. I guessed she'd been polishing a patch of floor less than six feet from the phone all afternoon.

'He got so worked up he hit the steering wheel and broke his hand.'

'He's still angry?'

'No. Not with you. With himself.'

'Van, just tell me what he said.'

'No. He'll tell you. There's a big part of this story you don't know yet.'

'So tell me!'

'No. Idris will.'

'Oh, Van!'

'He's in a bit of a crisis. You'll have to be nice. Remember your promiscuous past.'

'What about me being pregnant?'

'He doesn't want it any more than you.'

'Does he think it's someone else's?'

'No. He never did.'

'OK.'

'I'll bring him to the surgery. Meet us. I've parked the van there.'

I handed Idris over to Tucker. He more or less fell into her arms and from there into the car. I'd lost the signal from the statues by then. Back to ketchup kingdom with the strain of not panicking in the face of Idris' tearful revelations. It was just possible that this situation could blow Idris and Elen apart. It was likely that they would resolve it and cope with the tornado. For several hours I'd been holding down the unspeakable beast of the 'possible' with the pragmatic fat bum of the 'likely'. But beasts struggle and get free, and I was afraid of what would happen between these two people who I loved so dearly and in whose joint life I was so enmeshed.

'Whatever's been happening?' said Tucker, closing the passenger door on him.

'Lots. Ask Idris.'

'Are you all right, Van. You look awful.'

' 'Sright. Tired. I'm going. You know. Home. Now. Bye.' That was it. I didn't even wait to see them drive off. I got into the van and drove away fast, as if I was speeding away from an unexploded bomb.

Fat comfy 'Likely' made a rapid exit from my mind and the nasty pointy 'Possible' bounced and leered in my face all the way home. I saw Tucker curled alone in the middle of their big bed at night. I heard Moffy and Jelly talking about their barely remembered daddy. I saw Idris downing the last of the Jack Daniels and turning out the tilly in his tent. And I saw myself down the years, listening to each of them recount the stores of accumulated bitterness towards the other.

I drove on auto pilot my head full. So that when I walked into the cabin, for a split second I couldn't remember how I'd got there. I was suddenly dropped into an odd little time warp. It was one of those unlabelled moments, untagged with any particular time of day or life. The temporal equivalent of the sensation you get on waking in a hotel bed sometimes: you open your eyes and don't know what that wall is doing there. I forgot for half a beat of a heart where in my life I was.

For that tiny time after I opened my door and stepped inside Peter was still alive, just out of sight somewhere close by. The two empty coffee cups and the rolled up bedding left from the night we'd spent outside sleeping in the dunes. In half an hour we'd be walking on the beach, or sitting and watching the storm and I'd be telling him about Idris and Tucker's crisis. And he'd be saying, 'Sure they'll scream a little. But it'll be fine. Honey, trust me. Just fine.' He'd rumple my hair and stroke my neck and it would be fine. Because Peter said so.

My heart finished its beat. The coffee cups were David's and mine. The cabin seemed chilled and profoundly empty. Usually whenever I got back after a night away I'd walk in to find something of Peter in the air. I'd make tea, or a meal and play some CD of him whilst I cooked. But now there was nothing. Desperate to feel his presence even in the form of some mad grocery list or doggerel about domestic appliances I ran about the cabin searching. I opened all the doors, peered into the mirrors. I fetched his T-shirt from my bottom drawer and breathed and breathed through it, trying to find some trace of his old scent. But there was nothing. I wrapped it round my neck and face so that if the smell came back I would know.

Then I sat at the piano and began to play. All the songs he loved. The same favourites almost as my mother's. 'You're The Tops', 'What a Swell Party', 'Don't Fence Me In'. But I could summon only ordinary memories. I could see Peter rumbling out the words to 'You're The Tops' up the mast of a yacht; teaching a boat load of pacs 'Don't Fence Me In', but I couldn't hear his voice. They were scenes I could look in on but not feel. Then I tried the strongest spell I knew for summoning the dead: 'Do I Love You?'. After the first bar it did its job: it summoned Peter. A very dead Peter, not the resurrected one I'd wanted. Another digitally remastered CD began to play, and when I saw what it was it was too late to stop it. Like a bunch of kids playing with a Ouija board, I'd called up something bad that wouldn't go back.

It was the day before Peter's funeral. I was in the 'chapel of rest', the tarted up morgue at the back of Owen's Funeral Directors on the way out of town. Peter, the skinny version of him, lay in the box in his best suit. The woman who'd laid him out had done a good job. I could only guess at the nips and tucks she'd taken in the suit's back to make it seem as if it wasn't borrowed for the occasion. His hair was neatly slicked down. Eyes closed. Mouth straight. His nails were cleaner than they ever managed to be in life. Sticking out of the white cuffs, his hands were like clerics, pale and clean. Blameless sort of hands. He looked better than he'd looked for months. Rested. I knew I looked appalling. Like a junior bag lady or a rock chick after a night with all the band and fifteen lines of coke. Unwashed hair. Face puffy from crying and lack of sleep. My body sour and stale from all the months of worry and dread.

I'd come to say goodbye. To send him off with my love. But he looked so good. Oblivious. Indifferent to all the pain his death was causing me. He looked pleased, somehow, as if he'd just managed to pull off something really clever. I was suddenly far too angry to say goodbye.

'It's all right for you!' I shouted. 'You can't feel anymore.' I slapped the side of the coffin and stalked around it. 'What do I do now? Eh? Without you? You're my life. And you're dead, you selfish bastard.' I hit his chest with the flat of my hand. It felt like a sack of wet sand. No spring, no breath to repulse the blow.

'Dead! Dead! Of all the bloody useless things to be! I can't be without you. You can't die. Fuck you Peter. Fuck you for dying.' I hit him again. And again. 'And you can stop looking so fucking smug!'

I slapped his face then. But there was still no response. My hand left a little impression in the yellow waxy cheek. But no blood rushed to the place. No hand retaliated. Peter was giving me the ultimate in cold shoulders.

The T-shirt smelt of the morgue, sickly sweet disinfectant and over cleanness. I tore it off my face and threw it across the room. I ran about the cabin shutting doors now, throwing cloths over the mirrors. Trying to escape the remembering I'd asked for. I went outside in the dusk and began to do the most strenuous yoga routines I could think of and singing along with the radio. Not a combination of activities that Mr Iyengar would approve. So I suppose that's why my hand kept hitting the dead flesh and my voice kept shouting.

Which is when William arrived. Halfway through a scrappy cycle of dog poses done to a ragged attempt to accompany Robbie Williams.

'Myfanwy? What the hell are you doing?'

'Yoga.'

'Turn that bloody thing off.' I hit the radio's off button. Got up and tucked my shirt in. The funeral parlour CD faded immediately to black, the moment William had spoken. Maybe that's what I needed more of. Just a bit of company.

'You look terrible!' he said accusingly.

'You'd look terrible after some of those yoga poses.'

'I dare say. Are you all right my girl?' He put a papery hand against my hot cheek.

'Yes, Daddy. I'm just fine. Cup of tea?'

'Well. I'll try.'

'What d'you mean, you'll try?'

'Swallowing's getting a bit hard for me. That's why I've come. I've got a bit of news for you, Myfanwy.'

Nothing like the present to stop you thinking about the past. That's the way it's supposed to work. But William's news was the sort of news that Dr Patel used to deliver. William had got thin because eating was getting difficult. It was oesophageal cancer. He had two choices: the surgeon's knife or starvation. He was going into hospital sometime in the next fourteen days. It was my job to take him. It was my job to tell Tucker and Idris. By Christmas, I thought, we could all have experienced a combination of death, divorce and departure. My present was unravelling along with my past. Down the plug-hole I washed, my life diluted to transparency by a new flood of loss.

And I would have washed a lot further down if it hadn't been for those two chairs in Graham's window. There would still be someone I could be when I wasn't William's daughter or Tucker and Idris' companion any more. There was a little life raft to the future. So I drove back from Graham's feeling calm. Equal to the task ahead. I rang Tucker to say I'd be up that evening. I had to tell them that, along with whatever else they might have planned – house sales, legal separations, christenings – we could all be organising a funeral again.

Chapter Eleven

You don't need detail to communicate about the big milestones of life. It's enough to say 'My child was born', 'My husband died', 'I fell in love'. But inside the milestone, when you're living it, and after, when you remember it, detail is everything. Detail holds all the meaning.

I can say 'My father William Bowen died' and it'll mean something to you. But when I remember it, when I remember that day, that moment, 'William Bowen dying' wasn't what happened. There wasn't a moment when he made an exit. There were things that occurred that amounted to him being dead.

The first thing I remember is the sound of the ventilator as it rasped William's chest up and down. A sound like nothing else. A sound so gruesomely eloquent that on first hearing, without any accompanying pictures you could tell just what it was doing. It stuck like some vacuum cleaner part over his throat and face. His chest moved so slowly. Resentfully. He looked like an experiment. There were tubes and wires and electrodes everywhere. Sometimes, sitting holding his hand I half expected him to sit up and say, 'Myfanwy! Look at this. I've been investigating the effects of breathing failure.' I sat in the shade-grey whispering ward, hour on hour, and the slow wet suck and grind of the ventilator filled my world.

The second memory is of my own hand clasped on Tucker's

substantial back, on the solid mound of flesh below her left shoulder blade. My long bony fingers twined into the deep blue of her sweater had a kind of desperate look to them. We held each other for quite a long time, sitting in the ante room outside intensive care. I'd known she was crying even before I reached her. She was folded up in that sickly light of hospital fluorescent strips, her head encased in hair, like a cloud round a mountain peak.

'Yo ho fucking ho,' she sniffed.

'How is he?'

'Going out. He's not going to regain consciousness, Van. Whassisname—'

'Mr Stanhope.'

'Yeah. He came in about an hour ago and told me.'

'How long?'

'Tomorrow. Maybe. Tonight.'

'Go home Tuck. Sleep. I'll call you all if he's. You know.'

'OK. Oh, Van.'

Later that night, when everyone had been called from their beds, the nice staff nurse George, herded us out whilst they took out the tubes. Once back in with William we stood round his bed. Then came the third detail I keep in this milestone: the girls' faces as they stood in a line at William's bedside. In size order from level with his shoulders to next to his knees; Agnes, Jane, Jelly and Moffy. I saw them from my side of the bed, where I'd bent to kiss William's cooling brow. They were like four moons, white and pink against the sad yellow horizon of William's chest and belly, and the over-washed blue of the blanket.

The facts were that William went into hospital two weeks after he came to tell me that swallowing was a problem. That he never came out from the anaesthetic. That the cancer was everywhere inside him. That he took a fortnight of having every orifice plugged with equipment, and then he quit. That the machines were switched off and sometime in the minutes that followed he became dead. But what I remember are those three things. That noise. My hand. Those faces.

We were all ravenous back at Tucker's after we left the hospital. Even the shocked and pale-faced girls ate two rashers apiece. We talked too much. Were all too loud. Julian told funny stories about his first week of term. Death's like that. Makes you feel more alive. But breakfast was the last bit of fuel in the tank for Tucker and the kids. Julian, the girls and their mum were all asleep within an hour of getting back.

Idris' plaster and splint were due off that morning, a Wednesday. We both felt awake so I took him back to the hospital to get his hand sorted then we went together to Owen's, to sort out William's funeral: William had been more than an uncle, Idris was nearer a brother now than a cousin.

In the time since Peter's death a new branch of the Owen family had taken over the business. The sombre oak-lined office where I had nigh hysterically chosen Peter's last rites had been refurbished. It now looked more like a cross between the set for a TV cookery programme and an impresario's office: 'Shots of the Stars' — the best selling coffins and commemorative plaques — framed in gold covered one wall. Another wall was taken up with white melamine cupboards with a marble look worktop, and a yellow plastic kettle and a coterie of flowery mugs. The lavish curtains around the big window were bright too — a William Morris design of flowers and birds. In the centre of the room sat the new Mr Owen, hugely fat and sparsely bearded, behind a large light pine desk. He wore a pale blue suit and a primrose colour shirt and tie.

'Do take a seat!' he beamed, gesturing to the yellow velvet-covered armchairs, with his tiny pink hands. Both of us sat down wondering if we had really come to the right place, or if we had accidentally walked into some sort of gay dating agency. 'You have, what shall we say,' chortled Mr O, ' "a dear departed"?' His delivery style was that of a small-time comic, trotting out *double entendres.* For such a substantial man he had an extraordinarily small and constricted sort of voice. I suppose it matched his hands.

'Yes,' I said, 'my father. He died last night. He was eighty-seven.'

'How marvellous! Eighty-seven! Well, my word. What a lucky gentleman to have lived to such a venerable age. Excellent! Jolly good! Well done!' He was so enthusiastic in his congratulations that Idris and I found ourselves muttering thanks. 'Now then. Let us see what sort of send off we can give your old dad, eh?'

'We want something quite plain. Straightforward,' I said.

'Okey dokey. First of all. Are you going to fry him or bury him?'

'Fry,' said Idris, 'I mean cremation. Then we'll bury his ashes at his home.'

'Marvellous. So nice to have customers that know what they want. You know people can be so unnecessarily maudlin in these circumstances, they couldn't make a decision to save their lives some of them.' He sighed then pulled out a couple of files from the drawer of his desk. He handed them to us. 'So, all we have to decide is what sort of gift wrapping you want him in. Mahogany, pine, whatever. Just take a look at these. All the prices there are quite inclusive. What do you fancy? I must say I'm partial to walnut with the "Delphinium Spikes" or "Pacific Ocean" satin lining myself. Nice with someone of my skin tone. I could get away with "Summer Skies" at a pinch.'

We fell out of Mr Owen's door an hour later having chosen 'a send off' for our father and uncle. We stood on the pavement outside looking back incredulously at the building from which we had just been expelled.

'Bloody hell fire,' said Idris, 'where the blazes have we been? Is that a parallel universe in there?'

'William would have loved it. Did you hear. When he asked what colours William usually wore!'

'God almighty. What is this planet coming to. Coffin as fashion accessory.'

'When I die Idris. I want to be buried in "Teal".'

'After that I'm going for bloody sky burial myself. Even if it is only the seagulls up the municipal dump!'

We waltzed up the street arm in arm, laughing like two kids in wellies escaped from the polite tea in the parlour.

There wasn't a lot to do to organise the funeral. Mr O booked the crematorium for half past two on the Friday. The rest William had all but done before going into hospital – just as well with only two days to do it all. I opened the letter he'd left for me 'In case I go cold camping on a permanent basis' and found instructions for his wake: 'Do a tea Myfanwy,' the letter said 'you bake a good scone and your Victoria sponge is almost as good as your grandmother's.' It was the only time I cried then. From missing him telling me the next theory he'd come up with. 'Get some sweet sherry,' he said 'and a bottle of Irish whiskey. You know where the good glasses are.' Even at his most eccentric and bonkers he'd been alive, really alive. None of David's dreaded 'second-hand living'. I cried for myself, but not for William. The odious Mr Owen was right. 'Excellent! Jolly Good! Well Done!'

William had sketched a map of the mysterious earthwork, showing just where he wanted his ashes buried. 'Do a good job. Make sure the place looks the same after the earth is put back. Re-lay the turf please.'

And there was a guest list, surprisingly long. Tradespeople he'd dealt with for years and come to know, scrap dealers who he'd bargained with since he began his sculptures. And a woman from the National Museum of Wales. 'I've been talking to her about the sculptures. The National Museum could do a deal. Invite her so she can see them. If she doesn't come, ring her.' On the list was David's name but I left the issuing of invites to

Tucker. I got stuck in to clearing William's kitchen and sitting room ready to take boarders.

I spent all Thursday clearing things out. Chucked out the cupboards full of take-away containers, the mountains of saved paper and crates of coat hangers. All the kitchen storage space was taken up with bags and boxes of saved junk: wrappers and boxes, folded tin foil, egg cartons, glue, nails, empty plastic bottles. It was like one of Peter's mad raps or Fort Knox for kids' TV 'makes', the repository of raw materials for every 'Tracey Island' in the land. Tea, coffee and salt were the only foodstuffs.

Stowed away on the top shelf of the deep cupboard by the old coal range I found all my mother's best china, wrapped in layers of yellowing tissue. I got it all down. Tea plates with little sail boats, serving plates with an embossed shell design round the edge. Three sets of bone china teacups and saucers. Things that had peeked out from the glass-fronted dresser in the dining room when I was a child.

It had never occurred to me then that they could be used. After all, Zoe and William didn't have a social life. The only people who ate and drank at their house were my friends, or the plumber standing in the kitchen with a mug of over-sweet tea. Perhaps Zoe harboured dreams of jolly parties with hordes of like-minded bonkers people, just as she harboured dreams of a metropolitan Pacific. But people who believed in a world like 'Stingray' made real, where the starving had been saved by a high-tech version of Marmite sandwiches were thin on the ground five hundred yards from the North Orbital in 1969.

I spread the china over the table and the kitchen looked alive for the first time. Like a real kitchen. It had looked a little alive during William's and my brief joint residence. I kept the range lit even in summer. William still had the flock and the land then and it was good for reviving chilled and sickly lambs. I cooked properly in the kitchen, leaving stews to cook all day until we both came in, baking fruit cake to keep my father stoked up on cold days.

Looking over all my mother's dusty hopeful china I felt that daddy's mourners should come to this little house at its best. Not as the cold husk of some eccentric old exile. But as it might have become, in time, if Zoe and William had been here together: with heart and welcome and hard work for all those plates and cups. There were after all families round about with eccentricities even greater than our own. Zoe might even have started a dolphin appreciation group. William might have started a science club for local professionals and saved them from intellect-death in front of the repeats on UK Gold.

So I found some coal and kindling in one of the old stalls and lit the range. It smoked so much that William's wake threatened to be a double dad and daughter date. But at last it was over the shock of revival, and began to warm the core of the house again. Everything creaked as the unaccustomed warmth spread through the rooms.

I sat at the kitchen table feeling it happen, as if all the stone and wood were relaxing, like a farmer coming in after a long day in the cold. I let the tiredness in, a rush of heaviness in my blood. It wasn't just the two weeks of living in the all-consuming sound of William's ventilator. Everything else had gone on unravelling too. Tucker and Idris stretching their bond to its elastic limit over their decision to keep their baby. Taking turns for a week at sleeping on the sofa at the cabin. Julian leaving for Oxford under the blot of William's illness. And then a call from a London dealer and gallery offering me an exhibition.

If it hadn't been for all the unravelling I would never have considered saying yes. Accepting would potentially change my life. I could no longer be a private potterer; a lucky amateur. The gallery's clout and profile meant that in that world I'd arrived. After the exhibition my chairs could be the sort of thing people would buy instead of PEPS or BT shares. Big companies would have them in their deep pile meeting rooms. It meant that instead of pretending I didn't have a phone I would have to own up and have a fax as well. And a computer with clever accounting software on it.

Before the summer of mad ghosts, unsuitable lusts and dying parents, saying yes would have been unthinkable. Like consenting to living in a permanent earthquake. But in a season of earthquakes, when nearly everything is broken it seemed like a little bit of uncracked land on the horizon. I said 'yes' without giving myself any time for thinking. I didn't want to ask any of the questions that a considered decision might raise. Such as how could I get fifteen chairs made by the end of February? Such as the revolting enquiries about how long might William take to die, and who would care for him if he didn't?

But now, William was dead. All the decisions that had pulled apart the weave of our lives were made. The painful yanking bit was done. Almost all the strands were disentangled. All we could do now was wait for the wind to blow them back into some other configuration. I banked the range so that it grumbled and chuntered slowly all night. And I slept in my old bed and felt like a girl again at home. Safe with my parents just the other side of a wall.

Deliberately I left myself a little too much to do on Friday morning. I baked cakes that were *better* than Elspeth's, and a mountain of fat gold scones. I washed dusty glasses and laid out plates and cloths and paper napkins. I lit the woodburner in the sitting-room and put some new light bulbs in the lamps. I nearly rang Tucker to ask her to bring some things I'd forgotten, then thought of getting David's voice perhaps. So I ran out to buy extra milk and cream and jam, and almost didn't have time to go home and change before the drive to the crematorium. All the way there I checked through the list of food and drink, crockery and napkins over and over like a mantra. Holding off the thought of those little curtains and the big box with William in it going through.

Idris and Tucker and the kids were waiting outside for me after everyone else had gone in. 'God, Van!' said Tucker taking my arm, 'you cut that a bit fine. I thought we were about to end up going in with the wrong corpse!'

Crematoria are enough to make you opt for self 'suttee' at the bottom of the garden the day after your diagnosis looks black. Pseudo churches fully of tacky borrowed symbolism. This one was no better than any other. I remembered it from Peter's cremation: everything looked plastic. Everything was a Styrofoam take-out of religious iconry. An invented version of the sacred, for people who think death is for suckers and God is just some form of finger crossing you might do to get a lottery win.

I'd been too limp to feel angry at it first time round, with Peter. But now I sat in my pew raging and seething at the whole thing. Its saccharin unreality devalued real feeling so much that even Idris reading William's favourite 'The Lake Isle Of Innisfree' seemed like a Thomsons Holiday ad. By the time the creaky little roller took William's mahogany veneer and 'Deep Forest' satin lining in to where the real business takes place I wanted the furnace to engulf all human life. I didn't speak to anyone. I just marched straight to the car, and drove back to the cake and scones.

The 'tea' that William had requested was a much more suitable send off. Marge and Tony had shut the beach shop for the afternoon to come. Their turnover of chicken tikkas and Cumberland pies was going to be sadly reduced from now on.

Greg and Mike from the breakers' yard on the main road out of Carmarthen had come. They never dreamed of the things that William had done with the entrails and severed limbs of cars. Their van almost stalled in surprise as they drove up the track past William's sentinels and postillions.

Martin from the builders' merchants in town, and his wife Tracey — enormously pregnant with what looked as if it could be sextuplets. Gillian from the fruit shop where William got endless little wooden boxes along with his half pound of tomatoes. Reg the plumber who'd installed William's electric shower, and Jonathan the TV repair man who was forever patiently adjusting William's tuning.

They'd come in their best clothes, all looking a little

constricted in suits and good skirts. All looking ill at ease, not sure if smiling was allowed at wakes.

But there were a few ancient neighbours, who remembered William and Rees as boys. These sturdy old farmers were funeral stalwarts. They knew how to have a good time out of someone's death.

'Any more sugar is there, Myfanwy love?'

'Very good cake I must say.'

'No, I wouldn't mind another scone if there's one going.'

'Oh, I like a good spread at a funeral.'

Their easiness made all the difference. Oiled the social wheels so that soon everyone was leaving their tea and taking Idris' offer of sherry or whisky in William's 'good' glasses. I whirled around, making more sandwiches, buttering more scones. As if I was a real old-fashioned sort of daughter who wore flowery frocks in summer and wiped her children's mouths with a hankie corner.

'I liked coming up to see your Da,' said Jonathan, 'he always had some daft theory about what was wrong with his telly. And he loved a good chat. Good listener. I came up here one time after my Gran died. He was kind, you know. Understanding like.'

'He was in the shop one time,' Gillian said, 'I dunno, getting boxes for something. He told me what for but I didn't understand. My youngest was with me. Home from school with adenoids again. She was watching him taking the wire bindings off some of the boxes out the back. And he got some of the wire and he made her this little owl, little shape and eyes. Really good. She's got it still.'

Listening to their chat, I found that William had had a solid place in all their lives. He'd provided some colour, some small example of a different way to be outside of the norm. The childlike quality of his enthusiasm for things had been infectious. People liked him just for that. And for the odd little acts of kindness he could perform. Things I'd never known about that made me want to call him back for another long look.

It wasn't that I didn't notice David, with only two different rooms to be in and fewer than twenty people to mingle with he couldn't be invisible. We were both on stage. He had his most feathery light charm on, drawing out stories of pulling sheep from drifts in 1963 and expressing interest in the scrap value of a Massey Ferguson. He smiled at me as I brought round plates of food as if I were indeed his half aunt's friend, a hardly known and tenuous relative.

A watery dusk brought it all to an end. Idris, David and Julian — newly manly in his black suit — helped people to their coats and back to their cars. Then Julian drove the tearful Vicky home in her parents' Rover. Agnes and Jane helped Tucker and me collect up the plates and David kept Moffy and Jelly amused playing dens with the cushions of the old sofa. William's house had never felt so alive. Even the mess and washing up felt like a good thing.

It was comforting to stand with my arms in warm suds side by side with my best friend and almost-sister, Tucker.

'Another two months and I won't be able to get close to a sink. This baby is growing like a weed.'

'You look so well, Tucker.'

'I stopped feeling sick the moment we decided to keep it. It was just all the stress and hassle. I suppose it's William I have to thank for that.'

'I don't think he ever claimed to have healing powers, Tuck.'

'No. No. I mean because he was ill. So ill. We knew he might die. It felt as if he was making room for this new one. A life for a life.'

'God help you if it's a boy. Might turn out to be recycled William.'

'If it starts knotting its Babygros together to make a fish net or twists its nappies into the shape of a bird, I'll know!'

'You don't need to do this. I can manage.'

'No. I'll do the washing up with you. But I will take the girls home then. We've got a lot of catching up to do. I put everything on hold while William was ill. I've got to get the house packed up and ready to hand over to the tenants by the first week in November.'

'Just say the word. I can help.'

'No. You've got all this muddle to sort. That museum woman didn't come.'

'I'll call her on Monday. See what she says.' Tucker put down the plate she was drying and turned to look at me.

'What?' I said.

'Why don't you come to Kenya, for good with us? In the spring, when all this is sorted and your big gig in London is done. Or in June when Julian and Vicky come out with me and the baby.'

'Thank you. No. I've decided I can't be a maiden aunt any more. I've got to get a life.'

'You've got a life. Your work. Your stuff is fabulous. You've got your big exhibition coming up. You can run the life of a successful artist from anywhere. That's the theory I'm working on anyway.'

'No, I mean a whole life. With people in it who matter and who aren't related to me.'

'Oh, Van. I'm going to miss you.' And Tucker enveloped me in a hug, pulling my soapy hands from the sink and dripping water over the floor. Good job she was going to be in Africa until this baby was due. Tucker on hormonal overload was just too much to cope with.

It was chucking it down by the time Tucker, Idris and the kids were ready to leave. Idris got the engine running and David ferried the girls out to the car under William's slightly broken black umbrella, to protect their best frocks and shoes from harm.

'I can come over tomorrow and help the clear out if you need,' said Tucker, standing at the door. 'Or I can send Julian.'

'Get out woman,' I said, 'all I've got to do is sort out clothes. William only had one of everything. It'll take ten minutes.'

David walked her to the car leaning the half moon brolly to shield her from the wet. I watched him help her into the car. In a moment the door would slam and David and I would be alone with our pile of unfinished business and unassembled components. But I was ready for it. I'd been ready for it since the day I'd tipped the little bee corpses from their hives.

The tyres crunched and popped over the stones in the yard and the rear lights went down the track, smeared in the rain. David returned to the porch, then stood with his back to me, ostentatiously shaking the brolly out into the dark.

'Stinking night. Glad I haven't got far to drive.'

'Are you staying with Tucker?' He hesitated, the tension of the shoulders inside the black suit changed.

'She's made up the bed, yes.'

'You don't need to go, just yet? Shall we have some coffee? I don't want to do anything more today.' He turned round, crumpled velvet forehead, alien eyes looking at me.

'Are you sure you don't want me to leave?'

'Yes. Put a couple more logs on the fire in the living room. I'll be in just now.' He smiled so widely, dropped every guard, every bit of feather for a moment, and bounced out into the rain talking over his shoulder.

'I brought one or two things from London. I mean food things. And some wine. Just in case.'

Out in the kitchen, dimmed somehow now all the 'company' had gone, I put coal on the range. Filled a kettle. Assembled a homely tray of plates and cups and cutlery. I moved as deliberately as I could. Making myself be the calm I didn't feel. David and I were finally going to run our course, whatever that was. There was no reason for my heart to pound. I breathed carefully, waited for the kettle to boil and looked at the window. Nothing showed in the black but my reflection, tired looking and a bit pale, strands of hair escaping from the plait.

Then I felt the unmistakable brush of lips on the back of my neck. Once. And once again. Peter had always been hard to resist when he really wanted me.

'How did you get to be so cute?' He was pushing me against the sink at the cabin, pulling my dress up, pressing his palms into my flesh. Turning me round so I could open his shirt and feel the thrill and lift I always did as I peeled back fabric to reveal his chest. How could anyone else feel this good? How could I ever feel desire like this again?

Bang. My hands slipped on the edge of the sink and my braced arms jolted into the water, soaking my dress to the sleeves.

'Oh, fuck!' Peter was gone. The kitchen was full of steam from the madly boiling kettle. All the time I had sat holding William's hand or sprawling exhausted on my bed over the last weeks I'd looked for the old solace that the Peter 'CDs' had given me. But nothing would play. All I could find was that funeral parlour and the smug corpse. Not a word, not a touch. I could raise no memory to comfort me. I knew, as I'd always known, that it was all in my head. All my own memory circuits playing tricks. But with the imprint of Peter fizzing on my body I felt furious with him. Angry that only when it was someone else's lips I was waiting to feel, he chose to come back like that. No better than a dog pissing on a lamppost. I was as angry as if he could choose. As if he could be 'he' with motives and aims. I made the coffee and took the tray to the sitting room. Determined not to let Peter control me.

Which made two of us determined: David had clearly experimented with lights until he found just the right combination of lamps and firelight. He'd arranged a mini feast on a low table by the fire and spread a couple of rugs next to it so we could sit in the warmth and eat. I smiled to see that in spite of everything he still hadn't given up. I put the tray on the table and sat down.

'I was just going to come and find you,' said David. 'What happened to your sleeves.'

'Oh. I forgot to roll them up.'

'Is this OK?'

'Ciabatta, paté, olives and a bottle of red? It's terrible. The sort of thing I can get at Marge and Tony's any day!'

'Ah, Marge and Tony! Yes, I heard about their new range of microwaveable meals. Sort of thing I'd have really gone for a couple of years ago.'

We laughed rather stiffly and David handed me a glass of wine. 'How are you? You did a terrific job today. I think William would have loved it.'

'Yes. I think he would. And my mother too.'

'Do you want to talk – about William.'

'No. Not now. It's fine. He died on his own terms. He had a long life, and he filled it well. We didn't have any unfinished business. I gave him the funeral tea he asked me to. It's all too close to speak about.'

'Tucker told me about the letter. He was very brave.'

'Very realistic for someone so out of reality most of the time.' Both of us were finding our wine fascinating, studying the way the light caught its surface in the 'good glasses'.

'You're de-ummed,' said David, in his best vicar-addressing voice. 'I've heard you talking all day. That's great.'

'I am! It's my longest remission so far. I don't understand quite how it happens but I just seem to get the knack of talking. It's like trying to wiggle your ears or something. One day your brain finds the right nerves and another day it won't.'

'Oh, right,' David said. I got the impression he hadn't heard a word. He downed his wine and reached for the bottle. The sound of the liquid pouring was grotesquely loud in the very quiet air between us. I studied my newly refilled glass a little more before speaking. I could feel a stutter creeping up from my belly. I had to beat it to my vocal cords.

'David. I'm sorry about what happened at Mandy and Clive's.' David snapped from tongue-tied wine appreciation, and began to talk very fast. A torrent of what seemed like relief.

'This is a cliché, isn't it? I was about to say how sorry I was for marching off. I was very stirred up. All that about my mother. I really hadn't let myself even think those things about her before. I was about to burst. It was a catalyst.' He stopped looking at his wine and looked at me: there was something new about him, a calmness he hadn't had before.

He went on, 'That night, you, it was the most amazing catalyst. I went to a therapist friend just after I stomped off. As soon as I got back to London. I won't bore you with it all. But I got rid of so much crap. I'll go on seeing her professionally until I go to New York.' He slowed, took another sip of wine.

'Everything's got better in my life since that night. Like Paul and the Damascus road thing. You put some last piece of jigsaw in place. I dunno what you did exactly. Even my back is better, my knees don't give trouble. It's not perfect, you know, I can't perform. But I can dance every day, go to classes, hold a job without hating the other dancers. I feel less trapped. I feel there is something in dancing still for me. I'm healed. Or at least healing. And it's all through you.' He reached for my hand and squeezed it awkwardly. I didn't pull away and in a second or two the wave of pounding in my head stopped.

'I don't know what I did.' But I did know. I'd levered him open, using his attraction for me like a gentle crowbar. And in the process shifted something in myself too.

'When are you due to leave for New York?'

'About the same time as Tucker and Idris leave. I've got two jobs to go to there now. That's the other amazing thing. One part-time for my father, choreographer and rehearsal director for his film. It won't last beyond January. And one as rehearsal director at Ballet Work, it's a really exciting company. It's such a break. After everything that's happened, I can't believe it.' He lowered his head and shook it. Then looked up at me, I'd never seen his smile so sweet and relaxed.

'You were so kind, Myfanwy. Putting up with me being so pushy. Objectionable really. I ruined things by trying too hard?'

'No. No, you didn't. You weren't pushy. I gave you green lights all the time.'

'And then red lights.'

'And then red lights. But that wasn't anything to do with you. That was my fault. But if you really thought you'd ruined your chances with me, why did you do all this, the food and everything?'

'While there's life? Dunno. Maybe you've made me newly optimistic.' He had my hand in both of his now, turning it over like a smooth pebble being examined on the beach. He pushed his straightened fingers over my palm and in between my fingers: the fairy lights flickered and came on.

'David, I have to explain something. About the red lights. First I found it hard to believe you were attracted to me. I'm so old. Especially in your world where there must be so many beautiful young dancers.'

'Yeah! Beautiful air-headed egotists.'

'Whatever. Anyway. I'd forgotten about being attractive. It was something I didn't need or use anymore. When I found I was attracted to you. It was a shock. I was so scared.' He put a hand on the side of my face, and looked at me.

'How could you see this face in the mirror and not know how lovely you are.'

'That's so good to hear. It's been such a long time. There's never been anyone since my husband. No one. Not an affair, not a one night stand. Nothing.' He dropped his hand from my cheek and stared as if I'd just told him I was a clone or a part-time werewolf.

'I see. I didn't know. I assumed that because you're so lovely, so beautiful that there must have been lovers at least.'

I shook my head. 'So with you I was frightened of what might happen. What I might feel. I was frightened of everything. You name anything to do with love or sex and I was scared of it.'

'We're both talking in the past tense. Do you still feel scared.'

'Not so much. Or rather I just know I've got to get over it.'

'And do you still. Feel attracted . . .'

'Yes. I do,' I said.

'But now I'm the one who's afraid.' The feather charm ruffled up. 'I want you. I think I'm falling in love with you. But I understand what I'm asking. It's almost like asking to be someone's very first. It's a big responsibility.'

'OK. Then think of it like this. I helped you. Now you can help me. You're not doing the asking. I am.'

'All right,' he said, 'and I consent to help.' But he didn't sound convinced of his abilities. We knelt facing each other, knee to knee. Stuck now in the odd formality I had created.

'I'm sorry,' said David, 'I don't know where to begin. I want you to feel OK. Not scared. So. What would you like?'

'I don't know. Perhaps if you held me?'

David knelt higher, and reached his arms around me, as if he were picking up a cross between a parcel in an outsize cardboard box and a cactus. I found myself squashed uncomfortably against his shirt and tie. The buttons dug into my cheek. An opening move as inducive of sensuality as a lecture by Dr Paisley.

'Shall we lie down?' David suggested.

We disengaged like spaceships ponderously undocking and lay down on the blankets. There was a slight but persistent draught under the living-room door, and no way we put our arms that seemed comfortable. My arms round his neck and his around my waist. One arm of mine under his neck and the other round his waist, both his arms between our bodies. One arm under my own head and the other resting on his chest. We experimented for ten minutes until we had both thoroughly bathed in the nasty little draught, and got bits of carpet and blanket fluff all over.

Then, we gave up. I'd made David feel he had to perform some miracle of sexual healing. I'd made myself feel that this first post-marital sex was going to be life changing. Both of us were almost hyperventilating with tension and embarrassment. Not a recipe for arousal and intimacy.

David sat up. 'Actually I am very hungry.'

'Me too!' I said. I wasn't, but I ate bread and olives out of misery. It was all awful. We didn't even seem to be able to look at each other anymore. I felt ketchup settling in my throat.

'More wine, Myfanwy?'

'Oh. Wine. Yes. A little. You know.'

We didn't touch again that night. I cleared away the food. We watched the late news — some woman in a bad suit interviewing a politician whose halitosis was visible — and went to bed. Me in my little narrow room at the back over the kitchen and David in the high creaky spare bed at the front.

'Good night, David.'

'Good night, Myfanwy.'

The moment I shut my eyes, Peter came back. It seemed like gloating, I thought. He whispered all around my head, words I couldn't quite catch, never quite touching me with more than breath. I fell asleep and into a series of old dreams about him. Seeing him at the end of the street, running and running to catch him, but when he turned it wasn't Peter. Swimming after him as he rowed away, calling to me. The same tired set of feelings and images. Even in my dream I was bored by them.

Worn out with all that hopeless wanting, fruitless searching. I dropped down deeper and felt all the light slip away. I was glad to drop into nothing.

I must have been coming up again, nearer the surface when the shearwater dream came back. I didn't recognise it at first: lying under the deck chairs on the poop deck, a set of ample calves blocks my exit. The pink and lime flowers of a hemline just skim into view and the flesh splays over the edges of the gold mules like over risen dough. This is a more perfectly reproduced memory than ever before. I crawl out beside the legs into the sun with one arm cradling a bundle of dark feathers.

'Oh, good grief!' The woman's blotchy mouth looms over the chins and leans towards me. I've seen her all week, sprawled in the corner of the bar, smoking endlessly and coughing her guts up. Dressing her eighteen stone in scraps of chiffon and making racist remarks about the waiters.

'Ughh! Whatever is that?' The disgust in her voice makes me furious. How does she dare to feel revulsion for something so obviously beautiful?

'It's a bird. And it's probably been thinking the same about your legs.' I got myself into a lot of trouble in my early days with remarks like that.

In the cool dark of our cabin I cut slivers of fresh tuna and put them down the rose pink throat. Next door Tom is playing Mike and Mechanics too loud. Again. All day I find excuses to slip below. I open the flaps of the box and the brown head tilts calmly and the round eye looks up. Appraising. Warily calm, like a political prisoner with an Amnesty profile.

I stand at the microphone in the lounge and make my announcement about releasing the bird. Horrified again by the awfulness of my voice all over the room. Peter, hair slicked, white shirt pressed for dinner, toasts me from the bar. His pursed-lipped smirk tells me 'You're getting the hang of it, honey. They love a little theatre.'

Lars drifts past and hums in my ear: 'Born free as free as the wind blows.'

The pacs assemble outside on the deck. A nice bunch mostly. Well-meaning citizens. Bankers, doctors, academics. At twenty-four I find their straight and narrow lives a horror of monotony. I don't know about necessity and disillusionment. I consider that I will grow old unconventionally, probably with large amounts of original wisdom and no wrinkles. Electricity bills, early stroke and divorce have never occurred to me. All the pacs sunburnt faces turn to me, they hold their glasses very still. Some of the husbands rest hands on their wives' shoulders, and some wives cover those loved hands with one of their own. All the eyes look to me for some sort of answer as I get the bird from the inside of the big dark box.

'Shearwaters are relatives of the albatross. The bird that

doomed the ancient mariner. They both belong to a group called the tubenoses. I don't know if you can see, but on this little chap's beak is a kind of second tier. Yes? That's used for salt extraction . . . they need to take salt from their blood because they don't drink fresh water. They also have a brilliant sense of smell . . . which they use to find food, and to find home.'

I hold the bird so that everyone can see the fine beak with its neat down-turned end. There are murmurs of acknowledgement. I continue, looking surreptitiously all the while for Peter, over the heads of the enraptured audience. Since his toast from the bar he has disappeared.

'In a moment, when I release the bird, you'll see it has long, rather narrow, straight wings. It's a first class glider. Picks up lift from the surface of the sea and can travel effortlessly with huge fuel economy' – titters at this minute witticism – 'for hundreds of miles. Now let's see if he's ready for home time.'

I hold the bird aloft, free to go. Its triangular feet paddle a little on my palm, mummified slices of Toblerone. It looks for all the world as if it is doing a dance.

'Ahhhh' sigh all the pacs.

Its eyes are very bright. It examines everything around it, every face, every feature of the ship, the sea far below, the pink and purple horizon.

Where is Peter? I can't release the bird, I can't make it fly. Peter will know what to do. Looking down at the sea as we speed along I am suddenly filled with panic that somehow Peter is lost, left behind, overboard. I look all around, at all the questioning faces, then back at the bird. Peter is there inside it! I know. *I know it. Inside the bird that won't fly. The bird I can't bring myself to throw into the wind.*

I woke up in grey light soaked in sweat, and shaking. David was sitting on the bed, in a pair of boxers and my old school swimming towel wrapped around his shoulders.

'Myfanwy. Myfanwy. My dear girl. You were calling out and shivering. Are you OK.' I sat up and wiped my face on the row of turquoise fishes without even thinking.

'Hold me,' I said.

'Of course.'

He held me, damp nightshirt and all. Close. Closer. Not at all like a cactus or a box.

'I'm cold,' he said.

'Then get in.'

He crammed into my tiny bed. Gently he reached for the row of buttons on my night shirt and asked, 'Would you mind if I undid these?' Half playful, half tender.

'No. Not at all.'

He pulled the shirt over my head. Wriggled out of his shorts. Skin on skin we were. Mouth on mouth. Like a top of the range Merc on an empty autobahn we went from nought to a hundred in six seconds. Raging with wanting. Shaking with it like struck strings.

My heart threw itself against my ribs in lust and fear. Fear of losing the past and fear of taking a future. Every step forward must be into a void. There was no way to feel 'sure'. No way to feel 'unafraid'. Only a way to feel alive. Really alive.

Chapter Twelve

She hadn't come prepared I thought. She wore a long knitted skirt and matching top that made her look like a crow. Warm enough, but mud sensitive and restrictive of movements greater than those required by a journey from desk to printer and back. I watched her getting out of the neat little hatchback, fastidiously avoiding the puddles in the yard with tiny black lace ups. At least they were flat heeled. I opened the door to greet her before she knocked.

'Hello! Mrs Draco?'

'Olivia, please. Lovely to meet you, Miss Bowen.' Her voice was low and strong, with a slight trace of a northern accent. Not the native North Walean Welsh speaker I had expected. She extended a very pale hand, tiny as a child's poking from the end of her sleeve.

'Myfanwy.' My rough brown fingers almost enveloped her whole hand. We both noticed that my nails were really none too clean.

'Ah, yes. Your father told me your name. I was so sorry to hear about his death.'

That was good, no euphemisms then: no 'passing aways', no 'departing' no 'leaving us'. She looked me straight in the eye, unworried by the last great taboo of British society. She might look like a rather emaciated china doll, with her bone china skin and eyes the colour of baby boys' bootees but she was tough.

'Thank you. I miss him. But he did the best he could with the life he was given.'

'None can do more than that.'

'Shall we have a coffee before we go outside?'

'If you don't mind I'd rather look at your father's work first. I saw the marvellous examples on the track. Perhaps we could begin with a closer look at those?'

'Certainly.'

'I'll get my wellingtons from the car.'

As I put my boots on and found a jacket and William's semi-functional umbrella I glanced at her getting ready. Every movement had a self-contained, predetermined quality to it. Like watching Japanese 'No' theatre, or a child solemnly pleased with her skill at doing up her own shoelaces. Daintily as one of David's dancing partners she inserted her narrow feet and legs into a pair of completely clean boots. Then hitched up the black crow jersey and turned the waistband of her skirt over until it had given her a spare tyre and her hemline was at her knees. Finally she took a small blue notebook and perfect tiny silver pen from the dashboard, and slipped on a large black cardigan, the last part of her three-piece outfit.

There was nothing wrong with her stamina. We must have walked down and up – mostly up it seemed to me – William's track ten times and her cheeks never even coloured. I wondered how old she was, but with that china skin and close-cropped colourless hair she could have been thirty-five or sixty. Looking at William's 'work' as she kept calling it she lost some of the control and reserve.

'Good Lord, I know what that is – it's the dough hook of a Kenwood. I used to have one myself! Some of these figures have the most lovely patient quality to them. Very peaceful.'

I began to feel hopeful. She'd written quite a lot with the little silver pen. But when she'd been back to look at the grizzly bear made of Astroturf for the fifth time I thought I'd better make sure she saw everything else.

'Look Olivia, I don't know how much time you have but . . .'

'I do apologise. I'm taking up your morning.'

'No. No. It's just that there's quite a lot more to see around the fields. And there's the earthwork.'

'Yes, Mr Bowen mentioned that several times. What exactly is it?'

'Well. We can talk about it when we get there.'

I showed her the series of increasingly abstract birds and flying figures that dotted the back yard and the approach to the top field. I showed her what William had called the 'Carton Crucifix', a huge human figure made of piles of his beloved microwave meal packets and spread-eagled on the end of the barn with a huge barbed wire and tin foil crown.

'Did he have strong religious beliefs?'

'No. Beliefs that were as strong as a religion: that criminals should be made to grow vegetables; that the starving could be fed on yeast; that all chefs were charlatans. Nothing approaching religion in scope really, but passionately held.'

'What was the motivation for this piece of work then?'

'Lots of easy dinners? A sense of humour. He used to say "Carton Crucifix" to himself a lot and laugh. He also referred to it as "Take Out Jesus" sometimes.'

'I see.' She smiled a bit, so perhaps she did see. I wasn't sure. She'd got reserved again. Inward. The notebook and silver pen were no longer in evidence. I began to feel pessimistic about my chances of turning William's home into a national exhibit. I felt myself and all William's creations slipping a little nearer to the estate agent with the low parting and slip-on grey shoes: 'I take it you, the vendor, will be disposing of the *items*, around the property?' I could hear him saying.

The earthwork was surely not going to help matters.

At least the weather had improved a little. The overnight downpour had passed over and a big blue patch was coming in off the Atlantic. From the top of the field above William's 'last masterpiece' there was a clear view in the beginnings of a limp-wristed sunshine. The valleys around were crowded with the crowns of trees, crimped and textured by the colouring and drying of their leaves. Browns and russets, all the colours of a hen pheasant's wing. The hills were still green, set off by the dots and commas of dirty magnolia sheep. In the groin of two hills exactly opposite the field was a perfect triangle of sea.

'What a marvellous view.'

'Yes. You can't see any roads. Almost no houses. Just the roof of my cousin's barn.'

Sloping below us the curves and dips of the earthwork lay over the field like the grassed-over casts of a gargantuan worm. William had planted the raised parts with bulbs of all sorts, that he said would colour in his picture from Christmas to Easter.

'We're too close to see here. Is there some vantage point from which to view the whole thing?'

'Any of those hilltops,' I said with a false kind of enthusiasm.

'Is there road access to any of them?' In other words could the grockels park somewhere to get a snap of it? Answer: no.

'Well. Not at the moment. William said that passing boats would see what it was.'

'And what is it?' How I longed to be able to tell her: an ancient Celtic fertility symbol; a Sanskrit proverb about the unity of all life; a line of Shakespeare; the Welsh flag; a portrait of Barry John as Jesus. Surely here was my last chance blown.

'I've no idea. He wouldn't tell us. I'm not even sure it's anything anyone else would understand. But I think whatever it is it'll look pretty spectacular from the sea.'

'Yes. Yes, I'm sure it would. All the same, it could be very useful to know at this stage what exactly it depicts. Never mind.'

'Would you like that cup of coffee now. Or tea?'

'No. I'm sorry. I've spent far more time here than I'd planned. I must get straight back to the office.'

The grey shoes were virtually wiping on the mat.

I'd had enough for one day. I locked up and left for the cabin almost as soon as the boxy little hatchback had driven away. There was a mountain of making to do, the whole stormy summer of salvage and rushes to turn into 'exhibits'.

As I walked through the cabin door the phone rang. I was getting more relaxed about phones. Several people who were not Tucker or Idris now knew my phone number and used it. I even had David's old answer machine.

Marcus from the Gallery left messages. 'Hi. Marcus here. Look, would a square footage available be a useful thing for you to know? Give me a bell. Ciao!'

Graham did too: 'This is Graham speaking. Those last lot of baskets went like hot whatchamacallits. I know you're up to your eyes like, but there's people wanting them for Christmas presents now.'

And of course David. 'Hi. It's me. Just came out of a class thinking most unspiritual thoughts about you. Two days 'til I'm there. I'll call tonight.' 'Hi it's me. I'm ringing to say I'm completely in love with you. Bye.' 'Hello sweetheart. Where are you? Out on some beach. Oh God I wish I was there. I will be. Just thirty-six hours and I will be.'

Peter hadn't used it once. Coming back into the empty cabin with the phone ringing had always made me shiver as if a cockroach was running up my spine. No such invertebrate sensations now.

It was just two weeks after William's funeral and I was in free fall. Like a lottery winner in the first week, buying every frock in Liberty's without a thought for the nasty meetings with investment bankers and the begging letters from third cousins twice removed.

The day David and I finally . . . hard to know what to call it; 'made love' isn't right, what we did had far too much of the quality of a flood barrier bursting to be that. 'Had sex' isn't right either because what we had was a lot more than just sex. Words like 'shag' or 'fuck' or 'bonk' have a kind of cartoon cavalier sort of atmosphere, and there was nothing comic about us that morning.

Something like 'ignited' or 'catalysed' would describe it better. We slept for almost the whole morning afterwards, and then lay crammed mouth to ear in the tiny bed, whispering our lives to each other: my parents and their bizarre DIY science; his rhinoceros grandfather with the soul of a butterfly; my wanderings on deck; his appearances on stage; my foraging; his dancing.

But not Peter, because that day I was flung free, shot out from the face of my life on a huge bungee-jump. To be touched, caressed, possessed for real again, blew me far from Peter. For all that first weekend, the one that followed and the nights on the phone in between, the elastic bungee cord attached to my past was slack.

So coming back from Olivia Draco's assessment of the posterity potential of my father's house, I picked up the phone without hesitation. Safe in the knowledge that the dead never call.

'Hello?'

'It's me. What's the matter? You sound worried.'

'I think William's mystery message may have just cost me the deal with the National Museum.'

'Oh, she came today. Of course. What happened?'

'She seemed keen, until I told her I didn't know what the earthwork was. She left pretty soon after that.'

'Oh, Myfanwy. I'm sorry. Listen I'm coming to console you!'

'When?'

'I flogged the car. Three grand! So there's nothing more I can do here. I want to be with you. I want to spend my last week there with you. I'm coming down tonight. Can I stay?'

'Can you stay! Of course. But what about classes?'

'It's just a week. I can hold things together for a week. And I've got a while after I get to America before things really hot up.'

'OK. That's wonderful.'

'My train gets into Carmarthen at 9.58. Could you . . .'

'Bring some ciabatta!'

'See you.'

'See you.'

I sat by the phone just feeling my heart pound at the prospect of David's arrival. With nothing to do this side of the plane to New York, released from the grief and guilt over his mother, David wanted to lap me up, to be full of me. Like a baby is full of milk.

We could probably have fucked in the car park if it hadn't been for the new security cameras. The buzzing vitality of David's body was apparent even through the big layers of baggy winter clothes. We delved inside each other's coats, squirming hands through the soft hot layers to get a single fingertip on skin.

'I wish you had a sports car. How long till we get to a bed?'

'Half an hour to the first quiet lay-by, an hour to get home.'

'I can't do all of what I want with a gear stick in the way. But maybe I can't wait to do "all" and I'll have to settle for "some".'

'Let's drive. I can probably do it in forty-five minutes at this time of night.'

By the time we got home the extra twenty feet to get to the bed was just too far. Even flicking the light switch was too long a distraction. In the pitch black of the cabin kitchen nothing existed except us. The objects we collided with, leant on, held to had no identity. We discarded our clothes as if we would never need such things again. It seemed like a long time before there was a word for anything.

'Something's digging into my back. Ow!' David raised the bottom part of his spine and rummaged with his free arm underneath. 'Buttons. Two buttons.'

'Off my shirt, I think.'

'Mmm. Too big to be my shirt buttons. Don't know where they went. D'you want some more coat over you?'

'Yeah! Go on then. Thank you.'

'Are you hungry?'

'Not now.'

'Not even for Carluccio's ciabatta?'

'Well. Maybe a bit for that.'

'Shall I put the light on?'

'No. I don't want to see what we've wrecked.'

'OK. I can feel for the bag. I'll get a blanket too.' David wriggled from the selection of garments we'd scraped together as a kind of nest, and crawled off. I curled into the satin lining of his coat, and pulled what felt like a jersey under my head. I was floating in a warm dark sea, that was nowhere in particular. Just here and now.

'You've been asleep.' David was lying by me feeling my face in the darkness.

'Ah, there's the mouth I want to kiss,' he said slipping a finger over my lips.

'I had. I had a kind of dream . . .'

'Shh. C'mon, I'll feed you little bits of ciabatta, and butter like cream.' The bag rustled and David giggled in the darkness. I could feel the loaf and the cold butter placed between us as he lay on his side, propped on an elbow.

'Listen,' he said, 'I'm breaking the bread with my hands. I can feel the softness inside. I'll scoop the butter out of the packet with my fingers. Here,' he put a fragment into my mouth, hard and crusty, springy and yielding, slathered untidily in a slide of fat, 'you'll have to lick my fingers.'

I fed David in turn, pushing the nuggets of bread into the butter first, then into his mouth.

In the dark our aim was poor. Crumbs and butter got everywhere. We did our best to eat them all up. And very soon things had lost their words again and there was no place on my body left unattended long enough for even a bread crumb to sit undisturbed.

I woke with my cheek touching the glass of the French windows. I was on my back with David's head pillowed on my belly. I was mostly cold, and had various small pointy things under my spine. I turned to the chill of the glass to wake me further, then opened my eyes. Almost too close to focus, was a face of unbelievable vileness. If I hadn't felt the window to be securely between us I would have screamed.

'Uuufff!' said the face, leaving a wet noseprint as it did.

'Bet! Bet! Get here NOW!' Graham's voice yelled to his dog from the door on the other side of the cabin.

'Uuuff,' said Bet and ran off to the sound of her master's voice. I had completely forgotten that Graham had said he'd collect the next batch of baskets that morning before opening the shop.

'Hello! Anybody home?' he called cheerily from the door. I sat up so suddenly David's head dropped onto the floor.

'Awww. Shit!' he said.

'Coming. Hang on.' Still not properly awake I was filled with the fear that Graham would suddenly walk through the door. The devastation that he would see was too eloquent. 'You've been burgled!' he'd say, and I'd have to say no. And then David would appear from the pile of clothes and blankets on the floor. 'Good morning,' the charm would chirp. The explanation for the tumbled furniture and the empty butter wrapper would then be obvious. Graham might even glance upward and see the bra hanging from the light fitment.

So without waiting to find my clothes I just struggled into David's boxer shorts and overcoat. I pushed my bare feet into my wellies by the door, grabbed the workshop keys and went out.

Graham was pacing nervously beside his van, blowing plumes of breath from his nostrils like a dragon. Bet was locked in the front, looking out lugubriously through the passenger side window.

'Hi!' I said as brightly as I could manage.

'Oh, right. Hi,' said Graham. He stopped pacing and glanced at my face briefly. 'I've, you know, come to get the baskets. I hope that's still all right.' Something about the car, the seated dog and Graham's apparently excruciating embarrassment told me that he must have been here for some time. He'd parked. Knocked. Got no response and come round the back to find me. So he'd seen everything. He'd looked away the micro second he realised what he was looking at of course. But he'd still seen. I pulled David's coat around me a little more efficiently and blushed.

'Of course. No problem. Sorry I took a while to wake up. Have you been here long?'

'Well. Yes. I mean no. Not very long.' I walked in front of him to the workshop, and unlocked the door.

'Here we are. They're in here.' I unhooked the finished baskets from their places on the wall, chattering about each one as I did so, feeling my back scoured by Graham's eyes. Why did I feel the throat-tightening desire to apologise for having David in my house without having told Graham?

'There we are. That's the lot. I'll carry them to the car for you.' Graham stood in the door without moving, looking down at his feet, hair flopped out of place and over his forehead.

'Look Myfanwy,' he said, still looking down. 'I'm so sorry if I intruded. I mean I had no idea you had, a chap.'

'Well, it's been rather sudden. I mean . . . I didn't. You know. Have. A boyfriend. Until. Just very recently. No. I'm sorry Graham. I've embarrassed you.' He looked up from his feet then to my surprise, as I struggled like a fly in ointment with a sudden stutter revival, he smiled, a wide easy smile,

'No. No. I'm not so easy to embarrass as you think. That's not what I'm apologising for. I just didn't know that you . . . had someone.' This was another bit of Graham to surprise me. I remembered, just, to shut my mouth. He took the baskets from my arms and hooked them all onto one of his. 'Come and have a cup of tea at the shop, eh? Sometime?' Then very lightly he pulled something from the front of my frizzled and escaped hair, 'Bread in the hair, now that's a new one even on me. Thanks for the baskets. Bye.'

I stood inside the workshop until I heard his van go over the first cattle grid. Then I went inside. David, dressed in his own shirt, with my cardigan wrapped like a loincloth around him was tidying up, speaking over his shoulder as he picked stuff off the floor.

'Who was that?'

'Oh, Graham.'

'Ah, Graham the shop. The boring guy with disastrous sweaters. Yeah?' I felt an unreasonable rush of irritation.

'No, actually. The surprising man with the extraordinary smile!' I snapped.

'I'm sorry. I was just repeating what you told me!'

'No. No, *I'm* sorry. I'm feeling guilty for bad mouthing him. He's OK really. I need caffeine.' David came up behind me as I stood filling the cafetière.

'I found your knickers on the kettle. I don't think you've got anything on under that coat of mine.'

'Give me my cardigan back and I'll show you.'

It was cold out. Threatening rain anyway. We didn't miss anything being indoors all morning. All weekend.

My big break exhibition had begun to make its presence felt. To generate enough material I was going to have to churn out the work. One chair a week almost, until the day it started. I couldn't spend a whole five days in bed with David. On Monday morning when I said I had to spend the day in the workshop, I expected a little of the 'we only have days together!' melodrama. But there was nothing.

'I know you have to work. Don't worry. I can amuse myself. I'll go shopping for nice food. And I'll recce somewhere to work out, maybe. Can I take the van?'

David tootled off quite content to do his own thing and I lit the woodburner in the workshop, and wiped the misted windows so the light came in. I was filled with the same surprising sense of contentment that I'd had on the river with David sitting on the bank. It was easy to not think of not thinking about Peter. He was there behind me somewhere, but at least for a while I could have a rest from looking.

I began to assemble the ingredients for a new chair, fetching various likely looking bits from the piles at the end of the workshop and the rush store. I leant them in the centre of the floor, walking all around them to see if they got on together. I loved this stage of the making, when unexpected combinations of materials could spark wild ideas. After an hour I'd discarded the two wooden rakes and the sawn up bits of driftwood sleeper.

I took my big drawing pad and sketched the new chair from its components: a twelve-foot section from an old wooden boat; bundles of rush with the black plumes of flower heads still attached; an old glass float; a sea-bleached oak stump that I'd had cut into five fat slices like the layers of one of my grandmother's cakes.

Sawing, planing, drilling; modifying all the parts just enough for them to fit together with a snug solidity. I like my chairs to be able to survive a twenty-foot fall but still look as if all the parts could have washed up on a beach together.

Making that day was like yoga is supposed to be, all my brain cells chanting the same thing like a monastery of monks. My heart beat very loud and slow. Far away on some sort of internal horizon a tiny sharp figure – William – was making all his things along with me, the Astroturf bear, the carton crucifix, the birds. I didn't think at all. I just did and lived my doing, one moment and then the next. And the next.

David came and found me at the end of the day. His knock on the door and his voice reached me like waking sound penetrating a deep sleep. I saw the dark outside the windows and found it for a moment totally inexplicable. Until David told me it was six thirty and I had been working without a stop all day.

'I looked in at lunchtime. But you didn't seem to hear me. So I thought, well maybe this is just what she's like when she's working. I went away again.'

He was tentative and crushed velvet looking, worried.

'I've never done that before. A straight eight hours!' I told him. 'It's a one off. I've done loads.' I walked around the chair in amazement: I hadn't expected to be that far on before about Wednesday night.

'I think I could give myself tomorrow off!'

'Come on. You must be exhausted and you need to eat. You need me to take care of you.' He wrapped his arm round my shoulders and turned off the lights in the workshop behind us.

I was dazed all evening but David was sweet and patient. He coaxed me back to the world with chicken risotto, candlelight, and happy tales from his day of adventures in rural retail in regions the sun-dried tomato has never reached. He'd found a gym to go to, taken some clothes to be dry cleaned and charmed every bird out of every tree between the garage on the way in and the supermarket on the way out. We finished the bottle of wine toasting ourselves in front of the open woodburner, happy as a matching pair of buttered crumpets. A gale had come in with the darkness and was tugging petulantly at the shingles of the roof.

'I'll take you foraging tomorrow,' I said. 'This gale'll bring in some good stuff on the beach.'

'I'll keep off the sandbank this time.'

I was in a kind of shock. I had never expected to feel so totally comfortable and content in the presence of another human being again. We nuzzled into each other in the firelight and heat like puppies, twining round limbs and bodies with a pleasure that was only sexual after a while. David was so good at physicality, he could put all his inner life into his body, distributing emotion and thought like blood pumped to every cell by the finest capillaries. He drew me out into my body too. With David I felt the life I'd held fortressed inside stream out through me like a blush. Wherever I touched him I felt my energy rushing to the spot: my cheek against his chest tingled; my fingertips on his thigh felt too full of blood; my mouth on his neck felt as if it might begin a life of its own.

I snapped from my daze as the sensuality became sexual. We pushed against each other's strength. We felt equal. Almost David's size, I could hold him, pin him, turn him just as he could me. We tried to hammer each other into the floor. We screamed and cried together, swore eternal love and fell asleep on the rug again, wrapped in another lot of improvised bedding.

Hard cold floors are not good places for highly tuned and slightly damaged bodies to spend the night. David was wrecked in the morning, walking with a limp and miserable as a lump of chewed gum. He said two hours in the gym would put him right but I made him an appointment with Tucker's osteopath first.

I postponed our day off until he got back, and went into my workshop. I lit the stove and soaked up the remaining trance-atmosphere left from the day before. I thought about how loving David and accepting the exhibition were the same thing – steps into the unknown. I felt pleased with myself that every day I managed to be less fearful. But I was only doing it through the careful application of blinkers: I could look at 'now' but not at 'tomorrow'. I thought I might have given yesterday the slip, but the elastic rope around my ankles was just waiting to tighten.

I lifted a big grainy plank onto the bench and switched on the table saw. I needed two short sections with the best grain for part of the back of the chair. I marked them, lined them up and got ready to push the wood over the spinning blade. Without any warning Peter's fingers pushed tenderly between my own. Then palm to palm, squeezed as he would sometimes do when we were making love. It was such a tiny thing. So small a detail to hold so much. The texture of Peter's skin, the size and strength of his hands, the contained quality of his strength.

Suddenly every note of the love I was playing with David had sprung a sharp sad counterpoint, matching every touch and word with their parallels in the past with Peter. Loving David made Peter alive, and dead all over again. The plank jumped, slipped and I nearly took six inches off my left arm.

It took me two hours to stop shaking and half an hour more to stop swearing. Peter had oozed through, like sap, between me and my life again. No wild raps, or whisperings from receding boats this time but something so small and sweet it would be hard to sweep aside. If Peter could have chosen a moment, it would have been a good one to choose. *If* he had *chosen* he would have been wilfully getting in my way. If.

There was no more oozing. I focused fiercely on my grainy plank, and how its sections would fit into the chair. When David returned, mended, bright and bendy again we went out onto the beach.

The wind was razor cold, sand dry. High white clouds ran over the sky – reinforcements rushing to a war somewhere over the horizon. The sea was having its first big nervous breakdown of the winter, waves and swells all over the place, seaweed debris everywhere. It couldn't even stay the same shade of blue for more than a minute at a time. The tide was far out but the wind had spread a film of water over the last five hundred metres of sand. This mirrored the panicking clouds and created the odd illusion of a still lagoon. Stranded in the wet mirror surface edged in reflected light I could see all sorts of intriguing shapes beckoning me. David lengthened his stride to keep up, now that I was snatched up in the beachcomber's hopeful excitement.

'What are we looking for?' said David.

'The unexpected. That's the best you can find.'

'Right! OK!' The wind unravelled his scarf for the third time and he shoved it determinedly into his coat.

There wasn't any of the unexpected at low tide. Three bits of railway sleeper and a broken orange fish box. None of the objects that had looked so promising were anything out of the ordinary. The farthest and most interesting looking one turned out to be three pairs of large white Y-fronts sewn together and clogged with sand and seaweed. I imagined some oil tanker crew, bored out of their brains on another Atlantic crossing had played some joke on a new boy. By the size of the underpants, I guessed it must be the cook. Each cheek of a bottom that size would take ten years of greasy breakfast scraps to construct.

David flew up and down and across the beach, retrieving his ever escaping scarf and pouncing on every new piece of flotsam with the enthusiastic optimism of a seven year old.

'What about this? Looks a bit like a giraffe without legs? No? Oh. OK.'

I wanted to find something fabulous. Something I'd never found before to prove to David the fascination of this game of marine serendipity.

We searched the high tide line. It was what I called a housekeeping storm. There was lots of wood: for the fire; two good solid fish boxes: general storage; and a large unbroken section of fishing net — for rush drying. But there was nothing magical. No objects from Davy Jones. We walked back for the wheelbarrow to cart the haul home.

'I'm sorry there wasn't anything exciting,' I said.

'What do you mean? I think it's exciting that you can use all that stuff. The sea provides. It's sort of biblical. Hey. Great barrow.'

'It copes with the waves in the hard sand. I can stack it like a haystack and it still moves.'

'Get in.'

'What?'

'Get in. Hasn't anyone ever given you a ride in a barrow.'

'Not since I was six.'

'Then it's time you had another one then.'

We took turns to ride all the way back to our pile of booty. At first I pushed very sensibly, going for smoothness and safety. But that was too boring for David. He demanded twists and turns, variations in speed. When he wheeled me he provided sound effects too, and a rather too exciting crash landing at high speed to finish off.

'I've got a mouthful of sand!'

'Roughage.'

I stacked the wood to dry and came inside.

David called from the bathroom. 'Kettle's on. The ansaphone says it's got three messages.'

I pressed the replay button. 'Call me Van. I've had a surprising call from someone called Olivia Draco. And can you come to supper on Friday. It's our last night. Bye.'

'Miss Bowen. This is a message from Olivia Draco. I have a proposal to put to you. I wonder if you could call me? I shall be in the office until 6 this evening.'

There was a crackling on the tape. 'Hey! Thought you said three messages!'

The crackling cleared, and a male voice spoke: 'Hi,' it said. I sat down, every hair on end. It was American sounding. Quite deep, a little hesitant at the start, as he might be. 'Hi', all of heaven and all of hell in one syllable.

The voice went on. 'If you get this can you call me? I'm on the usual number.' The whole sentence revealed a voice more English than American, more tenor than bass. Not Peter then. David emerged from the bathroom.

'Oh, God. My father and his ego. Why doesn't he ever just *say* his name?'

'That was Dick? Your father?'

'Yes. Myfanwy! You're white! What is it? Are you hurt?' For a second I thought that I'd tell him. It sounded like Peter, I'd say. But that didn't seem like enough explanation, and the whole story was too much.

All I wanted to feel was love for David. Just one simple emotion. So I said, 'I stubbed my toe, it's agony. It'll pass. Will you make the tea?'

'Of course!'

David made the tea and wittered on about the great man his father. I quelled the wave and called Tucker and then Olivia.

Olivia's proposal needed immediate discussion. Tucker was in the cabin within an hour.

'It's got such potential, Van. All the outbuildings could be workshops or galleries. You could run courses there, all sorts.'

'Wait a minute. I'm not going to run anything necessarily. I don't have to have any day-to-day involvement unless I want to. That's what Olivia said.'

'For God's sake, Van, I'm not suggesting you run the bloody tea room. But if you're chair of the Trustees you could have a lot of influence.' Tucker smacked her mug of tea down on the table for emphasis. David's back winced as he stood at the stove making supper, and stoically ignoring us.

'Look, Van. This could be brilliant for you: a permanent showcase for your work and a way to get to know all sorts of other artists. People who aren't me or my relatives you said.'

'I don't know. I'd thought that if the Museum took it on then I could just forget about it. Not have to be responsible in any way. Turning the whole place into a centre for Welsh Art . . . I don't know if I want to be involved.'

'Anyone would think you were signing a contract in blood. If you don't like it you can stop doing it.'

'OK. OK, Tucker. I will think about it. But the point is you're happy with the plan to include your work in the permanent exhibition?'

'Yes. Delighted.'

'I'll call Olivia tomorrow. The lottery fund application has to be in by the end of the week.'

'We'll see you Friday?'

'Of course. Is there anything we can do?'

'No. We're remarkably organised really. Just be there on Monday to hand over the keys to the tenants, take the Land Rover that's it. I must go.'

'I've cooked lots, Elen. You're welcome to stay.'

'No, thanks, David. I promised everyone fish and chips. I'll go into town now. Bye.'

As soon as Tucker was gone I could stop pretending that I had any ability to think about my future life. I put Olivia's idea to one side easily: I probably wouldn't have to make a decision, I thought. Olivia wouldn't get the money and I'd have to sell William's home through the man with grey slip-ons. Solved. No thought required.

I brought my time horizon closer again, into tomorrow. Another day with David. Another day with Tucker and Idris just up the road. Every day now it would have to be hauled in, until it would be in the next second, my last second with David before he climbed onto the plane.

Over dinner David was quiet. He was pleased that there was a chance to keep all my father's work together he said. Only when we went to bed, really in a bed this time, did he say what he felt.

'You don't have to stay here, Myfanwy. You could make a life in New York. I love you. I want to be with you.'

'You will be,' I said, 'you will be.' But I was fixed on my time scale; the next hour, the next day.

'How will I be? How will I be if you stay here?'

I didn't answer. I couldn't answer. Anything that wasn't 'now' had started to be like numbers above four to a rabbit: 'one, two, three, four . . . lots'. 'Now, in an hour, in a day . . . sometime, someplace.' I kissed him instead. Every time he tried to speak, I took the words into my mouth and swallowed them away.

Much later I woke up. David was in the bathroom. I could hear him. I felt a hand on my thigh, so solid that I gasped. Not even dancers had arms that long. I pulled away and the hand came too, stroking now with Peter's unmistakable strength, warmth and experience; persuading me out of sleep some night in our past 'C'mon babe. All you have to be is a little awake. I'll do the rest. Huh?'

He'd been drinking with Lars, out on deck. He was hot. They'd finished that bottle of Southern Comfort. He was hot and drunk. Big. A little dangerous.

Stroke, stroke, stroke. More deliberate now. Kneading flesh. Working like a masseur.

'There. That's good. That's all I need. Hold it there.' The stroking stopped. There was a textile rustling as Peter took off his trousers.

'David! David! Come back quickly!' I screamed.

'I'm here. Sweetheart. Calm down. I'm here.'

I leapt up, clinging to David, holding him tight to squeeze Peter away. But I could still feel Peter's hand on my skin, feel him finding his way inside. I've never been keen on threesomes. Particularly involving dead people. Feeling a third hand on your body when two others are occupied elsewhere is at the very least unnerving.

'Make love to me, David. Please. David, please.'

'But we've only just . . .'

'David, just fuck me!' I guess desperate fear is enough like desperate lust. David beat Peter to it, out-manoeuvred him, drove him away with solid physical presence. But where my shoulder blades pushed into the mattress I felt for a moment Peter's caress. It spread a chill of loneliness and empty longing down my spine.

Chapter Thirteen

'I've got money for you. Lots of it. They'd all gone by Wednesday.' Graham's shop looked a bit bare without any of my baskets strung from the ceiling. I followed him to the little back room. He put the kettle on and reached into his jacket pocket for the cheque book. Business as usual, Graham as normal: jovial, superficial and even a bit dull. He didn't have the ghastly jersey on though. A rather nice jacket and thick cream shirt instead.

'I can't make you any more Graham . . .'

'Did I ask? Look, I know you're up against it. Your show coming up and all.'

'Who told you?'

'The place I bought your chairs from. Dropped me a line: did I know that Myfanwy Bowen – in big blue letters mind – had an exclusive show starting on the fifth of March.'

'Oh God!'

'What's the matter? You should be over the moon.'

'I've got too much on. I can't make enough pieces in time.'

'You could always use old stuff you know. Save a bit of time like.' He handed me a mug. 'How long does it take to make a chair?'

'A week, ten days, a fortnight. Depends.'

'OK, well I can save you at least two weeks then. Take my two for the show. Mark 'em "sold" mind. I want them back!'

'Graham. Thank you. That's brilliant. I've got all my dad's place to sort out. There might be a lottery grant to make it into a gallery and a kind of arts centre, so we could keep all his sculptures.'

'That'd be fabulous.'

'Well, yes.' Yes, if it weren't for my lover going to New York and my best friend going to Kenya and my dead husband trying to shag me. Yes. With less than twenty-four hours before Tucker and Idris leaving, and two days before David was due to go, I was losing it. My time horizon was slipping further away than I wanted it.

Graham turned to refill his mug. 'How's your chap then?' he said, clearing his throat to cover the tightness in the question.

'Oh, fine. In the osteopath's. He's a dancer. Got an injury. I dropped in here. While I was waiting for him.' Graham's sudden awkwardness was catching, I felt my tongue and my vocal cords getting out of synch.

'Is he down for long, then?' He stirred his sugarless tea with great concentration.

'No. He's off. On Monday. New York. For work.'

'Oh. Right. So we'll be losing you then?'

'Oh. No. I don't think so.'

'Good. Good. I'm glad of that anyway.'

'How's the piano?'

'Good. OK.' he held up his right index finger and wiggled it. 'Beethoven's Ninth with one finger. You'll have to come for a recital!'

'Yes. I'd better go. Thanks for the chairs. The baskets. I'll try and do some. Little ones. Before Christmas. You know.'

'Lovely. Ta.'

Tucker hadn't forgotten her skill for travelling light. She'd pared down everyone's baggage to the bare minimum. Even Idris who wouldn't normally travel without material preparation for flood, fire and ice, had just one normal sized suitcase.

Veterinary equipment, books and artist's materials had gone by freight two weeks earlier. Everything now, children and luggage, would fit in the hire car.

I knew Tucker would be well prepared so I was ready to see everything loaded for the off when we arrived for an early dinner on Friday evening. But there was an unexpected extra load for the emotion circuits: the girls' teddies lined up on the luggage shelf. Transitional objects ready for their biggest challenge yet.

I told David who they were: Agnes' Blue Duck, veteran of many near disastrous sea voyages in Aggie's improvised boats; Jane's 'Wurse' who had once been recognisable as a horse before reenacting the autobiography of a pit pony down a muddy hole at the top of the orchard. Moffy's 'Jeff' reincarnated from a previous existence as Julian's very posh teddy 'Duke', now sans practically everything except for one ear and a teaspoonful of stuffing. And last of all, Jelly's 'Baggy', a cloth bag made from a scrap of Granny Elspeth's old kitchen curtains, and now containing who knew what strange shamanic objects — a split marble, a Smartie top with the letter J, a pigeon's skull — with which Jelly daily saved the world from evil.

'I met Wurse the first day I came to Elen's. Jane put him on my bed to say "welcome". He has a serious BO problem.'

'He never dried out after the pit pony thing.'

'I didn't know about Blue Duck. Aggie's always too busy trying to impress me with her maturity, I suppose.'

'She's had that bird since she was smaller than he is. I have a photo of the girls on the beach with their special toys. Having a very serious pretend tea party together. But only the toys wear the sunglasses. Even Baggy had some.'

'It's hard to look cool when you're only a bag.'

'Yeah, but he manages it.'

'I liked being in a house with all those kids. I never knew kids could be enjoyable,' said David, 'I'll miss them. I feel as if I've only just found them and I'm losing them again. Maybe I'll go to Kenya and see them. Maybe we two should go together?'

The toys looked back at us, if a bag can look, brightly lit in our headlights. Already they seemed to be trinkets from a lost time.

'Oh, bugger,' I said, 'I'm going to miss them so much!'

'They aren't going for ever,' David said, 'they will come back.'

'But they won't be *little* any more. I'll never know anyone else's kids so well.'

'What about your own?' He put his hand on my thigh and squeezed gently. 'What about *our* own? There's nothing to stop us. It's not as late as you think, love.'

No, I thought, it was even later. I might slip in a little late career bloom, but a child? I would be sixty pretty well, by the time it was out of university. And no sudden surge of broody sentimentality brought on by a gaggle of barely stuffed animals was going to stop David being in New York by Tuesday night. It was later than either of us thought. Well beyond the last bus. Yet the aphrodisiac power of David looking at me so earnestly, and saying he wanted to give me a child was enormous.

'I've left the chocolate behind,' I said, squeezing his warm palm between my thighs.

'Have you?'

'I might have done.'

'Shall we fetch it?'

'Yes. But we'll have to be quick.'

He didn't move his hand. I drove. Not far, into an overgrown lay-by halfway home. And we were very quick. It was far too cold in the van to be anything else: like the Canadian Air force fitness exercises; brief but very intense.

Back at Tucker's the house echoed inside. The furniture was left of course, but stripped of its encrusting layers of life. The coats from the hall, the slippers from the groaning table. Books were on shelves and there were no signs of toys having the usual gruesome adventures that they suffered under the care of

Tucker's girls. The whole surface of every table was visible, including the big circular dining table which, for all of Tucker and Idris' marriage had been the house library, supporting open copies of books on mastitis in Jerseys, European Expressionism between the wars and Topsy and Tim Move House.

The wellies in the porch were the same, left in their size specific slots, as essential to any family in the house as knives and forks and a kitchen table.

'It's not actually clean yet,' said Tucker, 'the agency will come in tomorrow when we're gone and do all that. All the cupboards are cleared. We filled a skip last week.'

'I'd like to see it at the end of tomorrow,' said Idris, 'clean for the first time since my mother died. Bit of a novelty for the old house.'

The house didn't look keen on the idea to me. Grumpy and sullen I thought. Neither house nor its family seemed comfortable together now.

David had made a huge and beautiful sea food lasagna to feed us all and have only one thing to put in the oven. I'd brought the chocolate and fruit so that the children could share our secret fondue ritual with their parents. We had proper champagne and ate in the real dining room for the first time. But it wasn't a happy meal. We were all subdued and awkward. Everything had changed already. Idris had taken his family away from their cosy past but none of them had yet arrived in their exciting future. They were in a rather cold and draughty limbo, with the door closing on what seemed, when viewed through the narrowing gap, to be a warm and beckoning 'yesterday'. Even Idris' enthusiasm for life on the Serengeti plains was a bit dampened. I was sure that on his last night in his family home, for perhaps years to come, Idris was thinking fondly of the comforting familiarity of Friesian orifices.

The same nasty draught was blowing on me too, from the space in my life where Tucker, Idris and the girls had once been.

It didn't help that the kids had been over-excited for weeks.

They were tired and quarrelsome, and still too full of cakes from the send-off tea party they'd been given by their school friends.

They whinged over David's lasagna, 'What are the red bits?' moaned Moffy.

'Food, Moffy,' said Idris in a 'say-another-word-and-you're-dead' tone.

'Stop looking at me, Jane.'

'Who'd want to look at you, *Ag Bag.*'

'Mummy, I don't like the red bits.'

'Eat up Moffy. David's been very kind to cook such a lovely dinner for us.'

'No, really. That's fine. I won't be in the least offended if . . .'

'She has to eat what she's given, David.'

'Right. Right. More bubbly anyone.'

'But I *donliketheredbits.*'

'OK, that's *it*. Moffy. Get down from the table and go to bed. I've had enough whinging.'

'But I want the choklit.'

'Idris! Let her stay. It's our last meal here all together!'

'I don't care if it's the last bloody supper with the five fishes and loaves. Moffy *get down*.'

'That's not fair, Daddy.'

'Don't you tell me what's fair, Agnes Tucker.'

'Well, if Moffy's getting down, then so am I.' Agnes took Moffy's hand and made a dramatic exit, closely followed by Jane and Jelly.

'Well done, Idris. An excellent moment to assert your fatherly authority.' Tucker snatched the not yet empty plate from under his nose. 'I'll clear the plates, shall I?' She wooshed out to the kitchen without apparently touching the ground at all.

'Oh, God! I'm sorry David after you'd gone to all that trouble. I think we're all too wound up.'

'No, no. Really. That doesn't matter at all. My cooking's improved so much that lasagna is easy. It wasn't any trouble.'

David raised the full plumage, every quill perfectly placed and overlapping.

'David, I think we should go.'

'Yes. Let these poor people get their rest before that horrendous early start.'

'There's no need, Myfanwy love.' Idris looked ready to burst into tears, but he was admitting I was right. They all needed to be asleep before the stress of leaving induced any more damaging scraps.

'You lot have got to leave here at dawn,' I said. 'We'll go. Get our goodbyes over with. I'll pop up and see the girls now.'

'And I'll help wash up whilst you do. Come on Idris. Let's take these crocks to Elen.' It was strange to see David sweeping the tired and overwrought Idris under his wing.

When I was a kid the attic of Granny Elspeth's house was still an attic with one tiny window and rickety, uncertain boarding that could drop you through the plaster into the bedrooms below. There was nothing there but dust and spiders crazed by starvation. Yet it was still a delicious little festival of the spooky to climb the ladder-cross-staircase affair and push the trap door up into the perpetual twilight. Idris would take me up there. But he made me go first up the ladder and through the door.

'If you fall, I could catch you see?'

Safety was nothing to do with it. Idris only went into the attic when I was there to be taken. Opening the trap door I always felt I had nearly seen something, nearly caught the 'whatever it was' that lived in the attic 'at' whatever it was that 'it' did up there. I loved that fear and curiosity cocktail. Idris only liked it second-hand and mixed with a little pseudo-parental responsibility.

When the loft was converted to a real bedroom with windows and a proper floor, Agnes and Jane had chosen to keep the wooden ladder-stairs and the trap door. I climbed halfway towards the little square of light and heard their voices trickling down to me. With my eyes just at floor level I could see the girls sitting on the rug between the two beds. They were playing Snap. This was Jane and Agnes at their most benevolent. United by their noble stance against the Oppressor Father they were filled with protective sisterly love for their little twin siblings. Normally Moffy and Jelly would have been greeted with a slammed trap door, and the sound of Jane and Agnes throwing things at each other from behind it. And as for playing Snap! *Snap*? Only *babies* ever played *Snap*.

'Snap!' shouted Moffy.

'Snap!' shouted Jelly.

'Snap snap snap!' they shouted together, slapping their hands down on top of the cards and each other. Jane and Agnes exchanged the long-suffering sort of look seventy-year-old maiden aunts might share over a teenage niece giggling about her latest 'beau'.

I emerged through the floor and said hello. All their faces turned towards me, unsmiling, uncertain for a moment, looking out from the pool of light to the dark I stepped from. I felt that at last I had caught the 'whatever it was' doing the 'whatever it did': always, it had been these other children, waiting up in the attic to be born into their family. And after tonight they would be gone.

'David and I have to go home, so you can all get a good night's rest.' They ran around me then and stuck like limpets.

'Will you come and see us in Africa?' said Agnes.

'Of course. But not for a while. Not until next summer.'

'But *will* you come?' said Jane.

'Yes.'

'Will David come too?' said Moffy.

'Well. Perhaps. Yes. Perhaps.'

I hugged them all at once. 'Bye bye. I love you all very much.' There wasn't any more to say or do.

They walked me to the edge of the trap door and I walked down the steps. Just as I reached her eye level Jelly said, 'Myfanwy, sshhh.'

'What?'

'Here.' She pulled something from her pocket, clutched in a sweaty little hand and pressed it to my face. It was a rather dishevelled black feather. She whispered to me in that whisper you could hear five streets away.

'It's one of Baggy's things. 'Smagic.'

'Right. Thanks Jelly. I'll keep it safe.'

There were definitely a few of William's genes in this great niece.

I didn't know how to say goodbye to Idris and Tucker. It was too big a thing to manage. I couldn't even see all of what it was to say goodbye to them and their life in that house. I did what I could: 'Write to me you rat bag, send me a painting,' I said to Tucker.

'No good doing that, you won't even know which way up it goes, you fucking philistine.'

'Mark it top and bottom then.'

'OK.'

'Tell me what it's like up a wildebeest's bum, Idris.'

'I'll send a blow by blow account. So to speak.'

We hugged each other very quietly. And they hugged David. And then David hugged all the girls, lined up quiet and solemn at the door. And then I drove us home, because I'd been too sad to drink and David had been doing mine for me.

The stove had burnt out while we were at Tucker's and the cabin was like ice. If I'd been alone I might have left it that way to match my outside to my inside, cold and leftover as Sunday's joint in Monday's fridge. But I didn't like the thought of David shivering under the blankets so I went out to fetch more wood and kindling. When I came back in David had moved every scrap of bedding he could find in front of the stove ready to be warmed when it relit.

'We'd end up here anyway so, I thought, might as well be a bit more comfortable.'

He sat on the piano stool in his coat while I laid the fire.

'Are you OK?'

'I'll live.'

'Can I help?'

'No. I'll light it.'

'I'm going to have just one little fag. Is that OK?'

'You know I don't mind. Rolys don't smell like packet ones.'

The fire was sulky. It didn't want to wake up again. I had to coax it. Staring into the little black hole of scrumbled newspapers and wood shavings I didn't notice David fiddling with the music in the drawers of the stool.

'I get no kick from . . .' he began

He didn't sing it, and his playing was hesitant and inaccurate but there it was, the melody strung up with the accompaniment. If I looked at the piano now, who would I see? Peter and William, a double ghost, from the day they'd fetched the piano from the junk shop in Haverfordwest. Brought it all the way in the back of William's pick-up, covered in an old tarpaulin. It needed more than tuning by the time it reached the cabin: open heart surgery and a Reichian therapy poor thing. But the notes all played, even if all the c's played b flat and the d's played z's and other things out of some alternative scale of music.

'Play something!' Peter had commanded.

'No. Not until it's tuned.'

'Come on, Myfanwy love,' said William, 'we've slaved to get this blessed thing here!'

Grudgingly I played something I knew by heart. One of the old Cole Porter's that Mummy used to like.

'I get no kick from champagne . . .'

It was barely recognisable, physically painful almost to me but they loved it. They sang along hesitant at first, each of them camouflaging his good voice with self conscious macho growliness. Then the song drew them out, and they sang, sweet and tuneful. So although the c's went on playing x's and the f's playing t's, I heard their voices, remembering nearly all the words.

I didn't want to hear them singing again, so I kept my attention on the fire until my eyes were so hot they stung. Either I had to cook my corneas or to look up and risk the double ghost. I looked. It wasn't there. Instead David was squinting at the score in the poor light, his cigarette stuck in the corner of his mouth. He kept going wrong in the same place. Three times he went over 'You're standing . . . no . . . stand . . . ing. No! stand . . . ding here . . .' mouthing the words, shaking his head and screwing his whole brow into its crushed velvet look.

'I get a kick . . . out of you!'

He looked mad and lovely, coat all rumpled, whole body crabbed over the keys, eyes huge, sparking like Tucker's Liebig hair. Coloured perfectly beautiful by my relief at not finding dead people leaning on my piano.

'Bryan Ferry used to play this with a fag in his mouth too,' he said.

For the first time I saw him moving without elegance, as the struggle his hands were making of the music spread through him. It was strange and touching to see him so willing to be bad at something, yet still enjoying it.

'I didn't know you had all this music. I'm a load of crap at piano. I gave up when I failed grade four, I bet you play beautifully.'

Noticing me watching he began to camp it all up, the badness of his playing, his rucked-up coat, the cigarette stuck to his bottom lip. He took possession of it all: the piano; the music; the room; the moment. He was reminiscent of nothing. He'd never happened before, nor had anything he did. Under the layers of clothing and the tension of trying to play, his body was being clever again, even his shoulder blades could do comic parody.

The awkwardness itself became performance. It was like the day at the river when I'd watched him posing on all those gates and felt I was spectating some natural phenomenon, like a geyser or a lava flow. Except that now, the 'phenomenon' had been in my bed. I had some sort of stake in him, definitely something proprietorial. The feeling I had looking at David then wasn't something cloud-like and fluffy, not a 'love' feeling. It wasn't warm like 'tenderness'. It was hard and hot. I looked at David and felt quite simply 'mine'. And as all the remaining people to whom I could attach the prefix 'my' were about to leave the country it made me feel better. It was of more solid use to me that night than chiffon strands of romance. It was a handle holding me in the world.

'I get a kick . . . out . . . of . . . you!'

My ears woke first the next day. The quiet sounded to me as if it had just had Peter's voice in, or his footstep, or the sound of his duff right knee cracking. Somehow I'd just missed him and with everything but my hearing still sleepy I felt sorry, if only I'd woken a moment sooner . . .

I had one ear over David's heart and one covered by blankets, so that his voice came rumbling through his chest.

'It's our last day,' he said.

'Yes.' But it didn't feel like yes. I was in a limbo land still, a place 'after' and 'before' and 'between'. Only when I was obviously alone again with whatever might be left behind would I really know that, *yes* this *had* been our last day.

'But it doesn't have to be our last day,' David said. He pushed the blanket back off my face.

'It won't be.' It wouldn't be because to me then, it wasn't.

'Won't it?' He prised me off his chest, holding me cradled so he could look at my face. He was waiting for me to say I would follow him to America to stop any day being our last.

'I'll visit you. You can visit me, here.' Visit was a good word. Vague but promising. There were a lot of possibilities in visit, but it made David slump.

'I want a *life* with you, Myfanwy. Not *visits*. Come to New York.'

'I can't. What about William's house. And my chairs.' The practical arguments were a bit true. But not as true as my need to see what happened when everybody had gone – William, Tucker and David. What or who would be left? My chairs? Me? Peter? Telling David that seemed unkind, pouring a big cold black hole all over his gorgeous supernova of passion.

'You don't have to be involved with the house. Let Olivia run it.'

'There's nowhere to forage in New York.'

'Everything washes up in New York. It's the best place to forage in the world. You could sell chairs there for thousands of dollars.'

'Maybe. I don't know.'

'What about last night? What about all the other times? You might be pregnant already. What if you have our baby?' Of all the unrealities floating outside my limbo that was the most unreal of all.

'Then the baby can visit too,' I said. Yeah, along with the little pink and white stripy giraffes, and Diana and Dodi incognito.

'I don't want to be like my dad. I want to be with my child.'

'You will be. Would be. Look. David. Planning your career as a parent before I've even missed a period is a bit premature. I'm not going to be pregnant!'

'Why not?'

'I'm too old.'

'You're not!'

'David, this is bonkers.'

'Do you love me, Myfanwy.'

'Yes.'

'Then come and live with me.'

'It's not that easy. Give me some time. I *will* think. I *will* visit.'

'When? When can we be together?' I wriggled out of his arms and sat up.

'Right now. Now this minute. Here and now. We're seeing each other. You're always saying be alive. So be alive. Now. We are together. We are alive. So this is our life together. Now do you want a cup of coffee?'

'Yes. I do. I'll make it for us. For you. I'm sorry. I'm pushing too hard.'

It turned into a quiet day. By afternoon there was no wind or rain. Even a little apologetic sunshine dissolving its way through the resentful slab of cloud. We walked along the coast path on the other side of the estuary where the cliff is low, just a metre above the sea. On a rough day you get surf soaked. The rocks are very folded and pitted and there's an island a few hundred feet offshore, about the size of a tennis court. The place has an odd feel. A meeting of marine ley lines perhaps.

All sorts of things turn up there. William and I found a swallow still just alive, cowering under a lip of rock on Christmas Day. A jellyfish big as a car washed up there one summer when I worked in the sail shop. And on our first trip home after Peter's months in Antarctica an albatross spent a night on the island, lost at the wrong end of the planet. Seals always come there. So do people. Sometimes I think both sets of beings come to look at each other. The seals are the most often disappointed if that is the case, especially on November Sundays; seals don't know how roast lunches keep the humans inside on such days. So, as the only attraction for them that afternoon, they seemed more pleased and curious than normal. David had never seen a wild seal before.

'Do people feed them here or something?'

'No. They're just nosy.'

We found a flat rock to sit on so David could stare. Four — perhaps more — came and stuck their heads out of the water beside us. Their round grizzled heads were splodged with dark markings. 'Hey,' Peter used to say, 'somebody finally got really pissed at Gorbachev. I guess they chucked him in the ocean off Archangel and here he is!'

As David and I sat and looked so did the seals, eyes steady on us for minutes on end. Then suddenly they'd tip their heads back and go down black nose last. 'It's no good,' they'd be saying to themselves, 'I can't make head nor tail of the damn humans. They never do anything.'

Peter had told me so much about seals. I always got some echo of it looking at them, some voice fragment telling me facts: 'Their nostrils close automatically when they go down.' 'The babies are born white because they evolved from seals that pupped on the ice.'

Sometimes it was like an induction loop commentary at the zoo. But David's presence was a good exorcism, I only heard faint words coming up with the waves.

'They're so close,' said David, 'I can't believe they're wild!'

'They know all they have to do is dive to get away. It makes them bold.' David turned from the seals and mined my hand out of the layers of sleeve.

'Would you be bold if all you had to do was dive to get away?' He began to talk very fast, like the night at the cabin when I'd hauled him out of the sea. 'I won't hold you to anything. If you come to New York, I won't try and make you stay if you don't like it. You can dive. Get away. You can keep an escape route if it makes you feel safe enough to come close. Just tell me that you'll come. Soon.'

'I thought you said you wouldn't push me anymore.'

'Myfanwy. I'm leaving in the morning. I need to have something to hold on to. To know when I'll see you again.'

'I can't tell you.'

'Why?'

'There's so much to do here.'

'That's not it.'

'No.'

'Then you don't love me, do you? That's what it is.' He leapt up. All the seals dived in alarm, one of the humans *had done something*. 'You don't love me. You want me to go so that it will end.'

'No, David. No. I do care about you.'

'OK. Then leave here and come to America.'

'I'm not a clean slate.'

'I don't understand.'

'No. Neither do I. You have to give me time.'

For the real David I knew under the feathers, the fierce high leaping David, waiting without knowing was impossible. But he took my arm as we walked back to the car, and the next morning at the station he kissed me without asking anything more. Prepared to give 'impossible' a go. Watching the train disappear I thought of myself at twenty-three, exploding with love for Peter, unable to comprehend his forty-five-year-old caution. I felt a huge tenderness for us all, youngsters in helpless love and oldsters just as helpless but negotiating with the past.

Chapter Fourteen

'Oh, wow!' She's said it at the sight of every one of my father's sculptures.

'Oh, *wow!* These are just *amazing! Wow!* If it hadn't been so sweetly genuine I might have found the repeated 'wows' irritating.

'This place just *has* to be on a ley line!' With more pentangles woven into her layers of bright jerseys and skirtage than you'd get on an All Souls picnic, and more crystals about her body than the average geology museum, she should know. But in spite of being an economy-sized packet of assorted New Age philosophies, it was hard to dislike anything about this young woman. She was obviously popping with a lot more than one person's share of the celestial life force. Several souls had been crammed into her for recycling, I guessed. She was compulsive viewing, giving the impression that she might do almost anything at any moment – take flight, or morph into a giant luminous tiger – I felt I had to watch in case I missed something.

Olivia had simply said there was someone she wanted me to meet. 'She's a young sculptor called Lucy Becket. Talented. Very mature for her age. She's finished college and a year's travelling. She'll be big one day, but she's just starting. She needs space to work and an income. She'd be the ideal person to live in William's house as caretaker, and run the sculpture side of the Centre's activities.'

It seemed a bit premature to be talking about such detail but Olivia was already confident about full funding; she was she said 'going to get *all* the money from *somewhere*'.

And it was going to cost a bomb. The big barn would be a gallery at one end and restaurant at the other. That would be the permanent home for some of Tucker's pictures. The other barn would become a 'teaching space' where courses and demonstrations could be run. Then the old animal stalls would be extended to provide combined workspace and shops for any artist or crafts person who could prove their worth. It was a huge logistic undertaking. Where were cars going to park? How many times a day would ten loos flush? I'd had to run a telephone extension cable into my workshop so I could keep up with all Olivia's ideas. At first I'd tried to keep my distance from it all, 'honorary trustee' handing over the reins of my father's estate.

But Olivia kept phoning. Phoning and phoning. And sending people to visit so that I could show them William's work and explain to them Olivia's visions. In all my years of solitary foraging it had never occurred to me that the hills and coves all around were stuffed with other lone makers, all just waiting for something to bring them all together, and make them a true community.

I was caught up in Olivia's dream of what William's house and land could become. The product of my father's mad old age was going to be a kind of refuge for all sorts of creative people, a place to make and sell, teach and learn. I suspected that for all her black crow designer wear Olivia was a product of the sixties, and still held the belief that it was possible to change the world. In her head perhaps, she referred to the whole project as a commune.

So Lucy wasn't the first I'd met and shown round William's stuff. First to come was Rollo, a potter from near Pen y Bryn. Rollo's quiet and mouse-like exterior masked a raging exhibitionist interior that came out in his pots – jugs the size of amphorae with handles like monkeys' tails and colours like parrots, huge platters with swirling explosions of glazes. It was quite alarming to think that this quiet man, dressed like a junior accountant on holiday, should harbour such fantasies of rampant jungles.

Next came Rollo's friend Eleri, tall and skinny with dyed red hair and a ragged little three-year-old child in tow, whose gender I never quite worked out. She made stringed instruments, viols and old style violas, beautiful creatures that looked as if they could sing on their own.

After that came Jennifer the basket maker, Mat the weaver, Phil the dyer, George the furniture maker, Mary the clothes designer. It was like a sort of alternative Happy Families. I imagined all of us transposed in cartoon form onto a set of playing cards and arranged in our new little 'homes', pigeon holes in William's old stalls, busily making.

I even began to think that one of the stalls could contain me. More than half of it was Olivia being clever. She packaged up a new sort of life with a new set of people in it for me, and dangled it like bait.

Lucy had saved her ultimate wow of all for the earthwork. 'WOWWW!' It didn't even look that good on a drizzly misty day. More like random molehills than ever, I was beginning to think.

'I wish I'd met him! Just to think all this time I've been living just down the road almost. And I missed him. Damn. I can *feel* how amazing he must have been,' she said, closing her eyes and pressing her fingertips into her temples.

'He was pretty mad actually.'

'Olivia told me you make chairs like sculptures.' Lucy's eyes, absolutely black, snapped open. Not dreamy any more but alive with professional interest. She turned my way and made me feel illuminated, but not like a spotlight illuminates. More like the sun on a plant making its flowers open and its chlorophyll whizz. 'She said you've got a big show coming up. I'd really like to see your stuff.'

* * *

I stepped into the workshop ahead of Lucy, whilst she was in the loo. Peter was sitting in one of the two most recently completed chairs wrapped in the dress that had disappeared in the cavernous washing machine of the *Princess* more than ten years before. Worn like a sort of sarong crossed with a loin cloth, with the buttons cleverly done up, it was quite a natty fit on him. Around his neck was a frayed length of bright blue baler twine with a fat cowrie, probably retrieved from the beach where we'd left it for some long deceased hermit crab, strung on its end. He looked exotic, wild, but still handsome. I couldn't help staring at him a little.

'Wow!' said Lucy. 'Wow wow wow!'

It would have been the right response to a large dark-haired dead man sitting cross-legged with nothing on but a pair of kecks improvised from a lost frock. But she was looking at my chairs. I just had enough time to throw a large sheet over the chair and Peter. I didn't want to know if she could see him or not. Or if I would go on seeing him whilst she was there. I didn't want to know too much about how mad I was getting. I'd worked like an ant on cocaine since David's departure, stopping only for Olivia's ideas or the people she sent me. I'd finished three chairs in two weeks and a bevy of little Christmas present baskets for Graham to sell. It was all going well. I was more than on target. I slept pretty much where I fell, wrapped in sacking in front of the workshop fire, or on the sofa in the cabin. But only for a couple of hours a night, my adrenaline was running too high to let me rest for longer.

I had Peter to thank for my manic productivity. He'd been there since the morning I came back from the station, and found him leaning against the kitchen window gazing out onto the beach. He looked so real and solid, wearing the suit and tie he'd got married and got burned in. I was halfway across the room towards him before I remembered, before he turned to me. He didn't really look in my direction although he seemed to have his face towards mine. When he spoke it wasn't to me; a string of gibberish, nonsense derived from the last sparks of a dead brain.

'Mangotoffee, mozzarella, mangotoffee,' he said, quite insistently to no one in particular, 'mozzarella, mangotoffee, matzominge, mollify.' I couldn't get any closer. He was as untouchable as ashes. I tried speaking his name. I tried making sense of what he said. Almost the whole of Monday went by with me locked at a point four feet away from him trying to work out code versions, anagrams, hidden meanings for mozzarella and mangotoffee, as if they were spell-breaking clues.

Nothing of course worked. At some point I went to the loo, came back and he was gone. Immediately I wanted the nonsense rapping ghost back. He was more solidly whole than any Peter CD I'd summoned or any fragmented apparition that had come on its own. It had been lovely just to look at him, Peter standing in our house again.

I went to bed and woke at some horrible hour of body clock; two or three perhaps. He was back. Still in the suit but lying on the floor now mumbling, moving his lips inaudibly. I had to take a wide detour to get out of the bedroom and back again. He didn't move or react to me. In the way you think impossible things at that time of night I thought he might have reconstituted himself from his ashes like mashed potato. It gave me a little lift of the heart; a Peter rehydrated from ash would be real, in a way, with a body made of proteins and membranes and crystals of bone. Not a ghost with a body made of prism images from the slide show of someone's mind. But I checked under the bed and the carved box was still full, no sign that any of its contents had been spilled or wetted.

I sat perched on the end of our bed wrapped in the duvet like a big cloak and looked at him. I wasn't frightened exactly but I didn't know what to do. Peter was lying on the floor of what had been our bedroom in what had been his best suit. He looked absolutely like himself. But he wasn't behaving like a proper, all-pancakes-present-in-the-stack Peter.

Peter no longer had any presence in the world of chairs and tables, beans on toast and HP agreements. So this Peter on my floor could only be the product of someone's imagination. Mine most probably. Or Peter's. This Peter could make no difference to my life. Couldn't fill the space left by the real one. The way to deal with him was to to get on, keep busy and ignore him, as much as I could. I switched off the light and lay down.

Lying in bed and trying to sleep with a live dead body on your bedroom floor is hard. With the live dead body of the man you loved for most of your life it's impossible. I wanted to sit and look and look. It was such a relief to look at him after so long of looking at him inside my head. So I got up and began my work marathon instead.

Peter followed me. Not that he got up and walked. He'd just be there when I looked up from a saw, or a bundle of rush. Sometimes spouting gibberish or the lists of things I'd become familiar with in the summer, but devoid now of any grammar, or even verbs.

'Palomino, Potsdam, Pretoria, . . .'

He dressed more and more bizarrely, as if my trying to ignore him was driving him mad. I didn't ignore him altogether. I couldn't. I wanted to look. I wanted to talk to him and I did try again a couple of times when he was mumbling away about soffits and brass screws.

'Contiboard, cathedral hinge,' he whispered one night in my workshop. He was perched, impossibly, on a high shelf, lying with one crooked arm supporting his head and wearing a silk kimono that my mother had worn out in 1973.

I stood below the shelf and looked up at him. 'What do you mean contiboard, cathedral hinge? Eh? What are you talking about?'

He didn't react even though I was shouting.

'You never cared about hinges and shelves. Why do you go on about them now?'

The workshop door was knocked on loudly and then opened.

'Hello? Myfanwy? Are you all right I heard you shouting?' It was Graham. Cagouled and floppy haired against the drizzle outside in the dark.

'Oh. You know. I just. Shout. Sometimes when I'm working.'

'Oh. Right.'

'You'll want your baskets?'

'Yes. Yes, please.'

'They're up on this shelf.' I pointed above me, without looking to see if Peter was still up there amongst the little rush circlets and boxes that I had ready for Graham's Christmas trade. 'Here's the steps, would you mind getting them down?'

I kept my back to the shelf as if my spine was braced in steel and unable to turn. I began moving tools and materials back and forth across the room, just to keep moving and busy until the shelf was no longer the focus of attention. When Graham finally got down and came to stand next to the stove, I stopped the frenetic activity and looked at him intently.

'OK?' I asked, as in *seen any dead people sitting on high shelves?*

'Oh, smashing. These are great.'

'And everything else?' as in *are you sure there wasn't someone sitting on the baskets?*

'Yeah, fine. Business is good, you know. Piano's coming along. "Country Gardens" with two hands now!'

For him there had been nothing on the shelf but 'seasonal goods'.

'That's marvellous. Tea?'

'Don't suppose you've got anything stronger? I've just been loading a new lot of stuff into the barn. It's brass baboons out there let alone monkeys.'

We settled on two sawn-up lengths of old pew, with mugs of Laphroaig and our faces to the opened stove. Our backs firmly to Peter. I downed my whisky in one. Horrible. Like cough medicine. 'You needed that then?'

'Mmm.'

I did. As I'd looked up from my mug I'd found Peter sitting on my workbench, three feet from Graham and unavoidably in both our eyelines. It was a shock to find that whoever's imagination was conjuring the 3D version of Peter, it kept it up in the presence of a third party.

'Are you all right, Myfanwy? You look, well, a bit tired.' I was really very close to asking Graham if he'd noticed my dead husband besporting himself on my workbench between two vices and the glue gun, crushing my ansaphone under his substantial arse. After a week of Peter's company and almost no sustaining activities like sleeping or eating, I was mad enough to believe that politeness might be all that was keeping Graham from asking Pete if he too wanted a slug of Scotch.

Then the phone rang and a little elastic band of tension stretched between Graham and me as he waited for me to answer it.

Six rings. Eight. The phone was underneath Peter. There was no way to answer it without touching him. Impossible. I shut my eyes.

'Shall I get it?' he said. The ansaphone cut in at ten rings. 'Hello. This is Myfanwy Bowen. Please leave. A message. After the tone.'

'Hi. I'm worried. You're never there.' It was David, ringing on a line too clear to be real from the other side of the Atlantic. He sounded discouraged and sad. It was my fault. In more than a week I hadn't returned a single call; the disembodied voice of the live boyfriend had lost out in the competition with the dysfunctional hologram of the dead husband. 'Please, please phone me at my father's. Same number. I've booked you a return ticket to New York for ten days time. It'll be at the airport. The flight details are in the post. I won't call again until you call me. Bye.'

The phone clicked, the ansaphone did its little official whirring. Graham studied the fire and the inside of his mug, then coughed and shifted in his seat.

'Shall I go?'

'No. Just look at the phone for me will you.' I kept my eyes shut.

'What?'

'Does the phone look OK to you?'

'Yes.'

'There's nothing, unusual about it?'

'No.'

'It looks like a phone?'

'Yes.'

'And it hasn't looked unusual to you at all?'

'No'. Graham was genuinely mystified and uncomfortable. Perhaps he really hadn't seen anything. Perhaps, I thought, Peter was so unreal that he was only there for me. I didn't make the necessary leap to the fact that I might simply be going round the bend.

'Right.' I took a breath and looked up. There was my bench, my two vices, the switched off and gummy glue gun and the rather grubby phone with no one sitting on it. Relief and disappointment together. I didn't know what to do with the mad mumbling ghost but when he went I found myself frightened that he wouldn't come back.

'Right,' I said. 'Good. Well, let's have another drink.'

We did. Several. I got Graham chatting about the new lot of furniture he'd bought. I told him Olivia's plans for William's place, and he pricked up his ears when he heard about the possibility of 'retail' going on there. I showed him the faxes from Tucker's girls – pictures of the animals they had seen, and Idris' excellent representation of a wildebeest's rear.

To me it felt a good approximation of normality. But as he left with arms loaded with baskets he said, 'I think you badly need to get away, Myfanwy. I think you should go.'

'What?'

'To New York. I think you need a break. You don't look well. I'll look after anything you need doing here.'

I nodded and smiled. But David and New York were in someone else's life. The chairs, the cabin, the winter empty beach and Peter's dictionary-spouting shade were all I had in mine.

*   *   *

By the time Lucy was wandering around my workshop I'd had another week of insomnia, starvation and 'mangotoffee, mozzarella, miffymopp'. She asked about the rush, the driftwood, the split stone, my diamond cutter, my jigsaw, my precious perfect chisels, gougers, planes all laid out in rows.

In my strange state I felt porous, with all my tools, materials, products, and Peter too, pushed into every hole. The two fears; that she would see Peter, and that *she* wouldn't and *I* would, towered up inside me like a pair of adders fighting in spring.

She sat in the chairs and said 'Wow!', and walked to the one where Peter sat.

'Can I look at this one?' she said, resting her hand on the cloth covering Peter's head.

'No. Next time maybe. It went a bit. Wrong.'

'Oh, go on. I'm sure it's still great. I bet your idea of wrong is like amazing really!' She was already pulling off the cloth, and staring down at the top of Peter's head. I was impaled to the moment. Stuck like a midge on treacle. The slippery satin of the cloth slithered off the chair. Peter turned to the window as if presenting Lucy with his best profile. The dress was now draped around his shoulders. He sat cross-legged still, but naked. The blue baler twine was wrapped about the most spectacular erection he'd ever had, with the cowrie balanced on its apex like the blob on the top of the Post Office Tower. 'Tango, Tobermory, Totnes,' he said in a commanding flat voice, like a magician reciting a spell in Latin, 'Transylvania, Tartary, tits!'

'Oh, my God!' Lucy said and clutched at her belly through the draping layers of woollen jerseys made to fit someone with the dimensions of Cormoran.

Peter's voice rose, he stood up on the chair, arms wide, cowrie teetering, 'Tombola, trigonometry, tuxedo, Tanzania!'

Lucy gave a little shriek. 'Oh God,' she said again, holding her stomach now with both hands. She sat down suddenly on the floor, curled into a ball looking down at a point just between her splayed thighs. I couldn't breathe properly but I managed to speak, in a tiny hoarse voice that was audible only because Peter had shut up.

'Can you see him?'

She didn't hear me. She was panting quietly and very pale. I crouched beside her, the hairs on Peter's bare legs just inches from my face.

'It's all right. There's no need to be afraid,' I said unsurely. Peter was my responsibility I had to reassure her no matter how bad I felt myself. She smiled up at me.

'No, I know. I've never been worried about going into labour. All my mum's babies came very quickly. And I'm in such an amazing place. This must be on a very powerful ley line too! It's just a bit early, that's all.' I stared at her as if she'd just spoken to me in Japanese.

'What?'

'I'm in labour. It's due in three weeks. Just when you showed me the chair, I got a huge pain. My waters have gone, I think.'

Now that I looked at her I could see she was very pregnant. With her long skinny legs, her big clothes, and my preoccupations I hadn't noticed.

She was panting again. The contractions were clearly very close together. She was going to be like that woman on the *Princess* whose baby popped like a melon pip against the door of the shower one morning off Mahe. I looked at Lucy's closed eyes, slightly damp lids and shiny forehead. A baby was going to be born right next to the big hairy legs and misbehaving penis of my dead husband. I tried to think of a way to make him move, or get dressed at least. I could try and cover him with the cloth but how do you drape satin over what must be thin air?

Lucy was tugging at my sleeve. 'Can you get me my birthing crystal? It's in my bag in the car?'

'Right. Of course.'

It took me a little while to find her bag. When I came back from the car she was screaming.

'Phone a fucking ambulance!' she said and flung the red stone against the wall with amazing force.

When Peter had been dying I'd wondered how an ambulance would ever find us fast enough if he collapsed. With Lucy's screams in my ears I called the ambulance and the surgery. I've no idea what I said. It must have been more coherent than I imagined because the GP and the emergency medics did both arrive. Eventually.

Peter was still standing erect in every sense on the chair when I got back to Lucy. I cleared a space, a little distance away from him and spread a tarpaulin on the floor. I got Lucy onto it. She was starting to be senseless with pain and the work her body was doing to expel the baby in what seemed like a bit of a rush. I couldn't remember anything about the first aid aspects of delivering children. But I did at least work out that giving birth with your knickers on wasn't easy.

I helped her get stripped for battle, out of the soaked layers of skirt, and huge jerseys. I put two old T-shirts of mine on her top half. I didn't dare leave her side, so the workshop stayed cold, without me to attend to stoking the fire. But Lucy was burning with the effort of birth. There wasn't much of a break from pain it seemed. I'd always thought contractions had gaps, where women lay back and looked strained but perfect.

In spite of all Tucker's birth horror stories I'd retained this image that all you had to do was lift your broderie anglaise nightie, and pop, there you were, a clean round baby. Lucy lay on her side and clutched my arm in hers and screamed. The tarpaulin was awash with blood and water and shit. I swished it away from her as best I could with whatever I could reach with the hand that wasn't holding hers.

'I've got to kneel,' she slurred, after the only little lull in what seemed like days. I thought I heard the sound of the ambulance siren passing by the right turn, completely oblivious, on up the road. Stupid bastards, I thought fiercely.

'Hold me,' said Lucy, 'behind. No behind.' She shouted at me until I got it right. Her kneeling up, me supporting her with my arms under hers. I had to stand with my legs wide apart, her folded calves between them, her back against my torso. I felt all the huge shuddering effort go through her. When she screamed I wasn't sure if it was me or her. She shook as if she would shake herself apart and screamed as if the world would shatter.

Then she said, 'It's coming.' The distance between her vagina and the floor was more than a foot. I moved quickly, leaving her swaying unsupported. I crouched behind Lucy and caught the head, the shoulders, the toothpaste squeezed body, wet, slippery and red in my bare hands. The little girl writhed in fury at being born and the fat umbilical cord moved as if it still had its own life. Lucy's backside quivered over my arms as I passed the baby back between her mother's legs and up to the waiting hands and breasts at the front of the body she'd just vacated. I had enough energy just, to shout 'In here' to the ambulance men and the doctor.

'Triceratops, tumult, tetanus,' chanted Peter slowly as they moved in with the stretcher.

I saw Lucy safe into the ambulance still in the T-shirts but wrapped in hospital blankets with the crumpled little face tucked under her own. What a strange and surprising bond we had forged between us.

'Come and see me, when you can,' I said.

'I will. Thank you.' Lucy's voice was stretched thin over exhaustion and exhilaration.

'You did it. I just watched.'

She closed her eyes and smiled, 'I'm going to care for all your dad's stuff,' she said, 'it's going to be fine.' As the doors of the ambulance came between us she lifted her head as she remembered one more essential thing to say. 'But you must tell that man in there, in the workshop, to go away.'

I stood, not really seeing the ambulance draw into the drizzle. Her words suddenly concentrated my world to a single point, the way a needle piercing the flesh focuses all experience onto a square millimetre of pain. Amidst all the dark messy tangle of frenzied working, dreams of craft's Utopia and somehow getting Peter back from the fairyland of tumultuous triceratops and non-being, a tiny white laser-point of light came on. I let it blind me to everything except shoving clothes in a bag, grabbing my passport and wallet and locking the doors.

I called Graham from the airport.

'I changed my ticket. I'm going to New York early.'

'Thank God for that. Thank God you're getting away. You were going mad in that cabin.'

'I know. Can you keep an eye on things. The chairs mostly. The key's in a child's pink welly in the old chest in the garage. The details of the gallery are by the phone. If you call them they'll arrange to pick up the finished chairs.'

'Righto. No problem.'

'Thanks, Graham. I'd better go. Flight's been called.'

'Right. Right then. Have a good time. Rest, you know. Let me know when you're coming back. You do know that I hope you come back? Come and see me and the piano. I'm learning carols for Christmas.'

Chapter Fifteen

All the plants in David's father's apartment were carnivorous. I spent my first afternoon in New York with them. They waited on the deep window-sills and gathered in the little conservatory twenty floors above the traffic. Most were pitcher plants, green flutes savagely spotted with white and red. They looked like the rearing heads of venomous snakes or the glasses that witches use to drink a virgin's blood. Too clever to bother simply with photosynthesis, they'd ditched their place in nature and turned to darker pursuits.

The pitchers weren't the worst. It was the sundews I really hated. Spiked all along their leaves and dotted with jewels of fluid that caught the light. They just pretended to be still. But really they could move. Not honest and fast like an animal. But slow. Taking all the torturing time they wanted to wrap around a struggling victim caught on one of the sticky diamonds.

David had told me sometime that Richard had dropped his old family's nickname of Dick when he came to America and reinvented himself. He was *Rick* now. As I wandered around the bright clinical spaces of the apartment I began to feel how everything about him was 'Rick'. The beautiful clothes hanging in the closets. Quiet colours and a little crumpled so as not to shout the name on their label too loud. The aesthete's decor with the dark-stained floors and the square clean-lined furniture.

I guessed his friends were 'Rick' too. Not too young to be loud, nor too old to be unfashionable. They'd come in a nice balanced array of tasteful professions and personalities, they'd turn up at the right moment and always leave just a little soon. David, the grown up son, David the dancer, David the feather charmed must have fitted in very nicely to the universe of 'Rick'. So much so that it was Jed, Rick's driver and 'general factotum' (as my father would have said), who'd come to meet me at the airport.

I was searching the faces crowded at the arrival barrier, desperate for the big 'Close Encounter' eyes and the velveteen head. Instead I found a stranger holding a card – bright red and adorned with a rim of stick-on silver hearts – with my name on it. He wore the look that old people have when they think they may have just missed a bus. He was too small, fat and vulnerable looking to be a New Yorker. The fact that the person meeting me was neither David nor American was very worrying under the circumstances: I had spent the flight struggling to diagnose reality. At one point I became momentarily convinced that the clouds were just an extension of in-flight entertainment. David and Peter became interchangeably real. So did this harassed looking non-Yank mean that David wasn't real? Or that America wasn't real? Or wasn't really populated by Americans?

Whatever he signified, from the fictional quality of True Love to the non-existence of the 'US of A', the man seemed disproportionately pleased to meet me. When he spoke I realised why.

'Hi, Myfanwy? I'm Jed. I'm Rick's gofer. David sent me.' As I'd arrived it meant he could stop holding up the card bearing my name, Jed was from Liverpool and men from Kirby didn't stand around with poofy signs waiting for girls.

'Pleased. To meet you.' Groggy from the plane, my high-speed decision and two weeks in the almost exclusive company of a zombie I was a little ketchupped.

Jed took my bag. 'Is this all?'

I nodded. It was just a small bag and looking at it hanging at the end of Jed's solid overcoated arm I couldn't remember what was in it. At least something warm I hoped. By the looks of Jed's layers of clothes, outside it was like the Ross Ice Shelf in June.

He steered me out to a waiting car, through swirls of faces. Outside it was so grey and dull we seemed to have walked into a monochrome version of the world, an end point of entropy where all colour and heat had drained away. It *was* like the Ross Ice Shelf, complete with a sad trickle of snow, like the last few flakes at the bottom of a packet. Jed folded me into the back of a shiny dark car. The door clunked and the world became warm and coloured again; velvety, dark red seats, russet mock wood, blue cigarette smoke.

'Bleedin' snow. You'd think they'd never seen it, like. But snows every year. And still they're surprised. Even Liverpool council can grit the roads in time! Oh. Nearly forgot.' Jed plunged a hand inside his overcoat, a garment so marvellously capacious that he could have been concealing the entire cast of the Bolshoi in there. 'David said to give you this.'

I read the letter as Jed drove. Pulling the Technicolor car through the blank grey world outside. Condensation misted the windows, and the windscreen wipers cut the settling flakes.

'You're here, you're here! You're really here!' the letter shouted. 'Oh, my love, I can hardly believe it. I'm in a huge warehouse with my father and a ridiculously large number of other people. I didn't really know how huge a feat of organisation it would all be until we started shooting. We should finish here at around eight thirty. Rick – Dad – is dying to meet you. I suggest we meet up at Marana – a restaurant near here at nine. Jed will come and get you from the apartment. Longing to see you and hold you, among other things. So get some sleep in now if you can. Love love love. D.'

'Good job your plane got here when it did,' said Jed. 'Another hour and they'll close the airport. Pathetic. They get ten times this snow in Chicago and nobody gives a bugger.'

* * *

It was a long, long time since I'd been in New York. Peter took me there one June after an emergency stand-in trip to the Caribbean. We stayed in an apartment in Lower Manhattan with a college friend and his wife who'd never quite made it on the city's writers' scene. The place was full of crumbling piles of books – reviewed, about to be reviewed – and magazines which might one day take one of their articles. Life had moved to the centres of all their rooms as the stacks of publications moved in, towering and teetering from the edges.

It was impossible to get to any of the windows to admire the view from God only knew how many floors up. It had been so long since the windows had been looked through that they had acquired a yellowish layer of dust, the dry sputum of so many cantankerous old volumes. An atmosphere of competitive neurosis pervaded everything, including the towels. The weather was muggy, even the top of the Empire State Building afforded no view, just a sea of intangible fug.

The only things I remember from the four-day trip are the books falling on us as we fucked in their sofa bed and the fact that I left my favourite shirt on the back of a chair in a diner on what I'd remembered as being Fifth Avenue.

We drove through the packed nervous traffic in the feeble snow, and Jed's seamless guide book commentary slipped past my ears like a draught. I was back in the dusty dimness of Peter's friends' apartment with its smell of unattended books, so at odds with what I'd thought of as the essence of New York: neon signs, stilettos and bagels.

'Here we are!' said Jed, pulling into the underground parking for Rick's swanky apartment building. As we swooped down into the fluorescent-lit dark I realised I'd only thought as far as leaving where I'd come from. I didn't really know where I'd arrived or even who I'd really come to visit.

* * *

David was late. I'd pulled apart rolls and sipped into the second half of the bottle by the time I saw him, shouldering his way deftly through the waiters and between the tiny rickety tables packed too tightly into the long corridor-like dining room. Finally real. Finally solid in what seemed like rather more than just three dimensions. More possible than back-projected clouds or a nation full of scouses putting on Texan accents.

As I watched him weaving towards me, his body graceful and humorous at the same time, the images of Peter – on my bedroom floor, adorned with string and seashells in my work-shop – went flat and mute. They stopped shouting in my head, and the volume of the real, the present flipped up. Here was David. My lover, eyes hot as a well-laid barbecue and that divine body only just beneath the surface of clothes. Very close now. This was why I'd come.

I'd been sandwiched into the corner, pinned to my seat by the table, so I couldn't get up and hold him. He leaned into me, snaking an arm around my torso and almost lifting me from my seat.

'You're wearing a dress. I've hardly ever seen you in a dress.'

'It's practically the only thing I brought with me. I left in a hurry.'

He sat down opposite me. The table was minute, hardly room for the wine. Our knees overlapped underneath it. He slipped one hand underneath the cloth and under the hem of my skirt. The other I held in both my own.

'I didn't think you'd come. I thought I'd lost you. Or never had you even. Why didn't you call me back? Why did you come now?'

I didn't want to even think about home. How could I explain? *Seeing my dead husband, mostly naked, appearing in my house wasn't too bad. But when a woman was in labour on my workshop floor and she saw him too, I knew I needed a little break?* No.

'It doesn't matter. It's too much to tell. I'm here now.' He struggled. He wanted more explanation. Probably rather more reassurance too. But he got by without it, smiled even.

'I'm not hungry,' he said, 'and if I sit here with my hand on your leg any longer I might just have to fuck you on this ridiculous table. Can we get a cab to Rick's place?'

'Yeah. And I'll tell you on the way how a woman gave birth in my workshop.'

'Jesus! That sounds good. I'll need some fairly substantial distraction. It's fifteen blocks to get home.'

'What about Rick?'

'He sends his apologies, he had to go and view rushes.' Yeah, and sacrifice a few new borns for his plants. 'See you at breakfast he says.'

Good. I wasn't anxious to make chit chat that night with the master of the pitchers and sundews that had watched me, waiting for a false move all afternoon, whilst I'd been alone with nothing else for company than my last sleeping pill.

David's room in Rick's flat was blank and almost the only room without menacing pitchers or sundews. A floor-level bed and a huge built-in cupboard: it could have been featureless without the wall of glass, floor to ceiling, a window onto the black space between the great buildings. Lights swam in lines along the bottom of the black and dotted the verticals with yellow.

That first night the snow turned to rain and smeared the outside of the window, leaking the lights into shapes like inkblots. No part of Peter was there. Nothing of him had caught up with me, no watching eye, no creeping fingertips. There was no third party involved in what David and I did.

'Take me where I can't think,' said David.

I was a light burning in the black. No past. No future. Just a 'now' of the senses.

I met Rick well before breakfast. I walked into him at three a.m. outside the bathroom, and thought, as my totally naked body collided with his, 'Oh, it must be Rick!' But when I opened my eyes in the twilight, I saw naked Rick didn't fit with 'Rick'. Not the sinisterly youthful and gym-toned suavity I had expected. His body was one big inconsistency. It didn't tie in with the decor, the clothes or the friends I had imagined for him. Huge, shuffling, ten to two feet, legs like knotted drinking straws topped with a lumpy sagging pear of a body and more straws for arms. I couldn't even detect a penis and it wasn't that dark.

His genes did not contribute much to David's construction I thought. Except the ones for charm. The fact that we were both as bare as shelled peas he took completely in his stride.

'Myfanwy!' he exclaimed, in a delighted whisper. I don't know who else apart from David was asleep in the apartment, but whispering at three a.m. seems appropriate in any case. He shook my hand. 'So marvellous to meet you.' His voice was a kind of Oxbridge Washington cross, but with a warmth that Tucker's stories hadn't led me to expect. This was, after all, Richard the bastard. First cousin to the kind of Richard who had little children murdered in towers.

'I'm so glad you're here. David believed you'd forgotten him.' His manner was something like a slightly more worldly academic — a person who might keep *The Peloponnesian Wars* by the loo but also know what Ginger Spice did next.

'No, I'm no good at forgetting.'

'No? I'm a little too good at it myself. So I'm pleased to find you here. Are you sleepless?' he asked, 'I have some excellent pills . . .'

'No. Just going to the bathroom.'

'Just so. Of course. Well, see you at breakfast. Ta ta.'

Ta ta? Why had Rick constructed some of himself from forties radio scripts? Shuffling feet at odd angles, he toddled down the corridor waving a huge bony hand over his shoulder, his buttocks showing their contractions with a slow deliberateness. I lay awake for a long time thinking about the man who'd left his young son to cope with a manic depressive mother and about that bottom, slow and human and somehow sweetly self-deprecating.

It was strange how much that single little intimacy of a naked mid-night wee influenced how I reacted to Rick. At breakfast the next morning he was back in character with his Armani soft suit, gently fussing over his plants. But I knew that imperfect body was underneath the cloth, keeping a check on his ego. It made me inclined to like him, even without the layer of intelligent charm.

'You're welcome on set if you'd like to come. You may be bored,' said Rick on that first morning over a cup of coffee.

'I'll come. I want to see David working.'

So David, his reacquired father and I went downtown in a big blue car with a refugee scouse for a driver, an air of camaraderie amongst us quite out of proportion with our degree of acquaintanceship. It established a pattern, so that afterwards I could say: 'Every morning Jed would pick the three of us up . . .' as if it was a routine that we'd followed for years, like the civil servant sitting in the same carriage of the tube from the September after his Oxford first until his double bypass.

David and Rick sat in the back and talked about the shoot, Jed drove and gave me more running commentary about the history of his adopted city. I tuned out all the words until they were just a pleasant cushion of sound. I looked out of the windows at the buildings rising on either side like something created in expectation of a wholly different scale of human existence. The city had a completely un-human feel, like a mountain landscape, or ruins on Mars left by some alien race of giants. It made me miss the beach and the Peter's Pimples less. The humans here were improvising in a wilderness, like Innuit in the ice fields or Yanomami in the Amazon.

I had absolutely no curiosity about the geography of the city. Bundled in the hot vehicle, in borrowed outdoor layers, I accepted the daily journeys like a baby in a car seat. Here was the big grey building with the blue neons, after that was the shop with the bright green coat in the window, then the wide road, like a hat brim. Once or twice in traffic I spotted other outsiders like me, looking up from the windows of their cars at the city, with the same face as they'd look up at the Grand

Canyon, or Ansel Adams' Yosemite. We scooted along the ravines, out onto some freeways then dived back into a landscape of faceless boxes, cheap warehouses and deserted straight roads.

And then we arrived at a huge slate blue metal box into which I could have fitted the beach, the dunes, William's track and house and the earthwork and still have had room for a drive-in McDonald's and a couple of all-night petrol stations.

Inside it was a world. A series of sets – interiors of houses, dance studios, stages – built to represent the twenty-third century. In reality of course, more a reflection of the designer's preoccupations in the present, like the silver suits we were all to be wearing by the year 2000 according to the sci-fi directors of the 1970s. The sets were just the heart of the world inside the warehouse, around them were the other organs, Portakabin dressing rooms and make-up rooms, huge metal cages with props and lights and fat cables coiled like pythons, all with their attendant humans already busy. I followed David, weaving again like a thief through the casbah. Rick had gone in the opposite direction to fulfil his role as controlling god of this strange universe.

Between two Portakabins, by a canteen van, a flock of little white tables had gathered. Some witty props person had put two big artificial palm trees at their centre so the scene had an odd jaunty holiday resort feel. Twenty dancers were getting coffee, stretching or sitting slouched horribly on the little wire chairs. They were all beautiful. Even under the ugly jogging pants and ripped sweatshirts it was obvious. What wasn't obvious was their gender. They all had long hair, and bone structure to kill for, perfect skins in colours from magnolia to midnight.

'Are they girls or boys?' I whispered to David.

'Some of each. They were cast for their androgynous looks, it's pretty striking isn't it? I forget sometimes which is which!' As David dropped the old suitcase that passed for kitbag and document wallet onto a tin table, they all stopped what they were doing and turned towards him. I saw the switch inside him flick, the surface of feathers now as tight and shiny as a fish's scales. I sat back and watched as David beguiled, waking them up to their own desire to dance, reminding them that amidst all the repeating and fussing of filming, dancing was what they were there to do.

He told them the day's schedule, which sequences would be rehearsed and shot, when, where and in what costumes. I didn't notice him glance at his notes once. It was all in his head; every choreographed step, every shot. When he ran the warm-up and rehearsal, he used his whole physical and emotional self. He cared for every body in the room as he'd learned to care for his own.

If one of them had a problem with a step, with a stretch he stood very close, talking very softly, giving one hundred per cent attention. He watched them: assessing; sympathetic; precise; but without any shadow of envy at their greater suppleness and stamina. I could see what a long way he'd come since he'd fallen at my feet on that sand spit in the summer. He'd found his new way to be.

I trailed him like a ghost all day. I lurked at the edges of big sprung board rehearsal spaces, sets awash with lights, fringed with fretful technicians and governed by the presence of Rick, standing intent in a little pool of space and silence. David never lost his cool or his concentration and his dancers drew the same calm and lightness out of him. I began to wonder what this talented saint was doing in love with me.

At the end of the day we fell back into the blue car, and drove up town in the sparkly wet darkness. This time no one spoke except Jed.

'Greenwich Village, now you've heard of that haven't you? Did used to be a village outside the city . . .'

Rick and David were too tired to go out to eat and too hungry to wait for a take-out to be delivered. We foraged in Rick's freezer. Its contents reminded me of William – an eclectic selection of meals for one, balti prawns, Lebanese chicken, macrobiotic tofu — we all stood watching our meals go round in the microwave spotlight then ate perched on stools at the perfect black slate worktop. The tiredness of father and son was like treacle in the air around us. It made them affectionate and giggly as if they'd smoked a joint. We found a huge tub of ice cream too; Rick dolloped it out with glee.

'Your mother and I used to eat a whole block of Wall's Neapolitan ice cream out of the cardboard as a treat when you were a baby and we were broke. One pack, two spoons and the radio on in the kitchen so that if you began crying we wouldn't hear.'

David laughed. A real laugh. Rick was lucky. David had done all the work required to allow him to feel able to laugh over his father's affectionate reminiscence of the wife he'd left. I wondered what Rick had done to be able to reminisce at all about David's dead mother. Some emotional sleight of hand? A conversion to sin-confess-sin Catholicism? No, this was New York; Rick's easy ability with his past was the product of expensive therapy.

'This isn't too much of a vacation for you,' said Rick, over a bowl of double choc and raisin ice cream. 'All you've seen is the inside of three things: an apartment, a car and a warehouse.'

'It's a different world. So it is a holiday. I love seeing David work.' I couldn't help sounding like a besotted sixteen year old with nothing in her life but her teddy bear collection and her GCSEs. After a day in the warehouse as a spectator I felt that I didn't even have a teddy to talk about.

'Yeah. He's rather good isn't he?' Rick looked at David with the sort of open approval that matched the bare buttocks but not the slate worktop and the sundews.

David was basking in his back pay, fifteen years' worth of fatherly encouragement in one big dose. He said nothing, just looked back, like a sunbather under the lamp.

'Well, I'm going to commune a little with my sarrecenias then I'm going to bed. We have another sickeningly early start tomorrow. You can lie in Myfanwy, then go shopping. I thought all women came to New York to shop.' He didn't wait for any denial, just tootled out of the kitchen, all the spring in his step saved until the next day. 'Good night.'

We went to bed and I closed the door behind us feeling newly self-conscious of the consummate professional I'd seen all day. But the overlapping charm scales that had held David in all day fell off at once. He kicked the wall. I noticed there was a mark there already.

'Fucking hell. This bollocks film stuff drives me nuts. I could have broken that fucking cameraman's neck when he asked for that eighth retake. They were knackered.'

He crackled and boiled for half an hour and I came and lay beside him and held him and felt that I knew a bit more now about this funny layered mixture of man.

'Let's have a shower,' I said.

'Carwash, you mean.'

'Carwash. Mmm. In memory of Jules and Vicky.'

The next day was the same and the next. Standing on the edges and watching was something that almost everyone on the set had to do sometimes. So they began to talk to me. The make-up girls and boys, the dressers, the lighting lads, the electricians and carpenters, warmed and melded in the autoclave of a movie set into a little improvised community. I was invited into Porta-kabins for cups of herbal tea, and offered cold Coke from the back of props cages. When they found I'd run from Wales with almost no clothes, people came the next day with a skirt, or a sweater or a pair of shoes that might fit. In two days I had a new persona constructed from a short black cashmere skirt, a blue sleeveless turtle neck and a pair of spike heel mock crocodile shoes.

I spoke to more people in a day than in five years of hermit life at the cabin. And I loved it. I didn't ketchup, I didn't stutter,

I talked as easily as I had to the pacs on my first ship. But mostly I listened. I heard life stories, sob stories, hard luck stories, I heard who was going to bed with who and what everyone thought about it. I heard who would like to be going to bed with whom. I heard the universal obsessions of city dwellers: transport, crime and getting an apartment. I found myself absorbed into another safe little world cut loose from everything at home but held, complete and contained as an egg.

First the ship, then the cabin and now this. I told myself that this was my future; I was in it. David's world where I could just forget about Peter, William, Olivia, Lucy, Graham, the chairs, the gallery. I could coddle myself in this cosy little world for ever.

David fed my escapist fantasy by loving having me constantly within reach. Every break he would come and twine an arm around my waist and introduce me proudly to yet another set of people. If the dancers were stood down for half an hour or more, he'd catch my eye if I was near, or come and find me — having my tarot cards read or my hair French plaited. He didn't say anything. We'd just go back to his dressing room. The walls and floor were flimsy, they shook at a footstep so we had to be more gentle than we wanted. All the same, one afternoon the door fell off.

Everyone knew, but we were the Mascot Lovers, the director's son and his aging beauty girl friend. It appealed to everyone's sense of a movie fairy tale.

Then one night, over a table in Marana the size of an ashtray, Rick said, 'You know more about what goes on in my set than I do. I think it's about time we put you to work.'

'I'm on vacation, Rick. Remember!'

'No, I'm serious. I have a favour to ask you. David showed me some photos of your work.'

'What photos, David?' My chairs were from that other life. I didn't want to think about them.

'Don't be cross, love. You had some duplicate slides remember — the ones for the gallery? I borrowed them. I wanted to show Rick what you did.' David's feather scales were up, defensive and shiny. He was very uncomfortable about something.

Rick meanwhile seemed to have developed buns of steel. I imagined now a Schwarzenegger body beneath the grey fuzzy jacket. There was a tone of iron in his voice.

'Whatever.' He was anxious to ask his favour. David and my relationship could wait. 'The pieces – the chairs – are amazing. I need them.' Rick said 'need' as if it were the ultimate imperative, as if it were the one statement in all the world that could make anything possible, compulsory. 'I need six. They are perfect for a scene I want to shoot next week. It's our last one here before we do the exteriors in California. Can you help? I'll pay you handsomely of course.'

'All my chairs are in the UK. And the ones in the photos are all sold. I don't have access to them.'

'You don't need to get one you've already made. I want you to make me six chairs. Or rather, supervise the making.'

'By next week!'

'Yes.'

'It takes at least a week to make *one*. It takes a whole year to gather the right materials. The wood and the stone come off beaches in Wales, Rick! Where am I supposed to find driftwood and rush in Manhattan?'

'You don't need to make a real one. I have these fabulous model makers. They'll copy anything. Anything. They can make a Louis-Quinze commode from a Hershey wrapper. I want you to supervise them. That's all.'

'I don't know that it's possible.'

'It's possible. These model makers are astounding. They can copy any three-dimensional object. They have your photos but they'll do it better with your advice. Please.'

I could feel a cold tide of reality creeping up my legs, but I still said 'OK.' I didn't feel I had a choice in the face of David's round eyes pleading at me, and Rick's requisition.

'Oh, great. Great! Jed'll take you down there in the morning.'
'You assumed I'd say yes?'
'I'm an optimist, Myfanwy. It's how I get through my life.'

It was another, much smaller, warehouse with a selection of vehicles outside that would have looked happier in the Waltons than on a light industrial estate in the Bronx. Inside, it was divided into a series of open plan workshops like giant cattle stalls. In one, a stiletto ten feet high was being painted glittery purple. In another a fat guy in a check shirt was gluing the teeth into a dinosaur skull, and in the last, two women were running fifty-dollar bills off a metal printing plate.

A skinny, earnest looking black man with receding hair and little metal glasses came and shook my hand.

'Myfanwy. Hi. I'm Den. I'm so glad you could come. We're a little stuck. We don't seem to be able to get the same textures and feel into the chairs.'

Stuck on the first day didn't sound hopeful. But when I followed Den to meet his colleague Martin, also earnest and receding but white, I saw it wasn't their first day.

They had already built the basics of the six chairs. They couldn't possibly have done so much since the day before. Rick had been more than optimistic. All of them were the large nest-like designs. They hadn't been built from scratch, rather the appearance had been superimposed on a polystyrene frame.

'How long have you been working on the chairs.'

'When did we get the photos?' Blow-ups of the pictures David had given Rick were pinned up on their fabulously messy notice board, along with two pink slinkys, plastic flowers, hotel bills and taxi cab cards.

'Maybe ten days?'

Ten days ago, before I arrived Rick had decided to use my designs. He could lift them, copy them and, a hermit on a Welsh beach, I would never know. There would be no extra cost involved, no awkward copyright disputes. He must have been quite pleased when David despaired of my arrival. Did David know, I wondered? Had he made his father admit that he needed my chairs? Or if Den and Martin hadn't got 'stuck' would I ever have known my designs were being stolen.

I stood staring at the pictures of my chairs. They were worth something. It meant something to make them. It meant me, myself for myself. And I had been prepared to leave them behind. To enter into David's world and simply be a part of it as I had entered Peter's and become a part of his. I had been ready to drop my identity for the sake of escaping from Peter's memory. If I valued it all so poorly how could Rick be blamed for being ready to steal my ideas as if they were nothing, as if they didn't matter? I stood and stared, furious with myself and furious with Rick. Cold, awake and finally out of the dream I'd been wandering in. I must have looked as if I was about to shout at poor Den and Martin because they came and stood beside me, slightly stooped like cringing puppies.

'We really love your work,' said Den.

'Yes, it's extraordinary. Feels all wrong to be making it of plastic.'

'And it looks all wrong too. Come on, you two, we are going to search for the proper materials and make these chairs as real as we can.' Rick was going to get his money's-worth and I was going to get a Hollywood movie-sized advert for my work, and get paid for it.

I led those poor guys into bits of New York they never even knew existed. They knew back alleys and lots, lumber yards and rubbish tips, craft shops and warehouses, reclamation yards and stonemasons, but for every one they knew I made them find two more. At the end of it all we had wood that their expertise could distress into something from a beach, stone that could be cut to pebble proportions and best of all twelve bundles of real rush. It cost a fortune but it was good. At the end of two very very long days, I had assembled in Den and Martin's warehouse some real foragings, something with more bite than plastic and rafia.

'I don't know, Myfanwy,' Den looked at the haul and bit his nails, 'I don't know if Rick will stand this cost.'

'You wait till I've finished with him. He'll offer you extra. Early start tomorrow, guys. We've got a mountain of work on.'

I was plugged back into my own life, through the wood and stone and rush. I had repossessed the ideas that Rick had planned to take without notice, the identity I had been prepared to throw away. But I might have known that as I'd come back to myself I had to come back to Peter too. As I got out of the cab and paid the surly driver, I saw him disappearing down an alley with my old dress around his neck like a scarf, and I'd run fifty feet after him calling before I remembered again: Peter's still dead. Or rather undead and unburied.

I paced the lobby a little after that until I'd killed all desire to go out in search of Peter's shade. I needed a steady heart to face David and Rick. I'd slept in the guest room the night before and left them a note of excuse to avoid speaking at either the end or beginning of the day. Now, I guessed they'd both be home and I wanted to be feeling strong and sane when I walked in. At last I took the lift to the twentieth floor and found them eating a Chinese take-out in the living room with TV on. Without the clothes and the Italian leather sofa they could have been Bart and Homer.

'Can I switch this off?' I asked, switching it off. 'Den and Martin are great. They've been working on the chairs for some time. Ten days they said.'

David shifted slightly in his chair turning a millimetre away from his father beside him. There was at least one answer: David had known all about the chairs all the time. Rick said nothing.

'It was the rush look they got stuck with. You can't fake it. So we went and bought five hundred dollars' worth today. Is that OK?'

'Fine.'

'And I'm right in thinking if they hadn't hit a problem I wouldn't have known about you copying my designs?'

'I understood you were coming on vacation. That you wouldn't want to work. And I forgot. Once I gave the pictures to Den, I just forgot about it.' Rick looked up from his knees, sweetly innocent, charm on maximum. 'I'm good at forgetting.'

'And I'm working on my forgetting. So I won't say another word. My fee is six thousand dollars. That's three days' work. I want a credit and I want two VHS video copies of all the shots of the chairs.'

'OK.'

'I'm going to bed.'

'I'm coming too.' The look that David gave his father was the other answer I needed. He'd made Rick come clean. The 'I told you so, pay up and shut up!' was all there.

We closed the bedroom door. David came and sat behind me on the bed as I looked out into the dark, and the swarming lights, wondering if Peter's face would swim up to me again.

'Myfanwy. What can I say?'

'You don't have to say anything. He just tried something on with me and he didn't get away with it. It's not your doing.'

'I would have told you, if he hadn't.'

'Would you?'

'Of course.'

'I don't know, David. I think you have a lot of catching up to do with Rick. You need his approval. You won't always. But you do now. That's why you didn't tell me before.'

'Nothing's more important to me than you.'

'Not dancing? Not what you do on that set every day? Not your Dad? I can't replace all that. It's all important. Not one bit more than another. That's why you were prepared to give my chairs to your father.'

'I would have told you!'

'It's OK. I'm fine about it. You were in a very difficult

position. He's a tough customer. He did something sneaky and I caught him. It doesn't matter. It's been good for me anyway.'

'How?'

'It reminded me of *my* life. Of foraging. We did foraging today, Den and Martin and me. In dirty junk yards and posh shops. There was no wind, and no sea and no sky. I like my life in Wales. I like the plans for William's place. I can't live here with you and be myself. I'd just be being a part of you. Remember what you said that first night we met? You have to "do" to be alive? I can't be with you here and "do" my life. I followed Peter around the world for ten years. I didn't "do". I was a part of him. Now I want to be me. I need to "do" being me.'

'So this is over? All those nights, it didn't mean anything to you?'

'It's not over. It's just not going to be the way you imagined it. It doesn't have to be all or nothing.'

David's alien eyes filled. But he didn't turn away. He held my hands more tightly. The anorexic cherub that stringily presides over moments of insight hovered briefly over mid-Manhattan.

'OK', said David, still looking open-eyed at me, 'you're going back then. To Wales.'

'Yeah. I can see now what I need to do. Finish things off.'

'So you will come back?'

'Sometime. But I don't want to live here.'

'Do you believe that I love you?'

'I didn't. You're so marvellous and alive and magical some-times, it seemed impossible. I do now. But I can't be all you need. You can't live my life and I can't live yours.'

'Do you love me?'

'I think so. But even if I was sure it wouldn't change things.'

'I want you to be sure. I want your love. I want to have children with you. I want to make a life. A family.'

'Maybe I'll want that too. But whatever we do, it won't be like you plan. It'll be something, it'll be good but different. Not what you expect.'

'You're asking so much.'
'I know. I'm sorry.'
'That's OK.'

Sometime in the night I woke with David spooned along my back and his arms around my chest.

Peter lay on his side very close to me in his hospital gown, curled foetus-like, his arms cuddling himself. He looked in possession of his marbles but he said sadly, 'Mollymork, Manitoba, marketing.'

'We're going home soon,' I told him, 'to bury you.'

He looked right at me then, like the night he inspected my ribs for signs of bee legs, and he blew a tiny kiss. Lips pursed, eyes smiling. Then he closed his eyes and went to sleep.

Chapter Sixteen

I went from the chemist to the public lavatory in the car park then back to the post office. I put the little plastic stick with the two telling blue lines in an air mail package with a note scribbled on a postcard of Newport beach.

'See? You already have some of what you want. See you Christmas Eve. I've booked your flight and the train. Hang on. M.'

It was all I felt I could say. I enclosed the instructions for the test too, so that he would at least understand what he was seeing. I had too much to do to think about saying or doing more. Or even feeling more, all I could think of was my 'finishing things'.

The removal men were already there when I got to the cabin, stamping around on the frozen crusty sand and breathing white into the frosty air. A tall quiet lad with crew cut blond hair and a fat mouthy foreman who swaggered up to me belly first.

'Where shall we start then, love?'

'In the workshop, then the store room and garage. Everything's to go except the firewood.'

'What about the house? Furniture, beds and that?'

'No. It's all staying.'

'Any chance of a brew, love?' he said, ogling my breasts as I zipped up my jacket over a sweater. He managed to be lascivious, rude and patronising at the same time. But it served a purpose; I marched to the door of the workshop grated with irritation, so that my attention was a little distracted from the thought that Peter might be inside, reclothed in baler twine and sea shells.

'Yeah,' I said, 'when you've done some work. You can start with the table saw in here.' I snapped on the workshop lights, and looked around. Nothing but work and tools, sawdust on the floor and three neat spaces where the finished chairs had been.

'They all your hubby's tools, then?'

'No, mine. I slice stones up with them.' *Stones as in testicles.* I'd managed to get David's trick of making one word mean something completely different. He shut up. Between me and the cold weather I don't think he found his willie to wee with all day.

I felt more cheerful after that. Lighter. The rituals I'd planned were, after all, to a positive end. I made a pot of tea for them after a while, but I gave the only two chocolate biscuits to the lad.

'Don't worry about him, missis, he's just a bit sexist, like,' he told me quietly.

'Thanks,' I said.

It took them most of the morning to move the big stuff like the pillar drill and the table saw and all the driftwood timber, straining and instructing all the time.

'To me Lennie, bit more. Right.'

'Heavy bugger this, innit Darren.' Whilst they struggled, I wrapped my tools carefully in layers of old newspapers and laid them in boxes like a trousseau in a bottom drawer.

The men whispered over the crates of odd-shaped pebbles and lumps of sea-worn glass. By the time they got to the tray of dried birds' wings and the crate of miscellaneous weathered plastic, my transformation in the eyes of the older, Lennie, was complete: from aging totty to witch. I didn't get called 'love' even once more. But Darren was more and more curious.

'What's all this stuff for.'

'I just like collecting things I find on the beach. I make stuff with it.'

As we loaded the bundles of rush Lennie quipped, 'You got Moses in here or what?'

But Darren said, 'They smell nice, these do. What do you do with this? Baskets is it or what?'

William's sentinels were still sparkling with frost as I drove up the track with the van behind me. In the rear-view mirror I could see the faces in the cab behind peering anxiously at the sculptures as they passed. When we drew up in the yard behind the house, young Darren leapt out of the cab and ran to my car.

'Did you do those?'

'No, my dad. He died in the autumn.'

'They're fabulous. Really cool. He must have been mad though, eh?'

'In a nice way, yes.'

'You're going to make things up here now aren't you, like your dad?'

'Some of the time. It's going to be a kind of arts centre this place. Lots of people are going to come here to make things and sell them.'

'Can I show you something?' He was running to the van and the mystified Lennie before I could answer. He came back with a folded cloth of ripped T-shirt which he placed in my hands.

'I make these, they're traditional sort of, but I make 'em a bit different.'

Inside the folds was a love spoon, displaying all the features of the master carver's craft, wooden chains, interlocking spirals, a ball in a cage, all carved from a single piece of wood. But Darren's work was more than just a whittler's sampler; snakes and little lizards swarmed in asymmetrical delight over the basic design with a spoon bowl shaped like a heart. It reminded me of the pillars of the Gaudi cathedral in Barcelona.

'Are all your spoons this good?' Darren blushed but he looked at me straight, lifting his chin just a tad.

'Yeah. Some are even better. My imagination runs away with me sometimes.'

'Right. OK, well I know someone who would like to see your work.' I felt sure here was another potential protégé for Olivia.

I'd planned a reverential afternoon of ordering my new work-space and thinking about my dead dad. But Darren was all curiosity now he'd lost his reserve. He chatted to me as he and the silent and sulky Lennie installed my workshop in the more solid of William's barns. I told him all about the plans for William's house, the gallery, the workshops, the people.

Olivia and I had agreed that building work shouldn't start until early spring, which gave me time to finish preparations for the exhibition and do one or two commissions afterwards before I lost my work space to the builders for a while. Lucy would then move into the caretaker's flat, at one end of the converted barn, and I could occupy the house for as long as I wanted, and take one of the stalls as a workshop. None of which committed me to being anywhere all the time.

As I locked up in the falling dark and cold, I was whistling, thinking about the buildings filled with happy families of dyers, and carvers, and weavers and potters. And thinking how much visiting dancers might enjoy such a thing. I even smiled at Lennie as I gave him and Darren their tips.

'Can I bring you some more spoons to show?'

'Yes. And call that woman, Olivia. Maybe you could sell your stuff here. Talk to her about it if you want to.'

'I dunno. I'd like to, but can't see it would make money.'

'I think your spoons could sell for a lot of money. One day.'

*   *   *

I'd expected to gather a kind of emotional momentum towards the end of that day as I drove back down the familiar track to the cabin. Instead I got slower and slower. When I got out of the car to open the last gate I stopped completely. The moon was well up and bright enough to rival the last bit of wintry daylight lingering around the western horizon. The marram looked navy blue against luminous sand and the sea was a sheet of foil. The rooftops of my old refuge cut hard lines against the metallic ocean. I'd planned a 'last night'. The ingredients for a solitary meal lay in the fridge. The wood was stacked for the stove. The bed made up with clean sheets. Even the music was ready on the piano. A last night to try and make all the old Peter CDs play as they used to; beautiful, comforting and all firmly inside my head, under my skin. Then in the morning I'd get up and make a bonfire against the wooden walls and burn the whole place to the ground.

But I didn't have the appetite for it any more: not any of it, the memory fest or the cremation. The whole thing made me feel tired, sick to my bones. It was all the wrong medicine, a finger stall for a headache, an aspirin for a cut hand. What the hell would I tell the insurance company about how a bonfire came to be lit against a wooden building anyway? I got back in the car and reversed up the track.

'Myfanwy! I didn't know you were back.' Graham had his outdoor coat on, a navy nylon parka from the market with a scrap of artificial mange-cat fur round the hood. (William had worn one – 'such a bargain, I bought two.') 'I've only just got in from the shop.'

'Graham. Could I invite myself to dinner?' Close your mouth Graham, something may roost in there, said Tucker's trite little voice in my head. 'I'm sorry to ask. But I just don't want to be in the cabin tonight. It's a long story.'

'Oh, God. I'm keeping you standing on the doorstep like this. Come on in. It's lovely to see you. Tell me all about New York.'

The ugliest hound was beside herself. I don't know what Graham had been telling her but she was very pleased to see me.

'Get a grip, Bet for God sake,' said Graham, 'bangers and mash all right? They're the ones from that organic place, with the hippies. You know other side of Brynberian.'

'I used to get honey there!'

'Well, they've gone for pigs now. Meat's OK apparently, as long as it had a happy life first.'

'And died of natural causes?'

'Oh, yes. These sausages are made from very elderly pigs who died in their sleep, dreaming of truffles and sows with fifty teats.'

'I've brought some wine.'

'Great! Well, let's drink it then.'

I sat on the kitchen floor with Bet sprawled in ecstasy on my lap: a glass of wine in one hand and a dog's ear in the other. Graham cooked and I told him about New York. About Rick and the carnivorous plants, about studio gossip and how my chairs were going to be movie stars. We ate in the kitchen and he told me about Birmingham coach parties, about my baskets disappearing like pixie dust and about cross purposes conversations with Max from the gallery in London when he dispatched the chairs.

'He thought I was trying to sell him my two chairs. Took me two conversations to get through. He's a headless chicken!'

'Yes. But he's quite a nice headless chicken. So have your chairs gone with the three.'

'Well, no. Not until after Christmas. They're all here. I'll take care of them, you know. Come and see.'

The five chairs took up all the space that the baby grand didn't. The lamp light shone through the glass pieces on their backs and made blue and green patches on the walls.

'I'd buy the lot if I had the money. You'll be rolling in it after this exhibition and the film.'

'I ought to make one for myself sometime!' I curled up in the largest and most nest-like one that Peter had stood on the day Lucy had her baby.

'Right! As you're sitting comfortably, you can be my audience. I've been practising.'

He sat down at the piano, and lifted the lid. I could see the effect it had on him; instant relaxation, as if the instrument breathed out some soporific gas.

'Recognise this one?'

> Mama's little baby
> Loves shot'nin shot'nin
> Mama's little baby
> Loves shot'nin bread.

Very simple, not many notes, but perfect, two hands and all the right intonation.

'This is my favourite carol, but I've only just started it, I can't do the left hand.'

Hesitant, with two bum notes on the first line he began. But I recognised it. Not one of the well-worn dirges, like 'Come All Ye Faithful' or 'Hark the Herald Angels' with all that distasteful imagery about virgins' wombs. This was a humbler tune, simply feeling its way along like a child's footsteps. The words came up to my lips without asking,

> In Bethlehem did shepherds keep,
> Their flocks of lambs
> And feeding sheep . . .

I came to stand by Graham's piano.

'Start again. I'll do the left hand. We can sing maybe.'

'In Bethlehem did shepherds keep . . .' My out of practice mezzo, Graham's hopelessly inaccurate baritone, combined quite sweetly.

I stand by another piano, a Christmas in my twenties, at sea, the Sula Sea three days out of Brunei. Ten of the Filipino crew lined

273

up in best white dress uniforms, singing the two carols Peter and I had taught them. All of them so near to their homes and families and all with another eight months of duty in front of them before they would see their wives and husbands and children. And all of them singing now so sweetly, the words from someone else's culture to this audience of well-meaning and ignorant westerners. My voice is catching on the second verse with the thought of it, the love and the longing in their singing.

> There were three wise men from afar,
> Directed by a glorious star . . .

I am singing and playing. Singing those words with all my heart, for I am directed too, directed by the glorious star of my wonderful Peter, in his tux so handsome and large and full of living. I am drawn and enveloped, warmed and lit by Peter and how I love him. Outside of this moment there can be nothing.

> And when they came unto the stall
> Where the blessed Messiah was
> They humbly laid down at his feet
> Their gifts of gold and incense sweet.

Graham played the last notes, then looked up from the keyboard, smiling, delighted.

'That was great. You've got such a lovely voice! Myfanwy! You're crying! I didn't think my singing was that bad! What's the matter.'

'I sang that such a long, long time ago Graham . . . on a ship with my husband. It made me remember.'

'Your husband? I heard. About him dying a few years back.'

'Yes.'

Clever Graham. He didn't shut the piano and change the subject.

'Shall we sing it again?' he said gently, 'it's nice to remember, even sad things. Come on, you do that left hand, we'll sing it through and then you can tell me about what you remember.'

So we sang and out the memories came, 'gifts of gold and incense sweet', all my best times with my lost and beloved husband: unsullied and unspoiled by the swearing, peeing, farting, chanting of that mad spirit and the strings of matching words; uninhibited by the devaluing of endless replaying to fit the requirements of a stiff kind of solace. I told all the seas, all the shores, all the snow and sand and ice and darkness, the lists in hospitals and the comforts of honey. I talked until there wasn't any more and my eyes were almost closed with the first real crying they'd done in five years.

'God, he was a lucky man!' Graham said, handing me another bit of lavatory paper to blow on.

'Yeah. He got to see most things he wanted to!'

'Well, that was lucky too. But he had you. That was his best luck.'

Never in all the years I'd been with Peter, never in all the years he had been dead, had I thought of him as the lucky one. I was the one who was lucky, the unformed child found and made, and whisked around the magic earth by 'The Peter', the big man who knew everything. I had been lucky because he had shaped me and shown me. But looking at Graham's thin earnest face, seeing the conviction in his words I saw that it was true. Peter had been lucky to spend those years with me – so young and adoring and beautiful as I had been. He'd had a second chance at life through me. Close your mouth, Myfanwy, there's chickens looking for a place to roost!

'I think you need to sleep. Right now.' Graham got up. 'You just tuck down here. I'll be out in the barn if you want me. OK? There's blankets already on the futon.' He was suddenly brisk, making haste, getting away before temptation got the better of him I thought.

'But you'll freeze!' He was already taking the torch off the shelf and a sleeping bag from a cupboard.

'Don't be daft. After what we've had to drink? I've got too

little blood in my alcohol to even feel the cold. Sweet dreams Myfanwy.'

I pottered about the room, touching the chairs, taking off a few clothes, feeling light and blank. I felt as you do after illness as a child, the day when you get up, wobbly legged and quiet, and think a little toast and butter might be nice. A little real sleep might be nice. Very nice. A white sleep, like a bright sheet of paper with nothing on it. I lay down on Graham's bed, rolled myself in blanket and closed my eyes.

'It's related to the albatrosses. The tubenoses as they are known . . .' Everyone I know seems to be on this particular trip. Tucker, Idris, William, Zoe my mother and the great nieces she never saw; Agnes and Jane, Jessica and Molly, Julian and Vicky, holding hands at the back, Clive and Mandy, Lars. Graham's come too, standing at the front with a cocktail in his hand. The glass is packed with a ludicrous number of fruity bits and a silly parasol which keeps getting in the way as he sips. David's there, but he's not listening, leaning over the side he's looking at the sunset and down at the sea surging past. I lift the shearwater from its dark box and show them all its long straight wings.

'Just like a mini albatross,' I tell them.

It's eaten a lot of tuna today and it shits on me. Everyone laughs. I wipe my hands in turn on my T-shirt and find I'm wearing the dress I was married in. But it's a dream so I don't worry about this.

The sun has gone down, there's just a big pink stain left in the sky and the sea is already dark, dark blue. Soon no one will be able to see if the bird flies or not. I can't stall any longer, wherever he is, Peter isn't here. He's not coming.

Very gently I hold the bird out over the sea and let it sit on my hands. It looks all around as always. It dips its head even and unfolds its wings a little, making them stick out like bony wrists.

But then, it changes its mind, and settles onto my hand, nestling. The little webbed black feet fold, each around a finger.

I'm lost. I don't know what to do. Peter has told me all I know. But he didn't tell me about this part.

'You have to *ask* it to go.' It's Zoe speaking. So long since I have heard her voice that at first I look in the wrong part of the crowd for the source of instructions.

'You have to ask it to fly. *Tell* it what to do.'

The bird itself looks sad and confused now, if something so impassive can look confused. I bring it close to me. Holding it in one hand I gently stroke its soft round head with one finger. It is perfect. The ideal curve of feathered skull and neck. It turns, sideways and up, like Vivien Leigh tilting her chin in *Gone With The Wind*, to look at me with one of its eyes which are blue. Forget-me-not blue.

'Tell it what to do,' Zoe says again.

I take the bird's body in my hands, fingers cradling it beneath, thumbs a light restraint above. I lean far over the side of the ship, so far I must fall, surely. But I don't. I can make a huge arc now from the ship's side to the zenith that my arms will reach. I hold the bird down, arms straight, down as far as I can. I breathe. It's getting darker. Everyone is leaning over the side too. Watching. Fast, very fast, so as to give the bird the biggest momentum I can, I swing my arms up and up. It is quick but it feels slow and heavy, as if all my life is weighting my arms, stretching them like the lead on a plumb line. The bird in my hands is so heavy. It's nearly pulling me out of the arc, to fall down to the sea with my hands still clutched around it. As I reach the highest point my arms are pulled by a huge g force until they ache in their sockets.

And then, I just part my hands. Easy. The bird is catapulted up and out. Up a little further carried by my throw, but then even faster down. Its wings are still folded. It's falling!

'*Tell it what to do!*' says Zoe again, 'tell it to fly. *Tell it by its name.*'

'Fly away,' I shout. 'Fly away Peter. Fly away.'

The bird's wings snap out, the fall is more than broken, it's annihilated. The bird floats buoyant in the air, knowing its home now. Over the waves a black spot only just darker than the sea.

'Fly away Peter.'

There were earwigs in the sails, and a nasty smell of mustiness, but otherwise Peter's dinghy was as ready to sail as she'd been five years before. The trailer still ran easily over the path and down onto the shore. The beach was wet with the retreating tide, shiny in the early light and empty. I felt as clean, as sweetly blank as the sand, washed smooth, ready to take the first imprint of a new day.

It was cutting cold, but I didn't plan to be out for long. It was a good breeze for a sail across the bay and back. I got a bootful as I launched her. Peter would have laughed, he always managed to leap deftly aboard and keep his feet dry whenever he took her out. The wind was perfect, with the sail up she leapt away. The water had that surface fizz that you can only see when you are close to it in a small boat. Ships are too big, the mood of the sea is too intimate a thing to see at a distance of fifty feet.

I sailed straight out without looking back for a while, then I took down the sail in a flurry of flapping and hove to as best I could in the little fibreglass walnut shell. I looked back to the beach, the smile of sand, the ruffled dunes, and the cabin peeking out of the marram. Behind the beach the land began to rise in a crescendo of hills, random humps and little slopes of fields building to the precipitous tractor-tipping hill meadows, and then after a few miles, Peter's Pimples, the Preselis. The gradation of colours from beach to hills to sky was like a practice sampler from a watercolour class: white sand, pale-green, deep-green, blue-purple, mauve and back to sky so full of cold it was white as the sand. The depth of earth and rock, water and air was immense, humans just grains caught in the surface meniscus.

I took the wooden box from the bag, and lifted the lid. An eddy of breeze ruffled the top layer of the ashes and blew some into my face. Peter up my nose! I laughed out loud; after the trouble he'd given me it was appropriate. There wasn't any need for ceremony, no words: he was, after all, long gone. So I tipped Peter's mortal remains over the side without any respectful sprinkling. A slick of the lightest bits, hair perhaps, eyes, floated away. But the rest, a coherent blob with a silvering of bubbles caught on its surface, sank with a little effervescence, like liver salts. I threw in the box too, I knew I'd only get it back. But the sea would have a go at it first, effect some transformation.

I got ready to hoist the sail and head for warmth then I remembered the earthwork. 'The first bulbs will be up in December. Nerines,' William had said.

'What?'

'Nerines.'

'Sounds like a character in an Australian soap.'

'It's a white flower. It'll show the whole thing up beautifully. Wait and see!' I remembered the glee in William's voice.

The wind had drifted me far enough to see the meadow, the size of a small TV screen in my field of vision. The flowers were indeed in bloom. Neat lines of bright white in the sun, against the green, tracing out a pattern of greater intricacy than I had appreciated before. Or perhaps William had just lost it near the end and planted bulbs in the wrong place. The pattern didn't make sense, no words no symbols, nothing clear. We'd never know what had been in his mind. Daft old sod.

I raised the sail and turned the boat. I glanced one more time at William's 'greatest work'. This time the image fell on an eye without expectations, the white random tracery made sudden sense. My mother's face sprang out at me. William's specific instructions about the burial site of his ashes became clear: his final resting place was in her forehead. I tacked again and again to take me to and fro, to look and look. Each time I passed, the face I saw was different, like a figure you see made of speeding cloud. My own face. My father's face. Peter's. Idris'. Tucker's. David's. Graham's.

Perhaps William had formulated some theory of faces, some index of human recognition. Almost certainly he had thought so. I could imagine the endless scribblings on the backs of envelopes and cereal packets that had gone on in secret. How did he know it would look like this from so far away? Maybe he did have a pact with the little green men.

Whatever the mad science or chance behind it, my father had somehow found a universal face. The face we learn to see with love. One face containing all the true faces of our lives. A single face to bind everything together – yesterday, now, tomorrow.

As I tacked one last time in the stiffening breeze and the field disappeared behind the headland, I glimpsed a face I didn't recognise but knew at once. A child's face, with something of its mother and something of its father – my mouth perhaps and David's eyes.

Graham and Bet were there as I brought the dinghy in. They splashed through the freezing waves to help me ashore. Then we walked to the cabin along the strand line. The tide had brought in all manner of new possibilities, objects changed and reshuffled by their time in deep water. What better place to raise a child than a beach where there is space to dance, and every wave brings fresh magic and a new beginning.

Did you enjoy *Fly Away Peter*?
Here's a preview of Stevie Morgan's new novel
Back to the Jungle.

Chapter One

Just round the corner from Deacon Road Primary School, between 'Shorthouse and Shepherd' (suppliers of wheelchairs, bath lifts and motor-aided zimmer frames), and Firth's news-agents (suppliers of sweets past their sell-by date and time-warp stationery such as Animal Friends Calendars 1981), Samantha should be enjoying a private Sisyphean moment.

The other Mothers are enjoying theirs, as they disperse in all directions from the school gates, as separate and urgent as the splashes from a dropped pebble. It's not the demands of nine o'clock bosses or the breakfast washing up that makes them hurry so, with hardly a stop to chat. Nor is the weather sending them scuttling for the refuge of their cars and kitchens, because even though it is the first Tuesday of Wimbledon Fortnight, the weather is dry and warm. They rush away out of the desire to savour, without even the interruption of friendly conversation, the only time in their day when there is nothing that can be expected of them, there is nothing that they have to do. For the next few minutes, before they reach home or their workplace, they are free. They move quickly, walking fast or changing gear smartly at the green light, so that no one will guess that inside, they are slacking; that inside their heads, nothing is going on but a blissful blankness of white noise, or perhaps, at the very most, a little light fantasy of the silken sand and fluffy cloud variety.

But Samantha, Mrs Dale Cordellone, does not enjoy having nothing to do. She finds her own peculiar variety of freedom in the all-absorbing effort of pushing the rock up the mountain. When there is nothing that she has to do 'now', she thinks what it is she has to do 'next'. When there is no one to expect things from her, she tries to expect things from herself. So, as she crosses the road, leaving the alarming displays of chrome commodes and yellowing kittens behind her, she concentrates hard on improving the sound her new heels make as they hit the tarmac. She tightens all her muscles and snaps her upper spine straight, pulling everything inwards as if gathering her whole physical being inside a fortress of control. She adjusts the way her shoes impact on the ground, imagining a glass crushed to dust with every rapid step. Now, each time her heels come down, they do so with a satisfyingly self-possessed 'click'. Looking at her watch she is pleased to find that she is about to arrive at work a whole minute earlier than is usual.

Dressed in his brown stockman's coat, George is already out front, mustering the wire trolleys like a squad of unruly recruits. He pleats his forehead and pulls his brows down, glowering at the trolleys, daring them to misbehave. Hearing the sound of Samantha's heels he looks up. His whole face lifts, and becomes as bright and flat as smoothed tin foil. He taps his watch and greets her.

'Tad early today, Mrs Cordellone.'

'Just a bit, George. Must be my new shoes.'

'Ah yes!' he exclaims, his face even flatter and brighter as he grasps this little truth she has offered him. 'Yes! That'll be it.'

Samantha smiles back, acknowledging that only she and George could find the correlation between walking speed and new shoe leather logical and satisfying.

'Well, better get on, George.'

Smiling still, she walks on, leaving George to scold his trolleys and ponder the influence of new footwear on the world at large. The moment George began their customary morning exchange, Samantha lost the need to concentrate on the inter-action of sole and concrete. The day of providing for people's expectations has begun again, she has things to think about and things to do. The barricades in her mind can be left less heavily defended as she puts her shoulder back to pushing the rock.

Round this side of the building there are no windows. Only the little red security door in the huge metal wall, like a hole cut into a giant tin can. Samantha keys in the code and enters the fluorescent lit interior with its smell of fresh Dettol. The little warren of staff facilities and managers' offices inside feel as if they are the changing rooms of an old-fashioned girls' public school. Fresh-looking gloss covers the partition walls, snot green to waist height and dirty vanilla from there up and over the ceilings. The brown shine coating the concrete floors could be fossilised Bisto from a thousand school dinners. It squeaks faintly underfoot.

This little suite of rooms and corridors is really Samantha's favourite part of Stayfleurs. The atmosphere, reminiscent of stable and enclosing institutionalisation, is comforting, and the perfect antidote for the public part of the shop. After a few minutes in here she will be ready for 'out there', perched at a checkout surrounded by white melamine and saturated in light.

Samantha pushes open the door — in a deeper shade of green — marked Female Changing. Inside is a room like the rest — vanilla, snot, Bisto, Eau de Dettol — with the little addition of a row of neat brass pegs along one wall, above a slatted wooded bench. No need for the security value of lockers: theft here is unthinkable. Like swearing in front of the Vicar, or the Queen having sex. Samantha likes that unassailable respectability. It's not that Stayfleurs looks down on the rest of the world, retail and otherwise, it's more that Stayfleurs wills the world into non-existence. Such a level of self invention is something she finds admirable.

Three of her usual co-workers are already preparing for the day's work. They are not what you'd expect to find at a supermarket check-out but then Stayfleurs *is* a *better class* of supermarket. It flatters its clientele with a choice of three flavours of couscous, a selection of unpronounceable breakfast cereals and two sorts of air dried reindeer meat. This kind of thing attracts a *better class* of customer — people who look for the finger on fish and sigh with boredom over Australian chardonnay — and a *better class* of staff. There are no fat and feckless seventeen-year-old girls, nor droopy six-foot boys, giggling behind their acne with a packet of Marlborough Lites in their top pocket. Stayfleurs employs 'ladies' on its tills, women who would find the term 'woman' vulgar. Stayfleurs' ladies typically date from an age when middle-class marriage was a profession. But like miners and steelworkers they have outlived the industry in which they began their careers. They work here to escape their houses — big and empty — and their husbands' egos - ditto. At nearly thirty, which she feels is virtually the safe haven of her 'middle years', Samantha is almost the same age as their daughters.

They turn and smile at her as she comes in, then continue to slip the navy uniform housecoats over their Jaeger skirts and blouses.

'Oh, I think I must be electronic,' laughs Claudia as the material crackles over her arm and her newly coloured purple-brown hair stands on end. 'I do wish they'd make these things of natural fibres.' Claudia is an Amazon of a woman in her late fifties. She resembles a large sinewy horse. Quite a length of arm sticks out from the sleeves of the largest coats. Stayfleurs can offer. She must have been team captain of everything at school.

'You mustn't let a uniform put you off, Claudia, my mother refused to join the Salvation Army, all because she didn't like the hats. And she always regretted it.' Mary can afford to say this, of course, because she is small and neat, and the navy coat with its cream piping rather suits her pale, faded skin and white hair.

'I had an uncle in the Sally Army.' says Claudia, patting her static hair into place. 'But of course the men didn't have to wear those frightful bows.'

'Oh well perhaps they *do*, you know, *nowadays*.' Mary rolls her eyes and droops her right hand suggestively at the wrist, but Claudia stares blankly, blushing with discomfort because she doesn't understand the joke.

'Oh for Christ's sake Mary!' Liz, who has been rearranging her contact lenses until this moment, shuts her gold compact with a snap. 'Nobody makes jokes like that these days.' She tosses her head and stares contemptuously at Mary's rather lost-looking hand. 'I mean, don't you have any gay friends?' Liz, glamorously, brassily blonde, was an actress before Trevor swept her off her feet with his dentist's charm.

'Oh! Oh God! Silly me!' Claudia is laughing nervously now. 'Gay, of course. Queer. Oh I'm such a chump!'

This is the usual uneasy mixture of embarrassment and irritation that never quite crystallises into camaraderie. They're all too busy proving that they were really destined for better things than a supermarket, no matter how select.

Quietly tying back her fine brown hair Samantha has been waiting for five to nine, the moment when she needs to steal between their words and squabbles, to get them out to work. She knows what they need is a distraction, a shared sense of mild outrage. It's easy to provide it. Samantha places her words into the awkward little silence that follows Claudia's blushes.

'I think that Phillipa, you know the under manager from head office we had last Christmas, she was gay.' This is a fat worm none of the ladies can resist, there are appreciative gasps all round.

'Anyway, Ladies. As usual I think you look lovely in your uniforms. Shall we get ready to do battle?' United by a common sense of delicious scandal and a little frisson of genuine shock, Claudia, Liz and Mary walk to their work stations smoothed and content, like fed hens.

So far, thankfully, it has been a difficult morning. Samantha has hardly drawn a breath in two hours or put more than three customers' goods through her till without interruption. It began with twin toddlers running amok on aisle B and engulfing the freezer in a tsunami of mayonnaise. Once they'd thrown the jars they were no problem, being paralysed with the enormity of their deed. But their mother hyperventilated with shock and had to be sat down in the staff cloakroom with a paper bag over her head whilst Samantha rang her grumpy husband at the BBC.

'I'm calling from Stayfleurs, Mr Hannan. Your wife would like you to come and pick her up. Yes, I'm afraid it is quite urgent. There's been an incident with your sons and some mayonnaise.

Then there was a run on the Norwegian dried reindeer meat. Half of this morning's elderly customers have put at least one packet in their baskets (the Classic FM morning DJ announced casually between *Gymnopédie* and the *Moonlight Sonata* that Lapps don't get Alzheimers). When its barcode was scanned the computerised tills buzzed bad temperedly and flashed 'item not found'. Pensioners do not react rationally to computer glitches of this sort. They treat the bleeps and warbles of the discomforted till as an infringement of their rights as human beings, as indicators of the indifference of the modern world and harbingers of final social collapse. Seven times this morning Samantha has had to leave her own till to calm and almost self-combusting punter at someone else's.

'I perfectly understand your concerns about the future of society, sir, but really this is just a small temporary fault and if you could bear with us for a few moments you can complete your purchasing.'

But not even Samantha's most professional charm can pacify two of Liz's customers. A pair of old gents of military bearing vow to write to their MPs about this incomprehensible flashing, beeping delay, and demand to see the manager.

'Oh God, Mafeking all over again,' Liz breathes, rolling her eyes. Secretly Liz rather enjoys her barking elderly clientele because they make her feel young.

Luckily Mr Geoffrey is exactly the right figure to deal with the Sandhurst graduates of '41. He is the result of some strange crinkle in the time space continuum. He exists apparently as the thirty-eight-year-old manager of a modern supermarket, dealing effortlessly with computer stock control and business projection graphics. Yet he has clearly been lifted from a genteel department store somewhere in the 1930s. Samantha always thinks of him as wearing collar studs, and formal navy three piece pinstripes. His Marks & Spencers charcoal flannel sports jacket always surprises her. He obviously makes the same impression on the Colonel (rtd) and Lft. Colonel Smyth Parker (DSO); he is as they remember the managers of their youth. Although Mr Geoffrey says almost nothing — personal communication not being his strong point — his general atmosphere does the trick. The Smyth Parker brothers soften in a mist of remembrance of buying school uniform at Dickins and Jones with Mother.

'The trouble is,' Mr Geoffrey confides to Samantha, as the brothers leave with a complimentary packet of shrink-wrapped Rudolph, 'these old army coves think they're still fighting Hitler. I'm going to get onto head office about his bally reindeer meat. Could you hold the fort down here? You are so marvellously diplomatic, Mrs Cordellone.' And baring his yellow teeth in a what he believes to be a winning smile, he disappears through the doors behind the deli counter nervously readjusting his collar, his fingertips searching for the studs he left behind in a former life.

The tense atmosphere has got into the ladies' fingertips, making them jitter inaccurately over the till keys, so that Samantha has finally had to close down her own till to devote herself full time to trouble shooting with her master key for everyone else. Claudia is particularly disaster prone this morning, her awkward wrists stick out further and become pinker with every mistake. Inside that gung ho, jolly hockey sticks frame, beats the heart of a house mouse.

'I don't know how you stay so cool,' she says tremulously over her shoulder as she passes another trolley load of cat food and gin under the little red scanning light.

Samantha smiles professionally.

'Don't forget the "f" code on that alcohol, Claudia,' she says.

'Oops. Silly me.'

'And the "Delicat" is a special this week; it should come through on two for one, code four three nine.'

'Oh, oh, right. I don't know how you do it. Really I. . .'

'Code four three nine Claudia!' Whilst Claudia witters over her codes, Samantha steps forward.

'That'll be thirty-two pounds and sixty-three pence, please Madam. Shall I give you a bottle carrier for the gin?'

What no one understands is how relaxing stress really can be.

The offending reindeer meat has been withdrawn 'On Orders' and a lunchtime calm has set in. All the oldies are back home, sitting down to their reindeer and wet lettuce; the toddlers are safely parked in front of *Sesame Street*, whilst their mothers drink coffee at the kitchen table and wonder what it was they did with their times before kids. The only punters pushing George's trolleys are passing sales reps looking in vain for a simple cheese butty, husbands who have promised to cook dinner, and Women with Lists, shopping efficiently in their lunch hours. The reps and husbands wander the aisles with the same air of lost expectancy, hoping that some product will jump off the shelves and ask to be bought. The List Women cruise at speed, barely stopping to grab their usual items from the shelves, their heads full of the next six things they are going to do. None of them want to talk as they come through the checkout. They notice her 'good afternoon' as much as they notice the bleeping of the till. She's not drawn to look at faces now, only the middle bits of shirts and dresses as they pass the plastic screen beside her.

Samantha feels it is as if all the people in the shop, and in the streets and houses fanning out for miles around had turned their back on her. The demands of the external world become faint, they don't hold her attention. Inside she tightens control, reining in her thoughts, but it's like being in the basket of a balloon and looking down to see that the ropes holding you to earth and home are being cut, one by one. She hopes for a customer with a problem: a query about the next delivery of Dublin Bay prawns or a complaint about the selection of dessert wines, a gastric attack requiring naviation to the staff lavatory. Anything would do. Once, at a quiet time like this, a customer exposed himself to her, grabbing his sad purple penis and ordering her sharply to look at it. She had been positively delighted, the furore kept her busy for hours. But the pale blue eyes of List Women look clean through her and out to the world. As the basket load of olive oil, wholemeal pasta, quorn mince and mackerel pâté pass under the scanner, Samantha feels the familiar unease of an unauthorised Imagination Leak occurring.

At first it's confined to the back of the shop, where the aisles begin to fade into the dimness of artificial light. Out of the corner of her eye, Samantha can see that the shadows there are acquiring a kind of greenness. She can't help glancing that way between items to see that leaf shapes seem to be suggesting themselves, poking between the stacks of packets and tins. Then, a flash of movement catches her eye and she turns to glimpse a lizard's tail darting under the dried chillies. It seems that every time she turns her head a bright green gecko scuttles up the shelves, which themselves become taller somehow and then grow upwards quite unashamedly. Soon they are disappearing into a forest canopy that has spread high above all the aisles and is reaching for the front of the shop to feed on the light where the glass stretches from the ground to the roof.

The next List Woman to bring her purchases to Samantha's checkout is quite unaware of the slim green vine snake twining itself luxuriously through her thick red hair. As she checks the corn flakes, yoghourts, beans, marmalade, lavatory paper, frozen spinach, Samantha tries not to look up at what the snake is doing. But it is a particularly beautiful specimen: recently moulted, its lime green skin has a little iridescent lustre, and its head is a perfect arrow striking boldly through the deep auburn jungle. The woman puts her hand up to her hair, self-consciously checking that nothing real is drawing Samantha's gaze and knocks the snake to the floor. It takes some self control not to leap up and see where it went: Samantha concentrates harder on the parade of objects filing past her on the conveyor.

'Did you know that these ciabatta rolls are two for the price of one?' she says, without looking up. But her voice seems ineffectual and the woman with the red hair doesn't reply. Which is just as well as the vine snake has reappeared, popping asp-like from her cleavage.

Imagination started as 'her secret weapon', against little Dennis Williams, tiny wiry body, huge black eyes and lashes straight and thick as a wallpaper brush. At eight he was at the peak of his career with an empire that stretched over all three tarmac playgrounds and half way over the grass to the back of the Nissan huts. Life for Dennis would never be this good again and he was making the most of it. Kids just did what he told them to do. Enslaved by his wicked elfin charisma, they brought him sweets, toys, money and weaker children to torment. Samantha, tall for her age, too clever by half and stick thin, was a favourite pastime. In the middle of a silent ring of fascinated supporters he made her stand. Dennis was smart enough to know that words were Samantha's currency, so he never spoke. Just walked around her, slowly at first, then dancing and making kung fu kicks and karate chops, only some of which made painful contact with her shins and arms and head. The game was to make Samantha wince and cower even when she wasn't being kicked or hit. It became a regular feature of the day. Every morning playtime, Dennis's lackeys would come and round her up. She took to standing in the same corner of the playground to wait for them, because it was worse when they came and 'found' her wherever she happened to be.

Then one day her imagination just kicked in, unasked, like

adrenalin. She looked at Dennis's face and saw the most extraordinary thing.

'You've got spiders coming out of your eyes. Big ones.'

His eyelashes flickered, but otherwise he gave no clue that he had heard her.

'Ha! Ha!' he exclaimed chopping first the air, then her side.

'You have. Are you listening to me? You've got great big spiders just crawling out of your eyes and down your face.' Samantha could see clearly that first a hairy leg, five times the thickness of his eyelashes, would poke out, feeling around like a hand groping for a bedside light switch. Then, the lump of the body would show under the lid, stretching the skin so that the fine veins showed like web. Finally struggling to gain purchase on the smooth eyeball, the whole animal wriggled out, only to be followed immediately by another, just the same. By now Dennis's face was almost obscured by them. The early arrivals were having to negotiate the tangle of his hair.

'They're all over your face now.' Her tone was completely flat, but all the same informative, like a news reader saying that ten people were feared dead in today's train crash. Dennis stopped his circling and looked up at her. She noticed that the neck of his jersey was greasy and slack. A particularly fat spider squirmed its way grossly from under the lower lid of his left eye. Involuntarily, Samantha's nose wrinkled and in reply, a ripple of revulsion shivered round the ring of supporters. They turned questioningly to Dennis, leaning in to scrutinise his face.

Samantha waited in the corner of the playground at the start of break the next day, but no once came for her. A week later Dennis was running errands for a big boy with red hair. Dennis was smaller than ever and his jersey had gathered a few more spots of grease and egg. He turned his head from her as he ran past, and she felt suddenly that she must sit down under the weight of the revelation that had just landed in her lap.

*   *   *

Now, Samantha feels she has no one but herself to blame for the fact that there is a snake between the breasts of the young woman who wants pounds cash back please. Imagination may have come to her unasked in the beginning, but then she learned to let it happen, trained it to be strong. Used it at first just at school but later at home too when escape seemed the only option. It's her own fault that she never learned to control it better.

People don't know what they're talking about when they say 'a failure of imagination'. They think it means an inability to grasp things outside of the immediate material world. But Samantha knows the real meaning: that imagination fails you, however strong and clear it seems, it isn't. It's weak as water just when you most need it. It can't be trusted to protect you from anything that's outside your own head. It doesn't get you anywhere. It gets in the way.

But luckily at Stayfleurs nothing strays out of hand, not even Samantha's imagination. Something always happens that throws her runaway balloon a nice anchoring rope. And today it's George. Liz, just off her break, comes straight to Samantha's till, as the redhead and the snake duck under a liana leave the shop. Something has ruffled Liz's laconic exterior. She seems genuinely agitated. There is even a little flush in her nicotine-tanned cheeks.

'Mr Geoffrey says he needs you in the office. It's that poor creature George. He's practically foaming at the mouth.'

By the time Samantha pushes through the doors marked 'Staff Only' there isn't a leaf or a lizard left in the place.

George is sitting on the settee in Mr Geoffrey's office with his long arms wrapped around his own body, and rocking slightly to and fro. His face is a million creases. Mr Geoffrey leaps up from his refuge behind the large desk and glowing computer and comes towards her, sweating with relief.

14

'Oh, Mrs Cordellone. Thank goodness this happened whilst you were here.'

'I will still have to leave at three twenty-five, Mr Geoffrey.'

'Oh yes. But perhaps you could. . .' he trails off and looks forlornly towards George, still rocking and still staring into space. There is a short silence during which Mr Geoffrey looks expectantly into Samantha's face, before remembering that he is the one who needs to speak.

'Ah! Yes. You need to be "filled in". A boy returned his mother's trolley to the wrong place. The front of a line rather than the back. George moved the trolley to the back, and the boy returned and took it to the front. I believe this procedure was repeated several times. The boy became abusive. Erm. . .' Mr Geoffrey shifts his weight uncomfortably from foot to foot as if relieving the pressure of sore corns. This is testing his ability to relate to humans, rather than figure or computers, to the limit.

'And George got upset?'

'Well yes. He shouted at the boy, excusable under the circumstances. I don't think the mother will complain. I think she recognised that her child was rather in the wrong. Then he came up here. Well, as you see him now.'

'Would you give us just a few moments Mr Geoffrey?' He is out of his own office almost before she's finished speaking, relieved to escape.

Samantha sits beside George on the sofa.

'D'you think they'll make me early every day?' she says, stretching her feet out in front of her. 'I mean, they won't be new tomorrow will they?'

George stops rocking.

'Well. Not new as such. Not new per se. As it were.' His voice is shaky but his diction as distinct and tight as ever.

'It could be the style of course. So different from my old pair. It could be the style that's making me walk faster.'

'Well. That is certainly a reasonable and valid theory. It could indeed prove to be the style. It remains to be seen.'

For the first time since she entered the room George looks at her, blinking as if he has just woken.

'Would you like a lift home now, George? I'm sure it could be arranged. You have had a difficult day after all.'

'Ah. In that instance there would be no one to attend to the trolleys.'

'Mr Mullen from the deli counter would help out just this once.'

'Well. Yes. I am reluctant. It may endanger my position here. I may be seen to be surplus to requirements.'

'I'm sure that won't be the case.'

'No. No. Well. Home then. I think. A trying day!' George smiles at her.

'You just wait here, George.'

Mr Geoffrey took a little convincing that a taxi for George courtesy of Stayfleurs was 'appropriate'. So Samantha has had to run almost all the way to school. Her ponytail has worked lose and one bra strap is half way down her arm. As she comes through the side gate into the infants' playground, hair is sticking to her neck and face and her right breast is wobbling visibly out of its cup. She feels hot and uncontrolled. But it doesn't matter that there's no time to adjust her hairstyle or her underwear, because when she sees her boys there's no room in her for anything but the relief of being their mum again. No room for trying to pull her mind into a circle of control, no room for supermarkets full of tropical rain forest and retired soldiers. She fills up with her children and all she must be for them.

She's late and they've stopped looking for her. She sees them before they notice her. Joe is holding his thick brassy hair off his forehead with splayed awkward fingers and swinging his blue sweatshirt in his other hand. He looks sticky and crumpled. Samantha can feel his hot little palms in hers even at a distance of twenty feet. Tony is standing beside him, quite still. As usual Tony has come through the day untouched somehow, clean and unrumpled. One hand rests lightly on Joe's shoulder. Only she or Dale would notice the delicacy and the tension in that hand.

They are standing with Joe's teacher, Mr Hastings, who was Tony's teacher when he was in reception. Both of them are looking up to Mr Hastings with total adoration, like pet spaniels. Mr Hastings is young and rather handsome, he is always making his class laugh, and uses the same voice for talking to adults as he does for children. Tony's teacher Mrs Wiggins wears brown stockings underneath her blue sandals and plays songs on her guitar about how lovely The Lord is, in assembly. Tony says with contempt that she has a special 'slidey voice' for speaking to children. Mrs Wiggins doesn't mean to make anyone laugh.

The boys notice Samantha and launch themselves towards her at full pelt. She holds them in her arms, her eyes closed as if they had been apart for a year, not just a few hours. She is their mother again; defined by the food she will give them for their tea, the cotton shorts she will iron for them to wear tomorrow, the way she will stand in their room and listen to their sleeping breath.

'Mummy!'

Yes, that's right. Mummy. She has a whole galaxy of demands on her attention now and four little hands to rope her firmly to earth. She is sensible, efficient, loving. Totally in control of everything. She could list their every pair of socks, as well as recite their favourite stories. She is Mummy. At this moment Samantha can imagine that she was never anything else. Certainly never a child. Certainly never a person with a mother of her own.

She retrieves her bra strap and ties her straying hair. Then she takes Tony's hand in her right and Joe's in her left and they cross the road, and start to walk home.